"Oh, Beebs," Liz said over the phone. "I wish things could be different. I wish you could be here."

"Me too, kiddo." It had, however, long since been decided that their politics would not be a showcase for the family's black sheep. "How are the kids?" BeBe asked brightly.

"Bearing up well. Danny's a little tired. But I guess that's to be expected."

"And Michael? Is he going to be nominated?"

"It looks that way."

"And?"

"And what?"

"And he'll be running against Josh." She waited one, two, three seconds for Liz to comment.

"Congratulations," Liz said. "I see you're keeping up with the news."

Leaning back in her chair, BeBe put her feet up on her desk. She looked down at her legs, which had never been as long as her sister's, and at the pale skin that, despite living year-round in Florida, no longer tanned as it had on the Vineyard, but more often burned and made her sprout adolescent freckles that matched her orange hair. "Well," she said slowly, "it will be an interesting election."

Liz hesitated then said, "Yes. Well. That's one way of putting it."

BeBe's heart ached just a little. "Keep your chin up, kiddo, and everything will work out. It always has. It always does." She did not add, "But not always the way we want."

"I love you, big sister," Liz replied.

The
Summer
House

Jean Stone

BANTAM BOOKS
NEW YORK   TORONTO   LONDON   SYDNEY   AUCKLAND

THE SUMMER HOUSE

A Bantam Book / April 2000

ISBN 0-553-58083-3

Published simultaneously in the United States and Canada

*Bantam Books are published by Bantam Books, a division of
Random House, Inc. Its trademark, consisting of the words
"Bantam Books" and the portrayal of a rooster, is Registered in
U.S. Patent and Trademark Office and in other countries.
Marca Registrada. Bantam Books, 1540 Broadway, New York,
New York 10036.*

PRINTED IN THE UNITED STATES OF AMERICA

OPM 10 9 8 7 6 5 4 3 2 1

Prologue

 "Daniel is going to be president of the United States of America," BeBe said, skipping down the path toward their special cove, pulling the elastics from her carrot-colored pigtails. She scooped her hair into a French twist the way Father said made her look like a tart, whatever that meant.

It was not the first time that Lizzie had seen her sister do something against Father's wishes. It was, however, the first time she'd heard that Daniel was going to be president. She scooted quickly along the path on this bright, sunny morning and tried to catch up.

"How can Daniel be president?" Lizzie asked. "He's only sixteen." She was only nine herself (well, almost nine), but she knew enough to know that Daniel was too young, that he did not even come close to being the kind of old man it took to be president of the United States, an old man like John Fitzgerald Kennedy or Lyndon B. Johnson.

Slowing down to walk, BeBe replied, "I didn't mean today, silly."

Lizzie felt the tug in her belly that she always felt whenever BeBe or Roger or even Daniel himself called her silly or childish or anything that reminded her that she was the baby of the family, that she was the kid.

She pulled at a cattail, one of the tall, fuzzy-tipped weeds that rimmed Martha's Vineyard. This was the island where summers happened in big, gray-shingled houses, away from the city-street brownstones of Boston. It did not matter how elegant the Boston brownstones were, or how many generations of their family had endured the city summers: once the Steamship Authority had made the island comfortably accessible, the Adams family was ensconced there from June until Labor Day.

Lizzie ran the soft brush of the cattail along her August-freckled cheek. "Will Daniel be president after he graduates from West Point?" Congressman Carter and his gossipy granddaughter with the buck teeth had come for dinner last night. He had announced that in honor of Mother's clam chowder—"the best on the Vineyard"—he was going to see to it that Daniel received a commission to the military academy at West Point. Lizzie wasn't sure what that meant either, but Father had smiled and ladled more chowder into the congressman's bowl.

"He won't be president until long after West Point," BeBe replied now. "But I heard Father say that in the meantime, he'd make sure the congressman was re-elected."

Lizzie did not know how Will Adams could "make sure" that anyone was elected to anything. Everyone knew that voting was up to the people, and you could vote for whomever you wanted. Besides, Father was a lawyer, not a politician.

She tossed down the cattail, wishing she was older, like BeBe, smarter, like BeBe, and, like BeBe, had bumps on the front of her jersey.

"There's the president now," BeBe exclaimed as they

reached the end of the path where it opened up to the cove. The silver-dollar-like inlet sneaked in from Vineyard Sound onto land that still belonged to the Indians but that the Adams kids treated as their own. It was their secret place, where they splashed in and out of the water and had picnics along the scrub oak and tall-pine-treed fringes, away from the watchful eyes of fathers and mothers and adults of any kind.

In the middle of the water sat the old, green wooden rowboat. In it was President Daniel himself, along with Roger, the second-born brother, and a couple of fishing poles that dangled over the sides.

"Hey, Mr. President," BeBe shouted, waving her arms. "Any room in your boat?"

Daniel waved back and smiled his big, white-toothed smile that looked even whiter against his summer-dark tan. To Lizzie there was no boy alive more handsome.

"When I am president I shall make you both princesses," he exclaimed, clasping his hand to his chest, then pointing at Lizzie. "Especially you, Lizzie-girl." She giggled and shook sand from her pink and white rubber thongs. She knew there were no princesses in the United States of America, but here in their special cove, anything was possible.

Daniel picked up the oars. "Come on, brother Roger, let's save our two princess sisters from the enemies of the kingdom."

As he rowed the boat toward them, Lizzie squinted her eyes against the shafts of light that shot from the sun, sliced through the trees, and created a halo around Daniel's whole body. She leaned into her sister. "Do you really think he'll be president, Beebs?"

BeBe studied their brother a moment. She patted her French twist and nodded. "There's no doubt about it, Lizzie. It's exactly what our Lord-and-Father wants."

Lizzie knew that BeBe did not mean the "Lord" as in

God, as in Heaven, but *their* father, Will Adams, who always got what he wanted. Always. Every time. No matter what.

Despite the warmth of the sun in the late morning air, Lizzie shivered a little but did not know why.

Part 1

Year 2000

Chapter 1

 It had taken twenty-four years to get to New Jersey, twenty-eight if you started counting from when Daniel was killed. Which would only have been right, for that was when it had all begun . . . all of the planning and scheming and orchestrating that had landed Liz Adams-Barton here today, standing at a podium, acknowledging enthusiastic applause.

"Thank you," she said into the microphone at the Sheraton or Hyatt or Marriott, wherever she was. It was not her job to remember. Logistics was what her brother Roger was for: Liz merely had to show up and give a short, impassioned speech that would deliver the votes to her husband. Her husband, Michael Barton, who—not Daniel—was running for president of the United States.

This afternoon, her passion had been directed toward the Northeast Coalition for Handicapped Americans. For an hour now in the red-white-and-blue-decorated banquet room, the audience of eight hundred had been enrapt by her words and now cheered enthusiastically from their wheelchairs and walkers and crutches. They seemed especially delighted that Liz had brought Danny along, Danny, her twenty-two-year-old son—one of *them*—who sat next to the podium in his own chair with wheels. She glanced down at him. He responded with a hearty wink.

Liz smiled back at the crowd. They were not exactly exploiting Danny. He wanted to be there to help put his father—and all of them—into the White House and into the history books.

All of them included Liz and Michael and the three children: seventeen-year-old Greg, the politician-in-waiting; twenty-year-old Margaret—Mags—the spirited free-thinker; and of course Danny.

All of them also included Will Adams, Liz's father, who stood on the other side of the podium. At seventy-eight, he was nodding at the crowd, his faded blue eyes twinkling, the tired lines at the corners of his pale mouth turned up with the pride of accomplishment and the anticipation of a journey nearly won. He was entitled to be proud. Through every stage of the planning and the scheming and the orchestrating, Will Adams had propelled them here to New Jersey where the party's convention would convene tomorrow, where Michael Barton was expected to win the nomination for the highest office in the land.

And where Liz would take her own final lap toward becoming the nation's next First Lady.

The applause continued; the smile muscles ached in Liz's cheeks. She reached down and took Danny's hand. As she gently squeezed his strong fingers, she wondered what her brother Daniel would have had to say if he only could have seen them now.

"You were brilliant, Mom," Danny said as Liz slid into the backseat of the handicapped-equipped van next to her son. Further back was Clay, Danny's ever-present don't-worry-be-happy Jamaican nurse; up front were Keith and Joe, the Secret Service bodyguards assigned to Liz and Danny, their faithful companions, like it or not.

Liz sighed. "I wasn't brilliant," she said to her son, "but thanks for the kudos." During one of Michael's three terms as governor of Massachusetts, she had learned that politics was more about *presence* than it was about perfection. She pushed a shock of highlighted-blond hair from her forehead. In spite of the fact that the media proclaimed her "stunningly youthful," right now, Liz felt every day, month, and year of her forty-four years, *presence* or not. It had been a long campaign, and the real pressure wouldn't begin until the convention opened tomorrow.

"You're much better at this than you think," Danny continued. "You'd be perfectly capable of running for president yourself, you know."

She laughed. "And do what? Run against your father?" She did not mention that she could never run, not because the country wasn't "ready" for a female president, but because she had not been groomed to be anything but the physical, emotional, and spiritual support—the *wife*—of Michael Barton. He was the *man* with the schooling, the experience, and the backing of her father and his essential connections. Surprisingly, Will Adams had not foreseen that a female president would be possible, not in his lifetime or in Liz's either. It had been one of his few mistakes.

"Besides," she added, "why would anyone want to be president? With all those speeches and the long hours and lousy pay? And the way they scrutinize your personal life!" She let out a strained laugh and Danny joined in. Neither of them had the strength to rehash last winter's "scrutiny," an absurd tabloid scandal that had suggested Michael was gay because there was no evidence that he had ever had an affair or even considered it. The journalistic sensation had finally died down, deemed "unfounded" by the mainstream media and "simply stupid" by Roger, Liz's brother and Michael's campaign manager.

And Roger might have been the one to know. He had "come out" to the family two years ago when Michael was still governor and had asked Roger to be his presidential campaign manager. Roger had said he didn't want anything to hurt Michael's chances at the White House. His wife—who claimed she'd "suspected all along"—agreed to stand by Roger for the sake of the election.

And so, Roger's secret was harbored within the walls of the Adams/Barton family, where it was protected, and where it belonged. Their royal blue Yankee blood may have been curdling inside, but, by God, the world would not know it.

When the tabloid story on Michael broke, Will Adams himself went forth with a press release blasting the media for using the gay issue as the "last frontier" to discredit a candidate. The accusation was untrue, but even if it wasn't, he said, the issue of sexual preference should not be fodder for the media. His announcement was powerful, but still, the family had held their breaths for Roger's sake. And for all their sakes, because heaven only knew what the media might dream up next.

Thankfully, the attack had been dropped. Liz suspected untraceable money had changed hands or that Father had called in favors, but, as usual, she had not asked.

She shook her head now and patted Danny's arm. "How about you, honey? How are you feeling?" As with her father, the stress was beginning to become apparent on her son.

He ran his hand over what would have been thick, dark hair if he had not had it shaved to a trendy quarter inch. Liz liked the look. It enhanced her son's great bone structure and gorgeous brown eyes. "I'll be glad when we get to the hotel," he said. "I need a nap."

"Me, too." Liz gazed out the window at the Atlantic City boardwalk, at the beaches that crawled past in summer-heat slowness. For a moment, she envied the carefree, sun-hat-clad, ice-chest-toting people who strolled toward the gray sand. She wondered how many of them worried about elections or secrets or handicapped sons. "I wish your grandfather had come back with us. He looked as if he should rest, too." She had tried to talk Will out of going across town to meet Michael at a union rally, then from there to the convention center to schmooze for last-minute delegate votes. Not surprisingly, she had failed.

"Gramps loves the action, Mom. Hey—this is his dream, isn't it?"

Her smile was wry. "Sort of," she said. She had been careful not to emphasize to her kids that this had been Will's dream for Daniel, not for Liz, or rather, not for Liz and her husband. She'd been careful not to canonize Daniel, because he had been human, despite what Will Adams had thought, or still thought to this day. Besides, Liz had not wanted to give Danny anything unrealistic to have to live up to as Daniel's namesake. She had named her firstborn after the brother she had adored—long before anyone could have predicted the devastating football injury that had given her son a burden more powerful than living up to the legacy of someone's name. Even though that someone had been Daniel.

She looked at her son, who was gazing out his window. "Are you sure you're okay with this?" she asked.

"It's a little late for that, Mom. And no, I'm not always 'okay' with this. I'm not okay about a lot of things. But I'll survive."

Liz folded her hands in her lap and lowered her eyes, hating her own helplessness. She could not change what had happened, no one could. All she could do was give speeches on the topics of the day, smile and pretend to stay upbeat no matter how she really felt.

It was Danny's turn to pat Liz on the arm. "Sorry, Mom. Guess I'm really ragged out."

She rested her hand on top of his. His fingers were sturdy and masculine, callused by pull-ups and dips on the parallel bars in a daily upper-body strength regimen guided by Clay. She remembered that she must be grateful that Danny was only paralyzed from the waist down, that though his spinal cord injury had been precariously close, it had not been higher up on his vertebrae where more devastating, total-body damage could have been done. Still, when she looked at her so-handsome son, when she thought of his future or listened to his words that so often balanced on the rim of depression, gratitude was not always what she felt.

The van came to a stop. "All ashore that's going ashore," Keith called to the backseat.

Liz peeked out the window. They were not at the hotel, but at some kind of medical center. "We're supposed to be at the hotel." She couldn't help the whine in her voice.

"Your brother Roger called earlier. He arranged a last-minute appearance for you and Danny. Something in pediatrics."

Liz knew this had little to do with the sick children and more to do with feel-good photos for the evening news. She closed her eyes briefly, then looked at Danny. "I'm sorry, honey. Maybe you'll get that nap later."

Danny forced a smile and a shrug.

Long hours later, Liz was finally able to crawl under the covers and pull a scratchy hotel sheet up to her chin, trying to be quiet so as not to awaken Michael. The pediatrics appearance had left no time for a nap before a fund-raiser at the Guggenheim in Manhattan, then a guest shot on Letterman and back to Atlantic City.

She stared up at the dark ceiling. How had presidents been elected before helicopters were invented? When had it become the job of the First-Lady-to-be to keep the momentum going while her candidate-husband was stumping across the country or buried in strategy sessions? And yet she had to admit that there was something exhilarating about the attention . . . about having people smile at you, care about your every move, *listen* to what you had to say.

Breathing in the scent of commercially laundered linen, she closed her eyes. Tomorrow, the convention would open. Tomorrow, they would be cloistered in their hotel rooms, invisible to the world for four days until the candidate was officially chosen. Shutting themselves out from the world was part of Father's strategy toward building the drama and thus the momentum. It seemed like overkill, but Liz had to admit it would be four lovely, peaceful, media-free days. Maybe she'd even wear jeans. And sneakers. Yes, she thought, she would wear sneakers.

"Danny thinks you should be running, not me." Michael's words startled her. Even after all these years, she still could not tell when he was sleeping or when he was not. She rolled onto her side and reached across the king-size mattress until her fingers found the muscled-hard flesh at the top of his leg where it met up with his butt. There were few nights in these last many months that they had shared the same zip code, let alone the same bed.

She grinned in the darkness and lightly stroked him. "You have a great ass, Governor," she said. "I wonder if Roger should mention that in the press kit."

She sensed his smile.

"I expect no one would much care about my ass," he joked. "But they might be concerned that a word like that was coming from the lips of the next First Lady."

She moved across the bed, pressing her body against his nakedness. When they were first married, it had made Liz uncomfortable that Michael slept without clothes; now, she could not imagine him in bed beside her any other way. It was no longer as much about sex as it had once been; now it was about the warmth of his skin, the feel of his touch, the feel of her touch on him.

"What Danny said is true." Michael turned to her and encircled an arm around her tired shoulders. "I think your approval rating is higher than mine."

"I'm not sure Father would agree."

Michael kissed the top of her head, then fluttered a hand across her breast. "I disagree," he replied. "Something tells me your father would do just about anything to keep Josh Miller out of the White House."

Her hand froze on his leg. She wished Michael did not have to mention politics here, in bed. She wished that, just for a minute, he'd stop thinking about . . . work. She also wished he'd found a better time to mention Josh Miller than when her hand was making its way toward his penis and he was gently caressing her breast.

But now that he'd brought it up, she had to ask. "Do you really think Josh is going to be a problem? You're ahead in the polls."

"Not by much. And first I have to be officially nominated."

Michael's nomination was merely a party formality. He had swept the primaries, he had won over the delegates. It had not been as easy for Josh: he'd had a tough fight, but three weeks ago had captured his party's—the *other* party's—nomination.

"But how can Josh win? He's Jewish," she said, echoing her father's words, her father's thoughts.

"Kennedy was Catholic," Michael reminded her. "We never thought he'd make it out of Boston. But religion no longer matters. Nor should it. What matters is who is the best candidate."

Liz wondered if her husband really believed what he was saying, or if he'd simply been a politician too long. She moved her hand up to his back. "Let's not worry about the other side," she said. "Let's just take care of what we need to take care of." She hoped her voice sounded convincing.

"What I need to take care of right now is this erection you seem to have given me," he said softly.

Liz hesitated a moment and pretended not to know why. "Are you sure?" she asked. "You must be tired."

Without answering, he lifted her nightgown and slowly began kissing her face, then her throat, then the soft little places that lead to her breasts.

This is Michael, she told herself. *This is your husband, the man that you love.* But, even as her body moved in sweet rhythm with his, Liz felt an ache of dissatisfaction, followed by the sting of tears. Suddenly she wished that BeBe were back. Back in the world still ruled by their father, the world that seemed to be spinning out of control. Her sister, BeBe, was the only one who would understand how she was feeling. But BeBe was in Florida, safe from the "scrutiny" of the media, safe from the spotlight. Father had wanted it that way, and, as usual, Liz had not argued.

She cradled her face against Michael's shoulder. What would they think—Michael, her children—if they ever discovered that their mother was not as wonderful as they had thought?

Chapter 2

 "It's three o'clock in the damn morning," BeBe barked into the phone, her voice a husky blend of last night's margaritas and too many cigarettes, both of which she'd sworn off four times in the last month alone.

"But it's nine o'clock in Paris," said Ruiz, his voice as clear as if he were sitting in bed next to her. "The Loudets are waiting for your answer."

BeBe groaned, pulled off her black satin eyemask, and snapped on the lamp. "Ruiz," she said, "remind me to fire you when you get home."

"You cannot fire me. You are in love with my great Cuban ass."

Despite the hour and the slight headache that ringed her temples, BeBe laughed. "You're right." She picked up a glass from the nightstand and sipped some water. "I was a bad girl last night," she confessed. "I missed you so much I went to The Breakers and hung out at the aquarium bar like a trollop."

There was a pause over the line from Palm Beach to Paris. "What is a trollop?" Ruiz asked.

BeBe laughed again, though this time it was forced.

"Forget it," she said. She'd never been fully convinced that Ruiz's English wasn't actually better than her own. It seemed he liked playing the inferior one, the subservient employee to his lover-boss. It was a habit that was beginning to irritate the hell out of her. "Tell the Loudets I'm not ready to deal."

This time, the pause was not phony.

"Then why did I come here, BeBe?"

She took another sip of water. "You went because you wanted to get ideas for the new package designs."

"And to make French Country Comestibles irresistible to the Loudets."

He was right. BeBe had been toying with the idea of selling out to the Loudets, and Ruiz had been encouraging her. The French toiletries manufacturer had been courting her for over a year—ever since her brother-in-law had stepped into the international political scene and announced his bid for the presidency. Nor were they alone. It seemed that every opportunist with a fat wallet thought French Country would become more successful because of Michael's visibility. It was as if no one had noticed that it had been BeBe herself who had started her company with a single item: the most delectable, finely layered chocolate croissants on the face of the earth. BeBe had started it, and BeBe had turned it into a forty-million-dollar gourmet food industry whose exclusive products were available only through mail order or at the most discerning boutiques and department stores around the world. From her pear tart patisseries to her latest mandarin creme biscuits—all packaged in collectible tins of French blues and butter yellows and featuring the lovely designs of Ruiz—with each new item BeBe had grown more successful, alone, on her own. But lately no one cared that Michael Barton had absolutely nothing to do with the business.

And now, countless people wanted a piece of her, a

chunk of the action. Including the Loudets, who had offered one and half times what the company was worth. It was a difficult bid to ignore, even for BeBe, the independent woman.

Ruiz, of course, wanted her to take the money and run. "They won't keep the offer open forever, BeBe," he continued now. "This could be your chance of a lifetime."

She squirmed on the edge of the bed. "When are you coming home?"

He sighed. "Tomorrow night. I have some things to do first, then I'll see you about nine."

BeBe never asked what "things" Ruiz had to do. She assumed they had something to do with his Cuban refugee work, and the less she knew about that, the better. She helped back it financially, and that was enough. Uncoiling the phone cord, she let it spring back. "French Country could be worth more if Michael wins the election."

"And if he loses, it could be worth less. Or nothing at all."

BeBe stared at the floor.

"BeBe," Ruiz continued, "why are you stalling? Take the sure thing now. It will make you a very wealthy woman."

"I'm already a wealthy woman. Besides, without French Country, what would I do?"

"Stay home and let me make love to you every day."

For all his artistic talents, Ruiz would not have a problem being a kept man, as long as he was *well* kept. "I'm forty-seven, Ruiz. In a dozen years I'll be nearly sixty. You'll only be in your forties."

The pause came again. "Good-bye, Barbara Beth," Ruiz said brusquely. "I'll see you tomorrow night. In the meantime, I'll tell the Loudets to . . . how do you say it . . . kiss off?"

If she did not love his great Cuban ass, she would have told *him* to kiss off. "Just tell them I need more time. A couple of weeks." She hung up the phone. Maybe she was passing up the chance of a lifetime. Maybe it was time to let go of her business. But should she hold out for more money? Or was that being greedy? And greed was one of those seven deadly sins, wasn't it?

She threw back the covers and stepped out of bed. Greed was not the only deadly sin she'd come up against in her life, and so far, Barbara Beth "BeBe" Adams had survived.

Three hours later BeBe watched the sun haul itself up over the Atlantic and prepare for another blistering late-July day. She picked up the coffee mug that sat on her desk and tipped it to her mouth. It was empty. Sometime before dawn she'd finished her second pot of strong black java, between looking over the layouts for the spring catalog and reading proposals for a manufacturing facility in the Pacific Rim.

After her conversation with Ruiz, she had not gone back to sleep. Instead, BeBe had done what she did best: worked. Work was her salvation; work was her life. It was the one thing she could count on; it was the one thing that had ever made any sense, even though it gave her hunched shoulders and a stiff neck, daily headaches and, once, a bleeding ulcer.

Why would anyone expect her to give all that up for a mere sixty million dollars?

She set down the mug, remembering when she'd decided to go into business. She'd been between husbands number two and three. "Floundering" was the word her baby sister, Liz, had suggested; she had not been wrong. It was a condition not foreign to BeBe: it was as if her entire life had been spent on the cusp of something that never quite happened, at least not for long. It was as if her few times of settling down were just the halftimes in her permanent game of floundering.

So she'd been floundering again, between husbands, and had somehow decided that Paris was as good a place as any to do it.

For a few weeks she'd surveyed the haute couture and the Champs-Élysées and Luxembourg Gardens and the Moulin Rouge. Then she met a man who actually lived on one of those houseboats on the Seine, and she ended up spending four days and four nights there. His name was Pierre (no surprise there) and what was most memorable about him were the chocolate croissants he fed her in bed and the unique way he used his tongue to lick the delicate crumbs from all over her body.

When she tired of him or he tired of her (who tired first, she could not quite remember), BeBe walked the side streets of Paris. It was then that she saw the word "Comestibles" engraved on a wooden shingle. The sign hung over an old shop in a pale putty-colored building that hugged the curve of a narrow alley. Intrigued by the word, BeBe stepped inside the shop. There, amid cozy collections of gourmet treats, she found lovely, light biscuits and alpine-rich cocoa and marmalade made in Provence.

Comestibles. The word would not leave her mind, but continued to roll deliciously around in her mouth, even after she'd stopped floundering, even after she'd returned to the States.

Just before she met and (unfortunately) married husband number three, BeBe started French Country in the garage of her old condo in Palm Beach Gardens. In honor of Pierre, she began with chocolate croissants.

She supposed that when Father learned about her venture, he had not expected it would last very long. Which BeBe admitted to herself was perhaps the one reason she was determined to make it succeed. Thankfully, she'd waited until her next (and last) divorce before generating the big bucks. She'd moved up from croissants to tea cakes in lemon and custard and raspberry-almond. That's when she had the idea to pack her goodies in tins, thus escalating the retail price, the geographic span of the market, and the profits.

And now, here she was, perched on the edge of sixty million dollars, wondering if she should jump in or get off.

She stood up and decided that right now she was going to do nothing but shower and dress for the office.

She crossed the media room of her sprawling home, which, nestled as it was along prime Palm Beach water-front, was a few hundred steps up from the old condo in the Gardens. She absently picked up the remote and flicked on the television as she walked past. Out of the corner of her eye she saw Michael's picture. She stopped in the middle of the room and turned to the TV. She watched. She listened. She tightened the sash of her silk robe.

"We're all so pleased to be at the convention," Michael was saying to the crowd of reporters, micro-phones shoved at his face. "It's been a long journey to Atlantic City. In the next few days, we'll see where we go from here." He waved and flashed a wide smile. The cameras pulled back and BeBe saw Liz.

"Hey," BeBe called out to the wide screen before her, to her gorgeous kid sister who had come so far. Then BeBe saw Roger and his pain-in-the-ass wife, Evelyn, then Mags and Greg and Danny—Liz's kids, her nephews, her niece. But the smile that had come to her face vanished when she saw that next to Danny's wheel-chair stood Father, all puffed up and arrogant as if this were his show.

Looking at the eyes that looked too much like her

own, BeBe decided that maybe she *should* take the sixty million and run. Because for all of Father's connections and all his big-mouthing, she doubted if he had ever had such a sum. It would be revenge, and it would be sweet, but it would not be enough, never enough. With a slow, steady hand, BeBe raised the remote, leveled it at Will Adams's face, and pressed the OFF button.

If it hadn't been for Claire, BeBe would have lost her mind long ago, like maybe eight years ago when she'd decided she had enough products to begin her own direct mail catalog. Until then, French Country had been offered only through other people's catalogs and stores, other people who were making the real money, not her.

Claire was a single mother of three, struggling to make it on an administrative assistant's pay and no child support. When Claire showed up at the condo for an interview, BeBe was instantly drawn to her. It might have been the young mother's patently old, but neat and clean, navy blue suit—so uncommon in these days of nothing but jeans. Or it might have been BeBe's inherent attraction to the underdogs of life, with whom, despite the dubious "privilege" of her upbringing, BeBe had always felt she belonged. BeBe had hired her immediately, and had been happily increasing her salary regularly to numbers the woman had perhaps never dreamed possible.

However, Claire was a cynic who thought all men were scum (especially Ruiz) and detested politics (especially Michael Barton's politics), and she never hesitated to share her opinions with her boss.

"Your sister's on the phone," Claire said later that day. BeBe was sitting in her office reviewing résumés for much-needed additional chefs, trying to decide who could be trusted with her lavish, rich recipes.

"Lizzie!" BeBe said exuberantly into the phone. "I saw you this morning. You look wonderful."

"It's all done with mirrors," Liz replied. "The truth is, I'm beginning to feel older than dirt."

"What you need is some Florida sun."

"What I need is to talk to my big sister. Tell me this is all worth it, Beebs. Tell me everything will be okay."

It was a request BeBe could not even pretend to grant. "I'm sure Father has everything under control." She wanted to sound as if she'd meant it, as if it could give her sister some comfort. But, as usual, anytime Father's name was mentioned between them, a gap opened that could not be closed. BeBe had barely seen Father since Daniel was killed.

"Oh, Beebs," Liz said. "I wish things could be different. I wish you could be here."

"Me too, kiddo." It had, however, long since been decided that their politics would not be a showcase for the family's black sheep. "How are the kids?" BeBe asked brightly.

"Bearing up well. Danny's a little tired. But I guess that's to be expected."

"And Michael? Is he going to be nominated?"

"It looks that way."

"And?"

"And what?"

"And he'll be running against Josh." She waited one, two, three seconds for Liz to comment.

"Congratulations," Liz said. "I see you're keeping up with the news."

BeBe wondered just how much French Country's business might suffer if Michael lost the election, or worse, if ancient, dark family secrets were unearthed during the race. She supposed it was possible that her customers might choose to no longer deal with an Adams. She had a sudden thought of Billy Carter, and wondered what had ever happened to his beer.

Leaning back in her chair, she put her feet up on her desk. She looked down at her legs, which had never been as long as her sister's, and at the pale skin that, despite living year-round in Florida, no longer tanned as it had on the Vineyard, but more often burned and made her sprout adolescent freckles that matched her orange hair. "Well," she said slowly, "it will be an interesting election."

Liz hesitated then said, "Yes. Well. That's one way of putting it."

BeBe's heart ached just a little. "Keep your chin up, kiddo, and everything will work out. It always has. It always does." She did not add, "But not always the way we want."

"I love you, big sister," Liz replied. "Will you come see us when we're in south Florida?"

"What? Come to one of those horrible dinners with overboiled chicken and dishwater gravy?"

"Yes."

"The answer is no. Not on your life."

"Then I'll have to make time to come and see you."

"Please. And bring the kids. I love those kids."

"Me, too, Beebs. And I love you, too. You're the best sister. Guess I'd better go. Roger wants to give us an update."

"Kisses to him, too. But not to his wife." They both laughed for a second before hanging up.

Then BeBe looked down at her flame-colored manicure and wondered how Liz would feel if she ever found out that once, long ago, BeBe, the "best sister," had slept with her husband. That was before Michael had married Liz, of course. That was . . . before.

With a fast, forget-about-it sigh, BeBe sat up straight and buzzed Claire. There was no point dwelling on the stuff of the past. Not when there were millions to be made and work to be done.

Chapter 3

He hated being there. He hated the way his mother bowed down to his grandfather and the way his father acted like he didn't notice and the way his Uncle Roger juggled everyone and everything, a computer in one hand, a cell phone in the other. He hated the way his Aunt Evelyn paraded her martyred, "look at poor me, my husband is gay" self in front of the family, despite the fact that she would not agree to a divorce and lose her "status" (her word, not theirs) in life. Danny hated these things, just as he hated it that he couldn't even go down to the lobby for fear of a tabloid reporter and a pop-flashing camera. And he hated it that they were all as imprisoned in this hotel as he was in his chair.

Then again, Danny reasoned as he wheeled to the window and looked out across the skyline of copper and black glass and silver-fronted Atlantic City casinos, he hated most things these days.

He sighed. It was almost six o'clock. He'd already spent three hours online chatting the chat, and he did not want to join his brother and sister for a predictable *what if* session about the election outcome: *What if* they won't let us have our friends come to the White House? *What if* we want to have dates? Will the Secret Service come, too? Danny wanted to ask, *What if* by some miracle he suddenly was healed? Would they have to hide him until after the election because they'd lose too many sympathy votes? He supposed it was a tacky question. He did not want to be accused of feeling sorry for himself.

Besides, he had been taught that as the eldest child of Michael and Elizabeth (aka Ken and Barbie) Barton, he had to set an example. Doing that these days was tough, especially when he no longer gave a shit about much of anything, had not given a shit in the last three years, not since he'd looked at the world—and everyone in it— below the waist, no longer eye to eye, but eye to crotch. Danny recognized that few people were comfortable looking him square in the eye, anyway. Instead, they shifted from one foot to the other, trying not to drop their gaze to his dead legs, obviously relieved when they were able to move on.

From the other side of the wall came the sounds of his sister Mags's high-pitched, girlish laughter. Danny smiled. He had always wanted to be more like Magsie, more carefree and clever, more like Aunt BeBe. Instead, Danny guessed he was more like his mother, Liz, which was maybe why he got so upset when he saw her trying so hard to make everyone's life perfect, especially Gramps's.

The door burst open. "Hey, mon," said Clay, Danny's never-too-far-away nurse, "time to come out and play."

"A knock would have been nice." Danny spun his wheelchair around. "What if I was entertaining a young lady?"

Clay twirled a dreadlock around one finger. "If you was entertaining a young lady, I would have stood and applauded. But seeing you're not, how about if we work on some handstand push-ups?"

As part of his indefatigable quest to keep Danny in shape, or at least the top half of Danny in shape, Clay had developed a way to flip him upside down, lean him against a wall, and actually have him do push-ups as if he were in training for the U.S. men's gymnastics team. Danny had accused him of watching too much ESPN. Clay had ignored him, and in the end, Danny learned how.

"Not today, Clay. I'm tired."

"Tired my ass," the long-legged man called out as he loped across the room. "You're lazy, that's what. How do you expect to get to the White House if you're lazy?"

"I expect to be driven there in a big limousine by someone who's paid by the federal government."

"Oy!" Clay bellowed. "Remind me not to vote for you."

"Remind me not to run," Danny replied, then added, "No, never mind. You won't have to remind me." He looked around the room. "Three more days in this place?"

"It's what the mon said. You have to wait here until the last night, until your father is nominated. Your grandfather said no one can see the family until then."

"Jesus, you'd think we were getting married. The blushing bride not allowed to see the groom."

"Yeah, well, it's been a long time since you blushed, Danny boy. Now come on, let's get against the wall and give me ten."

"No, man . . ."

But Clay's hands were on the back of the wheelchair and he was steering it toward the wall. "I can't hear you," the nurse cried in singsonging jest.

Then, in what seemed like only an instant, Clay stopped the chair, tugged down Danny's shoulders, and flipped him against the wall. The blood flooded to

Danny's face; his legs were braced by his nurse who now chanted "Give me *one* . . ."

"Oh, Christ," Danny muttered. For a moment he refused to perform, and decided that among everything and everyone else, he now hated Clay as well. But as he stood there or hung there or whatever it was he was doing, Danny was reminded that without Clay he was pretty much helpless, that without him, he might just hang there forever or at least until he turned purple and blood came out his eyes and his nose and his ears. And oh, what a tabloid shot that would make.

Yeah, he depended on Clay. Then again, Clay had a pretty good job. A little PT, a little cleanup, a huge salary paid by a grateful Gramps—hell, Danny thought, Clay needed him as much as he needed Clay.

That's when he had an idea. "Clayman," he said, "I'm going to make you a deal."

"Your face is turning purple," Clay responded.

Danny smiled upside down. "I'll give you ten if you get me out of here. Just for a little while. A couple of days."

"No, mon, I can't . . ."

"Yes you can. I want to see the boardwalk. I want to see Atlantic City."

"And I want to see my next birthday. Have you seen the size of those Secret Service guys?"

"Keith and Joe? You could do them in a heartbeat."

"I'd rather not find out."

Danny wondered why he was feeling light-headed, when the blood was rushing up to his brain, not down from it. "We can go in disguise," he continued. "I'll leave my mother a note. Not even the Secret Service would do anything to upset my mother, and she never gets angry with me. Besides," he added, lowering himself on his hands, "if you don't help me, I'll see that you're fired."

"Bullshit," Clay said.

Danny let his arms collapse. The weight of his body followed.

"Sheeeeet," Clay said, trying to gather the crumpled parts of his patient.

With his face mashed into the thin hotel carpet, Danny asked, "Change your mind?"

"Okay, okay, mon," he said, sliding Danny up into the wheelchair. "You're a crazy man, but I'll try and figure something out."

Danny grinned.

In the note Danny left for his mother the next morning, he explained that he had to get out of there for a couple of days. "I promise, absolutely, double-deal promise to be back before the nomination," he had written on the back of a piece of hotel stationery. The "double-deal promise" was reminiscent of when he was in second grade, and he'd learned that a promise sometimes had to be broken (such as Dad "promising" to show up at his soccer game, but having to fly off somewhere instead). He decided then that the only way to be sure that a promise was kept was to make it, then double it, twice as solid, twice as apt to not come apart. It had made sense to a seven-year-old, and had tugged at his mother's heartstrings. Now, he was counting on its nostalgia to do that again.

So his mother was going to have to make excuses for him to his father and grandfather, not to mention Mags and Greg, who'd be pissed that he'd abandoned them in hotelsville. He adjusted the brim of the Yankees cap Clay had bought him and steered his chair toward the railing overlooking the beach, knowing that he did not could not would not let himself feel guilty. He and Clay would be back tomorrow night with a day to spare before the nomination: there would be plenty of time for remorse then.

"Are you happy now, Danny boy?"

Through his oversized, not-exactly-rose-colored sunglasses, Danny smiled. "Happy enough, mon," he said, watching two girls with bigger buns than bikinis bounce by in front of them, a much lovelier sight than his computer or room service, and a much more pleasurable pastime than doing ten for Clay. They had come almost all the way down to Ocean City: Clay said there were no rooms closer to Atlantic City because of the convention, but Danny suspected his nurse had wanted to get Danny as far from the place and the Secret Service as possible, yet still close enough for a quick return.

"For punishment," Clay said, "I think I will make you drive back."

Danny squinted against the sun's glare off the water. "Then I think I really *will* have you fired. I'll say this was all your idea."

Clay shrugged. "One can't blame a body for trying."

No, Danny supposed, one could not. Everyone in their own way—some subtle, some not—had been unsuccessfully trying to get Danny to drive the van that Gramps had ordered, the fully equipped, handicapped kid's set of big wheels. He shook off his annoyance. "Right now, what I want is a burger smothered in fried onions and ketchup," he said. "In fact, I want two. And a fat chocolate shake."

"Not good for the digestive tract."

"Tough."

"Why does it feel like you're holding me hostage?" Clay asked.

Danny smiled, then turned from the water. "After my burgers I want to stroll down the boardwalk and feed popcorn to the seagulls and play video games in the arcade and maybe even have the lumps in my skull read by a phrenologist with big, dangly earrings and a crystal ball. I want to be anonymous, Clay. Before the world becomes my permanent parasite, I want to have fun."

Clay smiled back. "You ask a lot for a man in a wheelchair."

Danny gave him the finger and headed for the hamburger stand.

He had a blast. They went down to Cape May—to the zoo and the lighthouse—then back to the beach for more lazy girl-watching. They cruised the boardwalk that evening, where the phrenologist told him he would have seven children. He won a half-dozen fake Beanie Babies playing old-fashioned Skee-Ball, ate two ice-cream cones and a cheese dog on a stick. Then he and Clay spent the night in a seedy motel where his mattress was springy and Clay's sagged in the middle and no one would have expected to see the son of a president. Which of course he wasn't yet.

It was all great, rebellious fun.

The next day began blisteringly hot. Clay let Danny forgo his morning exercise regimen and they set off on an ecotour of Great Egg Harbor. The only difficult part was loading Danny onto the pontoon boat. Amazingly, no one recognized him.

At four o'clock, Clay announced that no matter what threats Danny used, it was time to go back. "Tomorrow's the nomination," he said, which was no news to Danny. "Your father's big day."

They were riding along the beach road when it happened. Danny was in the back, gazing out the window, feeling the feel-good glow of adventure fade more and more as the miles shrank toward the convention center, toward his reality.

As if sensing Danny's mood, Clay snapped on the radio and scanned for a station. Between hard rock and country, they heard the announcement.

"About an hour ago at the Atlantic City Convention Center . . ."

The tuner skipped to the next station, where an oldies song played. But some kind of sixth sense had caught Danny's attention. "Go back," he said. "To that news thing."

Clay fiddled with the buttons, trying to find it.

"Come on, man," Danny pleaded. "Hurry up."

Clay flicked through the stations unsuccessfully and started to steam. "This is your goddamn van," he said, pushing another wrong button. "If you'd learn to drive it . . ."

And then, the announcer's somber voice was back.

"A seventh-generation American," the voice was saying, "he was instrumental in shaping much of the political scene as it is known today."

Danny would have sworn the chill that he felt dropped from his heart to his spine, into his dead butt and down his numb legs.

"Oh, Christ," he said. "Pull over."

Clay yanked the wheel and pointed it at the soft, sandy shoulder. The van slid to a stop.

Danny kept his eyes fixed out the window, out at the water, as the announcer continued. "It is not known how this will effect tomorrow night's nomination process. As of now, funeral arrangements are incomplete, but it is expected that William Woodman Adams will be buried in his hometown of Boston."

"*Sheeeet,*" Clay whispered.

Danny put his face in his hands. "Fuck," he muttered. "Fuck."

They sat there awhile on the side of the road, the silent nurse and his patient, the runaway grandson, who was too stunned to wonder how Gramps had died or where or when. He only knew one thing, and he said it out loud. "This is going to kill my mother," he told Clay, as if Clay didn't know. "This is absolutely going to fucking kill my poor mother."

Part II

1972

Chapter 4

"Where the Sam Hill is your sister?" Lizzie's father hissed beside her.

Lizzie Adams kept her eyes on the parade and bit her lip. "She'll be here, Father." Her spine stiffened as ramrod straight as the backs of the West Point graduates who were marching past them. "She promised."

"I shouldn't have let her come," he sputtered. "I should have known better."

Liz blinked against the bright sun, and tried to shield herself from the glare that hovered over the reviewing stand, its white-hot veil shimmering, marking time with the cadence of the rat-tatting, rum-tumming drums. Why did BeBe have to be late when she knew how important this was to Father? And why, in their second-row seats (VIP honored guests of the governor of New York), were they not exempt from the steamy weather?

Lizzie glanced in front of them at the governor and his wife, surprised that they remained cool-looking, unaffected by the heat. Then she looked down at her linen suit and wondered if the governor's wife would be as wrinkled as she surely would be by the time this long-winded ceremony ended.

"Why can't your sister be more like you?"

Her father's words made her back straighten again. She adjusted the small heels of her bone-colored shoes on the bleacher plank and clasped the matching handbag in her lap. "Father . . ." she began to protest, then quickly scanned the marching unit. "Look! There he is. There's Daniel!"

Although Daniel was in the same gray uniform as the other cadets, his chin was somehow higher, his body more square. His personal magnetism was almost visible as an aura around him. "Destined for greatness," Will Adams frequently said in case anyone had forgotten. "Presidential material."

Lizzie could see that the sight of Daniel had distracted her father from the subject of his absent wild-child. She tried not to sigh.

It was no surprise that her sister wasn't there. BeBe was nineteen now and she'd gone to a graduation party last night. She hadn't gone to the cotillion last week, of course, because only those lucky girls who had dates with cadets were able to dress like debutantes and float into the ball on a privileged cloud. No, BeBe had not gone to the historic cotillion, and when Father had remarked in private that Lizzie might attend with Daniel's roommate, Michael Barton, Lizzie had refused. She didn't refuse Father very often, but she had not wanted BeBe to feel left out. Inside, however, Liz had died a trillion deaths, because she would have loved the cotillion, she just knew she would.

She would also have loved to go to the party last night, but Father had said, "No. Absolutely not, you're too young." Chaperoned balls apparently were one thing; beer-drinking parties, another.

Father had not wanted BeBe to go either. But BeBe

went anyway. She could do what she wanted. She was a college student—at Mount Holyoke, no less—and "of age," at least in New York, where West Point happened to be. Lizzie, however, was doomed to dinner with Mother and Father and some "people" in the ancient dining room at the Hotel Thayer. It was elegant and quite grand, perched high above the Hudson, but Lizzie's evening could not compare with BeBe's good time.

Daniel, of course, also went to the party, as did their brother Roger and Michael, Daniel's roommate, who had ended up going to the cotillion with a girl from New Jersey. "She's ugly as dog breath," Daniel had made it a point to tell Lizzie, which did not say much because Daniel's taste was questionable: he'd taken Evelyn Carter, the granddaughter of the congressman who'd "gotten" Daniel into West Point. Her buck teeth had straightened out, but her personality had not: Evelyn Carter would always be one of those people obsessed with everybody else's business. But Daniel had taken her. So much for great destinies.

Besides, Lizzie didn't care who Michael had taken to the cotillion. He was simply Daniel's roommate, the other Massachusetts boy who had been appointed to the academy. "Michael Hamilton Barton," he'd introduced himself when he'd been a plebe and Lizzie was only twelve. She later learned that he was a "Barton of Lynnfield," which mattered to Father.

Just as Lizzie stretched her neck now to try and pick out Michael in the perfectly aligned ranks, a voice behind her whispered, "He's on the left. Third row. And he asked about you last night."

Lizzie blushed. "Sit down, BeBe," she whispered back. "Before you give Father a heart attack." She ignored the cold-as-ice glare that Will Adams gave BeBe and tried to find Michael among the other gray-suited graduates, secretly dying to know what else he had said.

. . .

Later that afternoon, Lizzie sat on the wide back veranda of their Martha's Vineyard summer home. It was a sprawling, gray-shingled, white-trimmed house set atop a sloping, velvet lawn that met a path that snaked through a thicket then sneaked to their cove and down to the sea.

It was a summer view she knew well, a view meant for just sitting on the white wicker swing on which she was sitting now and watching the sunsets, the seagulls, the tide, and, well, nothing special.

Nothing special, like the way Michael Barton and Daniel tossed a football now, back and forth, high into the pink and peach and navy blue end-of-the-day sky. By the sounds of their laughter no one would guess they had both come here to await their military orders, the word from the Army as to where they would go.

She pushed her feet against the porch floorboards and tried not to stare. But Liz couldn't help herself.

Like Daniel, Michael had changed since those early plebeian days. His chest was broader, his shoulders straighter, his voice had become grown-up deep. And he was . . . handsome. Handsome and smart and surely interested in older girls, surely not in the sixteen-year-old kid sister of a roommate, despite what Father seemed to want.

"All that money and textiles, too," Will Adams had said at least a dozen times, referring to Michael's lineage, which ran strongly through several renowned Lowell mills.

Lowering her eyes to the moist spot that seeped from Michael's chest through his T-shirt, Liz tried to decide what it would be like to fall in love with him and his textile mills. Love was unknown territory for Liz. For a girl from a proper Boston family who attended a proper girls' school, romance was restricted to infrequent dates and backseat kisses and groping between movies and curfew.

"No daughter of mine will shame the Adams name," she'd once heard Father shout at BeBe, when her sister had come home late—again. Mother had once told Liz that BeBe reminded Father of his dead sister, Ruth, of whom none of them was allowed to speak for some unknown, perhaps sinister, reason.

As Liz slowly rocked on the swing, she wondered why she had always felt compelled to follow Father's rules and BeBe had not, and what it had to do with his dead sister, Ruth.

"Go back for a long one," Michael shouted to Daniel. Daniel complied with four, five, six long strides backwards that landed him straight into the thicket of tall grass and scrub oaks.

He disappeared. For a moment, then another, Liz heard nothing. She smiled, suspecting what Daniel was doing.

Then he emerged. He was not carrying a football, however. Instead he was clutching the tail of a fat black-and-white skunk.

Liz squealed.

"Go back for this, Barton," Daniel yelled, twirling the skunk by the tail in a game he had invented that had sent his mother and most other sane people shrieking into the house.

"You're nuts!" Michael shouted but did not run away.

Daniel let out another yelp, twirled the skunk again, let it fly into the thicket, and raced up the slope toward the house, with Michael Barton in sudden fast pursuit.

"And that, my dear Lizzie," boomed the voice of her father, who had appeared beside her, "is the kind of tough stuff it takes to be president of the United States."

Liz nodded, because she and everyone—including Daniel—knew that he meant it. She leaned back on the swing and wondered if, *when* Daniel became president, she would have fallen in love by then, and if her children would be allowed to play on the White House lawn, and if Daniel would be too important to twirl skunks anymore.

She also wondered if Michael Barton would still be in their lives, if Daniel might appoint him an ambassador or something important, and if an embassy in an exotic land would be as elegant as the White House itself.

"And every president," came a voice from the doorway, the voice of Evelyn Carter, Daniel's know-everything-about-everyone cotillion date, "deserves one of these."

Liz's eyes dropped to Evelyn's hands, where she held a shiny, blue-silvery, hefty handgun. For a brief second, Liz thought it was pointed at Father. Then Father laughed and Daniel and Michael lumbered onto the porch, and Father said, "Let's have Mother bring us some fresh-squeezed lemonade."

It was a graduation gift for Daniel, a working antique that had been in Evelyn's family since World War I, maybe earlier, and it was called a pistol, not a gun.

"It's from Grandfather's collection," she explained, "He had planned to put it in the celebrity auction this Saturday, but he decided Daniel should have it instead."

That, of course, was an honor in itself. The annual Chilmark auction was famous for its social-register festivities, an occasion when those Vineyarders whose names or likenesses had ever appeared anywhere in the media had the "privilege" of donating goods or services. The money raised went to island youth programs; the prestige that it generated lined the egos of the rich.

"Grandfather would have brought it himself," Evelyn continued, "but he's still not quite right since the stroke."

Will Adams nodded understandingly. Daniel moved his eyes from the pistol to Father to Evelyn, then back to the gun. Liz wondered if he was worried that one lousy cotillion date had now locked him into a family-made match, the result of God only knew how many years of "favors" passed between Will Adams and Evelyn's congressman grandfather.

"He felt you should have it," she added with an over-eager bat to her lashes, "now that you're a soldier and all."

"Thank you," Daniel said. "And thank your grandfather for me, please. It's . . ." He turned the pistol over in his hand and studied the wood-carved handle. "It's great."

Great, Liz knew, was a neutral kind of word that Daniel used whenever he did not know what else to say, and in this case it must mean he was not impressed with Evelyn or her gift. It was an observation that made Lizzie smile.

Then Evelyn dug through the red straw tote bag that matched her red canvas shoes and withdrew a small box.

"Ammunition," she said, proudly holding the box toward Daniel. "Grandfather always says you never know what might happen next."

For a moment no one spoke, as if each was contemplating what, indeed, might happen next.

Then Father took the ammunition. "We'll need to keep this in a safe place," he said and reached for the gun. Daniel seemed glad to hand it over. "I'll lock it up in my desk in the study. But first we'll have young Hugh Talbot check it out for safety." Hugh Talbot was the new town sheriff.

Evelyn smiled and Daniel nodded and Michael took another drink.

It occurred to Liz that Daniel might be glad to get his "orders," so that he'd be able to escape Evelyn Carter now that he was a "soldier and all." Swirling the ice cubes in her glass, Liz considered where Daniel would go and how long it would be before he came back again and if the straw tote bag–toting girl would hang around and wait.

Then she stole a quick glance at Michael and wondered where his orders would send him and if she should write to him and if he'd write back. Just then a stranger appeared at the foot of the porch, and Liz forgot about Michael Barton altogether.

It was like something out of a movie, the kind you go to alone on a Saturday afternoon when you're feeling lonely and in need of a good pull on your emotions, maybe an opportunity to leave a few tears in the balcony.

"Excuse me," the stranger said. "I've lost my dog."

Liz did not know if everyone else felt the same slow-motion movements of the next few moments, moments that would be burned in her memory—the way the late-day sun seemed to melt into her face, the way it spread its heat all through her body.

Quickly, she put a hand to her throat and willed herself to breathe.

"She's a black Lab," the stranger was saying, though somehow it didn't seem right that he had a voice, because he looked more like a statue, a carved marble statue that wore cutoff jeans where a fig leaf should be. His chest, however, was bare and broad and shimmery in the sunlight maybe from lotion or maybe from . . . *sweat.*

Liz glanced at the others in case she had groaned out loud.

But their eyes were fixed on the stranger.

"No dogs around here," Father said. "We'd know if there were. My son is allergic."

The son he referred to was not Daniel, but Roger. Liz was surprised that right now she was able to remember that.

The stranger blinked. He was looking at her now; his long-lashed, deep-set eyes were as dark as the hair on his head and the hair on his chest, which trailed into a V and disappeared beneath his belt. "Well, if you see her," he said, "her name is Snuffy. She's real friendly."

Father gave a curt nod, but did not ask what to do if they saw her, how they could get hold of him, where he lived.

"Well, thanks," the stranger said. "Sorry to have bothered you."

Father stood, watching him leave.

"I know who that is," Evelyn said. "His family just bought the house on the other side of the cove."

Father raised his thick gray brows. Obviously, he had not yet heard the news.

"The Bentley place," Evelyn continued. "Well, it's now owned by the Millers. From Westchester. He's the son. And his name is Josh." She lowered her voice and added, "They're Jews. The whole lot of them."

"He'd kill you," BeBe said.

They sat in Liz's small room after dinner—the room that was tucked under the eaves. They sat on her small iron bed that smelled slightly of mothballs and dampness and everything summer.

"I'm sixteen, Beebs. It's not as if I'm twelve." Liz wrapped her old chenille robe—her "island robe"— around her more tightly, knowing that BeBe was right. Father would kill her if he had any idea she had . . . what? Fallen madly in love with this boy named Josh Miller? And why had she? She'd seen him for what—one minute? Two? They hadn't even spoken, and yet . . .

Was it his smile? His eyes? His . . . scent? She'd once read in a magazine that people emit scents just as animals do. That for every person there is a positive—and positively delicious—scent. Maybe if she explained that to Father, that it was all about nature, that it wasn't her fault . . .

"Besides," BeBe continued, "you don't know anything about him."

"I know he's gorgeous."

"Maybe he has a girlfriend."

"I don't care."

"He's Jewish."

"I don't care about that, either."

"Well, maybe he does."

Liz looked at her sister. "Why would he care that he's Jewish?"

"He might care that you're not."

Liz rose from the bed and paced to the window. She looked out onto the sandy earth below, lit only by the firelight that spilled from the living room downstairs, and by the half-moon that had risen high in the sky. "I've got to find a way to see him again, Beebs."

"You're smitten, Lizzie. It was bound to happen and now it has. Do yourself a favor and forget it. Trust me, it will pass."

Liz did not answer, but stared out the window.

"And aside from the obvious, don't forget that Father has picked out Michael for you."

"Michael is nice," Liz replied dreamily. "But he's not quite as . . . I don't know . . ."

"Hormonal," BeBe said, then moaned. "Oh, Lizzie, don't do this. Don't even give Josh Miller one more of your thoughts or Father will know, and Father will have him removed from the face of the earth."

Liz leaned against the window screen, breathed in a deep breath of cool Vineyard night air, and wondered if, in order to do that, Father would use the pistol that Evelyn had brought Daniel, the pistol with plenty of ammunition, because you never knew what might happen next.

Chapter 5

Late the next morning BeBe came outside, lit a cigarette, bent the match, and stuffed it into the grass. Father, of course, did not allow her to smoke in the house. She wondered if he considered smoking worse than being in love with a Jew. She inhaled deeply and thought about Liz. Her sister had finally grown into her legs and was becoming the kind of elegant beauty that would be perceived as classic, timeless, and all those other Romanesque words; refined beauty that attracted men for the long haul, way longer than one night; beauty that was very much unlike BeBe's own unique, ungroomed style.

So Liz had grown into her little-girl legs and now her heart had caught up. BeBe exhaled her relief on a slow stream of smoke, grateful that now the shock might not hurt if Lizzie ever learned that her sister, her idol, had slept with the boy that Father had chosen as Lizzie's ideal mate.

BeBe closed her eyes. She tasted the coarse taste of her morning cigarette, felt the dewy ground soak into her butt, and realized that "slept" was not exactly the right way to say it. "Had sex" was more like it. Or simply "fucked."

"We shouldn't be doing this," Michael had slurred after too many beers with tequila chasers.

They had slipped from the graduation-eve party and found a secluded dark spot on West Point's Flirtation Walk, under an oak tree, behind a stone wall.

In her heart, she knew Michael was right, but by that time she had pulled down her panties and was positioning herself over him. At that point she did not care whose penis it was, as long as it fit, as long as it would make her feel wanted and make her feel good, and smooth out—if only for a few moments—the rough edge that encircled her heart.

It did.

What had not made her feel good was that immediately after, Michael had asked if her sister had a boyfriend yet and if she'd be on the Vineyard with the family this summer.

He asked BeBe these things while her skirt was still raised and while she still had his wetness deep inside her.

But before she could answer, Michael passed out, drunk as the skunks that Daniel loved twirling.

BeBe had quickly dressed and told herself that none of it mattered; that she, after all, had been the one to pursue Michael at the party. She was not trying to steal him from Lizzie; she was trying to show Father that she was good enough to get a "good" boy, too, whether he believed it or not.

At least, that was how it seemed after several gin and tonics.

Of course, her plan had backfired, but after sobering up, BeBe told herself it was better that way.

Still, she thought now, taking another drag on her unfiltered cigarette, it would have been nice if Michael had been sober enough to act as if he'd liked her a little, as if she really was special enough to be liked by someone normal, an all-American boy.

She flicked a shred of tobacco from her lip and reminded herself that all-American boys did not go with girls like her: they were reserved for the Lizzies of the world—the Lizzies with the cheerleader looks and tightly closed thighs. Which might not remain closed much longer, if Liz had a chance at Josh Miller.

BeBe knew the signs, and she knew it was up to her to stop her kid sister before Liz's life took the same downhill course as her own. All she had to do was figure out how to divert Lizzie's thoughts back to Michael, even if it meant BeBe had to switch sides and agree with Father.

"You've got to help me," BeBe said to Roger. He looked up from the lilac bush cuttings he was transplanting behind the garage. Surprise showed on his face, for Daniel was the brother people always went to for help. Daniel, not Roger.

He set down his trowel and wiped his hands on his jeans. "Sure, Beebs. What's up?"

It occurred to BeBe, not for the first time, what a shame it was that Roger, one year younger than Daniel, seemed doomed to stand forever in his brother's huge shadow. Even physically he seemed inferior: where Daniel was sturdy, Roger was slight; where Daniel was handsome, Roger was . . . well, not unattractive, but plain. In the eyes of the family, he was number two next to Daniel, just as BeBe would always take a backseat to Liz. It was simply the way things were.

BeBe stuffed her hands into the pockets of her cutoffs. "It seems as if our Lizzie has a beau."

Behind the rims of his glasses, Roger's eyebrows went up. "Liz has a boyfriend? What's wrong with that?"

"The problem is not what, it's who." And then she told him about Josh Miller.

Roger agreed that Father would explode if he learned Liz was in love with a stranger, let alone a Jew.

"We need to do whatever we can to get her together with Michael," BeBe concluded.

"We could go to the movies tonight," Roger suggested. "All of us, if you want. Then work it so she has to sit next to him."

BeBe tweaked his cheek. "You're brilliant, brother. But not a word to anyone. It will be our secret."

He picked up his trowel and resumed his work. "Yeah, well, you'll have to find her first. I saw her head down to the cove after breakfast."

Michael Barton was not as good-looking as he had been yesterday. Liz maneuvered the rowboat around the small cove and let her thoughts drift from Michael to Josh Miller—the handsome, the untouchable, the forbidden. She set down the oars, closed her eyes, and let the warm remnants of sunset float over her, over every part of her.

She wondered what it would feel like to have his hands on her. She wondered what his fingers were like, if they were both strong and tender at the same time. She wondered what it would feel like to have his body above her, to have his dark eyes gaze into hers while he was touching her there and there and there, filling her with feelings and sensations and awakenings and . . .

Her eyes flew open. She glanced around to see if anyone was watching, if anyone could read what was on her mind by the flush that surely must be on her cheeks.

She touched a hand to her face.

Josh Miller, she thought. *Oh, God.*

She picked up the oars and began rowing again.

She had barely eaten dinner last night or breakfast this morning. Who could think of eating when all that mattered was when they would meet again, and where, and how . . .

She had decided how it would happen. She would be alone, at sunset, drifting on the water, as she was now. He would appear, slowly, calling for his dog. But then he would see her.

"Hey," he'd say softly. "Great night."

She would smile. "Yeah," she'd answer.

"I lost my dog," he'd say. "Again."

"I'll help you find her," Liz would reply. Then she would row to the shore. He would hold the side of the boat to steady it, then he would take her hand to help her out.

Their touch would be electrifying.

She'd reach up and pull the barrette from her ponytail. She'd shake her hair free. She'd look off to the horizon, but his eyes would not leave her. She'd nod toward the sky and say, "Beautiful sunset."

He would step closer, this hunk named Josh Miller. He would step closer and slide his arm around her waist. "Not as beautiful as the woman who's watching it," he would say into her hair. Then he would lean into her, his lips moving from her cheek to her ear, to her throat . . . then she would stretch her back in the slightest arch . . . then . . .

They would be married as soon as she graduated from high school. It would not matter that he was Jewish: the ceremony would be in the old South Church in Boston, and they would be so in love that no one—not even Father—could say they were not meant for each other.

And they would have children. Beautiful, olive-skinned children . . . and he would touch her forever, grazing his hand over and over her body, coming to know every inch of her being as if it were his own . . . and she would know his . . . the softness of a special place right there on his stomach, the firmness of his flesh that lay just below . . .

"Lizzie!" came a shout.

Liz jumped. One of her oars splashed into the water. Her heart pounded. Leaning over the boat, she reached for the oar. It was floating too far away. With the other oar, she tried to row toward it, but the boat went in a circle, no closer than before.

"Lizzie!" The shout came again, closer this time, and quite recognizable. It was BeBe.

"I'm here!" she called back, then stooped and reached again for the oar. This time, she fell in.

The water was early summer icy, its chill slicing straight to her bones. Breaking the surface, Liz saw BeBe standing on the shore, hands on her hips.

"What the hell are you doing?" BeBe asked.

"Hopefully not drowning," Liz replied, wiping the cold water from her eyes and kicking toward shore.

"Good," BeBe answered, "because we're all going to the movies tonight and that includes you."

The best part about The Island theater was that it was plunked on the corner of Circuit Avenue and Lake, next door to Darling's, home of the famous saltwater taffy and, even better, the rectangular blocks of popcorn in pink and in chocolate.

They bought their popcorn blocks first, then smuggled them into the movies, as if no one else in there was doing the same.

The theater was packed with summertime kids, who were there to watch or pretend to watch *The French Connection,* which had come out last year but had just made it to the Vineyard. "Slow boat from Hollywood," was how Daniel explained the delayed-movie phenomenon.

Liz followed BeBe down the almost-dark, narrow aisle, with Roger close behind. But when BeBe scooted into a row of empty seats, suddenly it was Michael who had moved in beside her. She sat down, took out her pink popcorn bar, broke off a piece, and pretended not to notice.

As the opening credits began to roll, something made her look at the silhouette of a boy as he moved down the aisle.

Then she realized it was *him.*

And he was holding out his hand to steady the elbow of a silhouette in front of him—a girl.

Liz's heart seemed to stop beating for one long moment. Then Michael leaned close to her and said, "If you want, I'll go get you a soft drink."

No, she did not want a soft drink. She wanted to know who the girl was with Josh Miller. She wanted to know why he was there with her and if he was in love with her. But all she said to Michael was, "No thanks."

The movie began. Liz did not pay attention. She was too busy looking over to where Josh was sitting. She studied the back of his head. It was hard to tell in the dark, but she didn't think he had his arm around the girl.

Maybe she's his sister, she speculated. After all, she was here with her brothers.

And with Michael.

A lump grew in her throat. Then, as she sat there, pretending to watch the movie, Michael rested his arm on the back of her chair. Her shoulders went rigid. A few days ago, Michael's gesture might have given her goosebumps, but today, she was afraid Josh might see it and think all the wrong things.

And they were wrong, weren't they?

By the time the big car-chase scene had everyone but Liz sitting forward on their velveteen-upholstered seats,

Liz thought she would die if she had to sit there any longer.

Then, thank God, the movie ended.

Daniel led them out of the lobby; Liz held back, lagging behind, doing whatever it took to have a chance to see his face again.

The chance came.

He moved through the crowd; he finally reached the spot where she stood.

"Hi," he said.

She smiled. "Hi." She was surprised that he was not much taller than she was; his broad shoulders made him look taller, bigger, than he actually was. And his skin . . . his skin was so smooth, so clear. She shifted on one foot. "Did you find your dog?"

"Yeah," he said. "Snuffy. She loves to run away."

His New York accent was mesmerizing. "By the way," she said, "I'm Liz. Liz Adams."

He grinned. "I'm Josh Miller." He kept his eyes on hers. There was something there. A magnet, maybe. A big one. With his eyes steady on Liz, he said, "This is Deborah."

The girl. Oh. She'd forgotten about *her*.

"Deborah's my cousin. She's here for a week."

The lump, the tightness, and every other foreign sensation that had invaded Liz's body now dissolved with his words.

My cousin.

Liz smiled.

"Welcome to the Vineyard," she said.

"I think she's bored," Josh said. "It's my first summer here, and except for the beach, I don't know what else to do."

Liz unlocked her eyes from his and tried to look as if she cared that his cousin was bored. "Saturday is the celebrity auction," she told him and explained what it was, though inside she was secretly amazed that everything she was saying made sense.

"Would you like to go with us?" Josh asked.

Her thoughts ground to a stop. *Go with them?* Was he asking her for a date? "I, well . . ." she stammered. "I would love to. But my family . . . we all go together . . ."

"Can we meet there?" he asked. "I'll buy you a burger and you can tell me about the island."

"Well," Liz replied. "I guess . . ."

"Liz!" BeBe's voice bellowed through the crowd.

"Got to run," Liz said.

"I'll see you Saturday," Josh said with a wink.

He had winked at her!

And as she moved on rubbery legs toward Daniel and BeBe and Roger and—oh, right—Michael Barton, Liz thought her heart was going to erupt it was beating so fast.

Chapter 6

It was hard to believe there could be this many people jammed onto the Vineyard and not have it sink into the sea. It was also hard for Liz to believe that Saturday had finally arrived, and that she'd survived the long wait. She stood under a canopy next to Daniel now and pretended she was scanning the auction crowd for potential bidders, not for Josh Miller. After all, Father had stressed the importance of this year's sale. He had decided to contribute an original letter from King George to Thomas Adams, the first of their ancestors to set foot on New World soil in Weymouth, on Cape Cod, not far from the Vineyard. Hopefully it would cause a sensation, bring in big dollars, at least a thousand, and warrant a photograph in the *Vineyard Gazette,* which was why Daniel was scheduled to do the presenting. If anyone's photo should appear as front-page news, it should be Daniel's.

Her eyes roamed the table where some of the offerings had been set out: a watercolor from a famous TV news anchor; an autographed collection of a Red Sox baseball player's cards; a sheet of original music from a mega–rock star turned islander. As she brushed away a small bee her gaze fell on Father, who stood laughing with Michael Barton as if they were old friends. On the other side of Michael was Evelyn Carter, who, for once, was not clinging to Daniel.

Liz adjusted her ponytail. Maybe Josh wasn't coming.

"Don't you ever get tired?" she asked, turning to Daniel.

He looked squarely at Lizzie, the way he looked at everyone who spoke to him—as if he or she were the most important person on the face of the earth. "Tired?" he asked her. "What do you mean?"

"Father is always making you do things. Just once, wouldn't you like to do something *you* want, not him?"

Daniel grinned and ruffled her hair the way he'd been doing since she was about three, in a way that, coming from anyone but him, she would have detested now that she was sixteen. "You make Father sound like an ogre."

"Sometimes he is. Sometimes I feel as if I have no right to my own thoughts, my own feelings. My own life."

He put a hand on her shoulder. "Lizzie, what's wrong?"

She wanted to tell him. She wanted to tell him about these strange feelings she was having about this total stranger named Josh, about this attraction she could not seem to shake, even when Father paraded Michael before her, even when Michael himself looked at her and smiled. She wanted to ask Daniel what she was supposed to do with these feelings, but she supposed his reaction would be no different from BeBe's. Liz had elected not to tell BeBe she'd be meeting Josh today: for the first time in her life, she had not shared "important" news with her sister. Neither could she now share it with Daniel. So instead of saying anything Liz just stood there, her eyes welling up with tears.

"Next we have Daniel Adams," a voice announced

over a rusty PA system. "With a most extraordinary offering. Daniel?"

He squeezed her shoulder. "Gotta go do this," he said apologetically. "Wait here, okay?"

Liz looked wordlessly at her big brother.

"Daniel Adams?" the voice crackled again. "Are you here?"

He touched a finger to her cheek, then turned toward the dais. "Over here." He stepped forward, the letter from King George in his hand.

The audience applauded. Liz blinked back her tears, looking absently over the crowd. Suddenly she stopped. She blinked again. There was Josh. He was standing by the homemade pie table, watching Daniel. And he was alone.

"You didn't bring your cousin," Liz said when she'd finally made it across the grounds to Josh. She tried to look pleasant and pretty, but inside she was a tangle of scared-child tremors.

"She went shopping instead," he replied.

Up on the dais, the bidding for King George's letter began at four hundred dollars.

Liz knitted her fingers together. "You didn't bring your dog, either."

Then he smiled and she felt she would melt right then and there, that she would turn into a small puddle at the bottom of his sneakers. "Snuffy?" He laughed. "She would have thought all these people had come to see her. She's better off when I can walk her along the beach at midnight. I do that sometimes, and it's just the two of us with no distractions, and no temptation for her to run off."

His voice was deep, deeper than Michael's, and his dark eyes sparkled when he spoke.

A woman in a pink-striped shirtwaist bid five hundred and fifty.

Liz motioned toward the dais. She felt oddly comforted by the sight of Daniel. "That's my brother," she said.

"Yeah. I know."

"He just graduated from West Point."

Josh nodded.

A man with a gravelly voice shouted, "Six hundred."

"I go to Harvard," Josh said.

That was a surprise. Somehow Liz had thought Harvard was exclusively for Yankee blue bloods, like the Adams family and other people King George had written to. Maybe Evelyn had been wrong and he wasn't Jewish after all.

"In fact, my father teaches there," he continued. "Hebrew studies."

"Oh," she said. *Damn, Evelyn was right.*

"Actually, Dad's retired. He worked for President Kennedy, then Johnson. As an adviser on Israel."

Liz nodded, hating that she had nothing intelligent to add, nothing important to ask. What did she know about Harvard except that it was across the Charles River from Boston? And what did she know about Israel? She'd long since given up trying to unknot the Middle East wars and peaces and everything in between. And all she knew about Jews was that Father would not want her hanging around with one, would not want her in love with one.

She turned her attention back to the dais. The woman in pink stripes jumped the bid to nine hundred. "Where do you live?" she asked. It seemed a safe question.

"New York. Westchester."

She knew that, thanks to know-it-all Evelyn. "Oh," she replied. "We're from Boston." Just as she said it, Liz spotted Father. He was not far from the dais, arms folded across his generous middle, eyes thankfully too busy staring at Daniel to notice that she was not where she belonged.

"One thousand," the gravel-voiced man, who was buried somewhere in the crowd, responded.

And then Liz heard BeBe's voice close in her ear. "Father planted that man," she said, moving to the other side of Josh. As Liz began to protest, Roger stepped in. BeBe and Roger, her sister and brother, now flanked Liz and Josh like unwanted bookends. BeBe continued talking. "Father never would have left his fate up to something as simple as a bidding process. Don't you agree, Roger?"

"Absolutely," Roger said. "But it's going great, isn't it?"

Liz was confused. She looked from her sister to her brother. What were they up to?

"I think the woman is from Smith College," BeBe said. "I wonder if she'll go higher."

Josh looked as perplexed as Liz felt. She forced a smile and gave a slight shrug.

"Come on, Lizzie." Roger grasped her arm. "Father will want us there when it's sold."

He tugged her—no, more like *yanked* her—from Josh's side; she looked back, but did not know what to say. As Roger pushed her through the crowd, Liz noticed that BeBe had changed her position and now blocked her view of Josh.

As they reached the dais the auctioneer announced, "Sold! To the lady in pink for twelve hundred dollars."

Evelyn surveyed the audience and savored the enthusiastic response to the King George letter and to Daniel as if she were the one being lauded, as if she were the one everyone loved. It was so apparent that Daniel would make an outstanding politician, just as Grandfather predicted, just as Will Adams demanded.

She sighed a little, wishing Grandfather could be there instead of in bed trying to regain his strength. And his mind.

Her eyes fell on BeBe Adams; no one could miss that pile of orange hair. Evelyn looked away, then back. She squinted, as if that would make what she was seeing easier to believe: BeBe was standing close to, talking to, *playing up to* that boy, that Jew from New York.

Evelyn caught her breath. It was easy to tell what BeBe wanted: anyone could see that Josh Miller was a hunk, though he wasn't as tall as Daniel. And it wouldn't take a genius to know that Will Adams would throw a fit if he knew one of his daughters was seeing—and being seen by—a Jew.

BeBe, of course, always went against her father's wishes, almost as if she did it on purpose.

Josh *was* a hunk. And everyone knew that BeBe "put out." As far back as Evelyn could remember, BeBe spent Vineyard summers doing every imaginable thing (and some that were not) to any boy who would let her, at least that's what everyone said. There was even that fisherman's son—what was his name? Tuna, or something disgusting like that.

She wondered how difficult it was going to be to have BeBe as a sister-in-law once she and Daniel were married and had a family of their own.

She was tired of being the good sister. Maybe that was what drove her to wait until everyone had gone to bed, then climb out her window—*climb out her window!*— and head toward the beach, where this afternoon Josh had said he sometimes walked his dog, Snuffy, at midnight.

Hopefully, tonight would be one of those nights.

Trundling down the moonlit path, Liz thought she must surely have lost her mind. It was bad enough she'd almost lost her leg when she'd crawled out onto the ledge of her second-floor bedroom then shimmied down the oak tree, scraping the inside of her thigh and turning her ankle a bit when she thumped onto the ground. But sneaking out with Mother and *Father* right there in the house?

Yes, Liz thought as the path stopped at the cove that led to the beach, this was certainly not proper behavior for a young lady from a ridiculously expensive Boston girl's school.

She smiled in the moonlight.

And then she heard panting and running—the sounds of a dog—followed by a splash into water.

"Snuffy!" she called out without thinking and then put her hand to her mouth. She listened. For a few moments all she heard was the dog happily panting as he swam.

Then, from a row of pine trees that curled around the water, she heard: "Liz? Is that you?"

Her heart began beating so hard she thought she might faint. She pulled the sleeves of her sweatshirt down over her hands and bit her lip, suddenly realizing what she had done, suddenly realizing that she was here.

"Liz?" he asked in a half whisper that floated in the near darkness.

She took a deep breath. "Josh?"

And then she saw him. He emerged a few feet from her, silhouetted in a sliver of moonlight, Adonis under the stars—the twinkling, broad blanket of silver Vineyard stars.

"Liz?" he whispered again into the warm night air, the sound of his voice melding with the gentle lap-lap of low-tide waves on the shore.

"Josh," she repeated. "Yes, it's me." She swallowed with difficulty. Her breaths became small. She wondered if he would sweep her into his arms . . .

"Hey," he said, moving toward her. "What are you doing out so late?" He spoke with candor, clearly and directly. He did not sweep her into his arms.

"Walking. It's a beautiful night."

He studied her a minute, then turned toward the water. "You've never met Snuffy, have you?" He clapped his hands. "Come here, Snuffy. Come on, girl."

The dog bounded out of the water, wagging and dripping. She raced up to Liz and shook herself all over, spraying Liz with water.

"Oh, shit," Josh said. "Oh, I'm so sorry."

"It's okay. It's okay." Liz laughed and brushed at her sweatshirt.

"Snuffy, come over here. Sit. Stay."

The dog did neither, but jumped back into the water and resumed having fun.

Josh ran his hand through his hair. "I'm sorry. God, I'm such an idiot."

Liz smiled. "Don't say that. Snuffy was just being friendly."

"But you're all wet. Your family will think you've been swimming . . ."

"My family will think nothing," Liz said. "They don't know I'm not home."

He frowned.

"I sneaked out of the house."

He smiled. "Why?"

She shrugged and walked toward toward the water, clapping her hands softly. "Snuffy," she called. "Come here, girl." Snuffy bounded from the water again, shaking and wagging and soaking Liz further. Liz petted the top of her head. "Good girl. You're such a good girl." She slipped off her sandals. The wet sand between her toes was still warm from the day.

"Are you in college?" Josh asked.

Snuffy ran back into the water. Liz picked up her sandals. "No. Two more years."

"Snuffy loves you. You should be a vet."

"You said Snuffy loves everyone."

"Yeah, I guess I did. But if not a vet, what will you be?"

She almost told him she was going to be a teacher. But that was what Father wanted her to be. Or, at least, it was what he expected her to *say* she wanted to be. What he really wanted was that she "marry well," *well* as in Michael Barton of the Bartons of Lynnfield, which was hardly something she would tell Josh. "I don't know what I want to do tomorrow, let alone for the rest of my life."

Suddenly, he was holding her hand. "I'd like to see you, Liz. I mean, on a real date. Could we do that? Would you like to?"

Would she like to? Was he crazy? Then she thought about Father. *He'd kill you,* BeBe had said.

Well, maybe BeBe was wrong. Maybe Father really wouldn't mind. Just because he and BeBe always clashed . . .

"If you don't answer me in five seconds," Josh said, "I'll take that as a no."

Liz shook her head. "No. I mean, yes. Yes, I'll go out with you. Of course I will."

"Tomorrow night?"

"Sure."

"Shall I pick you up at seven?"

She lowered her eyes to the sand. "Maybe we should meet somewhere . . ."

"What's wrong?"

Her mind raced. Tomorrow was Sunday. Perfect. Her parents always spent Sunday evenings at the Burnses, where they had supper and played whist as if they lived in the nineteenth century and sipped lemonade instead of single malt scotch. She raised her eyes to Josh's. "Nothing, nothing at all. I want to see you. It's just that Father has some funny ideas about dating . . ."

He studied her face a moment, his eyes lingering on her in the dark. "And I might as well tell you up front. I'm Jewish."

She hoped he didn't see the skip of her pulse.

"Will that be a problem?"

"No," she answered, perhaps a little too quickly. "I don't think so. It's dating in general . . ." She hated sounding so childish. God, she thought, I'm sixteen! "Seven will be fine," she blurted out. "I'll meet you on the road at the end of my driveway."

Before she knew what was happening, Josh had leaned down and kissed her on the cheek. Her knees grew weak. "You'd better get home," he said. "Before you get caught."

She crept up to the porch, her hand touching the spot where he had kissed her, her smile stopping just short of joy, stunted by the reality that Father might, indeed, kill her. Or Josh. Or both of them.

"Nice night for a walk."

Liz froze—as if moving would make her crumble, Lot's wife turned to a pillar of salt. Then her brain cells began to work. The voice was not Father's. The voice belonged to Daniel.

"What are you doing out here?" she asked.

He laughed. "I was about to ask you that."

"I . . . I couldn't sleep." She wondered if he was outside because he, too, had a midnight rendezvous, with a girl who was not good enough for Father.

Daniel leaned back against the railing. "It's a bit late to be off wandering, Lizzie."

She bit her lip. She had never, ever lied to Daniel, and did not want to start now. But she could no more let Daniel down than she could disappoint Father . . .

"I won't always be around to look after my kid sister," he said, sounding uncharacteristically somber.

"Sure you will. Who will do it if not you?" They both knew better than to mention Roger. Or BeBe.

"Lizzie. I need you to promise me something."

She wove her fingers together and stared at the ground, feeling certain that Daniel knew she had been bad. And that she intended to be bad again. "Cross my heart?" she asked.

"Cross your heart."

She did so.

He looked at her for a moment, then looked off toward the stars. "Lizzie-girl, I need you to promise me that you'll listen to Father. He may seem stern sometimes, but he has all our best interests at heart. And, believe it or not, he knows what he's doing."

She felt as if she were being reprimanded, the four-year-old caught stealing cookies. She thought of Michael, then thought of Josh. "I like Michael," she said, "really I do. But . . ."

Daniel laughed, then put his hand on her head and tousled her hair. "I'm not talking about Michael. I know you like him."

She swallowed her guilt like a wad of gum.

"I need you to promise me you'll listen to Father because I'm not going to be here for a while."

Suddenly, his words began to seep in. While she had selfishly been thinking of her own wants and needs, something else had been happening, something . . .

And then she knew. "Your orders," she said quickly. "You got your orders."

Daniel nodded. "Yeah, kid, I did. You're now talking to First Lieutenant Daniel Adams, battalion commander for Unit 112 of the United States Army."

She felt a slow numbness start at her toes and work its way to her heart. "Daniel?" she asked, wanting but not wanting to know.

He dropped his hand to her shoulder and pulled her close to him. "Yeah, kid," he whispered. "I'm going over. Uncle Sam is sending me to Vietnam."

Chapter 7

 The wail that came from outside woke BeBe and had her rushing out the door of her bedroom before she was fully alert. At the top of the stairs she collided with Father.

"What the Sam Hill is that?" he barked, as if the commotion were her fault, her scheme to shake everyone from their beds in the middle of the damn night.

She ignored him and ran down the stairs toward the sound, Father right behind, neither of them acknowledging that the wail sounded an awful lot like Lizzie and that Lizzie might be hurt.

Out on the porch, Lizzie was there, and she was crying into Daniel's chest.

The adrenaline that had propelled BeBe from her room now slowed to an uneasy crawl.

"She'll be okay, Dad," Daniel said quietly.

Father took a deep breath. "It's for the best, Lizzie. You'll see."

Bebe scowled; the screen door banged shut. Roger stood there in his pajamas, his hair askew. Behind him was Mother. "What's going on?" BeBe asked.

They were all looking at Daniel. Daniel looked at Father. "I think it's time I made some hot chocolate."

When they were kids, hot chocolate was the fix-it, the cure-all for scraped knees or neighborhood bullies. Daniel was always the one to make it: Daniel, the eldest, Daniel the comforter, Daniel, who was always there when Father was too brash and Mother too busy.

BeBe looked down at her nightshirt and her bare feet, then around at her family in various stages of dress and undress. "Hot chocolate sounds great," she replied, since no one else had. "But only if it means someone will tell us what the hell's going on."

They sat around the big table—the long trestle table—in the knotty-pine kitchen with the lobster buoys on the walls. It was rare that they gathered here for something other than dinner on evenings when the rain drove them in off the porch. It was not raining now, and it was after midnight, and there was not a full meal but hot chocolate and vanilla wafers.

BeBe shifted uncomfortably on the wooden bench.

"It's about me," Daniel spoke at last. "Liz was upset because of me."

The sink faucet dripped. Mother blew her nose. Roger stirred his hot chocolate too loudly. BeBe wondered if she was the only one here who had no clue what was happening, then she wondered where Michael Barton had gone.

"I got my orders today," Daniel said. "Looks like I'll be going to Vietnam."

BeBe blinked. The faucet dripped again. No one was speaking. Why wasn't anyone speaking? She tapped her mug on the table.

Father did not answer.

She looked at Father. "You're going to stop it, right?"

But still no one spoke. No one else even looked at Father; they stared at their mugs or their hands or the top of the long trestle table.

Father looked steadily back at BeBe. "I can't, Barbara Beth. Some things are beyond my control."

"Oh, come on, Father. Surely your friend Congressman Carter can do something. Why else did Daniel have to take his hideous granddaughter to the cotillion?"

"Evelyn Carter has nothing to do with this. Besides, her grandfather and I have discussed it, and he thinks Vietnam will be our greatest victory of all."

She might have thought Father was joking, except that he so rarely joked. "Congressman Carter is next to dead," she said.

"He's been a powerful man for many years, Barbara Beth. He knows what he's doing."

She did not—could not—answer. She held her mug with two hands to steady it. "So Daniel is going to Vietnam and it seems I'm the last one to know."

"We planned to tell you girls in the morning," Mother said, "so there would be less time for . . ." BeBe suspected Mother wanted to say there would be less time for tears, but her words were cut short by a small crack in her voice.

"It will be okay, Beebs," Daniel said. "Besides, it's better for my future. This country would never elect someone who had not served his time, especially during wartime."

BeBe scowled. "This is not wartime, Daniel. Vietnam is a stupid mess that's killing everyone it touches."

"You should be proud of your brother for serving his country," Father said, then added, "Besides, not that many are dying anymore."

Heat rushed into BeBe's cheeks. "How many are too many, Father? What makes you think Daniel won't be one of them? Because he's Daniel? Because you won't allow it? Well, I've got news for you. Vietnam is wrong. And I, for one, will not be proud to have my brother serve in that hellhole." She slammed her mug down, ignoring the splash of hot chocolate that splattered onto the table. She jumped up, stomped over to the back door, and turned when she reached it. "By the way, Daniel, where's your fellow soldier?"

Her brother met her eyes. "Michael? He left on the last ferry. He thought the family should be alone until . . ."

"Until you leave," BeBe finished. "And when will that be?"

He played with his mug a second, then said, "Tomorrow. I have to be at Fort Dix Monday morning."

BeBe grabbed the car keys from the hook by the door and stormed out.

When Lizzie was six Father had taken the whole family to Washington. It was cherry blossom time, spring vacation from school, and the air in the capital was thick and sweet and cotton-candy pink against blue sky. In fact, Lizzie thought Washington looked like a coloring book, with perfect colors of pink and blue and green for the grass and white for the monuments and big hollow buildings. (She later learned they were called *hallowed,* not *hollow,* buildings, even though the rotundas and the hallways did seem too big and too empty.)

Liz sat on the bed where she had sat not that long ago, watching the clock, wishing for time to pass quickly so everyone would go to bed and she could sneak out and meet Josh. Now, she only wanted the ticking to slow down long enough for her feelings to catch up with her brain, for her to grasp what Daniel's leaving really meant—for him, for her, for their family, and for this country where, in one of those hallowed buildings, someone had decided to send Daniel off to war.

BeBe did not believe in Vietnam.

Father said Daniel must go, that there was nothing he could do to stop it.

Daniel said a war hero makes the best presidential candidate.

Mother had nodded and Roger had said nothing and Liz had finished her hot chocolate in silence, feeling scared as a little girl and not at all like the daring woman who had just met a perfect stranger in the darkness of night.

Instead, she was feeling more the way Madelyn Reynolds—a girl from school—must have felt when her brother, Ronald, was sent to Vietnam and six days later was killed in a minefield. He came home in a body bag minus a few parts.

For weeks, Madelyn could be seen darting into the girls' room, gripping the porcelain sink, sobbing into the metal-framed mirror until her legs buckled beneath her and she sat down on the floor. No one had known what to say or do, Liz included.

She picked at the white knots on the bedspread now and wondered if she might end up the one on the cold, tile floor, and Daniel in the big, zippered bag.

BeBe drove to Menemsha, the quiet little fishing village that was so small it was hardly a village at all. She turned off her headlights so as not to awaken the neighbors, then drove down the narrow, cottage-clustered road until she reached Tuna's. Tuna was the island boy nicknamed for his prowess with yellowfin, the boy she'd known for many years, the one she'd depended on for a good screw every summer since she was fourteen and he, twenty-one.

This would be the first time she'd seen him this summer. She pulled onto the small lawn and parked next to Tuna's "rusted but ready," as he called it, pickup truck. Just being here made BeBe feel better already. She got out of the car and made her way up the flagstone walk that she'd walked up countless times, eager to see him, for he would distract her and nothing else would matter, not even the war.

She knocked on the peeling blue-painted door. A moment later a lamp was lit inside, then the door opened. But it was not Tuna who stood there; it was a young woman with long black hair, a quite pregnant belly, and a very traditional wedding band on the third finger of her left hand.

"Ah," BeBe, who was not used to stammering, now stammered. "I have a little car trouble. I know it's late, but I wondered if I might use your telephone." Peering into the room, BeBe saw the familiar homemade coffee table and the overstuffed, slightly torn plaid sofa.

"Sorry," the young woman replied with a sleep-weary smile. "We don't have one."

No, BeBe thought, of course they did not have one. This was only the seventies, after all, and the pay phone at the Texaco station on the pier worked just fine.

"I could wake up my husband," the mother-to-be continued. "Maybe he could help with your car. Is that a good idea?"

"No thanks," BeBe said. Definitely not a good idea. Then she apologized for disturbing her and pretended to walk toward the station, a bit sorry she would never see Tuna's penis again, for it was a good one and knew what to do.

Down at the harbor, BeBe sat on a rock and pulled up her knees, wrapped her arms around them, and rested her face there. *Dammit*, she thought. *Dammit, dammit*.

She let herself cry quietly, a weep more than a real full-blown cry, with babylike tears instead of real adult sobs. Barbara Beth Adams, after all, had nothing to cry about, did she? She was one of four children born with that great silver Adams spoon shoved into their mouths, and all the accoutrements, like a Mount Holyoke education and a summer house on the Vineyard.

No, BeBe had nothing to cry about. She was not one of the frail, almond-eyed women she'd seen on the TV news, the ones who had babies in rice paddies and spent every waking and probably sleeping moment in fear of the lives of their parents and husbands and children and selves. She was not one of the women Daniel was being sent to defend.

She had nothing to cry about, yet she could not seem to stop, as if fingers were tightly squeezing at the insides of her heart. She wondered why men like Daniel had to die for their country and women like her didn't have a chance even with a man like Tuna and a house with no phone.

What made her think she deserved even that? She was not smart like Daniel, not lovely like Liz, nor even content like Roger. She was simply the mediocre, trouble-making third child of Will Adams, with a special talent for finding trouble and for fucking almost any boy who asked, and some who did not.

She'd even fucked a girl once, no, twice, back at college, if fuck was the proper word for two girls together, sucking each other's dark, hard nipples and little pink places, pretending to do it in order to know how they tasted to boys, yet curiously savoring the warm rush of orgasms they each had created.

The girl's name was Nadine and she was a lot richer than BeBe, but her family was from the Midwest so they didn't count. Her father had invented some kind of equipment that increased the milk production of dairy cattle. BeBe wasn't sure, but she thought maybe the fact that Nadine had been raised on a farm had something to do with the girl's overactive imagination, which seemed fixated on sex more often than even BeBe's.

They met in the riding stables one afternoon about two weeks into their freshman year: they rode together through the yellow-red-orange trees and across the leaves that crunched beneath hooves. They became fast friends; even faster after they had fucked, that first time behind the stables, the second in Nadine's dormitory room. A few days later, Nadine's room was empty.

"Her father dropped dead," another girl explained. "She's gone home to Iowa."

BeBe felt sad for a few hours or maybe more, but she suspected it was probably all for the best, because she didn't really want to turn into a lesbo and with Nadine's sexy appetite and no boys around she supposed it was possible.

Beyond that, BeBe Adams knew she was not much good to the world or anyone in it. Certainly not good enough for even a tuna fisherman to want for a wife, nor good enough to stop a brother from going to war.

She was thinking these things between her tears, as she heard the approach of sneaker-soft-footsteps.

Chapter 8

"It's cold out, Beebs."

It was Daniel's voice. She did not look up. "What are you doing here?"

"Stupid question."

He sat down on the pier next to the rock where she sat. She still did not look up. "I took the car," she said.

"I noticed."

"You walked?"

"God, you're a genius."

"It must be three miles."

"Two, I think. I took the bike ferry."

Ah, BeBe thought, *the bike ferry*—the wobbly, barely-get-you-there raft that shortcutted the basin across to Menemsha and was especially essential when one had a mission. "You're an asshole," she said.

"So are you."

She stayed in her position, head down, cheeks now, she knew, streaked by her tears. She did not want Daniel to see that. She did not want him to think she'd been crying about him, or worse, about her.

"If you're planning to stay on this rock for a couple of days, we might need to borrow the car," Daniel said.

She listened to the water lap against the rock. "How'd you know where to find me?"

He cleared his throat. "Tuna," he said. "I figured you'd come and find Tuna."

They had never talked about BeBe's "friends." But BeBe had always known that Daniel knew, the way Daniel seemed to know everything. "He's married," she said.

"Yeah. I found out."

"Oh, God." BeBe looked up without thinking. "You went there too?"

"Don't tell me you were serious about him." And though Daniel could have laughed, he did not.

She thought for a moment, then shook her head. "Just humiliated, I guess. That even a tuna fisherman wouldn't want me."

"Beebs . . ." Daniel slid from the pier onto the rock and slipped his arm around her. "You didn't give a shit about him. And it has nothing to do with the fact he's a fisherman."

Her jaw tightened; she turned her head. "I take whatever happiness I can grab, Daniel. I'm not like everyone else in the family. I have no special talents."

"Yes you do, Beebs. You are a great and wonderful independent woman. Even the clothes you wear show the free spirit of your soul. If you let it, that spirit will take you far."

She closed her eyes and cried again, this time for real, this time for grown-up real. She cried into his broad West Point shoulder and wondered what the hell she was going to do if anything happened to Daniel. "You son of a bitch," she said, half weeping, half shouting. "You have no right to go to Vietnam." She smacked his thigh with a closed fist. He did not wince.

"It's my duty."

She pulled herself from him. "Fuck your duty."

"I'm trained for it, Beebs."

"Big deal. I can't believe Father couldn't stop it."

"Vietnam is bigger than Washington."

"I don't care about Washington. I care about you. It's going to change you, Daniel. If you come back at all, you'll be different."

"I'll be older. That's all."

"I watch the news. So do you." She looked down at her feet, then at the water that lapped the rock. She kicked at it, splashing it up onto her legs, up onto Daniel's. What she really wanted to do was dive onto the rocks and into the water and never come up.

"Maybe I'll be a hero," he continued. "Don't you want a brother who's a hero?"

She shook her head. "I want a live brother. Not a dead hero."

This time he did not respond, but his arm held her more tightly, as if maybe, just maybe, he was a little bit worried about that godforsaken hot jungle, too.

Tears stung the corners of Evelyn's eyes. She sat in the rocking chair of Grandfather's dimly lit, stale bedroom and tapped her feet to the erratic beat of his labored breath. With each tap, her anguish rose another notch.

Daniel Adams was off to war and she had to hear it from the postmaster who was also a neighbor and who had run into Michael Barton at the ferry; Michael, when questioned, had not denied that Daniel's orders had arrived.

Which, of course, Evelyn had prayed would happen because one did not get to be president by being a pansy, or at least that was what Grandfather always said. Still, Daniel should have told her himself that the orders had finally arrived. Then she wouldn't have had to call the

Adamses' house at seven o'clock on a Sunday morning and wake up the whole family.

However, she was not welcome to see him. "Family time," he explained, "you understand." Well, she didn't, not really, but he said he'd write when he had a chance. And he would, she knew he would.

In the future, after all, they would be together.

From across the room came the mournful sounds: hish, swish; hish, swish.

She looked at the old man who lay under the sheets, and ached with the fear that he would die before she and Daniel were married and that Daniel wouldn't want to marry her once her grandfather and his connections were gone. She'd be all alone then.

She closed her eyes and swallowed a small lump that had grown in her throat.

She supposed that technically, she already was an orphan. Her father had died his own hishy, swishy death three years ago from internal injuries from a Vineyard car crash that had killed her mother on the spot. Within forty-eight hours they were both dead, and Evelyn was left with Grandfather—and he was left with her.

Now he'd be gone soon, too. There would be the traditional funeral for a United States congressman, and Evelyn would be in the spotlight for one lousy day.

She opened her eyes and pushed back her tears.

Maybe Daniel would be allowed to come to the funeral from wherever he was. She'd have to remember to speak to Senator Jameison about that. She'd have to pull a few strings, but it should be easy, easier than being alone.

She looked back to Grandfather and realized that if he died he would never know she had given away his prized pistol, pretending it was from him. Grandfather would never know, so he would never be angry at her. But then again, maybe he would understand. Maybe he would even approve.

Summer Sundays on the Vineyard were usually filled with the aroma of Mother's fresh muffins, the intermingling rustle of *The Boston Globe* and *The New York Times,* and the chatter of who was doing what today with whom and at what time.

This morning, however, the air in the kitchen had the pallor of a funeral home and the waxy whispers of the dead, as if Daniel had already left for boot camp, as if he were already on his way. To make matters worse, Evelyn Carter had called at seven o'clock.

"More coffee?" Mother murmured to Father, who responded only with a silent shake of his head, as if he were really concentrating on the op-ed page he held in his hand.

BeBe noticed that Roger, too, was more silent than usual. Roger wasn't any happier than the rest of them that Daniel was leaving. Roger was—had always been—curiously content with position number two and perhaps even fearful to have the spotlight turned on him.

Lizzie was the only one who unashamedly showed her feelings, crying a little each time Daniel said something meant to make her laugh. At least she seemed to have forgotten about Josh Miller, thank God.

As for Daniel, well, he'd sat and stood so many times now that BeBe wanted to tell him to knock it off, but it didn't seem appropriate this morning, even for her.

She wondered if all families whose sons and brothers were going off to war were as off-centered as hers, poised in teeter-totter motion, waiting for one another to react.

"What time are you leaving?" she asked.

"On the two-fifteen out of Oak Bluffs." Daniel stood

up. "Hey, Lizzie, grab the Polaroid. I want to go out on the lawn."

"Why?" Mother asked.

"Just a little memorabilia." He kissed Mother on the top of her head and smiled that smile that always helped him get away with everything, the lucky shit. He was, no doubt, wanting to find one last skunk, for the record.

BeBe decided it was a good time to exit, maybe go down to the beach or into town, to be anywhere but here. She knew Daniel would understand. They had already said their good-byes last night.

BeBe didn't go to the beach. Instead, she decided it wasn't every day her older brother deserted her, and it wasn't as if Oak Bluffs was that far away. If the traffic was steady, she shouldn't have to wait too long.

Standing by the roadside, she stuck out her thumb, glad she'd worn her cutoff jeans this morning and the halter top that Father hated because he said it made her look like a whore.

Liz stood by the window of her upstairs bedroom where the dormer met the eaves, where the tiny-flowered wallpaper went up the walls and across the slanted ceiling— a trick that Mother thought made the room seem larger. It did not seem larger now, but instead felt stuffy and confining.

She held back the ball-fringed white Cape Cod curtain and watched Father steer the Buick from the driveway, onto the dirt road and toward the street, toward the ferry, toward Vietnam.

She had tucked one of the Polaroids inside Daniel's

duffel bag for good luck: she'd told him that any man strong enough to tangle with Vineyard skunks should have no problem with the North Vietnamese.

Then she had taken Father's keys and slipped the other photo into the locked drawer of his desk, next to the pistol that Evelyn had given Daniel—where it couldn't be damaged or lost.

"Be good," Liz had said into Daniel's ear at the front door. What she'd really wanted to say was, "Be careful."

When the Buick was out of sight. Liz pulled her eyes from the driveway and turned, looking around her room. A queer, lonely scent hung in the air, as if the house knew that something, someone, was missing, that Daniel had gone and things would never be the same.

The first to stop had been a decent guy in a pickup who was headed into Vineyard Haven. BeBe had him drop her off at the "Cross Island Parkway" as Daniel had always jokingly called the narrow road that cut across the Vineyard to Edgartown.

Waiting for her next ride, BeBe realized she was already thinking of her brother in the past tense, as if he had already been shot at, blown up, or bombed, and was a statistic on the *NBC Nightly News*.

Body count, she remembered hearing it called, just as another vehicle stopped—this time a station wagon driven by a small-eyed man who looked in want of something more than a passenger, and might be willing to pay if BeBe were so inclined, if she were that hard up.

She was not. She waved him away and started walking again, wishing she had worn something other than sandals, especially the sandals that laced halfway up her legs and were, like most of her wardrobe, built for style not comfort.

One car passed, then another and another. And then another pickup truck pulled to the side of the road.

"Want a ride, lady?"

BeBe turned and looked directly at Tuna. "I'm not sure," she replied. "How far are you going?"

He smiled. "Not as far as I used to. But hop in."

She climbed into the old truck where they had made love lots of times, back when Tuna still lived up island with his folks and they had nowhere else to go. Two years ago he had bought the cottage and, well, they'd no longer needed the truck. BeBe looked at the worn cloth seat and inhaled its officious sea-scent. "Nice wheels," she commented.

He put the truck into gear and spun from the gravel back onto the road. "Thanks for not giving anything away last night," he said.

"Yeah. Well, I kind of figured your wife had assumed you were a virgin when you married her."

"BeBe . . ."

She shrugged. "No problem, Tuna. Hey, we were summer friends, now it's different. It's okay. Honest."

He settled back on the seat. "You here until Labor Day?" he asked. As if she would be anything but.

Suddenly, however, BeBe wasn't certain. "I don't know yet," she replied. "I might go to summer school." With Daniel gone, and with Tuna up and married, what was the point of staying here?

"Would you like to come for dinner sometime?" he asked.

She looked out the cloudy window at the scrub oaks and the clear sky. She wondered how it was that men seemed to be able to do that—fuck you one day, then have you interact with their family the next, as if you were just pals, as if the fucking meant nothing, nothing at all. She thought of Michael Barton and was glad he had left.

"I think I'll pass on dinner," she said. "But thanks for the invitation." He nodded, and whether or not he understood, she didn't much care.

"I'm going into Edgartown," he said. "You?"

"Oak Bluffs. Would you mind dropping me at the turnoff?"

"Hell, no, I'm not going to do that. A little detour won't kill me."

BeBe nodded.

"Where in the Bluffs?" he asked.

"The ferry," she replied. "I want to make it in time to see the two-fifteen leave."

They made it in plenty of time. Tuna dropped her off across from the pier, waved, and acted as if he'd really see her later as he said.

BeBe shook off an impending depression by reminding herself why she was here. *Daniel,* she said to herself. *My big brother Daniel.* For one last look—just a look, no more good-byes.

After crossing the street, she stepped inside the Steamship office and checked the clock: one forty-eight. For once, for this one thing, BeBe was not late. And no one would ever even know.

She stared outside at the stream of cars that jockeyed for position on the long, wobbly pier, cautiously moving forward as if they were race cars waiting for the green flag. They jockeyed, then stopped, parked where they would stay until they were herded into the great steel cavity that would safely transport them across Vineyard Sound: as safely, she hoped, as one of those big cargo planes would take Daniel halfway around the world . . . and back again.

Then she saw them: Daniel and Father, crossing the street. There was an ache between her breasts as she studied her brother. He was wearing a khaki uniform she'd not seen him wear before and had on a small khaki hat and polished black shoes. He was no longer a carefree Vineyard boy. He was a soldier. And this was about war.

Father was walking close to Daniel, as if there were a big crowd—which there was not. As the men moved toward the boat, Father reached out and almost touched Daniel's arm—a hesitant hand that stopped somewhere in midair then returned stoically to his side. Even here, even now, Father couldn't express his feelings with Daniel, who was his pride and his joy.

She had a twinge of . . . what was it? Compassion? For Father? For the fact that despite all his power, he had not been able to stop his son from going to Vietnam?

In the distance now, close to the gangplank, Father and Daniel stopped. Father no longer hesitated, as if now it was okay: he put his arm on Daniel's shoulder. And then, Daniel hugged him. Father held tight. Tighter, longer, it seemed, than necessary. The knot in BeBe's chest grew.

The men broke apart and Daniel disappeared onto the ferry. Father stood waiting until the vehicles drove into the boat. Minutes later, the steel mass blew its long, foreboding whistle, then chugged slowly from the pier. Father still waited until the ferry eased its way across the water, growing smaller and smaller with each moment that passed.

Finally Father lumbered back toward land, his head bent, his hand passing over his face as if wiping away . . . tears?

For nineteen years, BeBe had wanted to despise this controlling, intimidating man who was her father. Now here he looked . . . lonely. And vulnerable. Feelings BeBe understood well. He looked almost human.

She lingered in the ticket office until she saw him cross the street, until it was safe to leave and try and hitch a ride. Then an odd thought came over her: *Father*. Should she ask Father to take her home?

She went outside and saw the top of his graying head as it moved toward the parking lot. She headed quickly across the street.

Just as she was about to catch up with him at the Buick, a woman appeared next to him. She was dressed all in white from her tank top to her capris to her high-heeled sandals, even to the chiffon scarf that tied back her long, blond hair. BeBe had no idea who she was. She did not look much older than BeBe herself.

And then the woman . . . *Holy shit,* BeBe thought.

The woman wiped the tears from Father's cheeks and kissed him, full on the lips.

Her first thought was to run. BeBe bolted as if she'd been shot in the head and the heart at the same time. She darted around the cars in the lot, bumping into side-view mirrors and stumbling over her sandals, her damn lace-up sandals that typified her "free-spirited soul," as Daniel had called it, and were in no way designed for running away, at least, not literally.

"Bastard" was the only word she could coherently piece together among the words and images that whirred in her brain.

William Woodman Adams, pillar of society, head of the most important family this side of the fucking Atlantic if you asked him . . . William Woodman Adams was nothing more than a two-timing, phony, lying piece of pretentious shit.

As she'd always suspected.

She wanted to run away and forget she'd ever seen what she'd seen.

Then she thought of Mother. Innocent, hurt-no-one, raised-four-children Mother. The woman who had endured Father's crap for too many years. And suddenly BeBe's desire to escape was replaced by another need: this one, to rip out the woman-in-white's bottle-blond hair, then kick Father squarely in his balls.

Taking a deep breath and rubbing her side, BeBe raised her head and marched back toward the Buick.

"It's not what you think," Father said when he turned and saw the look on BeBe's face.

The woman stepped forward and put her hand on BeBe's arm. BeBe recoiled. "My name is Lucy Talbot," she said. "I'm Hugh Talbot's wife."

"How convenient, Father," BeBe sneered, "that both of you are married." What a big, fat waste of time. She started to turn away; Father grabbed her shoulder and held her there.

"Just who do you think you are, young lady?"

She snapped back. "Don't call me 'young lady.' Why don't you tell your friend here what you really think of me? Maybe you can tell her over cocktails, while your family is home waiting . . . without Daniel."

"If we weren't on a public street . . ."

"Wait just a minute," Blondie interrupted. "Stop it, both of you. This is my fault. Your father got my husband a job. Thanks to him, Hugh is a sheriff. I was thanking your father. That's all."

BeBe frowned. *Talbot.* She vaguely remembered hearing the name. "Do you kiss every man who gets your husband a job?"

The woman shook her head. "You don't understand. Hugh was in the Army. He was on his way to Vietnam. But your father intervened . . ."

BeBe squinted. "Excuse me?" she interrupted. "My father . . . intervened?"

Father moved his hand toward the woman. "Lucy," he said, "I'd rather not . . ."

"No, Father," BeBe said, her lips barely moving. "I want to hear this."

The woman sighed. "Your father used his connections to get my husband out of going to Vietnam. Congressman Carter helped."

The breeze that perpetually blew off the water now stopped, or at least seemed to stop, turning the air suddenly quiet and still. BeBe pulled her eyes from the woman and looked at Father.

Father had found a way to stop this woman's husband from going to Vietnam.

"Lucy's father sent some business my way," Father was saying. "We needed a good sheriff here. Hugh Talbot was qualified . . ."

"And we needed Daniel," BeBe said. She pulled away from his hand. "But you let Daniel go off to war." Slowly she turned and began walking away, her sandals slapping the pavement.

"But Daniel is going to be president," Father called out, his words following her. "He will be a hero . . . Just you wait and see."

BeBe wrapped her arms around herself to stop her insides from spilling out onto the street, to try and hold back her wish that Father had simply been having a fling the way other men might have done. It would have hurt less. It might have even been forgivable.

Chapter 9

All afternoon the sun played that peekaboo thing with the clouds, as if unable to decide whether it should be happy or sad.

Liz sat on the back porch swing, her mood shifting as she rocked. Daniel . . . Josh; Daniel . . . Josh. The ache for Daniel was winning over the anticipation for her date with Josh, even though she'd spent over an hour deciding what to wear (jeans and a white, short-sleeved turtleneck) and how to fix her hair (long and straight with a beaded headband).

Father had not spoken since returning home from seeing off Daniel. He'd simply gone into his study and closed the door. Liz wondered if they should forget the summer and the Vineyard and go back to Boston where they could visit museums and shop and walk down Newbury Street and poke into the art galleries. In the city they could practically see a different movie each night; they could find street fairs and outdoor concerts and stroll from the Common to the aquarium and back again, or ride the T a whole day as she and BeBe had done a few years ago when Daniel bet them they couldn't. Or wouldn't.

There was so much more to do in Boston than here. The only problem was, Liz thought, swinging the swing again, Josh Miller was not there. He was here.

She met him at the end of the dirt road that led to her house. He drove a small, dark green convertible. Liz asked him to put the top up, terrified that Father would somehow see Liz speeding off with a boy who not only was not Michael Barton, but who was a Jew.

"I thought we could go to the Strand," Josh said, maneuvering the sports car down the winding, tree-lined street. "Have you seen *Cabaret*?"

Yes, she had seen the new film starring Liza Minnelli. And she could think of a thousand places they should go other than one of the two movie theaters in Oak Bluffs—right there on Circuit Avenue, out in the open. But when she looked into Josh's mahogany-colored eyes, what she said was: "I've heard it's good."

He smiled and shifted into third gear.

They never made it to the movies. After parking the car, they started down the hill, when Liz glanced in the window of McClelland's Café and noticed a familiar figure on a barstool.

"Wait," she told Josh. "That's BeBe. My sister." She slipped to his other side, trying to duck from view. "I can't let her see me."

Josh looked through the glass and frowned. "Maybe she's the one who should worry about being seen. She looks pretty drunk."

That surprised Liz. For all BeBe's shortcomings, drinking was not one of them. Well, not that she knew. She began moving toward the theater, but Josh reached out and stopped her.

"It looks like she's alone," he said. "She might need our help."

Liz was annoyed, Didn't Josh get it? She started to protest, when she caught sight of BeBe again through the café window. Her sister was slouched, head drooping, an orange-haired Raggedy Ann. On the bar in front of her were a tall, half-full beer and several shot glasses, some empty, some not. Josh was right. BeBe was drunk.

Liz took a deep breath. "You're right," she said. "I have to go in. Something must be wrong."

"I'll go," Josh said.

She began to protest, then changed her mind. Sooner or later BeBe was bound to find out about Josh. Right now it seemed more important to get her sister out of the bar.

Liz watched as Josh went inside. Without attracting attention, he approached BeBe and began talking. Liz wished she could hear what he was saying.

Then he took some money from his pocket, set it on the bar, and put his arm around BeBe's waist. He propped her sister against him and led her rubbery-legged body out onto the sidewalk.

"Hey, Lizzie," BeBe slurred. "What are you doing here?"

Liz shook her head. "BeBe," she said, "you're drunk. I can't believe you're drunk."

BeBe belched. She slumped against Josh then turned and looked at his face, as if seeing it for the first time. "Hey," she mumbled, "who are you?"

"That's Josh," Liz said. "Remember him?"

BeBe took a long look. "Oh, that's right. I know you. You're the Jew."

Liz grabbed BeBe's arm. "We need to buy you some coffee."

But BeBe's eyes remained fixed on Josh. "Did you see

him around here? Did you see my jerk of a father?" She began to wave her arms. "Over there," she called. "In the Buick." Then she passed out against him.

Liz wanted to cry. "Let's get her to the car," she begged, and tried to prop BeBe up.

"She needs to lie down," Josh said. "My car's too small. Let's get her to the beach."

Between them, they lugged BeBe across the street, past the ferry pier, and down onto the beach. Liz sat on the sand next to her sister, while Josh went back to the car to get a beach blanket he said he kept "for emergencies sort of like this." Liz tried not to think about what that meant, and instead, she focused on her sister. Her dead-drunk, passed-out, in-trouble-again sister.

"Father is going to kill us," she said. "Oh, BeBe, I have a feeling we're going to make an awful mess of things with Daniel away. Let's try not to, okay? Let try to make Daniel—and Father—proud of us. Let's not get in any more trouble, okay?"

Beside her, BeBe snorted.

"Oh, Beebs," Liz said. She felt a chill in the fading sunlight. "I didn't want to have a terrible summer. I wanted to have a wonderful summer. But it's all ruined now . . . now that Daniel's gone away."

Her sister moved. "Bastard," she muttered. "I'm going to kill the bastard for what he's done."

Liz leaned down. "Kill him?" she asked. "Kill who? Kill Daniel for leaving?"

Instead of answering, BeBe gurgled. She rolled into the sand and puked.

The next morning, BeBe wouldn't talk about it. She wouldn't tell Liz why she'd gotten drunk, why she was angry, or whom she intended to kill. She only said she was leaving the island: she was going to summer school at Mount Holyoke; she was not staying here another "goddamn minute" longer than she had to.

"You're leaving me, too?" Liz cried. She was standing at the doorway to BeBe's room, watching her sister pack.

"Believe me, kid," BeBe said, taking a second to touch Liz's cheek, "it's better this way."

It had been lucky for them that Josh got them home last night before their parents returned from the Burnses', lucky for them that Josh helped haul BeBe upstairs to her room and put her in bed before anyone knew what had happened, including Roger, who wasn't home either.

"You can't leave me," Liz pleaded. "Please say you won't."

BeBe shrugged. "You've got your boyfriend now. It won't be so bad."

"My boyfriend? I have to sneak out to see him! What kind of fun will that be?"

BeBe smiled faintly. "You may be surprised. Just be careful, Lizzie. That's all I can say."

"BeBe, please . . ."

But BeBe snapped the suitcase shut and lifted it from the bed. "I'm out of here, Lizzie. I called Tuna this morning and he agreed to drive me to the ferry. Say good-bye to Mother for me. And Roger."

She headed for the doorway. "And if anyone asks, just tell them I didn't feel like spending the summer hung-over."

When Roger Adams called and asked if Evelyn could drive him to the ferry, she was surprised and she was pleased.

"I need to go into town today," he said, adding that his father couldn't drive him because he was off-island, which Evelyn knew was a lie because Will Adams had called only ten minutes before Roger to ask about Grandfather's condition.

But Roger had asked and he was Daniel's brother. It certainly wouldn't hurt to score as many points as possible with that family, even though she was still angry that Daniel had not let her see him before he left.

Besides, driving Roger to the ferry would be a welcome break from her distress over Grandfather's deteriorating condition. The doctor had been by this morning and told her that Grandfather had taken a turn for the worse. The stroke had left him unable to walk or talk or do much of anything but hiss at his nurses and drool when he ate. *How much worse could it get?*

"Maybe I'll jump on the ferry and go to Boston with you," she said suddenly.

Roger paused. "I, ah, I have a meeting," he said.

Evelyn laughed. "I could go shopping while you're in your meeting. That way, you wouldn't have to take the bus back to the ferry."

Roger was silent.

"There's nothing wrong with that, Roger. I'll make sure Daniel understands that we are just friends."

Finally he spoke. "Do what you want, Evelyn. But I'm not sure I'll be returning tonight."

As she drove back on Route 128 south toward the Cape, Evelyn glanced at Roger. How was it possible that the son of God-and-country Will Adams and the brother of Mr. West Point Daniel could try and enlist in the Navy and be told he was 4-F? Not acceptable for duty. Impaired.

"It's my allergies," Roger had explained after Evelyn had pried out of him the reason he'd gone to Boston and she'd met him outside the recruiting office. "My stupid allergies. They don't care that I know how to take care of it. They just don't want me."

He looked like he was going to cry right there in the middle of the street. Evelyn knew that it didn't take a psychiatrist to figure out why Roger wanted to enlist when he still had one year left of college. It was simply a matter of Daniel, an effort to finally be like big brother. It had, of course, failed, because Roger was Roger, not Daniel.

She felt sorry for him, but did not know how to show it. Silence was better than saying something stupid, something that might add to poor Roger's distress.

So they made the trip back to the Vineyard mostly in silence, an accomplishment for which Evelyn applauded herself. When she dropped Roger off at the house, he asked if she would please keep his secret.

"If my father ever found out I tried to enlist, he'd kill me," he said, his face pale and distraught.

"I'm supposed to be the lawyer in the family. Daniel's the soldier. Father would hate it if he knew I was trying to change his plans."

It was hard to believe that even Will Adams had put such fear into one of his own.

Despite what Roger asked, Evelyn decided she'd ask Grandfather if he thought it was true. Besides, Grandfather could keep a secret.

This last thought turned out to be most assuredly true, for when Evelyn arrived back at her house, Congressman Carter was dead.

Chapter 10

He kissed her.

Three days after Daniel left and two days after BeBe did, Father, Mother, and Roger went up to Boston for Congressman Carter's funeral. Father had wanted Daniel to be there but it was too soon for him to leave boot camp. But even if Daniel had been there, Liz would not be. Instead, she had feigned menstrual cramps. Under ordinary circumstances, Father would not have allowed her to stay alone on the island overnight, but nothing about these days seemed ordinary. Father had barely blinked when he'd learned BeBe was gone; Mother had commented that summer school should be fun for BeBe. And then the congressman had died, and they had all left for the funeral, and Liz had waited for her chance to see Josh.

She had waited all day. She had counted the hours and minutes and once even the seconds until she had known Josh would be out walking Snuffy. Now here she was—here *they* were—standing in the moonlight by the old rowboat at the cove, and he had his lips on hers, and she knew there was nothing more delicious or wonderful in the whole world than his hands on her waist and their bodies pressed together.

It was Josh who pulled back with a low laugh. "Wow," he said. "I guess we'd better stop."

She did not want to stop.

He studied her face. With the lightest touch of his fingertip he traced her chin, her nose, her eyebrows, her cheeks. He took her hand in his. "I want to show you something," he said.

Holding her hand, he led her alongside the water. Snuffy danced in and out of view as they moved from the cove to the rocky stretch of beach that separated the Adamses' house from the others.

"Look." He pointed to a house that sprawled above the dunes. It was deep gray in the moonlight and the shadows, imposing in the night salt air; a house not unlike Liz's. "That's my house," he said. "My family's house."

"You're my next-door neighbor."

"It's more than a house, Liz. It represents lifetimes—generations—of struggle." She did not know how to respond because she did not know what he was trying to say. "All my grandparents died in the camps," he said slowly. "Birkenau. Auschwitz. Before they could be captured, my father and his sister were evacuated on the Kindertransport. Their lives were spared, but they lost everyone and everything."

Liz knew of the war; she knew of the concentration camps. But the only person she'd ever known who'd been connected to the atrocity was Mr. Goldman, the custodian at school. He was a quiet, small man who wore long-sleeved shirts even in warm weather. One of the girls said it was to conceal the blue-purple numbers tattooed on his forearm. But no one knew for sure: it was not something Mr. Goldman ever talked about.

"My father met my mother here in America," Josh went on. "She's Jewish, too. Together they have built a good life. Their family—and their beliefs—are held together by their faith." He turned from the house and faced Liz. "I'm only telling you these things so that maybe you'll understand."

"Understand . . . what?"

"Understand if, well, if I can't be as open about seeing you as maybe I'd like."

He touched the hair on her forehead again. "I took a risk when I took you out the other night. If my father ever knew I had a date with . . ."

Suddenly it all became clear. "With a girl who's not Jewish?"

He nodded. A knot tied itself around her heart. "Does that mean you can't see me?" she asked.

He shook his head. "But I feel really foolish. I mean, we'll have to be careful. At least maybe until I can find a way to explain to them . . . But I do want to see you . . ." He touched her cheek; he touched her lips. "Would that be all right?"

She smiled and squeezed his hand.

They found ways to be together. They met in crowded places like at the Fourth of July fireworks in Oak Bluffs, where they snuggled under the gazebo and no one paid attention. They found reasons to walk to the Chilmark General Store at the same time and steal an embrace by the fresh produce. And on special nights, Josh came by at midnight. He tossed a handful of sand against Liz's window; the fine pebbles grazed the screen and signaled her to sneak down to the cove for kisses and soft touches.

Sometimes when she was with Josh, Liz heard Daniel's words: "You won't always have me around to watch out for you." And she felt sad, because she missed him.

At other times she heard BeBe's warning: "Be careful." And so she was.

But most times she felt that God—the God of the Second Congregational Church of Boston as well as the one of Beth El Temple of Westchester—had sent Josh to her to help fill the void left by Daniel and BeBe. Because it was such a huge void, he'd had to send someone as magnificent as Josh.

One midnight in late July, everything changed.

The sand pebbles came, later than usual. But Liz was ready. She'd dressed in her ordinary denim cutoffs, but instead of a bikini top under her T-shirt or panties under her shorts, she wore nothing. She wanted to feel his love tonight: completely, fully; rightly or wrongly.

As she clambered out the window and down the tree, she remembered how angry Father had been about BeBe at dinner tonight, complaining that she might at least have the "goddamn decency" to call once in a while. His outburst had upset Roger, who'd quietly left the table. It had upset Liz, too, because she did not understand why Father hated BeBe so much. And it had made her feel even more guilty when Father had winked at her and said, "Thank God for you, Lizzie. Thank God I have one decent daughter."

So here she was, the one decent daughter, tiptoeing half naked down to the cove. Before she could dwell on the irony too long, Josh was there.

"My father wouldn't go to bed," he complained. "He kept talking."

Talking was one thing Liz was not in the mood for. She touched his hand. She turned his face toward her. She kissed him softly, gently, many times over. He kissed her back with want and with need. When his lips slid down to her throat, Liz gave a soft moan of delight. She fell into his motion and they slid to the sand of the dune, and she forgot about Father and BeBe and the whole Planet Earth.

Over and over, they kissed. He raised her T-shirt, and she

saw the spark in his eyes and the warmth of his smile when he saw she was naked beneath. He bent his head to suck at her breast. His hand caressed her thigh, his fingers stroking, ever so slowly stroking, then sliding under her pant leg, probing the soft, moist place. And the soft beating of Liz's heart, and the soft pulsating between her legs . . .

She thought about Father. She thought about the many ways BeBe had disappointed him. She stopped Josh's hand. "No," she said quietly. "No, I just can't."

He pulled away. "I'm sorry, Liz," he said, turning his face away. "I got carried away."

The night air was quiet, except for the peepers.

"I think I'm a little too crazy about you," he continued, still quiet, still gentle. He turned back to her and ran his fingers over her throat, down to her breasts. "You are far too beautiful."

"Oh," she replied, with a half moan. Then she touched his arm, and wondered if her heart would ever again beat in a normal manner. She arched her back slowly.

He stood up. "It's better this way," he said. "Not to, well, you know . . ."

Yes, she knew, but she did not know why. She lay there a moment, hoping he would change his mind, hoping she would. Then she stood up. She picked up his hands and set them on her breasts. She moved closer to him and kissed his lips. "No," she whispered. "It's not better at all." With courage she did not know she had, she slipped her hand down the front of his jeans and rested her palm against his hardness. And with his eyes on hers, he took her in his arms.

"We really shouldn't . . ." he said.

"I want to," she said. "I love you, Josh."

He kissed her, his tongue sliding like velvet against her own.

"Please," she said, gently pulling him back to the ground.

In an instant, her cutoffs were gone, her breasts, her belly, her thighs were covered by his mouth, his tongue, his eager kisses.

With one swift movement he pushed inside her, her virginity gone, bringing her to such a fever pitch of pleasure she almost didn't hear the shriek that rent the air—a shriek that could have been hers, but it wasn't.

Josh stopped moving. He shielded her body against his. "Go away," he commanded.

She realized he wasn't talking to her. Her body went rigid with fear, even as her heart still thumped with his love.

"Leave us alone," he said sharply.

"Jesus Christ." It was Roger's voice.

Then another voice, this one shaky, added, "She's no better than BeBe. She's no better than her slut of a sister." It was Evelyn Carter.

Then Liz heard them walk away. Tears sprang to her eyes. "They're going to tell my father," Liz cried, rolling onto her side and grabbing her clothes from the small heap on the ground. "Oh, God, Father's going to find out. Then Evelyn's going to tell everyone on the Vineyard. Why did the biggest mouth on the island have to find us? And why is she out here so late with . . . Roger?"

Josh looked at her and kissed the tears from her cheeks. "I love you," he whispered. "Everything will be all right."

"No," she said, standing up, pulling on her clothes, and pushing away tears with the back of her hand. "I can't see you anymore, Josh. I can't do this." She fled down the path.

Chapter 11

 Liz stayed away from the cove . . . for a few days, a week, two weeks. She and Roger avoided each other, and she dodged Evelyn whenever she visited.

Then the rains came.

In what was the wettest season the Vineyard had seen in years, there was little for Liz to do other than wear the letters off Scrabble tiles in games played with Mother, read through the musty paperbacks of summers gone by, and think about Josh and Daniel and BeBe and wonder why she was here and everyone else was out there living, loving, and doing something other than wasting time.

And then, Josh called.

"Liz," he pleaded. "I haven't seen you in weeks. Can we meet at the cove after dinner? I can't wait until midnight . . ."

She hesitated.

"I have to see you. Please. I have something to tell you."

But Liz did not dare, for she was not BeBe and she could not take the chance. She began to hang up.

"Liz," he said, his voice raised. "I love you, dammit."

She had not heard Josh angry before, but there was a harshness in his words now that let her know if she did not see him tonight, she'd never see him again.

Unfortunately, on her way out to meet him, she ran into Evelyn.

Evelyn stood at the back door, a small wooden box of numbered tiles in her hand. "Care to join Roger and me for a game of Rummikub?" she asked Liz with a glib smile. "It's a game from Israel." She held the box out toward Liz, whose face shamed pink.

Liz raised a hand and brought it down on the box. Tiles spewed out across the floor.

"I don't know what you're trying to prove," Liz said in a voice she didn't know she had, "but stay out of my life."

Evelyn looked coldly at her. "I'm only trying to help, Liz. I know how disappointed Daniel would be if . . ."

Liz leaned into Evelyn's face, her whole body trembling, her voice quaking. "If you care so much about Daniel, why are you hanging around with Roger so much?"

"I'm trying to help Roger, too. I'm trying to help all of you. For Daniel's sake."

"We don't need your help," Liz seethed. "And another thing, you're not Daniel's girlfriend. You're not part of this family." She grabbed a slicker, pushed past Evelyn, and went out the door.

"I love you," Josh said as they sat on the sand looking out at the sluggish gray sea that seemed tired of being rained upon, weary of the fog layered over its waves.

"Is that what you wanted to say?" Liz asked. She had not told him about her run-in with Evelyn; Evelyn, Father, all of them could go to hell. As soon as Josh told her why he wanted to talk to her, Liz would tell him it was time to stop hiding.

He looked up at the stars. "When I was a boy," Josh said, "my father used to tell me the story of Anastasia. Do you know who that is?"

"Wasn't she some kind of princess? A Russian princess?"

In the starlight, Josh smiled. "Anastasia was a Romanov princess. When the Bolsheviks took over the Russian Empire after the First World War, they destroyed the Czar Nicholas and his family."

"But there were rumors that Anastasia did not die with them," she said.

Josh nodded. "My great-grandparents—and my grandmother—lived in Russia then. They were lucky. They escaped the Bolsheviks. But my father said my grandmother always missed her little friend."

Liz gazed out to the sea. "Her friend?" she asked. "Anastasia was her friend?"

"Yes. My great-grandmother was the czarina's personal assistant. They lived at the palace."

"Wow," Liz said. "I can't imagine . . ."

Josh shook his head. "My grandmother said the paintings and treasures and jewelry and silver and gold were more than *anyone* could imagine. She and her family left the palace and went to Poland . . . and later, to the camps."

Liz shuddered. He slipped his arm around her and looked up toward the sky.

"My grandmother always worried about Anastasia. When word came that the royal family was killed, she didn't believe it. And when she learned there was doubt over Anastasia's death, she had great hope. She hoped her friend had somehow survived. Before Auschwitz she would sit on the fire escape of their tenement each night and look up at the stars and believe that Anastasia, no matter where in the world she was, might possibly be looking at the same stars. She prayed that Anastasia would know she was thinking of her, and praying for her, and hoping that, one day, they would meet again."

Liz had a strange feeling that Josh was telling her more than a fairy tale, more than a story passed down from his youth. "But they never did meet again," she said.

"No, sometimes there aren't such happy endings."

They sat quietly, Liz wishing he would kiss her, wishing he would do more than just stare off toward the sea and up at the sky.

"Do you suppose Anastasia is looking up at the stars right now?" she asked.

Josh chuckled. "Who knows. She might still be alive. But what's more important is that the stars are still here. And the stars are still there."

Liz was quiet a moment, then she asked, "Why are you telling me this, Josh?"

His arm tightened around her. "I'm not going back to Harvard in the fall," he said. "I'm joining the military."

Her heart sank. "No," she said. "Not you, too."

"It's not the same as Daniel. I won't be going to Vietnam."

"Not yet, maybe. But sooner or later, everyone goes . . ."

"I won't," Josh said firmly. "I've joined the Israeli military."

She thought she must have heard him wrong. "What?"

"The Israeli military. I've already joined."

He did not look in her eyes as he spoke, but kept his eyes fixed on the sky.

"Why?"

"Because I am Jewish, Liz. You know that. It is my duty to fight for Israel."

"You're an American. You were born here, weren't you?"

"Yes. But in my blood, I am a Jew. I tried to explain that to you. I must fight for my ancestors. And for generations to come. Can you understand that?"

No, Liz did not understand at all. She could only think of one more question. "When are you leaving?"

"Tomorrow morning," he replied. "Tomorrow night, I will look up at the stars. And I will think of you looking up at them, too."

She wondered if this was what it felt like to die.

Liz lay on her bed three days later—the bed she had barely left since Josh had gone—and stared at the ceiling and decided that death must be more peaceful than this, less painful than feeling as if there were only vacant tomorrows ahead, vacant tomorrows and an empty, long, outstretched highway of nothingness, pure nothingness.

She had even refused to look up at the stars because Josh had no right to leave her and she was not going to let him think that she cared. Not that he'd know if she'd looked at them or not.

Damn him.

Besides, it was hard to do much of anything but think about the ache in her stomach and the tears in her eyes.

She wished she were pregnant. If only she had gotten pregnant that one time they'd made love. But her period had started and erased any chance of that. But, damn, she thought, if she had gotten pregnant there would have been no way he'd have left.

Now, of course, it was too late. Because Roger and Evelyn had caught them and they'd not made love again, and now Josh was gone, like Daniel and BeBe and everyone who ever mattered in her whole life.

She told Mother she must have the flu. So Mother made chicken soup as was expected of mothers, and said she would phone the doctor if Liz spent one more day under the covers.

Only Roger seemed to know what was really going on. "You'll feel better soon," he said in that awkward brotherly way that boys used to address cramps or girl things in general. He had come into her room, delivering more soup.

Liz did not reply, but turned her face from the bowl on the wooden bed tray that had carried countless bowls of chicken soup and ice cream and hot toddies to four children over the years.

He sat on the edge of the bed. He smelled of dampness and fresh earth, of things real and honest. She briefly wondered why he was spending so much time with Evelyn, and if, in Daniel's absence, Evelyn had been allowing Roger, the other brother, to make love to her.

The thought made Liz's stomach roll. She turned from her brother.

"I know it's hard right now," Roger was saying. "But it will get better. Soon, you will have forgotten all about this mess of a summer. You'll see."

She didn't respond. In a little while, Roger gave up and left the room. Liz did not think that anything so bad could ever be forgotten, or that anything could possibly be worse.

She was wrong.

The next morning, as she lay in bed, staring at the ceiling, Liz heard the sounds of too many voices coming from downstairs; too many voices colliding with one another in short choppy sentences she could not make out.

She slid out of bed and went to the top of the stairs.

"It's bullshit," Father shouted below. "Pure bullshit."

Something slammed against something else. Something broke. "Bull-fucking-shit." Another crash, this one of glass.

"No!" The scream came from, of all people, Roger. "Father, stop it. *Stop it*."

Something else slammed. Something else broke.

Liz's body went numb with dull fear. Her mouth went dry. She crept down the first few stairs to listen more closely. That's when she saw her mother, cowered in a corner, her face in her hands, sobbing.

"Mother?" Liz called out, but Mother could not hear above the sounds of Father's crashing and slamming and shouting "Bullshit" all over the kitchen.

Liz moved down the stairs and into sight of her family, the remnants of her family surrounded by strangers, three men in gray suits.

Gray suits.

Oh, God.

"Mr. Adams," one of them said as he tried to hold Father back; but Father swung his arm and clipped the man on the shoulder, sending him reeling into the fireplace and down to the floor.

And that's when Liz knew. She didn't know in an instant, no, not quite that fast. But a big bowling ball grew in her stomach, as if her stomach knew first and then took its sweet time sending the information along to her brain. And that's when she knew her world was about to take one last leap around one last corner and leave innocence behind. Forever.

Roger spotted Liz on the stairs. He walked toward her in the slow, heavy motion of a dream. He walked toward her, the look on his face one that Liz wanted to erase, to rub from his eyes, to blot from his mouth.

"Lizzie," he said in the same slow motion.

He stepped onto the stairs and took her into his arms. Over his shoulder she could see Father's rage settling into his deep purple face, and see Mother's whimpers give way to pale immobility. Liz's own legs grew heavy, her own heart already starting to ache before she heard the words she somehow knew Roger was going to say next:

"It's Daniel," he said. "He's dead."

Part III

Year 2000

Chapter 12

The worst part about being in a wheelchair was that you got parked in the damnedest places, facing in the direction that the person who parked you wanted you to face. Or didn't want you to face. Or didn't much think about at all.

Right now, Danny faced the wall. He knew he was perfectly capable of turning his chair around—he was, after all, only paralyzed from the waist down—but he didn't much feel like staring at the black-veiled strangers filling the sanctuary, or the dark-suited politicians who'd come to pay their last respects to a man they either loved or hated, nowhere in between, or the stone-faced Secret Service agents who were only there because it was their job, a job that apparently did not include saving the life of an old man who had the misfortune of dying during a national presidential convention. Will Adams, Danny's grandfather, had died of natural causes. As if anything about Will had ever been natural.

Suddenly Danny's chair moved backwards, with the ghostlike motion he'd come to expect in the three years since his football injury.

"Why are you sitting over here?" came the voice of his sister, Mags, the mysterious chauffeur behind him.

"I guess Aunt Evelyn thought the congregation shouldn't have to look at me."

"Aunt Evelyn is wearing reinforced-toe pantyhose with sandals today. Which only proves what an asshole she is." Mags spoke with a matter-of-factness that amused Danny, even though he knew it created an edge that irritated their mother and did little to endear his sister to some people she encountered except, of course, Aunt BeBe, who was a different story altogether and who at least couldn't be stopped by asshole Aunt Evelyn from attending her own father's funeral no matter how much she'd disliked him, too. Danny wondered if BeBe's hair was still orange.

Mags wheeled him toward the side door of the small steepled church that had been built three hundred years ago and was probably not wired for the media presence today any more than the narrow white pews with the small wooden doors had been constructed to accommodate wheelchairs.

As Mags parked Danny under a stained glass window of John the Baptist, Danny wondered if their ancestors hadn't needed to accommodate wheelchairs because if someone became handicapped, they simply hanged him. No longer able to toil in the fields or defend the colonies. No longer necessary. Simply a burden.

He surveyed the church's white and maroon and mahogany decor that had not changed since the last time he'd been here, before the accident. Hell, it probably hadn't changed since the Adamses' ancestors arrived on Cape Cod in 1652 . . . or since the Bartons came a generation later. His mother, his father, families rooted so thick in New England soil that their tentacles shot downward to China instead of sprouting out toward the west, the wild, wild west. Pioneers, the Adamses and the Bartons were not. They were Yankees, rock-rigid, Boston-deep Yankees. Who ate their young and hanged their weak. And never—ever—discussed it with anyone.

The organmeister—a shriveled old man who perhaps had served at the Second Congregational Church of Boston since soon after the ancestors had arrived—pumped the pedals, and the recently refurbished (with Will Adams's money, of course) tall brass pipes came to life. "Amazing Grace," the brass pipes bellowed. Danny was surprised that Will had not had the words changed to "Amazing Will" in honor of himself. Perhaps he would have, had he known he'd have a massive coronary the night before the biggest night of his life.

Moving his eyes from the pipes to the altar to the purple-velvet-draped pulpit, Danny asked Mags, "Where's Mom?"

His sister leaned down, lips to his ears. "Uncle Roger said it would be better if she and Daddy came in last."

A sardonic grin passed across Danny's face. "A grand entrance at a funeral? Yeah," he nodded, "I suppose old Will would have wanted that."

Mags lightly slapped Danny's arm, which he would not have felt if she'd swatted him anywhere below the waist.

Below the waist. That mysterious place he once knew so well.

The organ music droned on.

Danny looked around at the dark suits and solemn dresses of the men and women of the funereal congregation. How many of them had taken a sidelong look at Will Adams's grandson, wondering if he had any sensation *below the waist*—specifically (because though most of these stiff-upper-lipped folks wouldn't admit it, what they really wanted was the *specifics*), could Danny get an erection and, if yes, could he feel it?

Danny would have given just about anything to be

able to crawl from his wheelchair, climb up to the pulpit, lean into the microphone, and shout: *The answer is no.*

Instead, he closed his eyes and tried to keep his mind from wandering to that long-ago, magical place of glorious sex, to that wondrous place of pulsing great hard-ons and panting hot heat, of newly grown coed breasts and wet places between legs.

How sweet the sound . . . that saved a wretch like me . . .

Danny's thoughts drifted to Anna, the young physical therapist at the rehab clinic in Switzerland where he'd spent two hapless years of costly treatment that went nowhere, though not for lack of effort on Anna's part. Especially when, just before he returned to the States, she'd sneaked into his room long after dark, stood by the side of his bed, watching him watch her as she stripped in the moonlight that leaked through the wood-shuttered windows, her lovely round breasts firm and eager for tasting, her taut thighs invitingly parted ever so slightly. Anna had tried, but in the end it had not worked.

"You will never feel complete until you feel it in your mind," Anna said as she tried to prod him. "In your mind is the only place it really counts."

But it had not counted in his mind—at least, not enough—and Danny had been left staring up at the ceiling, asking God if his life was worth living and hearing only the peal of Swiss church bells chiming four o'clock in response.

I once was lost, but now am found, was blind, but now I see.

"Fuck," he muttered.

"What?" Mags asked, leaning down to the wheelchair again.

He opened his eyes, shook his head, and slowly pulled himself back to today. "I'm going to miss Gramps," he lied.

"No you're not," Mags replied. "Neither am I."

Danny smiled and moved his gaze toward the lineup of the children of Will Adams who now filed in from the small chapel in the back: Roger, with Aunt Evelyn, leading the way, followed by BeBe, whose hair, hooray, still flamed like a sun-ripened carrot. Then there was a pause in the action, perfectly timed to the start of the final refrain of the hymn. His mother appeared. On her arm was the now-official candidate for president of the United States—better known to Danny as Dad—who had been unanimously selected in absentia while he'd been making funeral plans instead of taking bows. He'd been making funeral plans and trying to console Danny's mother, who, quite possibly, was the one and only person who would miss Amazing Will Adams very much.

Aaaaamen.

The house on Beacon Hill had taken on the same eerie pallor that it had after Daniel's funeral twenty-eight years ago: sunlight filtered in through the long lace draperies, the dust specks suspended over the polished mahogany woodwork, velvet sofa and easy chairs, and the century-old oriental carpets. It was a house of high ceilings and tall windows; a house that had once harbored Will and his wife and their four children until one of their children died, one left, and two married. It was a house where Mother had spent the ten years after Daniel's death mostly in the bedroom. A house where three years ago the steps from the cobblestone walk had been converted to a wheelchair ramp, but where inside, the book-lined, cigar-scented study still overlooked the Hill, the way Will Adams had planned it, the way Will Adams had lived it.

Liz moved around the kitchen knowing it was up to her to see that the guests were fed, even though she had the aid of six catering people, even though she was the potential next First Lady of the United States and might have expected to be waited on instead of waiting on everyone else. She did, after all, have another job: like preparing to hit the campaign trail with her husband tomorrow—somewhere in Illinois, Roger had informed her, somewhere where the swing vote was *critical*, as if it weren't critical everywhere Roger had organized for them to go, though some, he claimed, were more critical than others.

Michael had already lost three precious days of campaigning because Will Adams had inconveniently chosen now to drop dead.

Liz grasped the side of the counter, trying to quiet the wave of nausea that had been rolling within her since Father had turned gray and clutched at his chest. His death had been quick: the reporters had learned of the 911 call and one had even managed a shot of Michael administering CPR, a photo which saw Michael's rating jump six points. In fact, if Liz had not seen them lower Will's body into the ground with her own eyes today, she would have bet that it had all been an act—one more strategy in years of strategies choreographed by Father to ensure that his son-in-law and his daughter would make it to Pennsylvania Avenue.

"Dad wants to know if there's any bourbon," said Liz's youngest child, Greg, as he skittered his seventeen-year-old, always-in-motion body across the hardwood floor and into the room. "It's for Senator What's-his-name. You know."

Yes, Liz knew. It was for Senator Jameison, from somewhere in the south, who rumor had it dined on bourbon for breakfast and for most other meals, too, and spent more time juggling "favors" for the good old boys than working in his Washington office. Another wave of nausea rumbled through her. She wished that everyone would leave, that everyone, for once in her life, would just get out of the house and leave them the hell alone.

It really was their house now. Hers. Michael's. The children's. They had moved in with Father after Mother had died, bringing life once again to the old four-story place. *Saving my damned life,* Will Adams was known to have told others—especially reporters who might pick up on the image of family values and remember it when writing a piece on Michael.

"Mom?" Greg asked again.

She closed her eyes. "The bourbon is in the filing cabinet beside his desk," she told him. Though no alcohol ever passed his lips while in public, even Will Adams enjoyed a good shot now and then. Mother, of course, had pretended not to know.

In the same way Liz pretended so many things, in order to have peace in her life.

"Oh, Daddy," Liz whispered, suddenly longing for that controlling old man. While he'd been in charge, it had always been clear what was expected of you. There had been strength and security in his rules, as tough as they had sometimes seemed.

She opened her eyes and stared out the kitchen window, feeling not at all like a grown woman now, but like a little girl who wanted to sit on her father's lap and hear him tell stories of farmers and blacksmiths and brave young soldiers—stories of their hero-ancestors without whom surely the colonies would never have survived, let alone risen to power; stories that underscored the responsibility of their family name, and the importance of never forgetting it.

BeBe, of course, had long since forgotten it, somewhere around age ten, Liz suspected.

Roger had not forgotten, though he preferred to do his duty behind the scenes rather than at the podium.

And Daniel . . . well, Daniel was dead.

Gazing up at the pale summer sky that hung over the garden, Liz wondered what would have happened if Daniel had not been killed. He would have been the one on his way to the White House, and maybe then Will Adams would have found a way to survive until after the inauguration.

Daniel's funeral, of course, had been much different. The mourners had spoken in disbelieving, hushed voices marked by occasional outbursts of sobs and deep, painful wails. There had been no talk of what a wonderful life Daniel had had, for twenty-two years did not account for much of a life. And the house on Beacon Hill was not filled with senators and congressmen and people who mattered.

Even Will Adams had succumbed to a grief so penetrating that he could not share it with the world, could not exploit his son's death for the sake of front-page news.

At least, it had seemed that way until Will decided to place a gold star in the front window on Beacon Street— a World War II symbol meaning that a son had been killed in a war, defending his country.

It was that star that had driven BeBe from the house once and for all.

"Daniel was not killed in the war, Father," BeBe had said.

"He was killed during wartime, that's all that matters," Will gruffly replied.

"He wasn't even in Vietnam yet," BeBe hissed. "He was still in boot camp."

Father had not replied, and BeBe grew angrier.

"For godsake, Father," she'd shouted, "he was shot by an overeager kid from the Bronx who had an M16 shoved into his hand. He was shot by a *kid,* Father. One of *ours.* In boot camp, Father. *Not in the fucking war!*"

Father's face had turned deep purple; thick veins

appeared where Liz hadn't known there were veins. He pointed his finger in BeBe's face and yelled: "Your brother is a hero, missy. And if, for one minute, you don't believe that, then you don't belong in my house."

BeBe had seethed. "What I know, for a fact," she said evenly, firmly, "is that Daniel's death is no one's fault but your own. You know it, and I know it. You may as well have killed him yourself."

Liz could still feel the shiver that had run down her spine then, could still remember the cold, accusing look in her sister's eyes, and, worse, the way Father had stood statue-still, not denying her charges, not defending himself.

Liz had left the room, not wanting to know more.

That night, BeBe had left home and never returned, not until now, when it was no longer Will's house but Liz's. Liz and Michael's, according to the will. The star had long since been removed from the front window, and yet the scars forever remained: scars of Daniel, and now, scars of Will.

Liz closed her eyes to the ache in her head and wondered how she was supposed to get on a plane tomorrow and head for Illinois as if nothing had happened, as if she had no feelings inside her at all.

"They'll be gone soon, Lizzie," Roger said, carrying dirty dishes into the kitchen instead of leaving them for the caterers. "Then you'll be able to pack."

He set the dishes on the counter, and she stared at the remnants of brown "party" meatballs and bits of coleslaw. "I'm not sure if I can handle tomorrow, Roger."

"It's a National Businesswomen's Alliance luncheon. Followed by the dedication of a new Center for Handicapped Youth. You'll love it."

"I won't love it. I'm tired."

"You can sleep on the plane."

She kept her eyes fixed on the dishes. "You seem to be forgetting that Father just died."

"And you seem to be forgetting that the last thing Father would have wanted would be for you to stay here moping when Michael needs you out there by his side."

She blinked and looked up at her brother, at the angular-boned face she knew so well, framed though it was now by thinning, graying hair. She was not familiar with this strength in his voice. A thought flashed through her mind: now that Will Adams was dead, would the second son—finally, truly—become his own man after all? She looked squarely into Roger's eyes. "I don't believe it's called 'moping,' dear brother. I believe it's called 'mourning.'"

Roger recoiled. "I'm mourning, too, Liz. But the campaign . . ."

From the next room came the sounds of laughter. Male laughter. Good-old-boy, guffawing kind of laughter. Liz came precariously close now to a full, gut-wrenching vomit. "You see?" she cried, pointing toward the doorway. "The campaign. Everything is about the damn campaign."

"It's how Father wanted it . . ."

Heat rose in her cheeks. "Well, it's not what *I* want. Not anymore. I want some peace and quiet. I want some time without clusters of cameras around me and a bevy of Secret Service men in my face. I need some time, dammit. I need some time to grieve." Her lower lip quivered.

Roger held out his hand and lightly touched her cheek. "But don't you see, Lizzie? There is no time. Not now. After November you can grieve. After the election."

The voices guffawed again.

"No," she said, turning away from Roger. "I'm not

going to Illinois tomorrow, Roger. I can't. And if Michael loses the election, it won't be my fault." But along with the wave of nausea now came the fear that maybe it would be her fault, and that maybe the rest of her world would come crashing down, too, for maybe she had been a fool to think that it wouldn't. And maybe she had been the biggest fool of all to have allowed herself to live in the vortex—and by the directives—of Will Adams all her life. And maybe his death would signify the beginning of her own demise.

Liz grabbed the plates and scraped off the garbage as if it were poison, as if it could kill.

Evelyn, of course, had overheard the whole thing, because she'd always practiced the art of lingering in doorways. One learned so much that way.

And now she learned that her sister-in-law had decided not to campaign. God, she hated it when people were directed by their emotions.

As Roger emerged from the kitchen, Evelyn grabbed him by the medium-starched collar. "And just what do you plan to do about this?"

Roger blinked. "Evelyn, stop it. Let go of my shirt."

She released her grasp and pointed her finger close to his face. "You can't let her do this," she whispered hoarsely, making sure to keep her voice below the mono-tone cadences of the after-funeral visitors in the other rooms. "Your sister is as important to the campaign as Michael himself."

"Excuse me, but Michael is the one who will be elected, not Liz."

"You know better than that. Your father always stressed that the public buys not just the man but the package. Part of that package is the dead war-hero brother, the son in the wheelchair, and the strong woman heroine." She put one hand on her hip and stared into his eyes.

Roger blinked. "What do you want from me? I can't force her to go."

Sometimes Evelyn wondered why, when Daniel was killed, she hadn't just gone off and found someone else. But oh, no, not her. She'd been stupid enough to believe that being part of the Adams clan would automatically mean a future that mattered. And what had it gotten her? A husband who believed he'd rather be with a man and now a sister-in-law who wasn't thinking of anyone but herself. Where was their pride, their drive? Did no one else care what other people thought? A muscle tightened somewhere in her chest.

"Never mind," she said in disgust. "I'll find a way to take care of your sister myself."

Chapter 13

He was a son of a bitch who acted like God, but sent his son off to be killed and hated one of his daughters, namely her.

BeBe stood in the doorway of the room that she once shared with Liz, the room that now belonged to Liz's daughter, Mags. She thought about Father, and the many times she'd lain on the bed right here in this room and looked out the window and wanted only to escape from Beantown and Will Adams and all the trappings of wealth and privilege that came with being his daughter.

Unlike BeBe, Mags apparently had no intention of going anywhere, except the White House for four years, maybe eight. Where BeBe had once papered the walls with posters of places like Paris and Madrid, places as far from home as she could imagine, Mags had the walls covered only with Laura Ashley designs, with matching duvets on the twin beds, and coordinating canopies, draperies, and toss pillows, too. It was as if the room had been transformed from the bedroom of a very transient teenager into a Spiegel catalog spread. It had been a while since BeBe had seen Mags, but she hadn't thought the twenty-year-old had turned into Ms. Traditional.

"What do you think?" Mags asked BeBe now as she stood beside her, showing off her room.

"It sucks," BeBe replied. "I thought you were majoring in fashion design. You call this creative?" BeBe, of course, had left home and never finished college, but she'd had greater hopes for Mags—hopes that, one day, her niece's education would pay off in the world, that Mags would not have to hinge her future on a chance meeting with some guy named Pierre.

Mags laughed. "Isn't it gross? It was Evelyn's idea. For the funeral."

BeBe turned from the sight. "Excuse me?"

"Aunt Evelyn didn't think the press should have to witness my 'shrine to Brad Pitt,' as she called it." Mags frowned and pulled her hair away from her face, the face that looked so much like Liz's had that last summer they were on the Vineyard together, the summer that everything changed. "I wouldn't exactly call a couple of posters a 'shrine.'"

"I'd like to say Evelyn meant well," BeBe said, "but she never has."

"Oh, Aunt BeBe, I wish you lived closer to us. I wish you didn't live in Palm Beach."

BeBe smiled. "Apparently Evelyn thinks Palm Beach is more appropriate for me."

Mags tossed one throw pillow onto the floor and kneeled on one of the beds. "I can't *stand* her, Aunt BeBe. Why did Uncle Roger ever marry her, anyway?"

Crossing the room, BeBe pulled out the chair to the built-in desk and sat down. "Who knows? I guess he was bored. But it could have been worse. They could have had kids."

Mags wrinkled her nose. "Poor Uncle Roger. But why do they stay married? For godsake, he's gay."

BeBe liked the way her niece felt free to say—or ask—what she wanted. "I have no idea, Magsie," she replied honestly. "But I suspect it has something to do with being both stubborn and stupid. She proposed to him, you know."

"No way!" Mags shrieked. "*She* asked *him*? Gross."

"The day after Daniel was buried." BeBe suddenly remembered the flag-draped coffin, the twenty-one gun salute that felt as if it had been shot through her heart, and the hard stares from Father, as if she'd been the one who'd sent him off to be killed just because she knew the truth that Father could have stopped it, but chose not to instead. She cleared her throat and began again. "The day after Daniel was buried, Evelyn proposed to Roger. She told him that together they would be stronger than they would be apart, that she would help him get through the crisis."

"And he believed her."

"He was scared, I guess. We were all scared. Fear can really screw you up."

"I was scared when Danny had his accident."

BeBe was silent. Of course Mags and Greg must have been scared. Scared that their brother would no longer be the brother they'd grown up with, the older brother they could count on, no matter what. "You're lucky, though, Mags. You still have Danny."

"He's not the same."

"None of us are the same, honey. Life changes us. Always. Constantly. In my wildest dreams I never thought I'd live longer than your grandfather."

"You didn't like Gramps much, did you?"

BeBe stood up. "Gramps didn't like *me* very much," she said, then added, "I'd say we were about even." She looked out the window, down to the garden, where Liz stood now, alone. "I think I'd better go downstairs and talk to your mom. She looks in need of a friend." She headed for the doorway, then turned back. "Remember, though, Mags, I think your room really sucks."

Mags laughed. "And I think it sucks that you live in Palm Beach. We don't see you often enough."

BeBe felt the same way. Their twice-a-year visits were not enough. BeBe had relied on Liz to make the trip south—Boston and the Vineyard were simply out of the question as long as Will Adams still lived, as long as Will Adams still breathed.

"I think it sucks, too, Magsie. Maybe we can change that now." She wondered if Evelyn would try and stop her from being part of the family if Liz moved into the White House. Then she realized that Evelyn's opinion counted for shit now that Father finally was dead.

As if she'd been standing outside Mags's room listening to their conversation, Evelyn greeted BeBe on the stairs with a look on her face that was more sour than usual.

"Can't you talk some sense into your sister?" she demanded.

"Excuse me?"

"Liz is dodging the press, she won't sit with the guests, and I've just learned she won't go to Illinois tomorrow."

BeBe wasn't sure which of those mortal sins she was supposed to address with her sister. "This may surprise you, Evelyn, but there are more things in the world than a presidential campaign. Maybe my sister is grieving. She actually liked my father, though I've no idea why."

Of course BeBe knew why—it was because BeBe had protected her younger sister from ever learning the truth about Father, about what he'd done. But BeBe was not in the mood to discuss that with Evelyn, no matter how many "guests" Liz refused to sit with. Besides, it had been Evelyn's sainted congressman-grandfather who had assisted—or rather *not* assisted—in the deed that led to

Daniel's death. BeBe wondered, not for the first time, if Evelyn knew about that.

"I should have known you'd stick up for your sister," Evelyn snapped. "But this is for her own good. The race is tighter than anyone predicted. If Liz pulls out now . . ."

BeBe forced a sincere-looking smile. "Maybe she just doesn't like Illinois."

Evelyn glared. "It's not fair, BeBe. Roger went to a lot of trouble to arrange for her to speak at the National Businesswomen's Alliance . . ."

"Come on, Evelyn, I'm not stupid. I doubt it was much 'trouble' to arrange a free speaker. Especially someone in her position."

"That's not the point. The point is I'm afraid she's losing it. To desert the campaign now, when everything is so critical . . ." Her whine was pathetic.

BeBe sighed. "Did you ever hear the term 'fast-forwarding,' Evelyn?" Evelyn's eyes narrowed. In that instant, BeBe almost felt sorry for her, a victim of her own compulsions and need to control. "Fast-forwarding is worrying too much about the future before it gets here," BeBe continued. "Liz will work things out the way she thinks best. Give her that freedom and give her that respect and stop trying to run her life."

That said, BeBe pushed past her pain-in-the-ass sister-in-law and continued her way down the stairs.

"You don't understand," Evelyn called after her. "They're on the way to the White House . . . the stakes are much higher . . ."

BeBe shook her head but did not turn around. Talking to Evelyn was, as usual, worthless. However, maybe she should find out what was going on with her sister.

"I can't go, BeBe. I thought that, of all people, you'd understand."

Thankfully, none of the guests or the media or anyone had found their way into the secluded walled garden. "I know you're upset about Father," BeBe said, "but there are other things to consider."

"Such as?"

"It's no secret how Evelyn feels about me. It must have killed her to ask me to help. She thinks you're losing it."

"I'm not losing anything, BeBe. I explained everything to Roger."

"And he explained it to Evelyn. What you haven't done is explain it to me."

Silence hung over the garden the way it had earlier in church, as if this congregation of two now needed a pastor to tell them their next move. Liz did not reply. Her gaze dropped to the ground. She moved to a wrought-iron chair set at a wrought-iron table. She brushed the seat, examined it closely, then apparently decided it was too dirty to sit on. She walked to the stone wall and studied the ivy that crawled over it.

"You weren't this unglued when Mother died," BeBe said.

"Mother did not choose to die with an election hanging in the balance."

"Pardon me, but I did not notice Father's name on the ballot." She took a deep breath. "No matter how Father and I felt about one another, Lizzie, I can say this: he would have wanted you to go on. Having Michael become president meant everything to him."

It was sort of true. What BeBe wanted to say was that having *Daniel* become president had meant everything to Father, but by his own hand his plan had backfired from an M16 rifle into Daniel's young face.

What BeBe wanted to say was that Michael was Will's second choice, the runner-up, the person assigned to take over the duties should the first choice be unable. She wanted to say these things, but now was not the time for truth.

Liz plucked at the ivy. "I know it's what Father wanted, Beebs. It's why I've kept going all these years. It's why I stood beside Michael when he ran for governor, why I was still standing there when he resigned to begin this campaign. God, BeBe, that's all I've ever done was be Michael's support . . . not even so much for Michael but for Father. Because he expected me to." There was a slight quiver in her voice and BeBe wondered if Liz wanted to add that she had even *married* Michael because it was what Father had wanted, that everything she had ever done had been because Father wanted it. Well, almost everything.

But BeBe knew that Liz would not speak these things because they, too, were truths, and because Liz was Liz, the silly old fool.

BeBe went to her sister and drew her into a hug. "Do whatever you want, honey," she said. "Do whatever makes you feel right." She felt sure, that after a night's sleep, Liz would decide to go to Illinois with Michael, because that's how she was, always there for others, hardly there for herself. "As for me," BeBe continued, breaking away and wiping away a tear that had slid down her sister's cheek, "I have to get home. Business to attend to." She did not mention the offer to sell French Country, or her decision to wait. If Liz knew the election results might make BeBe rich beyond dreams, Liz would want that for her. And BeBe still wasn't sure what she wanted for herself.

Liz hugged BeBe back. "When will we see you again?"

She hesitated, then smiled. "When will you be in Palm Beach?"

"Depends on the polls."

BeBe smoothed her sister's hair and nodded. "Maybe we'll catch up before then."

"Wish us luck, Beebs."

BeBe looked around. "Hopefully," she said in a sober

tone that she knew her sister would understand, "you won't need it."

Danny was bored. Aunt BeBe was gone and Mags was staying in her room and even Dad seemed too tired from all the commotion to do anything more than sit with his feet up.

He, too, did not feel like getting on a plane tomorrow and schlepping off for some unknown city where his wheelchair was probably good for another one or two points, depending on the mothers who were polled. Lately he'd found himself imagining what it would be like to somehow stand up, wave his arms, and tell the crowds that this thing with spokes and an infernally humming motor was all a big, tasteless joke done for votes.

But he could no more stand up than he could survive without Clay, his cinnamon-skinned, yellow-haired nurse who did all the unmentionable things for Danny so no one else would have to, like empty his pee bag and clean up his crap and wash his crotch. And help him escape when he could no longer stand it.

He looked through the window where Clay, his hero, was talking with Liz, his mom, in the garden. He figured, of course, they'd be talking about him, the common denominator of their lives. Danny decided to wheel out and find out what they were saying and if any of it was good.

He maneuvered the chair through the narrow doorway, onto the flagstone walk. "Gramps would have liked the funeral, Mom," he interrupted. "A lot of people showed up."

His mother smiled and reached down for a hug. "You're right, honey. He would have enjoyed the show."

She stood up straight again and he tipped back his

head in the familiar position of speaking to anyone who was not sitting down. "So what next? Cleveland? San Diego? Beijing?"

"No. It was supposed to be Illinois . . ." Liz looked from Danny to Clay, then back to Danny again. "But I was just talking to Clay about a vacation."

Danny did not miss the way Liz wrung her hands together. He did not miss a lot of things from his perch on the chair. "A vacation?" he repeated. "So close to the election?"

"Just us, honey. I thought we'd go to the Vineyard for a few days. Would you like that?"

The Vineyard? Just them? Well, Danny thought, it didn't really matter where he spent his days, though he preferred to be out of the limelight, as if that were possible. But part of him thought his mother couldn't be serious, that they couldn't just up and drop everything in the middle of the campaign and take off for the island.

Could they?

Then he wondered if he wasn't the only one who sometimes needed to escape, and if his mother would wring her hands less if they went.

Sure," he said finally. "The Vineyard sounds great. But shouldn't Dad . . ."

Quickly, Liz shook her head. "I need a break from the campaign, honey. I thought you might, too." She glanced at his nurse. "And Clay, of course."

He did not know what this was all about, his mother's desire for a hiatus from, well, from her life. He wondered if, on account of Gramps's death, she was going to have a breakdown, and if he would know what to do if she did. On the other hand, could he use a break? Sure, what the hell, he thought. One less rubber chicken dinner, one less picture of him on the evening news, was fine by him.

Danny tried to act ponderous, then nodded at Clay. "Clayman," he asked, "ever been to the Vineyard?"

"No, mon. Not once in my life."

"Then get out your flippers," he said. "and I'll teach you to swim."

Chapter 14

http://www.rogerdodger.com

Uncle Roger had made Danny memorize the Web site address as if he were an idiot as well as a cripple, as if he did not have only thirty semester hours left to get his degree in pre-med and biochemistry if he ever decided to go back to college, as if he had not already been accepted at the top three medical schools in the country, accepted on his grades, not on his father's or his grandfather's name.

He stared at the screen of the computer he'd set up in Gramps's old Vineyard study—and wondered what he was supposed to write to Uncle Roger.

"You must keep me posted on your mother," Roger had said when he'd cornered Danny at the house on Beacon Hill yesterday. "I'll be watching the polls, and if they begin to dip, we're going to have to get her off the island and back on the campaign trail, fast. In the meantime, I'm depending on you to monitor her progress."

Progress? Danny thought now. Roger made it sound as if his mother had retreated to the island to knit an afghan or to paint the house. *She's on the right sleeve, roger-*

dodger, he could report. Or: *She's done with the dormers and is working her way to the roof.*

Tangible goals, tangible progress.

But grief? How does one *progress* through grief? A psychiatrist at the rehab center in Switzerland had told Danny that he needed to grieve, that the loss of the function of his lower body was, in many ways, similar to bearing the death of a loved one. The doctor had also said that Danny would not begin to heal—*mentally,* of course, because no one talked *physically*—until he'd put closure on the accident and could begin to walk (no pun was intended, Danny was sure) through the stages of grief.

He had been sitting in his wheelchair on the patio overlooking Lake Lucerne, staring at the picture-postcard landscape of the snow-capped Alps, and listening to the harmony of the bells of the cows grazing in the mountainside meadows. He had been sitting and watching and listening. Then he stared at the deep denim-blue water—"indigo," Ralph Lauren, the guy who made macho jeans for the machoest men, might have called it—and said, "Oh, sure, Dr. Weggis. I loved my legs all right. I loved my dick, too. Shall we have a funeral tomorrow so I can get on with my grief?"

Dr. Weggis had not been amused. But then, unlike Danny, Dr. Weggis was able to get up and walk back inside, and prepare himself a bowl of muesli with fresh cream instead of waiting for someone to serve him. He was also able to crawl into bed with his wife or his lover or whomever at night and do the things that one did when one had all working parts.

Arrived safely on the S.S. Steamship Authority, Danny typed now, watching each letter pop erratically onto the screen, wondering why a boy with 1548 on his SATs had never mastered the art of typing. *Subject in question appears normal. Is presently sitting on back porch drink-*

ing iced tea, probably trying to ignore baby-sitters. More later. Over and out.

He had already decided he was not going to share with rogerdodger the fact that his mother had wept silently on the ferry, that she had held his hand when they were disembarking or that when safely out of earshot of Moe and Curly (Danny's nicknames for the Secret Service "baby-sitters" assigned to rob them of their last bit of privacy) and Clay, of course, she had asked how Danny would feel if they lost the election and if he'd blame her. He did not share these things with his uncle because he felt it was none of Uncle Roger's damn business.

Besides, Danny wouldn't have minded at all if "they" lost the election. Maybe then there would be a chance for them to be together as some kind of family, to actually have time to do things together—things that had not been organized by a team of spin doctors, things beyond listening to speeches and posing for pictures.

London, for example. Danny had always wanted to go there, to see for himself the places he'd seen so often on television and in films—Big Ben and the Tower and Madame Tussaud's—maybe to find the cemetery plot of the last Adams to die there before their descendants bailed out for America. It seemed a bit preposterous that they'd never been. Then again, Adams/Barton family vacations had always consisted of summers on the Vineyard in this damp, gray-shingled old house, which for some stupid reason every one of them loved, where Dad and Gramps conducted politics in polo shirts instead of suits.

He wondered how much would change now that Gramps was out of the picture. For the first time, Danny wondered if his father really had the stuff to be president without the old man directing his every move. And if maybe—just maybe—his father was scared.

There had been a fleeting look in the eyes of the candidate after the funeral, a stare into space, a moment of blankness, then a blink back to reality and all that it meant. It had been just a brief look, but Danny had seen it, in the way his senses had grown more acute since his injury, as if the death of his legs had resulted in the birth of his eyes. It was a kind of "knowing" that he didn't always find comforting.

Danny shut off the computer, wheeled himself to the window, and looked onto the back porch where the subject of his e-mail indeed appeared normal. He folded his hands in his lap and decided that this wasn't so bad: at least he and his mother would have some time alone, at least he didn't have to face those god-awful cameras for a while.

The wheelchair whirred again as he rolled over to the French doors. He sat there a moment, surveying the porch. Moe and Curly ("Please call them Keith and Joe," his mother had asked)—so, all right, Keith and Joe— were stationed at the wicker table playing chess; Clay sat nearby wearing oversized headsets, tapping his foot, and reading a book on the occult. Closer inspection of his mother's iced tea revealed that the ice had melted long ago and that she'd probably not had more than one sip. Danny watched as she stood up, gazed out at the sea, then descended the steps toward the path to the dunes, her long legs moving mechanically, her head downcast, looking very much like any unhappy woman, not the one destined to become the next First Lady of America.

Just an ordinary day, rogerdodger, Danny thought with chagrin. *Put that in your dot-com and smoke it.*

She marveled at how the human body could shut down into a state of numbness, at how long one could sit or walk and think or not think, at how the world could turn or not turn and that it was possible to fully, completely, totally not care. Liz shoved her hands into the pockets of her cutoffs and stared at the sand that sifted through her toes.

It was good to have come. It was good to be in her old shorts, to be wrapped in one of Michael's old T-shirts from Menemsha Blues, to be barefoot. The Vineyard house had always seemed like home to Liz—their summertime, carefree home, not snarled with the time schedules of the city. Life was always so busy during the school years, so filled with the scramble of comings and goings; the only time Liz felt settled was here, on the island, where the cry of the gulls was as familiar as the laughter of her children, where the warmth of the sand was as snug as a thick down comforter fluffed by the sun.

She was glad they had taken the ferry. It had been years since they'd had the time: usually the vehicles were brought over by "employees" of Michael's or Father's, while Liz, Michael, and the kids were whisked from one place to another in somebody's borrowed jet.

Following the path, she stopped and looked at the clusters of Queen Anne's lace. They were the same white, intricately webbed blossoms that had adorned her wedding, along with plump pink and lavender hydrangeas. They had been flowers suitable for a wedding between the Adamses and the Bartons, the Yankee bloodlines maintained, the royal road paved to the White House.

For some reason she thought of her mother now, how beautifully she'd been dressed at the wedding in powder blue chiffon and Great-grandmother's pearls. For that one day, Mother had put aside the pain of Daniel's death long enough for a champagne toast, long enough for a smile.

It had pleased Liz that the wedding had made Mother happy, if only for that one day.

She and Michael had married four years after Daniel was killed. Liz was barely twenty and Michael twenty-six, but there had seemed no sense in waiting. The plans had been made, the future was set, the families were ecstatic.

So was Liz. Michael had been there at Daniel's funeral. Indeed, Michael had been there ever since, sometimes in closed-door meetings in Father's study, sometimes—though not often enough in recent years—walking the cobblestone streets of Back Bay with Liz, holding her hand, talking of life, of the world, of the future.

It had been, and still was, a good marriage, though not without compromise (as if any could be), not without frustration. *Overall contentment* was how Liz thought of their partnership, which like most things, she owed to Will Adams. Because Will had wanted their marriage. Will had expected it to succeed.

She closed her eyes and let the sun sink into her skin now, ignoring the footsteps behind her, footsteps that belonged to the Secret Service agents Keith and Joe.

"It's for your own good," Roger had told her when she protested having them follow her to the Vineyard, when she'd said she resented this intrusion into her own time, her own hurting time.

"You'd better get used to them," Michael had added, with a wink that reminded her that Keith and Joe, or others just like them, might follow her the rest of her life.

She knew it was for her own good. She knew that every presidential candidate since Bobby Kennedy was automatically assigned a Secret Service contingent. But Liz did not think she'd ever get used to their constant presence. It made all her visible years as a governor's wife seem private by comparison.

She walked across the sand. At least she was thinking again. At least she was focusing on something other than the image of Father lying gray on the floor, the commotion of Michael fruitlessly administering CPR, the EMTs strapping Father to the gurney and covering him with the sheet, while Michael directed them so capably.

"You're not afraid of anything," Liz had once commented the summer after Daniel was killed, when they were so young, when they were walking along this same beach, groping with words and feelings, trying to see how—if—each of them fit with the other.

Michael had smiled. "Of course I'm afraid. I'm afraid of a few things."

"Like what?" Liz persisted. "Snakes?"

Michael laughed. "No. Not snakes."

"Bats?"

He shook his head.

"Skunks? No," Liz answered herself, "you weren't afraid that time when Daniel was twirling the skunk."

They both became quiet, the mention of Daniel's name still awkward on their lips, in their hearts.

"I was afraid," Michael said finally. "But I didn't want anyone to know."

"Especially Daniel," Liz whispered tentatively.

"And you," he added. "I didn't want you to think I was less brave than your brother."

The way his voice cracked, the way he turned his face slightly from hers, had opened her heart and let him come in. Quietly, Liz took his hand. Should she tell him that she would never compare him with Daniel? Afraid to say the wrong thing, she kept silent.

They walked a few more steps, then Michael said, "I miss him so much, Liz. You think I am afraid of nothing, but sometimes I am afraid of that. I'm afraid of the fact that Daniel will never come back, and he'll never know how much his friendship meant to me."

It must have been then that Liz decided to marry Michael, to forgo the kind of schoolgirl passion she'd felt with Josh Miller for someone more acceptable, something much safer, someone whose hand felt very strong as it rested in hers.

As the path to the cove came into her sight now, Liz decided to turn back. She was not ready to relive too much of her life—not today, anyway.

Heading back to the house, she passed the agents and gave them a quick smile. Then she saw in the distance the wheelchair on the porch—the wheelchair that was unable to traverse the sand well enough to get down to the beach. The eyes of the young man sitting there seemed fixed in her direction. They were eyes that belonged to the one person in the world who would depend on her forever, the one person for whom she must pull herself from this depression.

Liz raised an arm and waved at her son. She remembered it was peach season on the Vineyard. Peach pie had always been Danny's favorite. As it had been of his Uncle Daniel before him.

Chapter 15

"I don't want to go," Danny said to his mother.

"I'm not asking you to drive," Liz replied, climbing the stairs up to the porch. She did not know why Danny refused to drive the van they had bought him, the one fully equipped for him, offering him freedom from a world of confinement. She often wondered if she would ever know her son again, if he would ever know himself. "Just come with me. You can't sit here all day watching Keith and Joe play checkers."

"Chess. They play chess. And I don't watch them all day; I go on the Internet."

Liz sighed. She did not know how far to let him go, when or how to force him back to society and life. She did not know where those boundaries lay and how far beyond them she should intrude. Danny, after all, was not like her other children; he never had been. He was the brightest, the most charismatic and energetic. He had also been the most challenging to raise, always inquisitive, always wondering how things worked and why. But his energy seemed depleted now, and if his mind was still sharp, he rarely let Liz see that. Perhaps he, too, had shut down into that limbolike state of disinterest. The difference was, Liz knew that, one way or another, she would feel again, she would one day—probably soon—rejoin the world. For Danny, the outcome was less certain.

"Clay!" she shouted to the far end of the porch. "Talk some sense into your patient." She was trying to act lighthearted, trying, as the psychiatrists had suggested, to seem normal and positive and not devastated for her child and his anguish. The trying was easy some times more than others.

"It's not Clay's job to talk sense into me, Mom," Danny answered for his nurse. "He's here to wipe me and dipe me and put me to bed, not to make me part of your human race."

Exasperation formed a small knot in her chest. It seemed that if Danny couldn't be civil to the world, he could at least be decent to Clay, whose patience with her son seemed to outweigh his salary.

"Okay," she relented, "but I'm going to make peach pie and you're going to eat it."

"You win, Mom," Danny replied, his words riding the wave of disinterest again.

Liz went into the house and grabbed the car keys from the wall hook. She didn't feel as if she'd won anything at all.

"You can't go in," Joe said to Liz as she pulled into the parking lot of the Chilmark General Store. It was the fourth time he'd said it since he'd jumped into the van as she was pulling out of the driveway. He'd threatened to force her to turn around. "The store could be unsafe," he repeated now. "It hasn't been cleared."

Liz turned off the ignition and looked over the rocking chairs that lined the front porch of the store, the hanging pots plump with geraniums, the people who lazed there munching sandwiches from the deli or walking in and out of the screen doors with the ease of a long summer day. She noticed the wheelchair ramp. *Handicapped accessible,* she thought, wishing it hadn't become second nature for her to notice these things.

"I have been coming to this store since before you were born." Of the two agents, Liz preferred Keith: he was close to fifty, soft-spoken, and calm. Joe was not much older than Danny, but brimmed with good health and vivacity. "Believe me," she bristled, "when I tell you the Chilmark General Store is safe."

Joe placed his healthy, young hand on her arm. "I can't let you go in alone."

"Please," she said, jerking open her door. "Don't be ridiculous. There are no evils lurking between the peaches and the corn on the cob." She got out of the van, slammed the door harder than necessary, and marched up the wide wooden stairs. She tried to block out the sound of the passenger door opening, then closing, and the feel—that damned pervasive feel—of footsteps behind her climbing up her heels. She put a hand to her forehead. Why was she being so uncharacteristically bitchy? She could not seem to help herself.

Liz opened the screen door and stepped inside, holding the door until Joe caught up.

She made her way to the back of the store, which she knew better than the large supermarkets in Boston, where she rarely went, but sent the cook. On the Vineyard, however, Liz had always been able to be herself, the keeper of her own kitchen, her own domain. She took a paper bag, then began examining the peaches, tucking the best into her bag, only the firmest—"not too ripe," Mother had instructed so many years ago.

Not too ripe.

Liz stared at a peach in her hand, struck by the realization that both her parents were dead, that she was a forty-four-year-old orphan now.

It reminded her of Christmastime when she was a child, when Will had packed his four children into the station wagon and driven them to the orphanage on the north end of the city. There they distributed dolls, toys, and games to the poor orphans and shared candy-cane cookies that Cook helped them bake. The next day their pictures always appeared in the newspaper, children of privilege sharing with the less fortunate.

Liz did not know how old she had been when she began to suspect that Father had them do this for the image it created and not for the good of the motherless and fatherless orphans.

Her hand closed over the peach. She felt the cords in her neck grow taut.

Enough, she said to herself, quickly dropping the fruit into the bag, and heading for the checkout. It was then that she noticed Joe speaking with someone . . . a young man as polished as himself, a man with a similar U.S. Marines buzz cut and nondescript clothes. Liz kept moving, hoping the agent was not hassling him, wasn't going to make a scene, right here in the Chilmark General Store where she had practically grown up.

She ducked down an aisle. Huddling against a shelf of soup cans, she heard Joe say, "No shit. You've got to be kidding."

Did they know each other? Joe laughed, but Liz could not make out the next words or who had spoken them. It didn't matter. Obviously it was just a friendly encounter and Liz was being paranoid.

She headed back to the cash register and paid for the peaches.

It was not until they were both back in the van that Joe grinned and said, "Unbelievable, I ran into an old friend in there. Rob Morrison. I knew him in Washington. We trained together."

Liz thought for a moment, then carefully steered the van out onto the main road, sensing something discomforting, almost foreboding. "He's with the Secret Service, too?" she asked quietly.

"Yeah," Joe replied. "Guess he'll be on the Vineyard for a few days. He's assigned to your husband's competitor."

Liz did not have to ask who he meant. Everyone in the world certainly knew by now that the candidate of the opposite political party also had ties to this island.

She steadied the wheel in her hands and struggled to keep her eyes on the road, wondering why Josh had chosen now to come to the Vineyard.

"Josh Miller is coming to the island," Danny announced from his perch in front of the television, where he half watched the evening news. There were rattling sounds from the kitchen. He looked toward the room but did not get a response. He turned back to the TV.

"Sources close to the campaign tell us that Mr. Miller will retreat to his summer home on Martha's Vineyard with his strategists in an attempt to find a way to bridge the seesawing gap in the polls, now at eight points between him and Michael Barton," the talking head at the anchor desk reported.

"Dad's only leading by eight points," Danny called out, but still his mother did not reply, as if she did not remember—or care—that right after Gramps died the difference had expanded from six points to twelve, and that now it had dropped back to eight. He also knew that an eight-point lead was not big enough to relax.

He stared at the television wondering who the people were who were polled, and why that was supposed to indicate how the whole country felt. It was like during that entire Clinton-Monica thing. At one point the polls said that, despite the scandal, his favorability rating was at something like seventy-two percent. But three-quarters of the people Danny associated with had not agreed.

Danny reached down and scratched the top of his leg, not because he could feel any kind of an itch, but because it was there. He wondered what life was like for the rest of humanity who did not have to deal with polls or men with dark hair and penetratingly black eyes, like the man on the screen in front of him now, the man whom thirty-eight percent of the people (with sixteen percent still undecided) preferred over his father.

Once, Danny had asked why they did not know Josh Miller. After all, the Millers and the Adamses had been summer neighbors on the island since long before Danny had even been born. He had never received a straight answer—something vague about the fact the Millers were from New York; something about the Millers being Jewish. "Not that your grandfather dislikes Jews," Michael had said. "He just doesn't trust them."

Danny thought it was stupid and had told his grandfather so.

"Good," Will Adams had answered. "When you're my age your grandchildren can think differently from you, too. And you can tell them to go to hell." He had then walked away.

On the screen now came a map of the country, with states that were Barton territory colored in red, those for Josh Miller in blue. The fact that Miller's states were bigger in size made it appear as if he were way out in front instead of eight points behind.

Danny thought about his mother, and wondered if Uncle Roger was right, if Liz should be back on the campaign trail. Did she no longer care about being First Lady? And what about Dad—shouldn't they be fighting harder?

Ten, five, even only a couple of years ago no one would have believed a Jew would even be a candidate, let alone win the race. But now here was Josh Miller, closing the ethnic gap with his grassroots charm and his tireless campaigning. The fact that he was a widower whose wife died last year of cancer leaving him with two young daughters only seemed to have increased his chances.

"Sympathy vote," Roger had said. "It can kill us if we're not careful."

Danny wondered if, now that Will was dead, perhaps they couldn't capitalize more strongly on the sympathy vote, too, more than the quick six-point jump that had since fallen by four. Then he wondered why he was doing all these ridiculous mathematical gymnastics and acting as if he cared.

Suddenly his father's face flashed on the screen, captured in the balance between air and air time, smiling in the balance between truth and the polls.

"My wife is taking a few days off from the campaign," he was saying into the camera, with just enough hint of gravity in his voice to let the folks know Liz was grieving, that Liz, after all, was one of them, the all-American girl. "As I'm sure everyone understands, this has been a difficult time for her. But she's with our son Danny, and I'm certain they will rejoin the campaign soon."

Danny scratched his leg again, unsure how "soon" would be soon enough to "rejoin the campaign." All he knew now was that his mother was clattering around in the kitchen, that for some reason she would not discuss the campaign, and that she was not even interested in the person named Josh Miller who could alter the well-charted course of their life if she didn't do something about it. And maybe do something fast.

. . . .

Evelyn double-checked her carry-on bag to be certain she had everything to make the long trip from Illinois to San Antonio productive: profiles on the organizations to which Michael would be speaking; head sheets and bios on the key players so he would be able to recognize them and act as if he knew them. It had worked at today's luncheon: no one would have guessed that only yesterday Michael had buried his influential father-in-law. No one who might have missed the news or the papers or the very trail of sympathy laid by well-meaning voters.

But Michael was a pro: Will Adams had taught him well. Still, Evelyn thought as she snapped her bag shut, she wondered why she cared when Liz no longer seemed to. Liz, the princess, who might just screw everything up because she was selfish and spoiled and always had been. Then Evelyn wondered if everything, from day one, was going to have been a big waste.

All these years she had kept quiet. All these years she had been the unimportant wife of the unimportant son, just because Daniel had gotten himself killed.

Even after Roger's "confession" about being gay, which she'd suspected for years, Evelyn had stayed Roger's wife because she had known that someday it was going to pay off. That someday Michael Barton would make Roger his attorney general (it had worked for Bobby Kennedy) or something equally impressive. Then she would become a grand Washington hostess, the one everyone would want to get close to because she was the sister-in-law of the president.

It had almost been worth it to funnel so many of her grandfather's millions into the campaign, no matter how many back doors she'd had to sneak it through, no matter how many favors she'd had to call in.

And all this time she had kept quiet about the young lovers whom she'd seen on that warm summer night long ago. And now the young lovers were on opposite sides, and perhaps only Roger and Evelyn knew. Roger had made her promise to keep the secret. It had been difficult, but she had done it for Daniel and for the family; she'd done it, of course, for her future.

But now Will Adams was dead and Liz had run off to the Vineyard, and suddenly the media was reporting that Josh was going there, too.

More than anyone, Evelyn knew that Liz was going to ruin everything if she didn't get away from her old boyfriend and back on the road, working for Michael. And she'd better move fast because time was running out. Eight points was a long way from victory.

As she walked down the jetway between Liz's husband and two of the children, Evelyn wondered what would have happened if she'd told what she'd seen that night at the cove so long ago. She wondered what would happen if she told about it now.

Chapter 16

She supposed he was a boy toy, but BeBe decided that wasn't a bad thing. In addition to doing those wonderfully erotic, make-you-feel-young-again things for which boy toys were created, Ruiz was actually a decent designer who put together packages that appealed to romantic emotions and turned even the thriftiest consumer into a French Country customer. It did not matter that the products were ridiculously overpriced. The cozy tins and oval boxes lined with fine parchment and tied with raffia made French Country the perfect gift for the *trés bon vivant,* or at least that was the perception they had succeeded in conveying.

In short, Ruiz Arroyo was worth nearly every dime she'd spent on the silver Mercedes convertible, the condo on the water a half mile from her house, and the frequent, substantial donations to his black market business of bringing long-lost relatives from Cuba by boat.

Of all his attributes, however, she preferred what he was doing right now: massaging her bare feet with a thick, sumptuous lotion he'd brought back from Paris. Slowly, he applied the lotion as if it were whipped cream, then lathered her arches, circled her heels, and fondled each toe, caressing with the gentle touch of a woman, and the sensuous strength of a man.

It made her trip home from Boston last night—in fact, the entire funeral process itself—seem like a dream—a hazy, unsettling dream that was at least a million lifetimes away from where she lounged now—on the chaise on the deck off her ocean-view bedroom.

"You're making me feel awfully good," she said, "You must want money. You want me to sell."

He examined her toes, one at a time. "The Loudets are nice people. They want to open new markets for their toiletries. French Country can do that."

She laced her fingers through his hair. "And part of my sixty million could bring a lot more boat people across the stream. Right?"

He stopped lathering, stood up, and walked to the railing that overlooked the Atlantic. "I try not to ask much of you, BeBe. I try and accept that some people have more than others do. I know I am lucky. I have my talent, which has, thanks to you, given me a good job and a wonderful life. But not a day goes by that I do not think of the others . . ." He looked out across the sea as if he were envisioning them now, those still in Cuba, doomed to smoke cigars, wear old, shapeless clothes, and left to drive cars from the fifties when cars were last brought by Americans. It conjured black-and-white images of old *Life* magazines; bleary photos of those left behind in time.

She listened to his words but kept her eyes glued to his great Cuban ass. It occurred to her that men, in their vanity, thought that women enjoyed ogling their crotches. Ruiz, however, somehow had learned that most women preferred looking at a tight, curvy butt. She suspected that was why now, when he was asking for money, he stood with his back, and his backside, in her view. "How much?" she asked. She knew there was more involved than financing a boat: the refugees must have papers, places to live, and food to eat until they could secure jobs.

He shrugged. "A couple hundred thousand should do it."

She closed her eyes against the hot summer sun. Now that Father was gone, there was no reason to keep her business in Florida, where the summer months smoldered. She could be in the Northeast, closer to Liz, closer to those she could call family. Whether or not she sold out to the Loudets or how often she supplemented Ruiz's twice-removed relatives, it wasn't as if BeBe couldn't afford to have someone shovel her snow.

But she was used to it here in the heat, with her hot Cuban boy toy who was asking for more money. She tried to focus on his butt, and on the lingering feel-good sensation in her toes. Life wasn't so bad here. "I'll have Claire take care of it tomorrow," she said. "Now get over here and take care of me."

"He's using you," Claire said the next morning after BeBe had requested the check for Ruiz.

"Save the editorializing for someone who will listen."

Claire moved closer to BeBe's long, glass-topped desk. "He's trying to get you to sell so he can have plenty of money and not have to work. Then he can spend all his time with those boat people, whoever they are. Have you ever even seen one of them? Has anyone ever come to thank you for your generosity?"

BeBe looked up from the stacks of paper in front of her. "I do not do it to be thanked. There's such a thing as helping humanity."

"Bullshit," Claire said. "You do it for the sex."

Swallowing a laugh and returning to her paperwork,

BeBe replied, "There are worse things in the world, my dear. Now write out the check like a good girl."

"Stop treating me like I'm a child. If anyone's immature around here, BeBe, it's you."

BeBe stopped what she was doing and peered over the tops of her half-glasses. "Would you have talked to your last boss like that?"

Claire scowled. "My last boss was an idiot. You're smarter than this." She thrust a piece of paper at BeBe. On it were several notations preceded by dollar signs. "I went back and dug out all your cancelled checks. In the past eight months alone, you've given Ruiz almost one and a half million dollars for his charity."

BeBe's amusement turned to a simmer. "This is the last time I'm going to remind you that this is my business."

Claire took back the paper. "It's just not right. You work so hard . . ."

"So does Ruiz. His designs have made us hugely successful. Don't forget that."

"He's an artist, that's all. Artists are a dime a dozen. And there are about a thousand out there who would do as good a job, if not better, for a hell of a lot less money."

"Just because you've had a couple of bad relationships doesn't mean all men are out to get us."

Claire stared at BeBe. "I'm only trying to help. You are more than my boss. You are my friend. And I think he's using the hell out of you." She turned and stomped out of the office.

BeBe watched Claire go and wondered who had hurt her so badly that the young woman could trust no one. She wondered if Claire hated Ruiz because he was Cuban like her long-lost ex-husband, because he was so much younger than BeBe, or just because he was a man.

Then she thought about Father and figured if anyone should hate men, it should be her. But like a fool, she loved men all too well.

Just then her office door opened again and Claire marched in carrying the oversized checkbook. She dropped it on BeBe's desk. "Fire me if you want, but I will not write out one more check for that man. You'll have to do it yourself."

"Now that my father is dead, there's no reason why I can't move the business up north," BeBe said later that afternoon to Ruiz when he'd stopped by her office for the money. He accepted the check casually—too casually, BeBe thought, then disregarded it as paranoia brought on by Claire.

He folded the check and slipped it into his pocket. "Are you trying to get rid of me?"

"Get rid of you? Why would I do that?"

"You tell me. Why do you want to move up north?"

"Because my family is there."

"Well, my family is here."

BeBe had never considered a group of refugees to be his "family." She sighed. "I've always hated the summers here, Ruiz. Now I'm free to suffer no more."

"If you sell the business you could travel all over the world to the best climates you want, whenever you want."

He meant, most probably, that he would go with her, travel on her money, live off her means. She ignored the tightness that had crept into her shoulders and reminded herself to forget about Claire. "Yes, well," she said, "it was just a thought."

"Think about this instead." He leaned down, kissed her, and took her breasts in his hands. "Tomorrow night I am going to drizzle sweet honey between your luscious legs. Then I am slowly going to lick it, until it is gone."

Ruiz might be a lot of things, BeBe knew, but he knew

how to please her. She placed her hands on the cheeks of his butt. "Tomorrow night? Why not tonight?"

He smiled. "Because I still have such incredible jet lag I would be no good to you."

BeBe had made the trip from Paris to Miami often enough to know what he meant. "Tomorrow night, then," she said, giving his ass a firm squeeze. "You bring the honey. And you'd better bring a lot."

BeBe was surprised, therefore, when, around eight o'clock there was a loud knock on her door. Few people but Ruiz ever came to the house.

But it wasn't Ruiz, it was Claire. There were tears in her eyes and a large envelope in her hands.

"These are pictures," she said, "in case you don't believe me."

BeBe wanted to ask what on earth she meant, but the words did not form. Perhaps she already knew what was coming next. "Ruiz Arroyo does have a black market connection with Cuban boat refugees," Claire said. "But he does not give them money. He takes it from them. That, along with the money he sucks off you, is apparently how he is able to own a mansion in Boca Raton . . ." She paused and looked away from BeBe. ". . . where his wife and four children live in great style."

Chapter 17

Out on the porch, he ate two pieces of peach pie, not because his mother wanted him to, but because if he couldn't have sex he might as well have peach pie. Warm. With vanilla ice cream positioned just so to melt around the edges the way Gramps had taught him. It had been one of the few things on which Danny and Gramps had agreed.

Tossing his napkin down on his plate, Danny smiled across the table at his nurse, who had devoured two pieces as well. "What do you say, Clayman?" he asked. "How 'bout a little surfing the Net?" It had been a waste of a day; Danny had taken two naps, but his depressed mother hadn't noticed.

Clay leaned back and rubbed his flat belly. "Got me a better idea, Danny. Let's go for a drive."

Danny knew what Clay meant. He wanted him to drive the van. He wanted him to learn how to use the push-button brakes and the hand-squeezed gas pedal. The tranquilizing high of the peach pie slowly dissolved into leave-me-alone melancholia.

"No." He put the chair in reverse and maneuvered it across the gray-painted floorboards and into the house.

Clay was right behind him. "Come on, Danny. Just once. You've got to deal with this . . ."

The nerves that inched up Danny's back—the ones he could feel—tingled. He wanted to shout, "You're my nurse, not my goddamn shrink." He wanted to tell Clay to get out of his life, and preferably take the van with him. He did not want to tell him that he was afraid. Afraid that once he gave in to such a proof of his condition that it would all be over, it would all be too real. He wheeled toward the computer. "Maybe Phaedra is online tonight."

"Phaedra's not real, Danny," the yellow-haired man on his tail retorted. "You've got to get out. You've got to get a life."

Danny laughed and snapped on the computer. "Doing what? Playing wheelchair basketball? Besides, you're no one to talk. You spend every day hanging out with a cripple." He double-clicked on the icon for the World Wide Web. "When was the last time you got laid, anyway?"

Clay sat in the chair beside Danny, stretched out his legs, and grinned. "None of your fucking business, mon."

Danny shifted his eyes from the screen to his nurse. "Are you queer?"

"If you mean am I gay, that's none of your business, either."

Danny shook his head and looked back at the screen. "My luck. My mother finds a queer to wash my dick."

You've got mail, the computer announced.

He moved the mouse to the mailbox. The message was from *rogerdodger.com.* He started to open it, then stopped. Just because Clay washed his dick and probably liked it didn't mean he should know everything about him. Or everything about the family, though Danny doubted that Clay would ever accept a million-dollar advance for a tell-all about the thrills and chills of the Adams/Barton family. What did Clay know, anyway, except maybe that Danny refused to drive the handicapped-equipped van? Any book of Clay's would definitely not be a best-seller. Hell, it probably wouldn't even get him a slot on Jerry Springer.

He clicked on his Buddy List. Phaedra was there. He created an Instant Message and typed: *I've just learned that my best friend is queer. What should I do?*

Beside him, Clay snorted. "I'm going to get even with you, Danny. I'm going to forget to empty your bag tonight and let you sleep in your piss."

Ding went the computer. *Come on over to my house, big boy,* Phaedra's reply read. *I can take care of you and your friend, too. Once he gets a look at me naked, he'll never think about boys again.*

Danny laughed. *Where do you live?* he typed.

Under a bridge. In Arizona.

There are no bridges in Arizona. There's no damn water.

London Bridge, she replied. *London Bridge is in Arizona. I'll meet you there tomorrow. I'll fuck your brains out.*

"Assuming, that is, that he has any left," Clay said, standing up. "I don't know why you torture yourself like this, mon," he said. "I don't know why you play with these people with no real names and no faces. Your 'Phaedra' is most likely a twelve-year-old boy getting his rocks off." He started to leave, then stopped. "You should quit thinking about all the things you can't have and start thinking about the things you *do* have."

Like a fully equipped van, Danny thought. Whoopee.

"And by the way," Clay said. "Not that it matters, but I am not gay. My brother was, though. He had AIDS. Which was why I decided to become a nurse. So I could help people like him. Like you. The difference is, he wasn't an asshole. He wanted to live. Too bad he didn't."

Danny stared at the screen. "Okay, mon," he said, clearing his throat. "I get the point."

The door slammed as Clay left the room. Danny sat for a moment, feeling like a juvenile, an infernal jerk. He turned off the computer, not caring what Phaedra or even rogerdodger had to say. Maybe he'd watch a little TV, then later he'd have some more pie.

Liz sat at the long trestle table that had been in the Vineyard kitchen ever since she could remember, listening to the music of being on hold, the telephone pressed tightly to her ear. She looked around the darkening room and wondered why her life had been reduced to making pies for one son, his nurse, and two military-like men. In this room that had once been filled with family she now sat alone—testimony to the passage of time and the emptiness it can bring.

Even the ghosts were unsettling. She could see Mother standing at the sink soaking clams for a chowder; she could see Father thundering in, asking what time was dinner as if it wasn't at six-thirty every night of their married life, even out on the Vineyard; and she could see Daniel. He was at the stove, tasting whatever was in the pot; at the refrigerator, holding the door open way too long but not being scolded; and he was sitting beside her, calling her Lizzie-girl, making her laugh.

And she could see Danny. At just a year old, his then-sturdy little legs taking one, two tentative steps, learning to walk.

She shuddered at the ghosts, the pieces of her family, now Jell-O-like bubbles, visible only to her.

"Mom?"

Her daughter's voice on the phone shattered the bubbles. "Mags?"

"Yeah, Mom. What's up?"

What's up? Why didn't kids realize that sometimes nothing had to be "up"?

"Nothing," Liz replied. "I made Danny peach pie." How could she tell Mags that she was just lonely? That she missed the other parts of her family picture, the only parts that were left for her to hold on to?

"Danny's going to get fat, Mom. He doesn't exactly exercise."

Liz did not mention that neither she nor Michael had been raised on a treadmill and had managed to stay slim; that her entire generation had not dropped dead in the pre-gym era, even without proper nutrition. She would have mentioned these things, but she was too tired. "I'll be careful, honey." She stared at the empty pie tin in front of her. "I didn't get to talk to Daddy when he called yesterday." It was not completely true. Michael had been on the phone when she'd walked in from the store, but she could not have spoken with him then: she was too stiff with shock that Josh Miller was coming back to the island. She swallowed and asked Mags, "How was the trip to San Antonio? Is Daddy there now?"

"The trip was boring," Mags said. "And Dad's giving a speech now—what else? I bailed out for a change."

"Is Greg with him?"

"And Uncle Roger."

"And Evelyn?"

Mags paused. Liz could almost see her daughter's noncommittal shrug. "I guess."

Liz changed the subject. "So how's it going? Do you miss me?"

"Yes, silly Mother. Are you coming soon?"

"I don't know. Not yet."

"Oh. When they said you were on the phone I was hoping . . ."

"I need a little more time, honey."

Mags did not say anything, at least not for a moment, as if she were trying to find the right words. Liz knew that there were no "right" words, but realized that her daughter might not know that, for until now, thank God, she'd not had to experience a death in the family.

"So," Mags said at last, "how was the pie?"

Liz closed her eyes to the now-dark room. "It was fine, honey," she said. "It was just fine." She wondered if the ghosts would have agreed.

BeBe supposed she should not be surprised. She stood there on the hand-painted, Italian-tiled floor of the foyer of her grand home in Palm Beach and felt the familiar ache of disappointment that came at the end of every love affair, of which there had been many.

Claire was long gone, having left BeBe holding the envelope with the "proof" of Ruiz's lies: photos, perhaps, of a smiling Cuban wife and four dark-skinned, black curly haired kids, well fed and happy, thanks to her money.

She wondered how long he'd been married, and how he'd explained the nights he'd spent with BeBe or at the condo she'd bought him for the sake of appearances. She wondered if his wife's name was Carmen or Lucia or Marlena. She wondered if he massaged her toes with thick lotion from Paris, or if he drizzled honey on her sweet, eager places. She wondered if he loved her.

BeBe sucked in a deep breath and held it a moment, then let it out slowly, wishing the pain would be released with it, the pain of, once again, having given herself to a man who did not love her. She had started with Tuna, way back when on the Vineyard, who had, at least, neither lied nor taken her money. It had been more than thirty years since then, and in that time she'd "progressed" to a gigolo whose greatest attribute was his ass.

And Claire was right. There were a thousand designers more talented than him.

Still, she thought, as she moved from the foyer and dropped the envelope into a wastebasket, it would have been nice if things had been different. It would have been nice if he really had loved her . . . if someday someone would love her . . . the way Michael loved Liz, the way Josh had, too. It would be nice, but . . . well, "nice" had not happened in her forty-seven years, and chances were, it would not happen now.

The quivers in BeBe's aching body won out, and slowly, ever so slowly, she dropped her head, sat down on the floor, and started to cry.

Fifteen hundred miles up the Atlantic coast, Liz stared out the window, off toward the shoreline, out into the night. She pressed her cheek to the cool, Vineyard-damp glass, closed her eyes, and silently wept.

Down the hall from his mother, Danny lay in his bed, his gaze shifting from the ceiling to the silhouette of his wheelchair, wishing he was someone—anyone—else, and wanting more than anything to have someone hold him and just let him cry.

Chapter 18

Josh Miller was wrapping up a three-day stint in Albuquerque and Michael Barton was in San Antonio for two days, or at least that's what the white-haired, thin-lipped reporter was saying as he spoke from the small box that sat on BeBe's kitchen counter. She poured another cup of coffee—her third of the morning. What was she doing watching the news when the damn sun hadn't even come up yet?

It wasn't as if she'd had any sleep.

At two o'clock she'd finally stopped crying. At three-fifteen she'd become incensed—she tore through the house, pulled out, ripped up, and shredded everything that belonged to Ruiz, reminded her of Ruiz, or even looked as if it might have.

She heaved everything from the balcony onto the beach below. Then, once again, she cried.

It had been all she could do to stop herself from calling Paris and grabbing the Loudets' offer, not because of the money, but because she did not want to look at one more of Ruiz's prissy yellow and blue designs. Common sense, what little she had of it, had stopped her from acting in haste.

It was that same common sense that had also stopped her from finding the son of a bitch and cutting off his balls. But BeBe decided there was time for that later this morning, when she had his office keys away from him and she was sure he could not hurt her or French Country.

"It's essential that Barton capture more of the South if he intends to hold on to his lead," the thin lips were saying now.

"That's right, Jack," said a blond-bouffant woman who had appeared beside him. "Barton's opponent has an increasingly strong foothold in the big states of Texas and Florida. It will be interesting to see what strategy Josh Miller develops in order to sustain that."

Barton two, Miller one, BeBe thought, wondering when the presidential election had begun to sound more like football than politics. Then again, maybe most people preferred it that way—as a high-stakes game where you were either a winner or a loser.

A winner like Liz who had the charming, successful husband and the three kids. A loser like BeBe, who had . . . no one.

She stared at the screen and thought about Liz. Maybe she should give her a call. It would not be that difficult to track her down. After all, Will Adams had always insisted they stay at Kensington Hotels: he had known the founder—hell, maybe he'd even kept the founder's kid out of Vietnam. Or seen to it that he'd had orders to go.

She wondered if there was a Kensington Hotel in San Antonio. Maybe the best thing she could do for herself right now was talk to Liz and remind herself of all those trappings of her sister's life that BeBe would never want to endure. It might make Ruiz's demise more survivable.

http://www.rogerdodger.com.

Danny logged on to Roger's Web site, went to the

mailbox, and stared at the blank screen. He was beginning to wonder if he should tell Uncle Roger what was
really going on . . . that his mother would not discuss the
campaign at all, that the day before yesterday, when his
father had called, Danny had lied and said his mother
was out, that she had gone to the store. She had, in fact,
already returned, and was standing beside Danny holding
a bag of peaches when he'd answered the phone. She'd
shaken her head and retreated to the kitchen, and Danny
had not known what else to say.

Did Mom and Dad have a fight or something?
he wanted to ask Uncle Roger now, figuring Roger
would know because it was Uncle Roger's business
to know everything and Aunt Evelyn's pleasure to find
out.

Besides, CNN reported that Dad was now only five
points ahead. He wondered if the Secret Service agents
really were spies, and if they were filtering word of
infighting among the Bartons out to the pollsters. He'd
like to ask Clay's opinion, but the Clayman still seemed
fairly pissed at him and would most likely not care if the
next president and his wife were at odds.

The truth was, though, Danny could not remember his
parents arguing very often. There was one argument, sort
of, after the accident when Dad wanted Danny to go to
the rehab center in Switzerland. Mom had wanted him to
stay home, had said she could take care of him better than
strangers in a foreign country. Danny had been in the
next room, alone in his bed, but he had heard their
voices through the thin walls of the old Beacon Street
house.

"He belongs here, Michael," Liz had pleaded. "With
his family, with us."

"More treatment might help," Michael retorted. "You
heard what the doctors said."

"I heard the doctors say he has about a two percent

chance of regaining normal function. Two percent is not worth having him gone for a year or more."

"But they're making breakthroughs in surgery."

His mother had made a scoffing noise. "It could be a decade before that is perfected, if at all. In the meantime, I want him home."

There had been a long pause. Then his father had said, "He needs to go, Liz."

If Danny had been in the room, he might have heard his mother sigh. What he did hear were her words: "Then I'm going with him."

There was silence for a heartbeat, or maybe for two. Then Governor Michael Barton spoke in the clear, direct, political-speak that always let one know exactly where one stood. "This is an election year, Liz," he said. "I need you here. Your father wants it that way."

There had been no further discussion. Danny had gone to Lucerne, his mother had stayed home, and Will Adams had, as usual, gotten his way. Michael had won a landslide victory in that November election and secured the party's good graces for the road to the White House nomination.

This time, Danny thought, they weren't fighting about him, at least not that he knew of. So maybe there was no point in alerting rogerdodger to the fact that the First-Lady-in-waiting might, indeed, be nuts.

He thought for a moment, then typed: *Gilligan here, stuck on the island. Just checking in.*

Just then an Instant Message flashed on the screen. *Yo, bro,* it read, *what ya up to?*

Danny smiled. There was nothing like contact with Mags to cheer him up.

Same old, same old. You in San Antonio?

Yeah. Do you have any idea how short Davy Crockett was?

LOL. You must have visited the Alamo.

Aunt Evelyn made us. She thinks it helps Dad's campaign to have us look like all-American tourist-kids.

Lucky you, you all-American, you.

F*!@ you.

Back at you.

I talked to Mom last night. She sounded like s*!t. When's she coming out of seclusion?

Her question startled him. Was Mags asking on Uncle Roger's behalf or for herself? *Today. Tomorrow,* he typed. *Maybe never. Who knows?*

There was a pause. His sister, obviously, was thinking about that one.

Don't let her stay there too long, okay, bro?

Now it was Danny's turn to pause. Then he simply typed, *Why?*

Because she's acting too weird.

He paused again, staring at the keyboard. *Let's blame it on global warming, okay? And by the way, you could call once in a while. We could be talking on the phone instead of in this detached, new-millennium method of communication.*

F*!@ you again. Gotta run. Aunt Evelyn booked us on a river ride through the town this morning. Yikes. Greg loves this s*!t. I'd rather be shopping. See ya. Bye.

Danny sat there, staring at the screen, a small smile sitting on his face as if waiting for the next message that was not coming. Finally, he returned to rogerdodger. He typed: *All's well. See you on the evening news.* Then he logged off, leaned back on the vinyl of the wheelchair and pondered the fact that Mags, too, had thought their mother was acting "too weird."

The Kensington Hotel in San Antonio was not being helpful.

"*Loooook,*" BeBe said, her irritation rising with every syllable she gave to the word. "Elizabeth Adams-Barton is my sister. I know she must be staying there. The Adamses always stay at a Kensington."

There was no response. At least it wasn't a negative.

"*Soooo,*" she continued, "if you will not put me through to the room, at least please leave a message. I must speak with my sister as soon as possible."

The voice was noncommittal. "If Mrs. Barton happens to check in, we will let her know."

"If you value your job, you will," BeBe said and slammed down the receiver.

She walked to the sink, dumped out the bottom-of-the-pot coffee, and slugged her way toward the bar in the living room. Swiping the hair from her face, she examined the contents and selected a bottle of coffee brandy. It seemed like a much better way to get caffeine this morning, if there was any caffeine in it, and if not, who cared anyway?

She pulled out a small snifter and filled it half full. She stopped, looked, then resumed filling it to the top. Just as she lifted it to her lips, the front door opened. She closed her eyes and took a deep swallow. The thick, burning liquid tunneled a path down her throat.

"Isn't it a little early for that?" Ruiz asked from across the room.

Her answer was to take another swig, a big one. Fortification was what she needed: liquid courage to control her anger and sustain her strength. Above all, BeBe knew she must not look at his ass.

That was how a huge part of her felt. Then there was the part that wanted him to walk over to her, envelop her in his arms, comfort her, say he was sorry, do all those things they did on those cable TV movies where the woman always got the man she wanted even though she did it in a very independent, I-really-can-live-without-you sort of way. She wanted him to tell her there was no wife, there were no kids, that Claire had made it all up.

But the bottom line was, BeBe trusted Claire more than she trusted Ruiz.

"So," BeBe said. She walked to the sideboard where he had dropped his keys and plucked them into her hand. "Are you over your jet lag?"

"Sort of," he replied as he moved toward the sliding glass doors off the living room. "Have you looked down on the beach? There's stuff all over the place."

On another day, at another time, she would have bitten back a smile. Now she simply removed the office keys and the keys to the condo from the silver ring she'd bought him at Cartier's. "Heads up," she said, tossing him the car keys.

He flinched, but his reflexes, like his penis, were fine-tuned. He caught the keys, looked down at them, then back at her.

"Thanks for the memories," BeBe said. "Now I'd appreciate it if you'd get your ass out of here and out of my life. Go back to your family. I'm sure you have enough money to last until the next sucker comes along."

He stood there without moving. "BeBe," he said, "this is not what I meant to have happen."

He did not try to deny it; goddammit, he did not even try. "No, I'm sure it's not." A hint of sarcasm heavily layered in Yankee pride crept into her voice. For once, she was glad of her Yankee pride, which helped her maintain that stiff upper lip and kept her from dissolving into sniveling girl-tears.

He stepped toward her, then stopped. He turned his face away.

"Ruiz," she said quietly. "Just go. I am humiliated enough."

He shuffled one foot. "What about . . . French Country?"

"I'll manage."

He did not respond.

A sick feeling rolled inside her. "What?" she asked. "Do you expect severance pay?"

He did not respond again, which she took for a yes. She wondered why she'd been so stupid that she hadn't listened to Claire long ago. "Consider the Mercedes your severance pay. And if you try and make trouble, I will go to the immigration authorities. I will reveal your little scheme."

His eyes narrowed. "Don't forget you invested in it. I could say it was all your idea."

"Just leave, Ruiz. Please." She was too tired to argue, too stung to spit in his face, although she knew she'd regret not having that satisfaction.

"You don't believe that I love you," he said quickly, and it caught her off guard, until she realized he was simply changing his approach.

"No," she replied. "Not for a nanosecond."

"You think I'm a man who uses women."

"Worse," she said. "I think you're an asshole."

They stood, staring at one another, her final words hanging heavily in the air. From outside the swollen surf crashed on the beach; a rumble of distant thunder passed by. *Hurricane season,* BeBe thought, *when anything can happen.* He stood staring at her, then jangled the keys. All that was missing was the ticking of a clock.

Then, instead of a clock, the telephone rang.

She pointed to the door.

The phone rang again.

He continued to stare for a moment, then marched angrily past her as if he were the jilted lover who had done no wrong.

She stood shaking for a moment after the door

slammed shut behind him. Then she slowly moved to the phone and picked up the receiver, her hand trembling, her voice ready to break.

"Aunt BeBe?" came the voice on the other end. "It's me. Mags. Did you call?"

BeBe made herself another drink, glad she had a cordless phone so she could stand at the window and watch Ruiz pick through his belongings on the beach while she half listened to her niece. Mags busily related an ordeal at the Alamo, trials with Aunt Evelyn and with life in general as BeBe wondered how she was going to put her life back together and how quickly she could get another designer.

"So we're coming to south Florida next," Mags jabbered with her twenty-year-old enthusiasm. "Please, please come, Aunt BeBe. Please come and see us at the hotel."

It started to rain, with the big raindrops so common in Florida, so common in hurricane season. "I'm not sure Evelyn would want me interfering with the campaign." Bebe turned from the window as Ruiz scurried toward the car, his arms overstuffed with trinkets, gifts he had given her, bought with her money, gifts he could now give to his wife.

"Interfering? Don't be silly, Aunt BeBe. You're family, you won't be interfering."

She wondered if Mags would feel the same way if she knew how many men around the globe BeBe had slept with, had even once slept with the candidate himself, back in the good old days, though only two people knew about that, and maybe only one of them remembered or had chosen to remember. She swirled the warm brandy around in her mouth and let Mags ramble on.

"Anyway," Mags continued, "I need you. You can't believe what a pain it is out here without Mom."

BeBe set down her glass. "Your mother isn't there?"

"No. She's on the Vineyard. With Danny."

BeBe frowned. She wanted to ask what the hell Liz was doing there, but decided it might not be an appropriate question for Liz's daughter. Not that that had ever stopped her before. But right now, other things seemed more important, like hearing the slam of a car door. She forced her thoughts back to Mags. "Well," she said, "I'm sure your mother appreciates it that you're filling in for her."

"Me? Hardly, Aunt BeBe. Aunt Evelyn is in charge—and if you don't believe it, just ask her. She orders Uncle Roger around like he's some kind of imbecile and she treats Greg and me like we're ten. 'Over here, kids.' 'Change your shirt, Greg.' 'Put on new lipstick, Margaret.' Yikes. She's driving me crazy."

BeBe closed her eyes, trying to focus on what Mags was saying. There was something slightly amusing about the predictability of Evelyn's asshole-ity, but she hated that Mags was now the brunt of it. And, distracted or not, BeBe also hated that Liz was not there. Her sister—the stable one, the lucky one—must be taking Father's death harder than BeBe had expected. She opened her eyes. "Have you talked to your mother?"

"Yes. She sounds weird. And Danny doesn't have a clue when she's planning to come back to the campaign."

"A presidential campaign is hardly the place to work through grief, Mags."

Mags sighed. "I know, Aunt BeBe. But it really sucks without her here. I hate all this smiling without her. Did you know that after every public appearance, when Dad isn't around, Mom makes up stories about the people who were there? She's got all us kids doing it now. It's so funny. She makes us laugh so hard."

BeBe laughed. It was not surprising that Liz would make up stories—it was such a "mom" thing to do, something that BeBe, the non-mom, would probably never have thought of. A car door slammed again; Ruiz must have loaded more things inside. She sucked in her cheeks. "What kind of stories?" she asked.

"Well, it started when we were little. The first time Dad ran for governor. We had to sit through this really long, really nasty rally. Mom leaned over and told us to think about the fat man with the bulging eyes. She said later she'd tell us a story about him and his rabbit."

BeBe smiled and sipped her brandy again. This was the playful side of Liz that she had not seen for years, the side that she would have thought was buried long ago beneath Father's saddle of decorum. "What about the fat man?" Without realizing it, she had strolled back to the window. The beach was nearly cleared now of all his belongings. He was poking through the remnants, his shirt soaked through, sticking to his back, his broad, tightly packed back.

Mags laughed. "I don't remember. But I do know that she took our minds off the boring stuff and got us focused on the guy. When we talked about it later, we all pitched in with our own ideas. Ever since then it's how we get through that stuff . . . knowing that after we'll make up stories about people and have some laughs about it." She paused, then giggled. "I suppose it wouldn't help Daddy's standing in the polls if the world knew what we do. But it helps us survive."

And *survival*, BeBe knew, was what life was about. She turned back from the window, wondering if Liz had developed the game after years of having to be the perfect daughter, of having to look perfect in the spotlight. She wondered if it was a game that Father had taught Liz. Then BeBe felt a sting of jealousy—that too-familiar, Father-likes-you-better sting she'd not let herself feel in years. Quickly, she changed the subject. "I suppose Evelyn has no sense of humor," she said.

"Yeah, well, that's putting it mildly. Would you talk to Mom, Aunt BeBe? I know she's upset about Gramps and everything, but . . ."

"I'll call her tonight. I promise."

"And will you come to the fund-raising dinner? It's at The Breakers. You know where that is, don't you? A thousand dollars a plate, but I can get you in free."

"A thousand dollars a plate? I didn't realize chicken was so expensive these days."

"Uncle Roger says the campaign has to raise a hundred thousand a day just to break even."

"I'll be there, honey," she replied. "And don't worry, I know how to get there." She did not add that she knew most of the bars in this town, because at one time or another, she'd picked up a man or two there.

She hung up the receiver and listened as the Mercedes roared to life, idled a moment, then squealed its tires and tore down the road.

Chapter 19

He was glad he had seen her naked. Danny closed his eyes and pictured Anna standing before him, lovely Anna the Swiss physical therapist. She had tried to restore his sex drive, which, according to the neurologists, had a forty percent chance of returning someday, but not that day . . . and it did not appear as if it would be this day, either. Danny looked down at the limp penis in his hand and wondered what demented spirit inside him even made him want to still try, made him want to take the hunk of dead flesh in his hand and pretend it would rise to the occasion, would become the angry, purple, pulsating beast that had thrilled more than one girl (well, only three in total, if the truth be known).

There had been Jodie, the fourteen-year-old who had more hormones raging than Danny, which was pretty unusual considering he was fifteen and thought of little else. Jodie went to Cambridge Academy, just across the Charles River from Harkness Prep. And Danny's mother would have killed him if she'd known that the son of the governor was banging a fourteen-year-old on the banks of the river every chance he got, which was pretty much daily, sometimes twice a day depending on their class schedules. It had lasted just a little more than four months, when Jodie's parents got a divorce and she was sent home to the West Coast to live with her mother full-time. Danny spent the rest of that year incredibly horny, missing their frenetic, amateur lovemaking and his daily sprints across the bridge. It was because of Jodie, however, that he'd developed a love of crew, having watched the long, flat boats skim through the water for Harvard or BU or BC. If he'd stuck to crew and forgotten about football, he wouldn't be in the wheelchair now. Jodie, however, would probably have gotten pregnant because they didn't always use protection, because there wasn't always time to buy contraceptives, and Jodie said her mother would freak if she went on the pill.

After Jodie, he spent the better part of two years either going into or just coming out of the blissful, yet lonely, state of masturbation, the *Commonwealth* of Masturbation, the boys at Harkness Prep called it, because they, after all, were the crème de la crème of the *Commonwealth* of Massachusetts, and were relegated (for the most part) to shooting their sperm into wads of tissue or into a warm bath, where the little buggers trailed through the water like long, white streamers of egg drop soup.

Then there had been LeeAnn, the tanned, long-legged island girl, whom Danny had known along with her brother, Reggie, during Vineyard summers practically all of his life. They'd been friends—summertime pals—until Danny started college and he chartered their catamaran to Cuttyhunk Island for a day. A dozen guys from Danny's environmental biology class had gone down to the Vineyard under the guise of studying the remains of Penikese Island—the neighbor of Cuttyhunk that had once housed the state's, or rather, the *commonwealth's,* infamous leper colony. In reality, the excursion resulted in more beer drinking than remains studying. When Danny returned to the boat the following day to clean up the mess, he'd run into LeeAnn and somehow they'd wound up in bed, or rather, in bunk, since they'd made love on the boat, safely tucked inside one of the pontoons that bobbed up and down with the rhythm of the waves and the rise and fall of their bodies.

For years they'd been friends and suddenly they were lovers.

LeeAnn was a perfect physical match for Danny; unfortunately, she was four years older and an islander. At the end of that summer, it had actually been Aunt BeBe who'd convinced him it was a match that was best left to memory. She said she'd "been there and done that" and that islanders and mainlanders simply did not mix for long. Danny was not sure if he and LeeAnn split up because they decided it would not work, or because Aunt BeBe's words had startled him. She had not elaborated. LeeAnn must have known, too, for though they had gone their separate ways, they'd returned to being friends. She and Reggie had even come to see him in the hospital in Boston right after the accident. Right after his world had fallen apart.

So there had been Jodie and there had been LeeAnn and the third, whom he guessed he shouldn't even count, was Anna. Anna with whom he had never consummated anything beyond manually manipulated leg lifts.

He studied his penis as it sagged in his hand and mourned the fact that he was the son of a famous man and therefore had been unable to be as sexually frivolous as most of his friends, or at least that was how Danny had perceived the responsibility to the Adams name back when he had a choice.

Now he wished to hell he had screwed everything in a skirt, long or short.

"Danny?" His mother's voice made him jump. Quickly, Danny tried to pull up the comforter. But he could not grasp it with his leg: it clumsily slid to the floor. He sat there, genitally naked for all the world—and worse, his mother—to see.

She moved forward, then stopped. He sensed her eyes fall to his lap. "Oh," she said. "Well. I . . . ah. . . . later. I'll come back . . ."

He squeezed his eyes shut. His chest grew heavy, the ache of a thousand humiliations not greater than this. "Yes, Mom," he replied, dropping his hands to his lap.

But his mother didn't leave. She cleared her throat. "Danny," she said, "it's okay."

The shades of his face must have shot up the scale from flesh tone to pink to beet red. Beneath his fingers he could feel the puttylike remnants and knew he was not— would never be—one of the forty percent, able to be a loving human being. "Please, Mom," he said. "This is embarrassing."

She nodded and, thank God, did not let her eyes drop to his lap again. She began to say something else, then stopped, and quietly backed out of his room.

When the door closed behind her, Danny put his hands to his face. "Fuck," he mumbled into them.

She felt as if she were going to be sick. Sick for Danny, that he would live an empty, childless life, without intimacy, without loving or letting himself be loved. She felt sick for Danny, her firstborn. And she felt sick for herself, that she had walked in on his private moment, that she had witnessed his failure and that he knew it.

Liz curled her feet underneath her on the swing on the back porch and sunk her teeth into her fist. Life, it seemed, was dealing one blow after another. Until now, she had been able to handle things. Or maybe reality was that, until now, she had kept herself so busy she had not noticed the pain, not let herself stop and feel the hurt. She had leapt from one campaign stop to another, one charity breakfast to one political luncheon to one fund-raising dinner to one whatever—anything to keep the dream in focus and the goal within reach. The trouble was, her own feelings had not played into the Day-Timer. There were meetings and "To Do's" all over the place, but no time for feelings, no time to . . . cry.

She wondered how often Danny cried. Did he weep every night before he went to sleep? Did he cry when he was alone in his room, when he tried to feel some sort of pleasure but instead had none? Did he sob into his pillow when he thought of his brother and sister and how healthy and whole they were and wonder why he no longer was?

The day that it happened had been the worst. The worst nightmare of a parent, the worst day of her life.

Liz and Michael were, of course, on the road. They were in Detroit, Michigan, of all places, at a governor's conference, it said on the news, but in actuality it was a conference to highlight Michael's state education agenda, which was being touted as a model for a national program. In short, it was just one more inch toward the White House.

She had worn a terra-cotta silk suit, trimmed in chocolate satin, which she would remember as well as she remembered the photo after photo of Jacqueline Kennedy's pink suit that Liz had seen when she was only a young girl and John Kennedy had been killed.

And though Liz was not Jackie and Danny was hardly the president (though Will might have had plans for him, too), the suit became a symbol of pain so great she did not think she would survive.

The call had come during the after-dinner speeches. A maître d' approached Michael and whispered something

Liz could not overhear from where she was sitting across the round table, in the politically correct mix-'n'-match dinner-partner style.

Michael's face grew as white as the linen banquet tablecloth. His eyes went to Liz. His mouth dropped open. He quickly stood up, threw his napkin on the table, spun on one heel, and left the hall in the middle of the governor of California's speech.

Liz did not have to be told something was wrong. She was right behind her husband, as if knowing that something tragic had happened. She did not want to believe it had happened to one of the children.

On the plane, he held her close. "I'll be okay, honey," Michael kept reassuring—her or himself, she was not clear whom.

But the words that played over and over in her mind were those she had heard at the airport: "Your father is with him. He had to sign the papers for surgery. They have to release the pressure on his spine."

Surgery.

His spine.

"He'll need several transfusions," Michael continued. "I wish we were there to give blood."

Blood.

Liz had frozen then. Gone into a seemingly semiconscious state of numbness, a place of shock, as if braced for the next bit of information that would assault her. She had clenched her hands together on the lap of the terracotta suit and tried to make it all the way to Boston without thinking or flinching or breathing.

"Oh, God," she moaned now, through her teeth, into her fist.

"Mrs. Barton?" a voice asked.

She blinked. The voice belonged to Keith, the Secret Service agent. She realized she had moaned. "It's all right," she said, standing up. "I'm fine." She smoothed the front of her shirt, thinking that she was glad she had thrown the terra-cotta suit in the trash.

"That's good," the agent said. "Because you have a visitor."

Liz scowled. "A visitor?" She did not need a visitor right now.

"We didn't know if you wanted to see him or not."

"Him?" Liz asked. "Who?"

The agent looked puzzled. "Well, ma'am, it's the other one. Mr. Miller."

She steadied herself against the swing. She closed her eyes.

"He wants to see you."

She had no courage to leave, and no strength to protest. Slowly, she opened her eyes and simply said, "Bring him out to the porch."

"I'm sorry about your father," Josh said once they had settled on the swing and convinced the Secret Service agents—numbering an absurd four now, two for each— to leave them alone, that neither was going to maim, kidnap, or kill the other.

Liz nodded and stared off across the dunes. She did not trust herself to speak out loud; she did not trust herself to look at him, at his tender, sensual face that she'd seen slowly mature in newspaper and magazine photos, on the national and international news. Josh Miller, the timeless reminder of earlier times, of lust-filled days and heated nights.

"I wanted to come to the funeral," he said, "but it seemed inappropriate. Besides, I didn't want . . . well, you know . . ."

Yes, of course she knew. Josh didn't want to turn Will Adams's funeral into a media circus any more than it already was.

Liz stole a look at him, the man who had once swept her off her feet. BeBe had once told her it was hormonal. If so, those same hormones were still there. She tucked her hair behind her ears and wondered if she looked different to Josh, and if the difference was good or bad.

He moved the swing. The sudden motion caught her off guard, and she gripped the seat.

"Your father was important to me in ways he will never know," Josh continued. "I used to be so envious of you kids. You were the ones with the guaranteed futures, with no obstacles before you. I guess I was angry about that. That you kids had it all and I . . . well, I couldn't even have the girl I wanted. Anyway, I think I set out to prove something to your father. And now look at us." He stopped the swing and placed his hand on hers. The warmth of it seeped into her skin. She stared down at his large knuckles, his thick, straight fingers, the tanned tracks of veins. "Who ever would have thought we'd be on opposite sides of the fence, Liz?" he asked. "On opposite sides, at the top of the heap?"

She forced another smile.

He looked down at her hand. Her eyes followed his. With the lightest, gentlest touch, he traced the lines of her fingers, the curve of her nails.

"You must miss your father," Josh said quietly.

"Yes," she said softly.

"Did he ever mention me? I mean, about the election. Did he ever . . . say anything?"

Liz smiled again, an image of scowling Father coming to mind. "Yes," she replied. "He said you were a sneaky bastard who should stick to your own kind."

Josh looked at her. Then he grinned. The tension dissolved and they laughed. He lifted his hand from hers and ran it through his hair, through his still-dark, still-thick hair. Liz tried to pretend that the back of her hand did not feel cool and abandoned and not as complete as it had felt when his palm rested there. Then he said, "God, he really hated me, didn't he?"

"Hate is just another word for fear," Liz said. "And for the record, as I remember, your family wouldn't have been thrilled to have me in your life before you . . . left."

His eyebrows raised. "So it was *my* family that stopped us? You mean your father would have let you . . . date me?"

She grinned a soft, childlike grin. "No," she replied. "Of course not."

"Romeo and Juliet," he said. "Destined to be apart."

The ropes of the old porch swing creaked.

"I'm sorry about your wife," Liz said suddenly, remembering that his wife had died, that he'd had his share of heartbreak, like most everyone their age.

"Me, too," he replied. "She was a good woman."

She pushed down a twinge of childish jealousy.

Josh laughed again. "God, that sounds provincial, doesn't it? She was my wife for twelve years. What else would I say? That we didn't always have the same parenting skills? That there were times I'd wished she'd been less domestic and more interested in the world?"

He shook his head a little, deep in thought.

Josh the thinker versus Michael the listener. For a brief second, Liz actually wished she could be an objective outsider, one who could judge the two candidates and decide which she preferred. She breathed a long breath of Vineyard fresh air. "It must be difficult for your daughters."

The swing creaked again as if in affirmative reply.

"What about your wife, Josh? What was she like?"

He paused and lowered his head. "She really was a good woman, Liz. She was the best."

Liz nodded, but this time she could not stop the tiny ache that had formed in her heart.

• • •

Josh Miller looked shorter in person than he did on the news. Danny was an expert on how to judge a man's height by the way he sat in a chair: so much allowed for the torso, calculated by how far the legs stuck out at the knees before the feet reached the floor. It was, he sensed, a foolish, weird game. But it helped pass the time some days and didn't hurt anyone.

From his position in the living room, Danny could see the other presidential candidate in profile, enough to determine that Josh Miller was under six feet—five nine or ten maybe, not as grand in stature as his opponent, Dad. Danny tried to remember a study he had read in college about presidential candidates and what the outcomes of elections were in relation to the height of each candidate. But he could not recall the results; it had seemed unimportant at the time, like so many things that had since found some meaning if only to give his mind something to do.

He wished he could read lips. He wished his mother hadn't closed the French doors. All he could tell was that they were both animated. Mom was smiling. Miller was smiling. But neither was revealing why Josh was here.

Danny wondered what this would do to rogerdodger's polls if anyone knew. And exactly how prejudiced Gramps had been. His mother had once said she hadn't seen Josh Miller in decades. So what were they doing now? Sharing old stories of shooting at squirrels (the way he and LeeAnn and Reggie had done) or clamming (ditto) or stealing the bike ferry and going past Menemsha for a picnic (double ditto)?

And, if so, why were they talking about such stuff when the future of a nation was at stake?

He realized that this was perhaps the first time he had thought of his mother—his parents—as being young,

young enough to be utterly stupid. It was not easy to imagine, not of his mother. Nor of this five foot nine or ten, slightly unpolished guy who now sat on their porch, though God only knew why.

Maybe Danny could learn something if he wheeled out front where the agents were hanging out in the driveway. By the sounds of the laughter coming from there, Moe and Curly seemed to know the others, belonging, as they did, to the mutually exclusive club of professional guardians. He wondered if they were talking—laughing—about them, if they were comparing the Bartons and the Millers, and who came up as being the bigger pains in the ass to guard.

He was wondering these things when the telephone rang.

Chapter 20

 She did not want him to go; she wanted to sit here and listen to the sound of his voice, the cadence of his words—poet's words, ebbing and flowing with the rhythm of the waves, riding the tide of the wind.

But for the sake of her sanity, she wished he would go.

"The second time I went to Israel, it was different," Josh said.

She wanted to block her ears. She wanted to hear no more. The second time he went to Israel. Yes, she remembered that, too. She had not—not now, not ever—wanted to remember that time, when he'd finally returned, when it had been—should have been—too late.

"I think it was only then that I realized we really would not be together," he was saying, then added, "God, it had been five years since I'd seen you. Wouldn't you think I'd have figured it out before then?"

Liz lowered her gaze to the gray-painted porch floor, as the painful memories flooded back, memories of the summer when everyone had left her—first Daniel, then BeBe, then Josh. She once again felt the huge, empty hollow of loneliness, and the way Michael had been there to help slowly fill it. Five years later, when Josh returned to the island, she was married to Michael, had been married a year, because Michael hadn't left her and because Father had wanted it.

"It had been five years since I'd seen you," Josh continued now, "but in my heart, you were always there."

He had been in hers, too. Which was why it had been so easy to love him again. "That entire five years," Liz said quietly, "I never heard from you. You never wrote."

He steadied the swing. "That's not true, Liz. I wrote all the time. It was you who did not write back."

She nodded. She had always suspected—hoped—that Father was destroying Josh's letters, because that was less hurtful than thinking he had never written. "Father," she said. "He must have found your letters."

Josh also nodded, as if he, too, had known, as if he, too, had accepted their fate. "So you never got my address, and you did not know where to write. And by the time I came back you and Michael were married."

"Was that why you returned to Israel?"

"Returned? I ran away, Liz. It was better than staying here, wanting the one thing I could not have. I tried to punish myself by rejoining the military. But I was given a routine patrol assignment on the Jordan River. It was mundane," he continued, "boring. Most of Israel's problems were with Lebanon then, so the river was safe. But it was incredibly quiet and brutally hot. In fact, the only excitement was the heat. At night the sky was so big and so black it scared me sometimes."

She tried to picture this passionate man who was active and curious and . . . loving . . . alone on the banks of the hot desert river. She thought of the stars in the wide dark sky, and thought of Anastasia, adrift and alone. Adrift and alone—the way she too, had felt when he'd left for good. Blinking back the images, she asked, "Why did you stay there?"

"Penance, I guess. For loving you."

They were silent a moment. Liz wished it was nighttime, so the sky above them would be big and black now so she would feel what Josh had gone through, and maybe have a better sense that he had loved her, once, long ago.

"On weekends, most of the soldiers went home," he said. "It was the only time they had anything decent to eat."

"And you?" Liz asked. "What did you do?"

"Sometimes I stayed. Our barracks were concrete huts, designed to keep out the heat. At night I went down to the banks of the river. I sat there alone. I looked up at the sky." He paused. "And then," he said quietly, "I met Rachael."

Rachael, of course, was the small, sweet-smiling woman whose picture Liz had seen hundreds of times when Josh was a senator. And each time she'd told herself it didn't matter that Rachael was his wife and she wasn't.

Josh continued. "Rachael lived in a kibbutz. They're the most honored, you know. God's chosen ones are born in a kibbutz."

"A commune," Liz replied, then wished her word had not sounded so negative.

Josh smiled. "Sort of. A holy one, though."

She shifted her position on the swing. "So you fell in love with Rachael and then you were married."

"It wasn't that simple. When I finished in the military, I came back to the States. Israel is my homeland, but America is my home. Anyway, by that time, Vietnam was over, but the only thing on my résumé was being a soldier. Rachael had an uncle here who lived not far from my parents in Brooklyn Heights. He was a dean at Columbia. I went there, then on to law school. The state senate came next. It wasn't until the late eighties—just before I was elected to the U.S. Senate—that I saw her again."

He did not elaborate on when they were married, or how joyful it had been for him when his children—the two girls, now eight and ten—were born. For that Liz was grateful.

"It must have been difficult," she said, choosing her words carefully, "losing your wife. And your children are so young . . ."

"It's probably why I've thrown myself into this campaign."

In another place, in another time, they might have been on the same side. They might have been fighting for the White House together, if things had been different, if life had not hurt them.

His hand returned to hers. His warmth covered her skin. "There are so many things I would like to tell you, Liz," he said. "So many things I'd like to ask."

She nodded and turned her face toward the dunes, off toward the sea. For a few moments, they did not speak, the swing creaking slowly, marking the passage of time, a reminder—as if Liz needed one—that their worlds, and their lives, were not, had never been, one.

"Mom?"

Both of them jumped. Liz turned her head toward the door and Josh pulled his hand from hers. Danny sat in his wheelchair at the open door, an odd, quizzical look in his eyes as he looked from one of them to the other. "Dad's on the phone," he said.

Liz rose too quickly from the old porch swing, as if Danny had caught her in a private moment, the way she had caught him in his.

"We're leaving here for south Florida tonight. If you meet us there, you can see BeBe," Michael said.

Liz tried to listen, but it was hard when she could see from where she stood in the living room that Danny had stayed on the porch, and was deep in conversation with Josh.

"Liz?"

Should she tell him that Josh was here? He was bound to find out and then it would seem strange that she hadn't mentioned it. She wished she could hear what Danny was saying; she moved closer to the glass and squinted, as if that would help. "I just saw BeBe at Father's funeral," she said.

Michael sighed loudly and tightly. "Have you talked to her since?"

Liz pulled back the curtain. Danny's wheelchair faced the swing. He seemed to be studying Josh. What was he looking for? She blinked, knowing it must be her imagination. "BeBe and I don't always talk regularly. You know that."

The sigh again. "Liz, the kids want you here. I want you here. I feel so . . . off balance without you around."

Off balance? Liz wondered if that was what Josh had felt when his wife had died.

"Danny said Josh Miller is there."

Michael's statement, combined with the laughter she now heard from the porch, from her lover and from her son, weakened her knees, her spine, her heart. Of course Danny would have told him, because Danny would have no idea there was anything to hide.

"What are you doing?" Michael continued, "fraternizing with the enemy?"

Liz leaned against the windowsill and toyed with the phone cord. "He came to pay a condolence call. In fact, he was just leaving."

What followed was silence. No sighs, simply silence.

"Maybe we could talk about this later?" Liz asked. "About me leaving the Vineyard?" From the window she saw Josh stand up. *No,* her heart cried out. *Please don't leave yet.* "Michael?"

"What," came his flat response.

"I said, can we talk about this later?" She wondered if it was her imagination, or if his tone had changed when he'd mentioned Josh. They'd never talked about Josh as a person, only as a competing commodity, like Tide versus Wisk, Scotties versus Kleenex. She had tried not to think about whether he knew more about that summer on the Vineyard, if Evelyn, in all these years, had ever told him what she had seen. She tried not to wonder if he knew . . . everything.

"I have a speech in five minutes," he said. "Another in two hours. When exactly is 'later'?"

Outside the window, Josh was shaking Danny's hand.

"Your father would want you here, Liz," Michael said, his tone softening a little.

"I know," she replied, feeling as if the air was being squeezed from her—the air and her soul and her *self.* "Father wanted a lot of things from me, Michael. And I always came through on everything. But he's not here anymore. And now I'll just have to trust my own instincts, and accept that I have my own feelings that I sometimes need to address."

After Liz got off the phone, she returned to the porch. Josh was joking with Danny, trying to convince him to change party allegiances.

"Sorry," Danny was saying, "I'm afraid my dad needs all the sympathy votes I can drum up."

Liz smiled. "You'll have to excuse Danny. His sense of humor is a bit twisted sometimes."

"Except with the media," Danny pointed out. "I'm always on my best behavior with the media."

"You learned from a pro," Josh said with a wink toward Liz.

"My mother?" Danny asked.

"Nope. Your grandfather. He was one of the last great political strategists. He knew what he wanted and he knew how to get it."

Then Josh smiled, and Liz smiled, and Danny smiled. And Liz knew Josh needed to leave now.

She folded her arms and thanked him for coming and left it to the Secret Service to escort him out of the house. She tried not to think about the fact that it might be another twenty years before they were alone together again, when they were old and wrinkled and no longer cared about what might have been.

It had been night and then it was day and then it was night again. BeBe worked much and slept little. There were things to do. She had to find a new designer, and was optimistic about one from a textile firm, one who specialized in graphics packaging with a soft, feminine appeal, and yes, she would be open to a deal. BeBe had also tracked down the Loudets in case Ruiz decided to seek revenge. Monsieur Loudet confirmed that, indeed, Ruiz had telephoned, but he had been out of the office, and, *Oh? You still have not made a decision? Oui, bien,* because he had the impression from Ruiz's message that BeBe no longer was interested.

Most importantly, BeBe had to try not to let her anger weigh her down, or allow that Cuban piece of shit to represent every man who had ever hurt her, which would have been easy to do but a big, fat waste of time.

The morning news had announced that some hurricane had just missed Florida and was headed for the Carolinas. But what had really caught BeBe's attention was the report that the Barton campaign had arrived in Palm Beach. BeBe realized she'd never called Liz as she'd promised Mags she would do. Still, she kept working into the evening, but she made it a point to clear out of her office, and drive through the rain to The Breakers, just before the thousand-dollar chicken-breast gala was to begin.

She sat at the aquarium bar now, tracing the movements of a bright yellow fish that darted and swam and darted and swam happily beneath the glass. She was waiting for her presence to be announced upstairs in the suite of the president-to-be, waiting for some Secret Service lackey to appear and escort her to them. She had not ordered a drink; she had not thought there would be time.

"So you're here," said someone beside her as a straw tote bag was plopped on the bar, causing the poor, startled fish to scatter. The owner of the trademark tote bag flopped into the chair next to BeBe. "What do you want?" she asked.

BeBe refused to give Evelyn the satisfaction of showing her annoyance. She looked again for the yellow fish. "Mags invited me," she said, then added, "not that it should matter to you."

"Everything to do with Michael's campaign matters to me."

"The last I heard, Roger was still Michael's campaign manager."

Evelyn turned her eyes to the bartender. "Give us a couple of margaritas," she ordered. "Strawberry."

BeBe did not know what Evelyn was up to, but decided to play along. She was too tired to argue.

Evelyn waited until the drinks arrived before she spoke again. "I came downstairs to tell you not to come to tonight's dinner."

That was no surprise to BeBe.

"With Liz still not with us, we thought it best for you to remain in the background."

BeBe had no idea what one thing had to do with the other. But she recognized Evelyn's usual maneuvering to keep BeBe out of the public eye.

She licked the salt around her glass. "You know, Evelyn, I'm not sure when it was that you decided to hate me. Maybe it was long before Daniel was killed. But aren't we old enough now to bury the rusty old hatchet?"

Evelyn blinked. "Leave Daniel out of this, Barbara. I simply feel it's in the best interest . . ."

BeBe raised her hand. "Let me finish that for you. You feel it's in the best interest of the campaign if the errant, unmarried sister—the one with questionable morals—remains in the shadows until after the election." She snorted. "I wonder how Daniel would have handled this."

"You're making fun of me," Evelyn seethed. "You never wanted me to marry Daniel, did you? You never wanted me to be part of your family. You just never understood."

BeBe laughed without meaning to.

"Oh, I understood that you had it all figured out. You and your grandfather—who was no better than my father. A couple of arrogant sons of political, string-pulling dickheads who always got their own way, no matter what the cost. Even Daniel's death didn't stop any of you. Just substitute Roger and rearrange the chess pieces a little."

"Don't speak ill of the dead, BeBe, God rest their souls."

BeBe stood up. "You're a fool, Evelyn. You've played a martyr for so long you've lost sight of the facts. Take Daniel, for instance. He would never have been killed if it hadn't been for favor-swapping, and I think you know it. You've always known everything. Well, honey, so have I."

BeBe picked up her purse, slung it over her shoulder, and stalked out of the bar, determined to find the presidential suite on her own.

* * *

The campaign was in south Florida now, and the Gallup gap had narrowed to a spandex-tight four points. What Danny had once taken as a joke now seemed uncomfortably serious. For he had met the enemy. And the enemy was not a bad guy at all. In fact, Danny had been impressed. Josh Miller was real and engaging and not at all like most of the snot-politicians who had circled the Will Adams/Michael Barton wagon as long as Danny could remember.

Danny logged on to the computer now and thought about how he would feel if his father lost the election, if, unbelievably, Will Adams had been wrong about a Jew becoming president. And how he would feel if his mother did not become First Lady, but just another ex-governor's wife, relegated to charity luncheons (for the handicapped, probably) and keynote speaking gigs at girls' school graduations.

He decided it would suck.

He maneuvered the mouse to rogerdodger's Web site and decided to cut the shit.

Tell me what to do, Uncle Roger, he typed. *I'll do whatever it takes to get Mom back in the spotlight.*

She could not make it back to the suite. Instead, Evelyn fled from the bar and ducked into the ladies lounge, her legs watery, her knees buckling. She brushed past a cluster of potted palms, darted across the white and gold marble floor to a louvered-door stall, dropped to her knees, and vomited into the pristine white bowl. Along with the vomit came only one thought:

God, how had BeBe found out?

Chapter 21

 She was tired of bullshit. When BeBe was finally cleared to enter the Barton suite she told them all so—Roger, Mags, and any of the Secret Service who cared to listen.

"I left your wife in the bar, Roger," she said. "I am sick of her treating me like a second-class citizen. All these years I put up with it because I found it mildly amusing. Now I find it a great pain in the ass. I have every right to be here with my family. And if she doesn't like it, she can go to hell."

They stood there, staring at her.

"What?" BeBe asked. "You never thought I'd get pissed? You never thought it bothered me that Evelyn—and my father—made it quite clear I was not welcome to show my face as the candidate's sister-in-law? Well, it's bullshit, and it's going to stop. As of right now."

Mags stepped forward. "Aunt BeBe, we never thought you shouldn't be here . . ."

"No, honey, I know you didn't. It's your charming Aunt Evelyn as much as it was your grandfather. Isn't that right, Roger?"

Roger closed his eyes. "Evelyn has some strange ideas."

At that moment Michael walked through the doorway, followed by Greg, the youngest Barton, the Michael clone.

"Michael," BeBe said, wondering if she should feel flustered, as if the king had just entered.

He checked his watch. "Dinner in half an hour, everyone. BeBe, I'm so glad you could join us." Something in his demeanor, his voice, and his wink, told BeBe that he had heard every word of the conversation, and that she should forget it—that all was well.

He went to her and kissed her cheek. "Long time no see."

As always, she was impressed by his ability to be a great politician. "It's been *days,* Michael," she answered. "Honestly, we must get together more often." She reached out and playfully pinched Greg's cheek. "You look more like your father every day. But lighten up, Greggie. You're too young to be president yet."

Greg laughed good-naturedly, and Michael smiled and walked to a gilded mirror where he quietly adjusted his tie. "Your father thought it was never too soon to begin."

BeBe turned toward him. "Father's presence must be missed out here on the road."

Michael let out a puff of air. "You have no idea, Beebs."

No, she had no idea. None at all. She looked at Mags, who rolled her eyes. "How's Liz?" BeBe asked, suddenly needing very badly to know how her sister was, suddenly aware of how strange it was that she wasn't here.

Michael hesitated a moment too long. "She's doing okay. I hope she and Danny will be joining us soon."

BeBe nodded, but the cloud that moved across Michael's eyes suggested he didn't have much hope for that to happen.

"We talked to her yesterday" Mags offered.

Once again BeBe was assailed by guilt for not having called Liz.

"Josh Miller was there," Greg added. "Can you imagine? Josh Miller at our house?"

There was an uncomfortable moment of silence.

Josh Miller. At the Vineyard house? Yes, BeBe could imagine. As much as she tried not to, her eyes flashed back to Michael. "Really?" she asked.

"It's true," Michael said with a hollow laugh. "I asked if she was fraternizing with the enemy."

"Well," BeBe said quickly, trying to cover up for the sake of the kids as well as for Michael, "Josh knew Father," she said lamely. "He was probably extending his sympathy. Are you still ahead of him in the polls, Michael?" she asked, trying to sound casual.

"Not by much," he replied.

"The competition is closing in," Mags said with a swoop of her arms. "Which is all the more reason we need to get to this dinner. That, and the fact that I'm starving."

"Right," Michael said abruptly. "Let's go, shall we?" He held out his arm for his sister-in-law, the woman he'd once slept with in a moment he'd undoubtedly done his best to forget.

But BeBe did not take his arm. "You know," she said, "I love you all dearly, but I just remembered something. I have to get back to my office immediately."

She rushed out of the room, not caring that she was leaving them completely bewildered by her behavior, as usual.

Liz was in that space between sleep and waking that was cozy and pleasant and filled with promises of sweet dreams. It had been a long, tiring, two days . . . the way she had walked in on Danny and caused them both deep embarrassment. Her argument with Michael. And seeing Josh. Josh. Last night and today she had thought of little else: she had tried to remember each word he had said, each gesture of his hand, each tilt of his head. She had tried to remember, then she had tried to forget.

She began to slip into dreams now, just as something skated across the screen of her bedroom window. Slowly, Liz opened her eyes. Had she dreamed it?

The sound came again . . . the sound of sand pebbles sifting through the screen, grazing the window.

Oh, God, she thought. This couldn't be happening.

But she knew that it could. She had hoped that it would. Somewhere deep within she had hoped so much that he would come, surely she had willed it to happen, surely this was no dream, surely this was real.

She got out of the bed and tiptoed to the window. She paused, afraid to look, afraid of looking and seeing—or maybe not seeing—Josh standing there below.

She took a deep breath and looked outside. She saw nothing except the darkness. She sighed. "Damn fool," she muttered. Of course Josh Miller would not be outside beneath her window. He was a presidential candidate, for godsake, and she, perhaps the next First Lady. People—adults—in their positions did not sneak around in the middle of the night, trying to recapture childish, romantic dreams.

Feeling chilled, she reached to close the window. And then she saw him. He was there. A shadow in the night. A shadow she would know anywhere, anytime, no matter how many years had passed.

She caught her breath. "Josh," she called. He just stood there.

"Don't ask me why, just believe it when I tell you I have to get to the Vineyard," BeBe barked at the ticket attendant at the Delta counter in West Palm. She had gone home and thrown some things in a suitcase, answered some "urgent" business calls, swallowed two glasses of wine and three forkfuls of last night's pasta, and begun the trek to the airport through increasing wind and blowing rain. She was not in the mood for an unsympathetic clerk.

"I'm sorry, Ms. Adams," the clerk said in monotone, "but the last flight for Boston tonight has left. And I'm not certain about tomorrow. There's a hurricane off the coast of North Carolina."

BeBe restrained herself from leaping over the counter and grabbing the neat-as-a-pin clerk by the lapels. "I don't care if there's a snowstorm that's the blizzard of the century. Get me on a freaking airplane, lady, or I'll charter one myself."

He took her hands. He took her hands there in the darkness of the moonless night. They stood quietly a moment. She wished she could see his face, every detail of his face, every timeworn line and dark beard stubble, every crease of the dimple in his right, not left, cheek, every long black eyelash that framed those deep, sincere eyes—eyes that had captivated so many American voters.

But this was not Election Day and Liz was no ordinary American.

Without words, he led her to the path that led down to the cove. It was different now, made narrow by undergrowth that sprawled along the sides. But it did not matter—this was the path that led to their cove.

When they got there, Josh locked his arms around her, buried his face into her neck, and cried.

"Josh," she whispered. "Oh, Josh."

He caressed her shoulders, her back, that little hollow in her spine just below her waist.

She felt the tears running down her face, too.

"I love you, Liz," he breathed. "I have loved you forever, I love you now."

She knew this was wrong. If nothing else, Liz Adams-Barton did know right from wrong. Her father had made sure of that, as he'd made sure of everything.

But she didn't care. She pressed against him, her breasts tingling through the T-shirt she had thrown on. She felt his hands move lower, cupping the still-round curves of her now-arching butt.

He kissed her mouth, full and open and moist with longing. His lips trailed down to her throat, making little sucking sounds that were incredibly erotic.

"Make love to me, Josh," she whispered. "Right here. Right now."

She slid out of her jeans, pulled the T-shirt over her head. She stood there, naked, before the one man in her life whom she had fully loved.

And then they were on the ground, a bed of pine needles and sea grass soft and smooth beneath her, the contour of the dunes sculpting against her back, cradling her. When he entered her, it was with a bold, desperate fever. She gasped, having forgotten how large Josh was, the way he filled her to the limit, the friction he created against the inside walls of her. She moistened to his touch in instinctive, wondrous knowing, knowing that he belonged there, that the joining of their bodies was the only right thing in her world.

"Michael Barton has picked up a couple of points again, and is now leading Josh Miller by about six and a half," the anchor said.

"That's right, Wendell. This race is getting more and more interesting. It could be that the decline for Miller is because he has stepped out of the limelight for a few days. The race is just too close for either candidate to take a break from the campaign trail."

"There's no word on how long Mr. Miller will be in seclusion," Wendell the anchor said. "We know he's gone to Martha's Vineyard. Interestingly, it has also been reported that is where Mrs. Barton is recuperating from her father's recent death." Wendell smiled.

Danny pressed the off button on the remote. He took a slow drink of coffee and wondered if he should check in with Uncle Roger. He still hadn't heard back about his offer to help: Danny knew Roger must be busy but still . . . well, it was now Sunday morning, the day his mother usually got up early and made breakfast of eggs and bacon. But so far, she was still sleeping.

He, of course, would not be up so early if it weren't for the Clayman's rigorous running schedule, which he did not indulge in until Danny's morning PT was complete. But after the gruesomely time-wasting leg-lift routine, unlike his nurse, Danny had nowhere to run to. There was simply a wheel to the remote or to the computer, depending on his mood.

God, he thought, closing his eyes, *how much longer can life be this dull?*

The telephone rang, as if in answer to his question.

"Danny?" The voice sounded familiar, but he couldn't place it for a second. "It's your Aunt BeBe."

His spirits immediately lifted. "Hey, Aunt Beebs. How's the orange hair?"

"Still orange. Listen. I'm coming to the Vineyard. I want to surprise your mother, so please don't tell her. Also, I'll need you to pick me up at the airport."

He took another drink of coffee. "You're coming here? When?"

"Today. I tried to get there last night but the closest I could get was New York and I didn't feel like walking from La Guardia."

"You're coming today?" Danny asked, even though that was what she had said.

"One forty-five by way of Boston. Meet me at the sorry excuse for an airport, okay? And remember, don't tell your mother. Don't tell anyone." Quickly, BeBe hung up.

Danny was left holding the receiver. How was he going to pick up Aunt BeBe when he'd yet to summon the courage to drive the van? She'd said not to tell anyone, which, he supposed, included Clay. God, was this a plot between his mother and his aunt?

The two hours and fifty minutes from West Palm Beach to Boston seemed to take two days. The turbulence of "unsettled air" all around them made her queasy, the first-class flight attendants drove her crazy trying to compensate for the bumps, and the in-flight movie was stupid.

BeBe almost wished she hadn't thrown Ruiz out for good. She hated to admit it, but sometimes life was simply easier with someone at your side, anyone, no matter how disreputable.

Still, every time she closed her eyes, she could feel again the little knife that twisted in her heart when Claire had said "a wife and four kids," that same little knife she always felt when she realized she was not quite good enough, that no man, not even a tuna fisherman, would ever want her, that she was the bad sister, and Liz was the good one.

But now it was time for the bad sister to come to the aid of the good, before she proved herself as bad as her sister.

She looked out the window at the bank of white puff clouds and thought about Liz. As different as they were, they had always been—always would be—blood sisters.

BeBe was counting on that to help Liz come to her senses, if, in fact, her senses had lapsed, or if she'd ever had any when it came to Josh Miller—the man who could ruin Michael's election chances once and for all, and make them all look like a bunch of fools.

A break came in the clouds and BeBe saw land, sculpted as it was along the coastline of the blue-gray Atlantic, the ocean she'd come to know so well, north and south.

She had not been to the Vineyard house since their mother had died. BeBe had not had the courage to go to the funeral in Boston. She'd told Liz she had a bad case of the flu . . . she could not tell her the truth, that she could not bear to look at Father and wonder if he was responsible for her death, the way he'd been responsible for his son's.

It had been late in October, when Will Adams's clan (or rather, what was left of them) had gathered at the house on Beacon Hill. BeBe had chosen, instead, to go to the Vineyard to say good-bye to her mother in her own way.

She had broken into the house, built a fire in the huge stone fireplace to lessen the damp island chill. She had curled up in an old comforter and sipped hot chocolate that she pretended Daniel had made, and wept for her mother.

In the morning she put on a soft flannel shirt and went out into the morning mist. She plucked a milkweed pod and walked to the top of a dune where, her eyes toward the sea and a gray, crying sky, she gently blew the angel-like wisps into the air. "Godspeed, Mother," she whispered. "I love you."

She had not returned to the Vineyard until now, that place where, she supposed, there had once been some happy moments, mostly with Daniel, sometimes with Liz and Roger. Some happy moments, but no great joy.

Only Liz could have brought her back. Liz and the first love she'd apparently never quite forgotten. But how could she have forgotten with a living, breathing reminder staring her in the face every day? The living, breathing reminder, Danny—the boy who was Liz and Josh's son, not Liz and Michael's. Danny—whose real father was Josh Miller, not the man he called "Dad."

Liz knew and BeBe knew, and she'd always feared that Josh knew, had known all along. But it was a truth that—for the sake of all those she loved, especially her sister, especially Danny—BeBe could not let come out. Not now. Not ever.

The big plane tipped its wing and began its descent into Logan. Hopefully, the twin-engine prop to the Vineyard would be on time.

Chapter 22

 "Where is my son?" Liz shouted into Clay's face. She had awakened late today, after ten o'clock, which was not surprising, for she'd not fallen asleep until almost dawn. She'd sneaked past Keith and Joe, and walked for a long time on the beach, thinking about Josh, about Michael, about her life.

She'd reached no conclusions.

When she'd returned to the house, the van was not in the driveway. Clay was on the back porch. Danny was missing.

"I'm sure he's fine, Mrs. Barton," he said. "Danny's handicapped, but he's not stupid."

"The van is gone."

"He must have decided to try and drive it."

At the base of her neck, veins tightened. "Without telling anyone? When you two took off in New Jersey he left me a note."

Clay did not answer.

Her blood pressure elevated. "What if he needs medical attention? What's wrong with you? His health is your responsibility. That's what we pay you for." She spun around to Keith and Joe, who had looked up from their chess game as if she were an intrusion. "And what about you two? You follow us around like pulp fiction private eyes. But Danny went out alone, and neither of you saw him leave?" She swept her arms in the air. "Is this what you all get paid for?" She was aware of the heat rising in her face, and of the fact she was creating what Father would call a scene and Michael, a waste of energy. But Liz could not stop herself. Her emotions, her anger, and her guilt balled up like a fist ready to strike.

From the other end of the porch, Keith cleared his throat. "Excuse me, Mrs. Barton, but I'm sure Danny will be fine. Maybe he needed a little freedom. You know, like this morning. You wanted freedom. You went down to the beach. Alone."

Her anger flared to think her private time had not been so private; that they had known all along where she was. Then she quickly wondered if they somehow knew about last night . . .

"Sometimes," Keith continued, "freedom is the best thing you can give a person. Any person."

She threw her hands up into the air. "You are impossible," she spewed. "You are all impossible." She shoved her hands into her pockets. "All I can say is that nothing had better have happened to Danny or you'll all be sorry."

With that, she stormed into the house, went to the kitchen, snapped on the faucet, and waited for the teapot to fill, all the while tap-tapping her foot against the hardwood floor, drumming her fingers on the countertop.

Freedom, she thought. How long had it been since she'd even known the word? Danny wanted freedom, who could blame him? So did she. She wanted the freedom to lie beside the man she wanted, the man she had never once stopped loving. She wanted the freedom—just once in her life—to be who she was, not someone she was supposed to be for her father or her husband or her children.

The water poured over the top of the pot.

"Damn," she said. "Shit, hell, damn." Then the teapot slipped from her hand and clattered into the sink. Liz stared into the stainless steel and began to sob.

"Well, look at you, all duded-up with a shiny new van." BeBe tipped her hat against the glare that flashed off the dark green, shining metal—the glare of the bright Vineyard sun.

"I even stopped at the car wash just for you, Aunt Beebs." Danny wheeled around toward the special sliding door that held the wheelchair lift. "It's my maiden voyage. My solo flight, in case you didn't know."

"I didn't know," she replied, bowing to him. "And I am thus honored." She moved toward the door, painfully aware that Danny had endured enough problems for life. He did not deserve to learn that his father was not who he thought . . . assuming, of course, he did not already know. She looked back to his wheelchair. "Tell me what to do."

"Nothing," he said as a big side door slid open. "Just get in. I need to learn how to do this for myself. That's why I even left my nurse back at the house."

She climbed into the passenger side of the van, remembering that Liz had told her at Father's funeral that Danny would not drive, that he would do nothing by himself except sit and sulk. BeBe had told her it would take time. It would please her if her impulsive need to get here had helped him break through. It would please her, because Danny was such a good kid. With so much to lose, even after having lost so much.

She heard the slide of metal, the whir of a motor, then a clank, clank.

"You all right back there?" She turned to find Danny at her shoulder.

"I made it," he beamed. "It's getting easier each time." He slid behind the wheel, adjusted his dead legs, started the engine, and, with his hand, pressed what BeBe presumed was the accelerator that rested on the dashboard. He did not act as if he knew any dark family truth, or as if his mother had just lost her mind.

"Nice job," BeBe said.

Danny shrugged. "All in a day's work."

BeBe smiled and touched his shoulder. "Well, I can see you're doing okay. How about your mother?" She hadn't planned to ask so quickly, but the question had tumbled out.

Danny flashed her a guarded look. "Geez," he said, moving his eyes back to the road. "Have you been talking to Uncle Roger? I e-mail him every day."

"I saw them last night at The Breakers. Briefly."

"Dad must be doing good in Florida. The polls are up a little."

BeBe drew in a breath. The more the damn polls favored Michael, the more she worried that Josh might play his trump card. She did not know which of the candidates it would hurt or help if he revealed to the world that Danny was his son, but in the bitter realm of politics, she figured Josh could come up with a way to use it in his favor, to make Michael look like a fool and Michael's wife, lower than that.

She turned her head and saw the familiar white pines and the soft, sandy roadside of the "Cross Island Parkway." "It's not the polls I'm worried about, Danny," she lied, then added, "I'm worried about your mother." That part, of course, was the truth.

"Me too, Aunt BeBe. Mom's been acting kind of weird. Not herself, you know?"

The catch in his voice underscored BeBe's own fears.

. . .

She was so relieved to see the van—with Danny behind the wheel—pulling into the driveway, that at first Liz didn't notice he was not alone. In the shadows of the afternoon sun, she did not see the van's passenger until the door opened, a large tapestry bag dropped to the ground, and an orange-haired woman—BeBe—stepped out.

"I don't know if I should hug you or kill you," Liz said, shaking her head at Danny as she went to greet her sister.

"Don't kill him," BeBe said. "He's my ride back to the airport when I decide I can't stand this island another minute."

"BeBe," Liz said, then stopped. She looked at her sister, at the one person in her life who had been there for her, who had let her be herself, even when she'd been wrong. And now BeBe was standing there, once more her rock. Liz didn't have to ask why. Surprising tears sprang to her eyes, floodgates of guilt opening wide. BeBe stepped forward and put her arms around her, and instantly, Liz had the urge to confess everything right there in the driveway, in front of everyone.

"I was in the neighborhood," BeBe said, "and thought I'd drop by."

Liz wiped her tears. "You are such a liar," she said. "Danny, don't ever listen to your Aunt BeBe. She is such a liar."

"Well, I'm not lying when I say I need a glass of iced tea more than anything in the world." BeBe turned to Danny. "Think you can spin that two-wheeler into the kitchen and rustle up some drinks for the old ladies?"

Danny turned toward the house. When Liz moved to go after him, BeBe stopped her.

"How are you, kid?" BeBe asked.

Keith and Joe were following Danny inside, and for this moment Liz and BeBe were standing alone. Alone, with the scrub oaks and the hydrangea and the clamshell pieces dug into the dirt driveway that she remembered so well from when they were kids who shared secret daydreams and needed each other.

She choked back her thoughts and picked up BeBe's bag. "I'm fine, Beebs," she said. "Really I am."

BeBe studied her face with an expression that said she knew otherwise. "Bullshit," she said.

Liz hoisted BeBe's bag to her shoulder, her need to confess now supplanted by a need to defend. "Did you come to visit me or harass me?" She wanted BeBe to say she had come to harass her, to save her from Josh Miller and from herself. But if BeBe knew he was there on the island—had been at the house—she was not saying. Instead, her sister simply looked at Liz with a small, fake smile.

"You decide" was all she would say.

The salt in the air—or maybe it was in her tears—stung Liz's eyes. Liz stood and stared at her sister. She gripped the strap of BeBe's bag as if it were a lifeline and she were on the Titanic. And then, her lower lip began to tremble.

"Oh, shit," BeBe said. "Oh, shit."

Liz set down the bag. Her shoulders began to shake.

"Oh, shit," BeBe said again, then put her arm around her sister.

Liz leaned her head into BeBe's shoulder. "I wish I could lie to you, Beebs. Oh, hell. Why can't I just lie to you?"

"Because you're kind and good and not a bit like me," BeBe replied. "And because if you lied, I'd know it."

So Liz did not lie. Instead, she just cried. And BeBe did not ask her why.

He'd give anything to know what the hell was going on. Danny wheeled from the bathroom, where dutiful Clay had just emptied his pee bag, and parked his chair by the window overlooking the driveway.

His mother was sobbing, Aunt BeBe was comforting her, and none of it made any sense.

Sure, Gramps was dead, but Mom hadn't seemed this upset at the funeral. Maybe she'd been hiding it.

Was that why Aunt BeBe was here?

Or had he been right in assuming Mom and Dad had a fight? And, if so, about what? Had Dad gotten caught up in that game of sex known to so many of his predecessors? Danny frowned. He'd never suspected his father of playing around—Dad simply wasn't like those other politicians: last winter's witch hunt had proved that.

Still, there must be some reason Mom had not returned to campaigning.

There must be some reason she was this upset.

Jesus, he suddenly thought, *what if Mom wanted a divorce?* Who would vote for a man whose own wife didn't want him? Especially when there was a viable opponent like Josh Miller on the other side of the ballot?

The anger BeBe felt rushed from her head to her heart to her fingers—which wanted to wrap themselves tightly around Josh Miller's neck—and down to her legs, propelling her across the dunes toward Josh Miller's house.

She had smuggled a little vodka from Father's study into her iced tea, drank it and made another, then told Liz she wanted to go for a walk—alone. Or, at least, alone with her drink. She had said it was difficult being back on the Vineyard, thinking about all those things she'd never resolved with Father, thinking that if only she had been a better daughter they could have had a happier life together, all of them. BeBe wasn't sure how much of it was crap to throw Liz off track about BeBe's real mission.

But as she trucked along the dunes, stopping for frequent sips from her glass, she knew it wasn't all crap. It was strange to be back on the island; strange to feel the damp Vineyard beach between her toes instead of dry Palm Beach sand; strange to hear the fat, gray gulls instead of skittering, light sandpipers; strange to see thick, purple-lined clamshells instead of delicate pink conch.

And it was strange to feel surrounded by generations of her roots embedded there on the island, instead of the rootless, shiftless, here-today-gone-tomorrow Ruizes of the world.

But with the old weight came the old ache, the ache that was too familiar, carrying with it memories of hundreds of summer nights, hundreds of long, steamy, usually miserable summer nights.

In fairness to the others, summers on the Vineyard had sometimes been fun, filled with swimming and clamming and saltwater taffy stuck in her teeth. But that had all been ruined those last years, when she could never do anything that pleased Father—as opposed to Daniel, who could do no wrong in anyone's eyes, including her own.

And now, the one Adams sibling on whom everyone's leftover high hopes had hinged, was about to fuck everything up.

"Stop right there!" The shout came from a dune up above, from a deep-voiced male who must have excelled in Gestapo training.

BeBe stopped. She looked up, shielding her eyes against the summer sun.

"Where are you going?"

"For a walk. I happen to own this beach, in case it's any of your business." She didn't really know if she owned the beach at all: she had never shown any interest in Father's property when he was alive and did not intend to start now—let Roger and Evelyn haggle with Liz and Michael over who was entitled to what. At the funeral BeBe had told Michael to let her know sometime if the old man had completely cut her out of the will or not, if he had ever gotten around to it, not that it mattered.

She stuffed her hands into her pockets, ignored the Gestapo, and kept walking.

"You'll have to stop, lady," the commando said. "You're too close to protected property."

BeBe stopped again. *Protected property.* Of course. Josh's property would be protected these days, and this man must be one of the gray-suited henchmen like those camped out with Liz and Danny. *Argh,* she thought. *Why would anyone want to be president?* She chalked it up to masochism, then put her hands on her hips.

"I am a personal friend of Josh Miller's," she said.

The henchman came down off the dune, speaking into a walkie-talkie, most likely to an equally nervous henchman on the other end of the beach.

"Give Josh a call," she said. "Tell him BeBe Adams wants to see him. I'm sure he'll know why."

The man reached her. "Please, ma'am. We don't want any trouble."

BeBe laughed. "I'm not interested in politics. What I have to say to him is personal. Damn personal."

The agent paused. He whispered something else into the walkie-talkie. In the distance, BeBe could see two other figures approach at a brisk clip.

"If you feel you must see Mr. Miller in private, you have to go around front like everyone else," the guard said. "We can't have just anyone walking along this strip of beach."

BeBe put a hand on one of her hips, looked out toward

the fast-approaching cavalry, and huffed. "Tell that to the seagulls," she said, and pranced off in the other direction, knowing there was more than one way to skin a Secret Service cat, and that'd she'd do it as soon as she figured out what it was.

Chapter 23

On the way back BeBe spotted the entrance to the path she remembered from when they were kids. The path led to the cove where she and her brothers and Liz often paddled the rowboat, where long ago they pretended they were on the high seas, trying to avert pirates and shipwrecks.

It was only a small cove, not like the ocean, but Father had forbidden them to take the boat on the open water. Once, BeBe supposed, she thought he was being protective. Later she decided it had been just one more way for him to exert control. Because while he certainly wanted nothing to happen to Daniel or Lizzie, if BeBe and Roger had been capsized and washed up on the cliffs of Gay Head, Father would not really have given a shit. Okay, BeBe thought, so maybe that was overstating it.

It was only a small pirates' cove, but it had kept the Adams children from drowning. And it was where Liz had met with Josh.

"Maybe we all should have drowned," BeBe murmured. She drained her glass, flung it into the brambles, and pushed her way down the path.

It was overgrown now with wild grape vines and sassafras and thickets of underbrush, some dotted with bright flowers of purple and yellow, some knotted with prickly-looking thorns that had dug into BeBe's young, summer-tanned legs more than once. Carefully, she pushed back the tangles and continued toward the cove. It had always been so secluded there—maybe if she went back to the scene of the original crime she could figure out what to do; maybe a Vineyard sea monster from their old pirate days would surface on thick, murky water and give her an answer . . . or maybe, she thought as she stumbled a little over a small rock, maybe she'd just had too much booze.

Seeing the majordomos on the beach today had reinforced the gravity of the situation. That and the fact that Liz had not been forthcoming, had only said she would not lie, but had not told all there was to tell. Nor had she said she did not plan to see Josh again. For all BeBe knew, they would be screwing on the dunes tonight and every night until one of the media piranhas caught them at it.

BeBe shoved another bramble out of the way and wondered if she should get on the next plane back to Florida where the stress of a sixty-million-dollar decision paled in comparison to this.

The underbrush finally opened and gave way to a small clearing—a clearing that BeBe did not at first recognize. Then she realized that this was it, the cove, surrounded now by trees that had grown much taller, shading the water and forming a canopy over the pine-needled earth. The water itself was no longer blue but slate-colored and dense with reeds and lily pads and cattails that formed a thick wall and seemed to have shrunk the size of the water to that of a large puddle. An unlikely spot for dreaming dreams or calling up memories.

Which was just as well.

Movement along the water's edge caught her eye.

Looking through the light that spiked through the trees, she saw a dog, a black Labrador retriever, with a long, thick tail that wagged and wagged and propelled him into the water.

As if being directed, her eyes slowly moved to a tree beside the place where the dog had jumped in. And there was a man. He was sitting under a pine tree, his head down, his body inert. BeBe knew in a heartbeat who the man was.

"Josh," she called out, stumbling around the cattails and through the half-sopping ground. "Josh, it's me, BeBe. Liz's sister."

He raised his head. At first she thought he would get up and run. Hell, she wouldn't blame him if he did. In fact, he probably should.

Josh stood up. He did not run. "BeBe?" he asked. "How did you find me?"

"No thanks to your guardian angels," she said.

His laugh sounded empty and distracted.

"I told them I was going for a walk. They hate that."

"Well, they will certainly never be accused of not being zealous enough."

Josh brushed a few pine needles from his pants, his neat, khaki twill pants, not the cutoff jeans that had been their fashion staple so long ago. She wondered what else about him had changed. Maybe not as much as one would think, judging by what little she and Liz and any of them had changed. An unexpected twinge for Daniel nicked her heart.

"So you were looking for me," Josh said. "Should I bother to say I'm surprised?"

"Save it," BeBe said, "and promise me you're not planning to use my sister to get her husband to lose the election."

Josh blinked. "What?"

That never-go-away need to protect her sister bubbled once more beneath the surface, mixing with the vodka and tasting like anger, if anger had a taste. "Isn't that why you came, Josh? Because you knew Liz was here, and that she'd be vulnerable and grieving and in need of . . . someone . . . to pay attention to her?"

He leveled his eyes on her. "You never really knew me, BeBe," he said.

She laughed. "I never had to. I know your type. I've known hundreds of your type." And suddenly the image of Josh Miller before her became not just the Jewish boy from New York of whom Father wouldn't approve, but every boy from every state who had ever decided that BeBe was good enough to bed down, but nothing more. Every boy, and every man, Ruiz included, for whom, like Father, when all was said and done, she had not been good enough. Her head swam a little; she steadied her footing.

"BeBe," Josh said, coming closer. "I would never hurt Liz . . ."

The words tumbled out, as if the more she said the more she needed to say. "Don't try to deny it, Josh. You knew Liz could never say no to you, you used her . . ."

"You're wrong," he seethed, his throat reddening through the open collar of his neat white shirt. "You're probably the only person on earth she feels she can trust. If she needs anyone now, it's you, BeBe. Not me."

She laughed again. "No, Josh, I'm not the only person. She has a husband, in case you've forgotten. She has a husband and three children who love her very much." She raised a hand to her forehead, shielding a dull gray glare that had clouded over the sun. She half closed her eyes. "If you think this is going to help you win the election, you're wrong, Josh. And I don't know what I'll do, but believe me when I tell you I'll find a way to stop you."

"BeBe," he said. "You're talking like a fool."

She tipped back her head. "I'm not a fool, Josh. I know as well as you do what's been going on."

He did not try and defend himself, which confirmed BeBe's fears. *Oh, Christ,* she thought, *they've done it again.*

"BeBe," Josh said, "I don't expect you to understand this, but I loved your sister a very long time ago. I think I always have."

The gray cloud grew grayer. The sky grew darker. "And you certainly picked a fine time to show how much you love her. Don't you care who you hurt, Josh?" Her voice turned to a sneer. "Who am I kidding? You're a man. That gives you license to hurt whomever you want. Pardon me for forgetting that."

"BeBe, please understand. Liz has always been in my heart. If it hadn't been for our fathers . . ."

"If it hadn't been for our fathers, what? You and my sister would have been married? Come on, Josh, what kind of a man are you? It seems to me if you'd loved her that much you'd have found a way to be with her, fathers or no fathers. It makes me sick, when I think of all she's been through . . ."

Josh's eyes drifted off to the cove, where his dog seemed to be managing a swim in the muck. "What Liz has been through?" he asked. "What about me? I wanted to marry her, BeBe. When I came home from Israel, I was determined. But she was already married. She'd married Michael without waiting to see if we could work things out."

BeBe looked at his face, which seemed quite sincere; but, then, he was a man and a politician on top of that and she wasn't born yesterday. Still there was something about the way his head tipped a little to one side, about the way his eyes seemed rimmed with red . . .

She remembered the way he'd been sitting quietly before she'd arrived, before he'd known she'd been watching.

Suddenly, things became clear. She dropped the shield from her eyes. "Josh," she said quietly, "please don't pursue this. Please. Think about Danny."

His gaze drifted away for a moment, then returned. "Danny? Liz's son?"

BeBe nodded. "And yours," she said. "I've known it, and I'd bet so have you. Please don't do anything to hurt him. Or her."

"What are you talking about?"

She closed her eyes. "It's okay. I know all about the fact that Danny is your son. Liz told me a long time ago."

The muscles in his face did not move. "Well," he said slowly, "I'm glad she told you. She never bothered to tell me."

The air grew silent and still, thick with island dampness, devoid of the music of birds, even that of the gulls, as if some invisible force had put life on pause.

And then the iced tea and vodka sloshed inside BeBe and she knew she'd been wrong: Josh had not known that Danny was his son; he had not been planning to use it against Liz, to use it against Michael.

She had been wrong. And now, she had fucked up. Big time.

BeBe turned around and headed back through the undergrowth, her stomach as tangled as the vines and the shrubs all knotted and webbed around the old pirates' cove.

He had thought his aunt BeBe was probably the coolest person on the face of the earth, which was why he had followed her, why he had tried to catch up to her and talk to her about Mom.

But he had not been able to make it as far as the cove. He had barely made it onto the path. But where his feet could not go, his ears could still hear. And now, from the place on the path where the hard-packed dirt turned to impassable sand, Danny sat without moving a muscle, not even the ones that still worked.

Had he heard what he thought he'd heard?

He'd heard the words.

But they made no sense.

Sounds of leaves crunching and twigs breaking came toward him. He had to get out of the way. He could not let anyone know he'd heard.

With frantic motion, he yanked at the wheels. He could not turn on the motor. He could not risk the noise. And yet . . . the damn wheel was stuck. Stuck in the rut it had made in the sand.

The footsteps came closer.

Danny pulled on the wheel, his body twisted. Just as he feared he would be caught, he noticed the brake lever. It was locked; he must have flipped it in his haste.

With a single thrust, he popped the lever. And just as he backed into the brush that, thank God, had him fairly well-hidden, BeBe passed by hugging her stomach, her orange hair limp, her freckled cheeks pale, her eyes so glazed she probably wouldn't have seen him if he was parked in the middle of the damn path.

It wasn't until she was safely past that Danny began to comprehend what he had heard.

Josh Miller was his father.

Josh Miller. Not Michael. Not Dad.

It was only one statement, one lousy bunch of words strung together. So why did the top of his body feel as numb as the bottom? And why, when Danny tried hard to swallow, was there no spit left in his mouth?

Chapter 24

It had started to rain. Liz stood at the window looking out toward the sea, toward the place where so many dreams had once begun. She could see the thicket where the skunks had once lived—those big, fat, furry creatures that Daniel had twirled by the tail, each summer getting a little braver—Daniel, not the skunks, though maybe they did, too. Maybe they knew Daniel would never hurt them, that he was the perfect son of Will Adams, that he would do nothing to mar the family name, because one day he was going to be president, in charge of the whole damn world.

She had wanted to name her firstborn after Daniel long before she knew that the father of the child would not be her husband. She had wanted to do it, and yet, she realized now, it was only what Father would have expected, in honor of Daniel, war hero or not.

Many years had passed now since that morning when Liz dropped off her urine specimen at an unfamiliar gynecologist's—unfamiliar because she had been so afraid that her own doctor would somehow know the truth.

So she had gone to a doctor's office in Back Bay, down

one of the narrow cobblestone alleyways that had been restored but had not yet been discovered by anyone she knew or who would know her.

She was volunteering at the museum then, even though she'd just earned an associate's degree in secretarial science—not exactly a teacher as Father had wanted, but acceptable enough. The fact was there was no need for the wife of Michael Barton, daughter of Will Adams, to have a real job. Later that day, she called the doctor's office from a phone booth outside the museum. The nurse said, "Oh, Mrs. Smith"—Liz hadn't given herself time to think of a more believable fake name—"I'm so happy to tell you that the test is positive. You are very much pregnant."

On the way home that night, Liz sat like one of the mummies on display at the museum, as she tried to decide how she—*what* she—would tell Michael. He'd been in China all summer at an exchange program for young international attorneys; they'd made love before he left and three months later when he returned. But he'd been home a month now and she was two months pregnant, not four, and not one.

"You can't tell anyone the truth," BeBe said. "Especially Michael."

Liz had telephoned her later that night, when Michael had gone off to a meeting at the state house. She had not had the courage to tell him at dinner, but she told BeBe, her trusted sister, her confidant. She also told BeBe that the baby was Josh's.

Her sister had freaked. "I thought he went off to Israel. For chrissakes, Liz, I thought he was out of your life."

Liz had cried. "He did. And he was. He joined the Israeli military. But that was after Daniel died, and then he came home again . . . and it's been five years . . . and, oh, God, BeBe, what am I going to do? When I told him

I was married he just about died. He's gone again. He went back to Israel. I'll never see him again."

"Which," BeBe said, composing herself quickly, "will be just as well." She then convinced Liz that it would be easier to pretend the baby came early rather than two months late. "Keep your weight down and no one will know. You've been married over a year, so no one will raise their eyebrows or count on their fingers. You can pull it off."

Liz wondered how other girls made out when they didn't have a big sister—the older, wiser sister always there to bail them out.

She pulled back the curtain now and watched the gray rain beat harder on the small-paned window, feeling that twenty-some-year-old kernel of guilt rise to the surface once again. She, indeed, had "pulled it off." It had helped that Danny was born two weeks late—or two weeks early, depending on whether you knew the truth or knew the lie. And she had kept her weight down—Danny weighed only six pounds four ounces, so no one assumed he was anything but an eight-month baby. Thank God, she realized now, no one back then had known enough to ask details.

Except, of course, Father, who had taken one look at Danny and known. Or perhaps he'd always known.

For a moment, only a moment, Father and Liz were left alone in her hospital room. "We will leave things as they are, Lizzie," he said. "No one will ever have to know."

She pulled her sweater closer around her now, feeling the sudden damp chill that always came with island rain. BeBe was still out walking and Danny was gone again. She hoped he was with BeBe, and that the two of them had found some shelter from the rain. Clay came into the room.

"Is there any boarding up we should do?" he asked.

"Boarding up?"

BeBe appeared behind him, her orange hair plastered to her wet head, her short cotton dress sticking to her body. "I haven't been here in almost over a decade. Leave it to me to visit the same time as a hurricane does."

"A hurricane?"

"It was a gorgeous, damn sunny day," BeBe muttered. "I should have known better." She headed up the stairs to her room. Liz turned to Clay.

"A hurricane?" she asked again.

"Hurricane Carol. Haven't you seen the news? She missed the Carolinas and is heading this way."

No, Liz had not seen the news. She had not wanted to hear about polls and politics and the chance that in a few more months, she might be the woman looked up to by so many women in America and maybe the world. She had not watched the news because she did not want to know these things. Any more than she wanted to hear now that a hurricane was headed their way.

As quickly as he could manage, Danny had climbed into the van, started it up, and raced down the driveway, the tires spitting up clamshells as he pressed his palm down on the fucked-up accelerator.

As he sped down the road around one winding corner, then another, he wasn't sure if that was rain on the windshield or tears in his eyes. He winced at the clichéd imagery, then blinked and decided it was both. If he could feel anything below the drawstring of his sweatpants, his proverbial belt, he wondered if right now he'd be feeling his intestines expand and contract, bail open then clamp shut, the way they used to when he had to speak in front of an audience, back when he had a real life and did those kinds of things. He sank his upper teeth into his lower lip, unable to hold back the rush of his thoughts.

Josh Miller was his father.

Michael Barton was not his father.

And Mags was not his sister.

And Greg was not his brother.

And his mother was a liar.

And Josh Miller was his father.

He took a corner too fast. He grabbed for the hand brake too late. Rubber hydroplaned across wet pavement. The trees on the side—big, thick—trunked trees whose leaves arched across the road—rushed up to meet the metal of the van. Then the brakes anti-locked and the van slid sideways. Danny held his breath and waited for the crash. It did not come. The van came to a stop within inches of a tree.

"Fuck," he shouted, staring at the brown, peeling trunk of the withered-up oak. Death would have been easier. Death would have been less painful to face.

He punched up "Reverse," jammed down on the accelerator, and jilted back onto the road. The rain was coming down harder now, sheeting up on the hood, smacking the windshield wipers. He whacked the shift into "Drive" and sped down the road, his adrenaline pumping, his anger blazing. All he could picture was the fat-assed TV commentator on the news: *Mr. Miller . . . Martha's Vineyard . . . It has been reported that is where Mrs. Barton is . . .* and then that smile. That godawful smile.

Did everyone in the whole fucking world know except him?

Did everyone in the whole fucking world know and keep it from him? Why? Before his accident had they ever planned to tell him? And now, no one wanted him to know . . . no one wanted to upset the poor crippled kid?

He frowned. "But what about the fucking election?" he screamed at the windshield, then banged his fist against the steering wheel. "How can any of them get away with this?"

He spotted the road to Lobsterville Beach. Without thinking, he ripped the wheel toward the road, the van's rear end fishtailing behind him. If he was on real land he would keep driving forever . . . to California, if possible, or even Alaska . . . as far as the van would take him, as far as he could get.

But he was stuck on the island. And all he could do was look at the sea . . . maybe there he would find an answer . . . or maybe he could pretend to get lost the way he had done so many times when he was a kid trying to escape from the watchful eye of Gramps and the constant feeling of responsibility pushed upon him just because he was named after Daniel and because . . . why? Because he was Ken and Barbie's son?

He wheeled around the corner and came to the dunes. The small, tired sand mounds that now stood in solitude were getting pelted in a steady staccato symphony, abandoned by all bathers who had the sense, unlike Danny, to go in out of the rain. Then again, he reasoned, they probably had homes to go to. Homes and families, families who really were families, not half-bred, lied-about people they thought they belonged to because they'd always been stupid enough to believe people, to trust people, for godsake, people like his mother and his . . . shit. Not his father. Michael Barton was not his father.

He came to a halt at the top of a dune overlooking the water, facing Cuttyhunk and Penikese Islands—Penikese, that wretched, untalked-about place where the lepers were once kept, lepers, society's dysfunctional, much like himself, those whom others did not want to face, did not want to see, did not want to look at lest they be reminded that there is pain and deformity and fucked-up shit in the world. And then, a disjointed thought rushed at him in an instant: Danny wondered if his father . . . if *Michael* knew.

His gut went empty. He did not, of course, feel it, but rather he sensed it, the way most men (or women, he supposed) sense there is a facial hair sticking out where it doesn't belong, or that a fly is unzipped when there is no breeze blowing. For at least two of these past three wheelchair-bound years, Danny's senses had been acute enough to know when he'd peed in his bag.

"Fuck," he said again, more quietly this time for he felt not so much angry now as ashamed. He looked down at the bulge in his pants that he knew wasn't caused from an erection—would never be from an erection—but from the clear plastic bag that was undoubtedly filled with warm yellow liquid, warm yellow pee.

He told himself it could have been worse, that it could have been brown, that it could have been shit.

Tears once again stung his eyes. He wiped them away and tried to take a deep breath, tried to figure out what to do next. Straight ahead was a bluff, a wall of sheer rock that dropped twenty, maybe thirty feet into the water. He wondered what it would feel like to go over the ledge, not in the van but on his own, in the wheelchair, in his own death trap. Would centrifugal force keep him tightly plastered to the chair, like that amusement park ride where people stood around the perimeter of a wheel and spun up and down and around and around without falling off? Would those same forces of nature make them—man and machine—tumble over and over, down to their fate? Or would Danny be flung from the chair, then crashed against the rocks and careened into the sea—never having felt the plunge or the slams into his body, the mass of broken bones from his waist down to his toes?

Who would find him?

How long would it take?

And would his rescuers already know that Josh Miller was his father?

Everyone on the island probably knew. The Vineyard had a way of protecting its own, even the summer people who had been there since God.

But if he killed himself, would no one be elected president? Would both Michael and Josh have to withdraw from the race in humiliation? Would someone like Pat Buchanan or Donald Trump or that wrestler guy from Minnesota step in and claim victory?

He stared off at the horizon, that never-ending horizontal line separating this world from the next, reality from the unknown. Then Danny realized that the responsibility of having a Buchanan or a Trump or a wrestler in the White House was not going to be his, no way.

Silently, he opened the van door, loosened his pants, and juggled the catheter that, indeed, was quite full. He dumped the liquid out the door, watching as it splashed yellow tears up from the pavement, the waste of a man with a waste of a life, reduced to performing such a menial, physical task that had become essential to perform if he wanted to live in this great thing called society.

He put himself back together—physically, anyway—and looked out across the sea, searching for answers where he knew there were none.

And then he saw the *Annabella*. Docked at the pier across the inlet was LeeAnn and Reggie's catamaran. LeeAnn and Reggie—his Vineyard friends! They must not have had a charter to Cuttyhunk today. Maybe it was because of the forecasted rain, which already was happening, or maybe they didn't have a party willing to pay a high enough price.

Well, Danny didn't give about the damn rain and, as he'd learned from Gramps, what good was having money if it couldn't buy you friends?

He backed up the van and drove down toward the bike ferry, where he could get safe passage across the inlet. Keeping his eyes on the *Annabella*, Danny smiled. Maybe there were at least two honest people left in the world, after all, a friend who had once been his good buddy, and the friend's sister who had once been a great . . . well, he thought with a shrug, she had been, back then.

Getting across on the bike ferry had been simple. He'd left the van and wheeled down to the small raftlike boat, removed the ropes, and started the engine with the key that someone—the owner, apparently—had left behind. Danny had never been sure exactly who owned this Mark Twain–like ferry, but as far back as he could remember it had been used on an honor system by whoever wanted to get from one bank of the Menemsha inlet to the other, pedestrians and bicyclists alike. But because it was free, and because it was used on a first-come, first-served basis, when the ferry sat on the opposite bank, hugging the charcoal rock-jetty that carved out the bay, that's when the hopeful travelers were SOL— shit out of luck, tough darts, better luck next time or next year or whenever you'd be coming back to the Vineyard again.

Danny was grateful he was not SOL today, especially because of the rain.

As simple as getting across on the bike ferry was, the rest posed a huge problem, that never-going-to-go-away problem that added to his pain right now and just simply pissed him off: where the ferry was easy to glide onto, the *Annabella* had a four-step step stool that Danny could not have traversed if his life depended on it, which, right now, it felt like it did.

"Fuck," he said, running his fingers over his rain-soaked scalp. With his hand still feeling the shaved stubble on his head, Danny had a sudden thought: *dark hair*. Unlike Mags, unlike Greg, Danny's hair was thick and dark, had always been thick and dark. *Thick and dark like Josh Miller's hair.*

He yanked his hand from his head and screamed into the water-drenched air. Why had his life become so fucked up and why was this all happening to him?

"Danny? Is that you?"

He lifted his eyes toward where the voice had come from. From the hole in the galley of the catamaran a head popped up. A head with dirty blond hair that hung straight and lifeless but framed a face that showed nothing but life. Life, a deep, sunny tan, and bright, sky blue eyes. "LeeAnn," Danny said. "Yeah, it's me."

LeeAnn pulled herself up from the hold. Gray sweats fell over her slim, well-toned body, the product of days on the water hoisting the mainsail and hauling the rigging, or whatever it was called by those real sailors who spent more than a few days each summer adrift on the water. "Jesus, what are you doing here?" she asked. "And have you noticed it's raining?"

The sound and sight of a friend was almost too much to bear. He bit his lip again and hoped he was not going to cry. "That's a fine greeting. I haven't seen you in almost three years and that's all I get? Besides, I'm the son of the next president," he added, pushing down the reality that those words would be the truth no matter who won, no matter who lost. "And yes, I noticed it's raining." He swiped his hand over his wet head again. "Where's Reggie?"

She slung her legs over the side of the boat and sat on the edge. "I'm not going to tell you if you're going to be such a dick. I guess all this notoriety was bound to change you."

Danny lowered his eyes, then raised them again. "Fuck you," he said, and was grateful she did not say "Been there, done that." Instead, she smiled.

"Reggie's over at the Texaco station listening to the shortwave. Rumor is there's a hurricane headed our way."

Great, he thought. *Just great.*

"Would you like to sit out here all day in the rain or come inside?" LeeAnn asked.

Danny mimicked a laugh. "Do you happen to have a crane that can haul me up the steps?"

"Shit," she said, not awkward, really, about Danny's problem. Not awkward, like so many others. If anything, she seemed a little embarrassed that she'd forgotten, which was, of course, the best Danny hoped for from people. *Just forget it,* he'd often wanted to say. *Just forget it, the way I would like to.* "Reggie should be back in a minute," LeeAnn continued. "He can help . . ."

"I can wait," he said with a shrug. "No charters today?"

She smiled. "Nope. We were about to stock up with food when the rains came. Not many tourists want to trek to Cuttyhunk in this weather."

"I do," Danny said, not knowing until this moment that he did, not knowing until now that getting off this damn island and away from having to face his mother and away from having to think about what had happened and all that it meant and would mean . . .

"Yes," he repeated, "I want to charter the *Annabella.* Is my credit any good?" He noticed that the rain was beginning to soak through his jeans now. He wondered if his legs were already wet. He wondered if he'd "catch his death of pneumonia," as his nurse in Switzerland had always warned of when Danny insisted on sitting on the balcony overlooking Lake Lucerne even on the dampest, wettest days. His nurse, Anna, so much prettier than Clay. And so . . . well, like LeeAnn . . .

"You want to go to Cuttyhunk?" LeeAnn asked. "Are you nuts?"

He needed to think for only a second. Then he shook his head. "Not Cuttyhunk exactly. Penikese."

"Nobody goes to Penikese, Danny. It's uninhabited."

"It was good enough for the lepers. I think it's appropriate for me. Will you take me over?"

"And do what? Have a picnic?"

"Maybe leave me there."

"You are crazy. Besides, it'll be dark in a few hours. And I told you, there's a hurricane coming. . . ."

"You said *maybe* there's a hurricane coming. And it only takes forty-five minutes. An hour tops."

"Maybe tomorrow, Danny. If it stops raining."

"Why? Because you're too chicken to go out in the rain? Reggie won't be."

Just then Reggie appeared, his long legs loping down the pier, his yellow slicker flapping behind him.

"Hey, Danny!" he shouted. "What brings you out on this fine day?"

"You," Danny said. "I need you to take me to Penikese."

Reggie laughed. "Gee, and I thought it was because you missed us." He gave Danny a slap on the shoulder.

"He's serious," LeeAnn said. "He wants to go to Penikese."

Reggie scowled. "Nobody goes there anymore, Danny."

"So I've heard. I also remember that you have always enjoyed being the exception."

"Except when it comes to Hurricane Carol. I just heard at the station. She's on the way."

"Will she be here by sundown?"

"Not until the wee hours."

"Then we have plenty of time. I only want to go across the sound, not halfway around the fucking world." He had no idea if he would want to return or not. He had no idea, and, right now, he did not care. "You can spend the time telling me what the hell you've been up to in the last few years."

"That would only take ten minutes. Twenty, if we include the part about how many times we wrote to you and you never wrote back. Or how many times we called and you wouldn't come to the phone."

"I was busy," Danny said.

"Yeah, sure," Reggie said.

"Leave him alone, Reggie," LeeAnn said, standing up. "Danny had better things to do than talk to us. He probably still does. But I'm not sure going to Penikese should be one of them. What if we get across and the seas are too rough to get back?"

Reggie scratched his one- or two-day-old beard growth. "LeeAnn's right, Danny. It's too risky."

Danny threw back his head, opened his mouth, and caught some rain. "Then fuck you," he said. "Fuck both of you." He put the wheelchair into gear and started to leave. Reggie caught up with him.

"Jesus, Danny, what's wrong?"

"Nothing's wrong, goddammit. I just came over here to ask a favor of my friends and they don't want to be bothered, that's all. Well, like I said, fuck you." He rolled back toward the bike ferry.

"Okay, okay," Reggie called out. "We'll take you over. God, you are such a spoiled brat."

If Danny had felt better he might have smiled. Instead, he felt a small sense of relief. Just getting off this damn island would maybe give him a chance to think.

He went back to the boat, where LeeAnn and Reggie

had the pleasure of lifting him out of his wheelchair, lugging him onto the catamaran, and dumping him in the wheelhouse where they told him he was lucky to have them for his friends and he'd better stop being an asshole and remember that. It was the first time in a long time that Danny had smiled and felt good about it.

Chapter 25

"I thought he was with you," Liz said to her sister, after BeBe had toweled off and changed into jeans and an old sweatshirt of Danny's.

Warmly tucked into the gray and crimson Harvard attire, BeBe wished she was eighteen again instead of ninety-five like she felt. "I haven't seen Danny since he brought us the iced tea," she replied, then added, "Do you have any brandy around here?"

"Brandy? My son has disappeared. Am I the only one who is concerned?"

"He hasn't disappeared, Liz," BeBe said, her words laced with exasperation. "He's obviously driven off somewhere in the van." Her head was throbbing now, from the sun then the vodka then the implosion of her sinuses behind her eyes thanks to the damn rain. Not to mention the aftershock of meeting Josh and the realization of what she had said, what she had done. She rubbed her forehead and wondered how she could ask Liz to please just shut up.

"Alone?" Liz asked from between nearly closed teeth. "God, Beebs, he never even drove the van until today. Until he went to get you."

"I thought you were the one who'd been hounding him to drive."

Liz sucked in a breath. "You don't understand. I'm worried about him."

BeBe did not point out that perhaps Liz was worried about the wrong thing. "Maybe he went back to the airport. Maybe he went to pick up someone else. Your husband, for example."

The color drained from Liz's face. She kept her eyes fixed on BeBe and winced.

BeBe could not believe her big mouth. She remembered the old gun that Evelyn had given to Daniel. She wished she could dig it out of Father's desk drawer, place it to her temple, and pull the trigger. It was the least she could do to spare her sister any more misery than she'd already created. "I'm sorry, Lizzie," she said, approaching her kid sister to give her a hug like old times.

Liz turned away.

BeBe pulled the long arms of the sweatshirt down over her hands and folded her arms. "Don't you get it, Liz? You weren't supposed to be like me. You weren't supposed to be the one with the fucked-up life. Your life was supposed to be perfect, unharmed, without scars."

Tears welled in Liz's eyes. "I know that's what everyone expected," she said. "But I'm human, Beebs. We all screw up stuff. Nothing has ever been perfect in my life. Especially since Daniel was killed. I thought, of all people, you knew that."

BeBe wondered if Liz could forgive her for telling Josh about Danny, by justifying that she, too, was human. "Yeah, well," BeBe stammered, "I tried my best to make things perfect for you, kid. To keep the dream alive for at least one of us."

Liz smiled. "It wasn't your job to make my life perfect, Beebs. Maybe Mother should have, but she was too busy either making life grand for Daniel or wallowing in his death. And Father was too busy with his own agenda, trying to get me to take Daniel's place, to live out the life Father had always wanted for himself, but had never dared to go after."

Never dared to go after? BeBe did not understand what Liz meant. Did Liz think Will Adams had once wanted to be president? And if so, did she wonder what had stopped him? BeBe suddenly wondered whether Liz had been more aware of Father's motives than she'd once thought, that maybe Liz, too, had learned that Father had not kept Daniel from getting orders for Vietnam, all for the sake of "credentials" to pave the road to Pennsylvania Avenue. But as BeBe looked into Liz's hurt eyes, she knew her sister did not know, could not have known. And BeBe had revealed enough secrets for one day, perhaps for a lifetime.

"Okay, Lizzie," she said, "so none of our lives has been perfect. Look at Danny's. He's stuck in a wheelchair. And now he's found a way to gain a little freedom. Don't take it away from him. And don't, for godsake, worry about him."

The tears dripped from Liz's eyes and she turned to the window. "I just wish he hadn't picked now to take off again."

BeBe looked out at the rain. "A little rain won't hurt him."

With her eyes lowered, Liz admitted, "It's not that. It's that I need him here now. I need him with me. He is more of my strength than he knows."

BeBe studied her sister a moment: her perfect sister, now standing there without makeup, without the help of hair stylists and wardrobe consultants, just a middle-aged woman out on the Vineyard, trying to make some sense of her life.

BeBe's head felt ready to burst. She thought about the look on Josh's face when BeBe told him that Danny was his son. Maybe Liz didn't need to know what she'd done so stupidly. Maybe Josh would keep it all to himself.

"Just be sure Danny doesn't know how much you need him, Liz," she quietly said. "Or you'll do to him what Father did to Daniel and what he did to you."

"You might want to ration that, in case the hurricane comes," said one of the Secret Service agents—the older one, who had introduced himself as Keith. He had a gentle accent that might have been rooted somewhere in the South.

BeBe had retreated to Father's study, and was pouring brandy into her glass. "Why?" she asked. "You can't have any, can you? Aren't you on duty?"

He laughed. It was a nice laugh, which she guessed might have softened from years on a job where he'd seen and heard more than maybe he'd wanted. She wondered how many family secrets—"first" family and otherwise—he held between his silver-gray temples.

"Wouldn't drink even if I wasn't on duty," he replied. "My father did enough of that for both of us. He fell off a bar stool when I was twelve. Cracked his skull on the floor. No one knew he was dead until after last call."

BeBe looked at her glass, then set it down. "Where are you from?"

"New Orleans. And before you ask, yes. The bar was on Bourbon Street."

She'd only been once, but remembered the noise and the heat and the stench. She raised her glass. "Then here's to fathers," she said. "May they all rot in hell."

Two hours later, Danny had still not returned. Liz had busied herself cleaning out closets, sorting through Father's Vineyard flannel shirts and sweaters for the

Salvation Army, a task easier to tackle with her mind on Danny, not Father, on Danny's life, not Father's death.

But the closets were clean now, and Danny had not yet returned. She had moved to the living room and was sitting quite still, unable to speak to either Keith or Joe or even to Clay: she was upset that once again they had let him out of their sight, they had let her down. She half wanted to call Michael and have them all fired, but the thought of talking with her husband right now was far too disturbing, as if he would know by the sound of her voice that she'd been unfaithful. That she had made love not just with her body but also—more sinful, perhaps— she had made love with her heart.

BeBe was on her third or fourth glass of something, Liz did not know or care what, but her sister insisted on sitting out on the porch in the rain, staring off across the dunes, which were no longer visible on the foggy horizon.

Liz stood up and went to the fireplace. She lifted the poker and shoved it at the fire, wondering when it would be legitimate to voice her concern. Was two hours long enough? Three? BeBe . . . all of them . . . thought she was being foolish. A hysterical mother not wanting to let go. But it wasn't true. She had always, of course, worried about the children when they were out. But Danny was . . . different. Yes, he was twenty-two. He was an adult. And he should be able to do as he pleased. But all that had stopped the day of the accident.

"He's going to need massive blood transfusions," Father had said, and the life and the soul and the spirit had drained from her body, leaving her smothered by a blanket of cold like she had never known. Cold for her child who lay virtually lifeless, cold for the fact she might have to tell them the truth. Tell them the truth that his blood might be different. It would not match Michael's; it would match Josh Miller's. And they might need to know that to save Danny's life.

She had stood in the white-on-white corridor of Massachusetts General Hospital, hearing the muted sounds of sirens in the distance, hearing, but not hearing, voices around her that sounded as if they were coming from deep inside a tunnel. She had looked down at her terra-cotta suit and wondered not what the people of the state would think of the governor's wife and her unmentionable transgressions, or even how Michael would react when he learned the truth. She had thought only of Danny. And Mags. And Greg. Of how this would hurt her innocent children and if she could ever forgive herself for what she had done.

But she had been spared. Blood was taken from the blood bank and Michael "replaced" it with his, as did Father, as did Mags, as Greg would have done if he'd been old enough. But Liz had been spared, and Danny had been spared, and the other children had been spared. And every person who believed in the Adams legacy and in the leadership of Michael Barton had been spared learning the pain that Liz had carried all those years.

She poked at the fire and warmed herself against the growing chill of the rain.

The polls, of course, would go wild if news that Danny was missing ever leaked out; if the world ever learned about Liz's renewed love affair with Josh, or that Danny was not Michael's son at all, but Josh's, of all people. The polls would bounce like a steel ball in an old-fashioned pinball machine, zinging and pinging all over the playing field, until the gossip finally settled on . . . Michael for sympathy? Josh as a victim, never having been told?

She stared into the embers and realized how sad the country was, that the choice of its leader could be so influenced by the behavior—then and now—of a scared, confused wife.

The perfect life. Oh, sure, Beebs, Liz thought. If I've had anything it hasn't been that. Then she thought about Mags. And about Greg. They had a different father from Danny, but she had loved them all equally and she still did.

She glanced at her watch. Another fifteen minutes had passed. She could not wait any longer. She had to call Michael. Because Michael was still Danny's father, and he had a right to know his son was missing. And a right to help her figure out what to do.

"He what?" Michael barked into the phone.

"I know that everyone here thinks I'm overreacting. But, Michael, it's almost two and a half hours . . ."

"Call Hugh Talbot. Hang up the telephone, Liz, and call Hugh Talbot."

Hugh Talbot was, as Liz and everyone up island knew, the sheriff, and had been for nearly thirty years.

"The van can't be too hard to locate, honey," Michael continued, his steady politician's voice wavering only a little, only enough for Liz to know that deep down, Michael was scared.

"But what if Danny went off-island? What if he . . . left?"

"There might be a hurricane, right? Maybe he couldn't get across. Maybe the ferry's shut down."

But Liz knew the weather had to be pretty inclement for the Steamship Authority to cease its shuttle. She also realized that Michael wasn't going to be much help in Florida.

"You're right," she answered abruptly. "I'll give Hugh a call. I'm sure Danny just ran into a few old friends or something. Besides, he hasn't driven in a few years. Maybe he's just enjoying the ride again." She wanted to add that his license must be expired, but decided that was unimportant, and would be a sure tip-off that she was faking unconcern.

"I'll give Hugh a call and let you know what happens," she said and hung up the phone, grateful that Michael did not point out that this would not have happened if they were with him campaigning as they should have been, grateful that Michael could not look her in the eye right now and see what she feared he would see there.

Hugh, however, was not available. "Folks are battening down for the hurricane," Hugh's wife, Lucy, told her. "Not that it's any of my business, but you should be doing the same."

"When you see Hugh," Liz said, "please ask him to keep an eye out for the van. It's dark green."

She hung up, feeling slightly annoyed that Lucy Talbot felt preparing for a hurricane was more important than locating a lost son.

Rubbing her arms, Liz went out onto the porch where BeBe was still stationed, trancelike, looking out at the rain. Liz sat down next to her sister on the swing, pushing away the thought that only the day before yesterday she had sat here with Josh.

"If he's not home soon I'm going to call the media," Liz said abruptly.

"What?" BeBe asked, sharply turning to face her sister. For all the alcohol Liz presumed she had drunk, BeBe looked as clear-eyed and sober as a Mormon on Sunday, or any other day.

"I said I'm going to call the media. It shouldn't be difficult. There must be an army of reporters stationed at Josh's. A lot of the media people have cars. They can help us search for Danny."

"You're going to call up a search party?"

"Don't make fun of me, BeBe. Danny is missing and, quite honestly, I feel as if something's wrong. In my gut, I feel it."

BeBe didn't answer.

"Are you with me?" Liz asked. "Will you help me find him?"

"Do you honestly think the Secret Service will let you leave?" BeBe nodded toward the house, where Keith and Joe had moved the chessboard inside and were playing a quiet, subdued game. "I'd put money on it that they've been told it's more important to guard you, not Danny."

"They don't have a choice."

"Yes, they do. Danny has the van and I'll bet they have the keys to the other car."

Liz's head began to throb with a dull ache.

"They have to let me go. Danny might need help." She stood up. "I know you're going to hate me for this, but I'm going to call Josh. I have his number . . ."

Suddenly, BeBe was beside her. "Don't," she said.

"Don't what? Don't call Josh?"

BeBe squeezed her eyes shut. "Please don't. It will only complicate things."

Liz felt a sting as if her hand had been slapped, as if she were that little girl again, the know-nothing baby of the family. "It will not complicate things, BeBe. But Michael is not here, and I need help fast. Josh has the connections. He can get it done." She started to move away, then turned back. "Besides, it's not as if he knows anything, BeBe. It's not as if . . ." It was the paralyzed look on her sister's face that cut off Liz's words. A look that said something, something . . .

"He knows," BeBe said.

Any energy Liz had remaining now left her body. She stood on the porch of the house she had loved for as long as she remembered, and slowly forced her eyes away from her sister, off toward the dunes, off toward the thicket, off toward the cove, and out toward the sea. She pictured Daniel there a moment, a brief moment. If he had not died, he would be the one running for president. If he had not died, none of this would be happening. None of this nightmare that had become Liz's life.

She looked back at BeBe. "How?" she asked slowly.

BeBe paused. She picked up her glass from the old wooden table next to the swing and took a drink.

"*How?*" Liz repeated, this time more insistent.

BeBe closed her eyes again. "I told him," she said. "This afternoon."

It was strange how quickly the wind had picked up and how quickly the fog was crowding out the daylight. Reggie had pulled in the sails and was tying off everything he could tie off topside; LeeAnn was with Danny in the wheelhouse, at the controls. She fought to steer, struggling, Danny knew, to keep the boat upright. He held on to the ledge that surrounded the windows of the small, square, all-weather-carpeted area and knew it was best not to speak. He was oddly grateful to be out of his wheelchair, which was folded up and stuck in the corner. Even though he could not feel the bench underneath him, it was good to know that something other than a flap of brown vinyl was supporting his dead little ass. He made a mental note to get out of the chair more often, if they ever survived this adventure across the high seas.

Through the rain-splattered window Danny could barely see land, a long, gray strip that would be Cuttyhunk Island. It did not look too far: it looked almost as if he could reach out and paddle a few strokes and the boat would be there. But Danny knew better than to be deceived by the ocean, especially when the ocean was all inky and rough as it was now, and when no man-of-wars floated on the surface, as they were known to do in this patch of water on sunny days, not on days that turned out like today, when even the most playful sea creatures knew the importance of being serious.

LeeAnn, for example. Danny glanced at the hard-working young woman whose eyes were fixed on the water. Usually, LeeAnn had the CD player blasting with reggae or Caribbean music—anything to make the passengers feel they were bound for a tropical island, a visit to paradise.

Today, she had not turned it on. She did not need to impress Danny. And she did not need to pretend that they were in paradise.

"I knew this was stupid," she finally said now. "We'll be lucky to make it to Cuttyhunk in one piece."

Danny didn't respond. Instead, he looked out the window again at the sharp, slanted gray rain and felt himself fill up with gratitude for these friends he had found, for LeeAnn and Reggie, who had always been there for him—been there to laugh and play when they were kids, been at his bedside when he lay crumpled and worthless, been there even after he'd been too despondent to write back or return their phone calls, and now, there for him when he'd been ready to end it once and for all. He might have been lied to all of his life, he might have a father he did not even know, but Danny Barton was lucky that he had friends such as these. Friends, dear Gramps, that he hadn't had to buy.

He looked at LeeAnn again and blinked back a few tears. Then he wished Reggie would hurry up and come in off the deck before he got tossed overboard and pissed them both off.

Chapter 26

BeBe had never understood the old cliché of feeling like a piece of shit. After all, what exactly did shit feel like? And who had determined that shit had feelings, anyway?

She'd never understood it, and yet, right now, it about described how she felt. After having spent a lifetime protecting her younger, presumably more fragile sister, BeBe had blown it, big time. She had betrayed Liz. Okay, it had been a stupid mistake, but what kind of excuse was that?

She went to the back hall to find an old yellow slicker. She slipped it on, inhaling the familiar dull scent, like tires on wet pavement, or the old inner tubes they had once floated on in the cove, until Father had decided it was too dangerous because the hard intake valve might poke out someone's eye.

Back in the living room, she went to the telephone. From the drawer of the small oak stand, she pulled out the phone book—The Island Book, it was called—which, of course, was still there, was always there, updated yearly. It only took her a moment to find the number she wanted.

"What are you doing?" Liz asked, walking into the room and eyeing her sister.

BeBe averted her gaze. "I'm going to find your son."

"Did you forget we don't have a vehicle, or are you calling a cab?"

BeBe knew the sarcasm in Liz's voice was propelled by deep anger, and she did not blame her. "There are probably only two men in the world I haven't totally pissed off yet," BeBe said. "One is your husband, only because he doesn't know what's really going on. The other is Tuna. Hopefully, he'll give us a hand. If he's still alive."

Tuna was still alive. He said he still drove a rusted-out pickup truck (though this one was black), and he was still married to the same woman (four kids, three grandkids now), and he said he was only too glad to help out BeBe and her famous sister. Besides, he added, he was sick of listening to everyone piss and moan about Hurricane Carol and speculate if she was really going to hit the island or not.

As for speculation, BeBe knew there was no time for any of her own—to wonder whether or not calling Tuna had been a good idea. Instead, she told Liz to put on a slicker, that Tuna would be there in ten minutes, thank God for old friends.

Apparently finally realizing that there might be reason for concern, Keith decided to drive into Vineyard Haven to check with the ferry to see if Danny had boarded. He had tried phoning first, but had not been able to get through. She could not imagine why Danny would have wanted to get off-island, but part of her hoped that he had. She hoped he had arrived in Woods Hole and kept driving, up to Boston, where he had friends, where he might decide to become part of the world again—the world away from the spotlight that shined off the spokes of his wheelchair, the world away from the political board game.

So Keith left, and Clay said he would wait at the house "just in case," and BeBe sat in silence next to Liz in the living room, where she felt once again like the family's bad child.

He had a few teeth missing and he smelled a bit like what might have been last night's beer, but Tuna showed up and for that Liz seemed grateful. She was not so happy, however, when Joe insisted on going with them. Neither did their chauffeur.

"There's no room," Tuna said. "You'll have to sit in the back."

The "back" turned out to be the open bed of the truck. Tuna tossed a rain hat at Joe and showed him a tarp that might help him stay dry.

Under other circumstances, BeBe would have cracked a joke and Liz would have laughed, and they would have become like silly schoolgirls again, despite their years, despite all they had been through in their lives.

But this was not ordinary circumstances, so BeBe simply climbed into the truck next to Tuna and, for once in her life, did not speak.

Tuna backed out of the driveway. "Where are we going?" he asked BeBe.

BeBe looked at her sister, saw Liz's pain, then quickly averted her eyes. "Where do you think Danny might be?" she asked.

"I have no idea," Liz replied. "I was always too busy to pay attention to his friends, or to what he liked—or didn't like—to do. I was always too busy, but I always trusted him. Danny was a good boy."

When Liz spoke of Danny in the past tense, BeBe

wanted to scream at her sister to stop being a jerk, to slap her and tell her to grow up, that none of this was her fault, that it was all Father's fault for screwing up all their lives. But of course she said no such thing.

"Let's start in Gay Head," BeBe said. "Danny always liked to look out from the cliffs." No one mentioned that it would soon be dark. "If he's not there," BeBe added, "we can try Oak Bluffs. Maybe he did something really simple like go to the movies."

"The movies?" Liz asked.

"This is his first taste of real freedom in years," BeBe said with more conviction than she felt. "He might want to have fun. Besides, the Strand is still there. So is The Island."

Liz looked at her sister, then looked away again, as if not wanting to remember those nights at the movies, the popcorn blocks, the saltwater taffy. And Josh.

This was her penance. Liz numbly stared out the dirty side window of the rattling old pickup truck and knew that this was her penance for being with Josh again, for letting herself succumb to lust or memories or vulnerability—whatever it was that had propelled her into doing what she should not have done, then, now, or ever.

It was difficult to believe that it had only been last night and that she had felt so happy, so blissfully content, as if she had come home, as if there had still been a home left to come to.

She didn't even know how she felt about him. Had she loved him all these years? She had, of course, thought of him often, more often of late, since he'd entered the race against Michael. Once, such a thing had been inconceivable. But Liz had allowed herself only a few moments of wondering if he had done it on purpose, if he were trying to prove he was good enough for her, if perhaps he still loved her, had always loved her, and this was his only way of proving it.

Then she had realized that was a feverishly selfish way of thinking, as if the world or anyone else's world revolved around her.

"You know, of course, that Gay Head's now called Aquinnah," Tuna said to BeBe.

Liz tuned them out, these two people beside her who she suspected once had been lovers.

Old lovers, Liz thought, and once again, an ache blossomed somewhere inside her.

She suddenly wondered if she should have told Josh that Danny was missing. Was that how it worked? Now that he knew Danny was really his son, was he entitled to know anything? And more importantly, did he *think* he was entitled to know anything?

She put a thumbnail into her mouth and slowly chewed the edge. Of course, Danny wasn't a child; he was a full-fledged adult, legally entitled to make his own decisions. Did that make a difference?

The windshield wipers creaked. The breath of three adults crammed into the cab of the old truck began to steam up the windows. Tuna laughed. Then BeBe laughed.

Liz squeezed her eyes closed. "Shut up!" she screamed. "Both of you, please just shut up!"

The laughter halted, chopped like a carrot by a ginzu knife on one of those TV infomercials that Liz sometimes watched in the middle of the night when she could not sleep.

Liz opened her eyes and was not surprised to sense they were wet, as wet as the pavement that stretched up toward the lighthouse, the empty pavement where no cars—not even pink tourist buses—were parked at the souvenir shacks. No cars, no buses, no van. For a few moments they sat there in silence, staring out at the vacant cliffs and the dark, choppy waters below.

"You'll have to excuse my sister," BeBe said softly. "She's so worried about Danny."

For all his seeming character flaws, Tuna at least had the sense not to speak.

Liz felt like a fool. "I'm sorry," she said. "I have a lot on my mind, but that's no excuse to be rude. I do appreciate your help, Tuna."

"Guess it's best to head down to Oak Bluffs," Tuna said, steering the truck around the big, U-shaped loop, the one that began the return to the island.

And then Liz remembered that Danny had once called this spot "end of the world," because your only choice was to turn back or to go forward, off into the sea. He had called it that long ago, back when he was a child, back when he was a whole child and would never have run off without letting his mother know where he had gone.

The boat pitched and rolled and heaved like a Disney World E-Ride gone out of control. Danny hung on to the edges of the bench where Reggie and LeeAnn had plunked him and tried to focus on not throwing up and on not looking to see if his catheter was full because there was nothing he could do if it was. It wasn't as if he could mosey out of the wheelhouse, walk up to the rail, pop the cap, and drain his pee into Vineyard Sound. It wasn't as if he could ask Reggie to do it for him, because Reggie had relieved LeeAnn and was now at the helm, struggling to keep the catamaran upright, struggling to keep them alive. He couldn't ask LeeAnn, either, because she had gone below to puke her seasick guts out, and Danny could not have followed her there, because there was merely a ladder from the wheelhouse down to the galley and bunks, and, well, ladders were pretty much out of the question for a guy with virtually no legs.

It was amazing, Danny mused, how focusing on battling the elements to stay alive took one's mind off other, less consequential things, like learning your father was not who you thought.

"If we make it into the channel we'll be okay," Reggie shouted above the whip of wind that lashed against the windows.

Danny knew the channel was Canapitsit, which, tucked between Cuttyhunk and Nashawena, provided the only access from Vineyard Sound to the town dock at Cuttyhunk. He knew all this because, back in his youth, he had made it a point to learn all about the Indians and their influence on the Vineyard because he'd been trying to score points with LeeAnn and make her think he was really one of them, not one of those summer people who only "took" from the island and never gave back. It had never occurred to him that she knew what he was and had liked him in spite of it.

"We're not going to make it to Penikese are we?" Danny asked.

Reggie pulled his eyes from the horizon and shouted above the roar of the wind. "Danny, my boy, we'll be lucky to make Cuttyhunk. The storm is kicking up sooner than expected. LeeAnn was right. We were stupid to try."

Danny dropped his gaze to the floor, to the wet, thin carpeting that had seen the feet of so many happy tourists. "Sorry, Reg," he said. "I was miserable and depressed and had no right to drag you two into my problems."

Suddenly the boat lurched on a wave that seemed as high as the Prudential Center in downtown Boston. Danny felt the roll come in a split second. He grabbed for the edge of the bench. But he was too late, and his body was flung onto its side and dumped onto the blue indoor-outdoor-carpeted floor.

"Fuck," he said.

"No kidding," Reggie said. "Hold still a minute and I'll get you up."

"Forget about me," Danny said, hoisting his upper body as upright as possible. "Keep us afloat. I'll be fine until we get there." With the force of his hands, that at least still worked, Danny tried to push his body around, tried to straighten the rest of himself so he would not be too twisted, so he would not break any bones if he already hadn't. Pain below the waist, like pleasure, was something Danny did not have to worry about.

He did, however, have to worry about the catheter, which he now could see quite clearly and see that it bulged. Just as he knew that the last thing he could do to his friends was release his pee all over the boat, they hit another wave, and the boat pitched again. Danny automatically clutched at the catheter just in time for it to pop open and empty its contents.

"Jesus, Danny, are you okay?" It was LeeAnn's voice, calling to him not from below deck where she should have been, but from the ladder she had climbed to check up on them.

He would have been more embarrassed if her face was not barf-seasick green.

"Just another day in paradise," he said. "Sorry, though. It seems I've pissed the bed."

Reggie glanced down at him, then back to the helm. "Jesus," he said.

LeeAnn's eyes fell to the floor, to the puddle of urine that surrounded him now, mixing with the rainwater and creeping up to his chest—he knew because he could feel its warmth there.

LeeAnn started to laugh. "This is absurd," she yelled above the noisy assault of Mom Nature or whoever was causing such chaos. "I'm downstairs puking my guts out, you're up here pissing your pants, and Reggie is barely keeping us alive. I say it's absurd and it's more fun than I've had in years." With that, she clutched her stomach, rolled her eyes, and ran back down to the galley, retching as she went.

"She's right," Danny admitted from where he was sprawled on the floor. "It's more fun than I've had, too."

"Which only proves," Reggie added, "that you're both assholes."

Danny smiled. The boat rose up again, then quickly slapped down. And Danny realized that if he died out here, if they all died out here, it was better to die happy with friends than to die miserable and alone . . . or even worse, with people who had spent your whole life lying to you.

Chapter 27

By the time they arrived in Oak Bluffs, it was dark. Like Gay Head, it looked like a ghost town. BeBe gazed at the huge Victorian homes that rimmed the water and were now boarded up with beige plywood eye patches that covered their windows, blocking their view of the blackened sea. The few vehicles on the streets were mostly all parked, abandoned like the houses, waiting for the wrath of Carol.

They circled around the Flying Horses carousel and drove up Circuit Avenue, past the movie theater on the corner, past the T-shirt and fudge shops and the bar where Josh had once extricated BeBe. There was no green van parked in any of the angled spaces that bordered the left side of the street.

"Stop," Liz commanded. "I'm going to go into the theater. Maybe he parked somewhere else."

BeBe did not point out how unlikely it was that Danny would park any distance away since he would have to wheel himself all the way.

Tuna stepped on the brake and stopped the truck. Liz pulled the navy-lined slicker hood over her head, got out, and slammed the door. The rumble from the truck bed told BeBe that Joe was following Liz.

BeBe dropped her face into her hands. "This is such a nightmare."

"Does her son run away often?" Tuna asked.

BeBe shook her head. "You don't understand. There's so much more involved. So much at stake . . ."

"Do you think Barton will win the election? Do you think he has a chance to beat out the Jew?"

BeBe winced at the way Tuna referred to Josh, at the prejudice that people like Tuna—and Father—could not seem to break through. Despite how she felt about Josh, the prejudice repulsed her. "I don't know if Michael will win the election," BeBe said quietly. "I don't know anything anymore."

Tuna parked the truck. "Come on, Beebs, I'll buy you a quick cup of coffee at Linda Jean's. And you can tell me how rotten your life is, and I'll tell you how perfect mine is."

After a moment of hesitation, BeBe agreed. Even if Liz came back before they did, BeBe needed a break. And at least Tuna would always be Tuna and never pretend to be anyone else.

"My wife doesn't understand me," Tuna was saying while BeBe stared into the mug of steaming coffee. She didn't know which was funnier—the outdated pickup line or the fact that Tuna thought there was anything there for his wife to understand in the first place.

"What's to understand?" she asked. "You like to fish, you like to fuck. What else is there?"

"Come on, BeBe, you know me better than that."

"No I don't. And you'd better not be making a move on me, Tuna, because now's not the time or the place, and I'm definitely not the right person. Besides, the last time I saw you, you were happy with your marriage."

"The last time you saw me was almost twenty-five years ago."

"Shit," she said, "we're getting old, Tuna."

"All the more reason we should take advantage of every opportunity that comes our way." He took a long drink of his coffee, plucked a thin paper napkin from a chrome container, and wiped the Formica table where he had spilled a drop.

BeBe was fairly certain he wasn't doing all this because he was neat. *He's thinking,* she knew. *He's thinking about making his next move.* She hated it that he was so transparent. She glanced out the window, wishing that *her* next move could be out the door, fast. Leave it to her to find the one man on the island knee-deep in male menopause, and to drag him back into her life. God, how she longed to be at her desk, consumed by her work, where the real world could not intrude.

"It must be exciting," he said, "this political life. Being out there campaigning, traveling around the country."

It took her a second to get what he meant. "Political life?" Then she laughed. "Not me, pal. I stay as far away from that as I can. That's my sister's life, not mine."

"But you must get into part of it. All the celebrities that do all those golf tournaments and things. All the singers who perform at fund-raising concerts. God, it sure is a lot different than being stuck here on a damn island."

BeBe leaned across the table. "Get this straight, Tuna. The last 'celebrity' I saw was James Taylor when he gave a benefit concert right here on this 'damn island.' I do not travel around the country. I live in Palm Beach, where I sweat to death in summer and work my ass off at my very successful business. I never have time to play golf; nor do

I care. And I'm sorry to disappoint you, but I like my life." As she said it, she realized she wasn't far from the truth. Well, not too far.

"Geez, what a waste," Tuna said.

"Not really," BeBe said, staring at him now, at the face that was leathered from too many years on the water, and weary perhaps from looking at the same wife for so long; the wife who probably also felt "stuck." "Thanks for the java." BeBe stood up. "But I need to find out what my famous sister is doing."

They left the restaurant, Tuna blessedly walking with distance between them, as if he had gotten the message, hallelujah. But BeBe felt a small seed of sadness for this man she had once known, sadness for his life, and for the lives, she supposed, of most people, whose lives had begun with so many possibilities that were now so few.

They made it to Cuttyhunk. The small hump of an island was barely visible through the heavy gray curtain that dripped with rain; the harbor itself was amass with few boats but hundreds of orange buoys that bounced with the chop, deserted by boat owners who must have believed that Carol was coming and they needed to get out of her way.

The *Annabella*, however, was, according to Reggie, too old and too mean to be dissuaded.

Once they were safely past the rock jetty and into the inlet, LeeAnn made it topside and helped Danny back onto the bench. She yanked off his shirt—the one covered with saltwater and pee—then washed his chest with a warm, wet cloth, dried him, and pulled a clean Black Dog sweatshirt over his head. Then, while Reggie steered delicately toward the pier, LeeAnn slid off Danny's pants and studied the mess.

"Tell me what to do to fix you up," she said, as if nursing duties were something she had willingly signed on for, simply by virtue of being his friend.

In another place, at another time, Danny might have been profoundly humiliated. But with Reggie at the helm and LeeAnn studying him so matter-of-factly, it did not seem humiliating. It seemed, instead, the most natural thing in the world.

He leaned back on the bench and told her what to do. Then he watched as she did everything perfectly, or nearly perfectly, and even told her it was a damn shame he couldn't feel her touching him because he'd like that a lot, because he knew her hands would feel better on him than those of his Jamaican nurse, Clay.

"Shut up and try to let one of us know when you intend to pee your pants again," she responded with good humor. She covered him in a pair of Reggie's clean, dry sweatpants. They were too long but it didn't matter, because it wasn't as if Danny had to walk anywhere, and, anyway, he doubted that the fashion police were holed up on Cuttyhunk Island.

He had a quick thought that Josh Miller was shorter than Michael Barton; that Danny was shorter than his sister, Mags, or brother, Greg. Shorter, and now he knew why: it was because he really wasn't one of them; he was one of the opposite party. He tried to push away his thought.

Warmer and drier now, he thanked LeeAnn and told her she'd make someone a wonderful wife. She gave him the finger, buttoned a slicker around herself, and went out on deck to help Reggie tie off.

Reggie and LeeAnn "borrowed" a golf cart at the marina, hoisted Danny onto the seat, put his wheelchair in the back, and headed for the Vineyard View Bakery where they hoped to get much-needed food and more-needed shelter.

The restaurant was closed.

Reggie banged on the door. No one came.

"They're home where they're safe," LeeAnn said. "They knew there wouldn't be tourists on a day like this."

The tourists, of course, only came and left Cuttyhunk: there were no hotels here, no welcoming inns. Danny had once heard that in winter less than fifty people inhabited the island. He would bet there'd be even fewer next winter if Hurricane Carol picked here to hit land.

Reggie climbed back into the cart and turned it around, the small canvas roof sagging from the persistent rain. He hooked a left and headed up a small hill—at one, two, maybe three miles an hour. Not that it mattered: the roads were deserted. It could have been No Mans Land—that spooky island south of here that was used for target practice in World War II, the place where few dared to go because of the rumored land mines and ammunition and ghosts that were there, ghosts that might have crossed the water and settled on Cuttyhunk for the lack of activity on the main street of town now.

The dim golf cart headlights revealed gray-shingled houses that dotted the road—many boarded, some, perhaps, in anticipation of Carol; some simply because they belonged to summer people who had already returned to the city.

They putt-putted through the wind and the rain until Reggie finally slowed. "Look," he said, pointing under the golf cart canopy. "People."

The "people" turned out to be three men, a woman, a child, and a dog, all standing on the porch of a building marked "Cuttyhunk Historical Society." They were looking off toward the Vineyard, discussing, perhaps, whether or not Carol would choose to land there instead of . . . there.

One of the men waved at Reggie, who waved back, pulled up to the white picket fence, and shouted, "Evening, friends. Nice day."

"Reggie Watson? That you?"

"It's us," Reggie replied. "Me and my sweet sister, LeeAnn, and our passenger, who wishes to remain nameless. Do you have any food in that joint or do you prefer to starve your tourists?"

Along with the laughter that rolled down from the porch came the friendly, small-town warmth that Danny had not felt in ages, not since his life had become hospitals and hotel rooms, wheelchairs and airplanes, not since his days were spent being shuttled between patient and poster boy, poor, helpless Danny and the politician's brave son.

Cuttyhunk was simple, and that was how Danny liked it. He smiled and wondered if he could stay there at least part of forever.

Until they rounded the corner and pulled into the driveway back at the house, Liz had not given up hope that the van would be in the driveway. But it was not there.

The dull ache in her head crawled down to her shoulders. She bent her neck to relieve the pain; it did not work.

She said mechanical thanks to Tuna and was vaguely aware of walking toward the house and of BeBe behind her. Inside, Keith was building a fire in the fireplace.

"Any luck?" he asked.

BeBe shook her head. Liz went into the kitchen to make tea.

"Me either. It's a mess at the harbor. Everyone's trying

to get off-island before the storm shuts everything down. But not Danny. At least, if he went, he didn't take the van. He could have bought a passenger ticket—they wouldn't have a record of that. But the vehicle . . . no dice."

"I suppose you checked the parking lot . . ." BeBe asked, while, from the other room, Liz tried not to listen. All she wanted to do now was burrow under the big puff on her bed; she wanted to burrow from the world and pretend that Father was not dead, that Josh had not learned about Danny, and that Danny was here, safe in his room. She wanted to turn back the clock to last night—or was it the night before—before she had once again found warmth in Josh Miller's arms. She wanted to pretend it had not happened, and yet she could not.

Setting the kettle on the stove, Liz fired the heat beneath it, and tried desperately not to think about what would happen if Josh Miller came forward and claimed Danny as his own.

Outside, the rain whipped a tree branch against the window. Liz wondered if Danny was warm and safe and if he'd be all right.

The teapot whistled. She poured the water into her mug and stood mutely watching, while the teabag steeped.

"Lizzie?" Her name was called so quietly, Liz barely heard it. She turned and saw BeBe standing in the doorway. Her sister's face was white.

Liz gripped the counter, afraid to hear what BeBe was going to tell her.

BeBe came into the kitchen and put her arm around Liz. "Keith saw Danny leave the house earlier."

"When?"

BeBe removed her arm and wove her fingers together, one by one, the way an ex-smoker or ex-drinker some-

times does when trying to substitute one action for
another.

"Earlier," she replied, "before the rain started. He
didn't think there was reason for concern at the time."

"BeBe, what's going on?"

BeBe shook her head. "I don't know. But I'm afraid,
Liz. I'm afraid this is all my fault."

"*What's* all your fault?"

"Keith followed Danny outside. He saw him going
down to the path."

"To the water?"

BeBe averted her eyes from Liz. "Yes. But he thinks
Danny turned off at the cove."

"How? The wheelchair couldn't make it down the
path."

BeBe struggled with her words. "When Keith was
driving to the ferry, he remembered that he'd seen Danny.
As soon as he returned from Vineyard Haven, he checked
it out. That's when he saw the ruts of the wheelchair.
They're now filled with rainwater."

"What are you saying? Is Danny still down there? Did
he fall into the water . . ."

BeBe shook her head. "No. The tracks don't go all the
way to the cove. But I'm afraid they went far enough."

"Far enough for what, BeBe?"

Silence.

"BeBe?" Liz asked again, wanting to shout, but afraid
it might hurt too much, afraid that she was going to need
all the energy she had to handle what was coming. "Far
enough for what?"

BeBe sucked in her lower lip. "Josh . . ." was all that
she could say.

Liz steadied her eyes on her sister and asked her in a
voice that was surprisingly even, "Danny overheard what
you said to Josh?"

BeBe could not seem to answer. She mashed her teeth into her lip. Her eyes brimmed with fat, wet tears. Her body trembled.

Liz's hand went to her throat. The blood in her veins seemed to bubble, coming to a rolling boil like the candy Liz used to help Mother make so often for Father and Daniel and Roger and BeBe in the safety of the house on Beacon Hill. *Bring to a rolling boil,* the cookbook read. If she hadn't known exactly what that meant before, Liz knew now. One by one, her body parts began to move. Her feet, her hands, her legs, her arms. Her head swiveled from side to side and up and down. Her facial nerves twitched and jerked. Then she pulled back one arm as hard as she could, thrust it forward with a might she hadn't known that she possessed and slugged her sister smack in the jaw.

Just as BeBe thudded to the floor without a cry, without a whimper or a scream, Joe appeared at the kitchen door. Beside him stood a man in a uniform. "Mrs. Barton?" Joe asked. "This is Sheriff Talbot."

The sheriff stepped forward and looked down at BeBe. "I've come for your sister, Mrs. Barton. She's wanted for questioning in the murder of Ruiz Arroyo."

Chapter 28

She wondered if this was where Ted Kennedy had sat back in the Mary Jo Kopechne days that hardly anyone remembered anymore, except maybe the girl's parents and the islanders who lived near where it happened. She wondered if there was some irony in the fact that she was the sister-in-law of a presidential candidate and he had been the brother of two. No, she guessed that was stretching things. She wondered if she would be thinking more clearly if her jaw didn't feel as if it had been broken in half.

BeBe sat forward on the narrow cot, rested her aching face in her hands, and tried to figure out why the hell she was here.

The murder of Ruiz Arroyo?

It was what Hugh Talbot had said. That Ruiz had been found this afternoon down in Palm Beach, and that he had been driving a Mercedes registered in her name.

Well, of course, she had given him the Mercedes. He had not been a bad lover, up until that last night. He had not been a bad lover, had not been a bad employee, and taking the car back had seemed so . . . juvenile, that BeBe had decided to just let him have it. Besides, the car enabled him to have fast transportation back to his wife and four kids and out of her life.

But now he was dead and they thought she had done it.

"I wasn't even in Palm Beach!" she shrieked in the cruiser all the way to the county lock-up in Edgartown. "I left there this morning!"

"They said it was an execution-type murder. Something about you hiring someone to do it."

"Who the hell would I hire? And why?" Her insides were trembling as much as her voice. She felt a sickening combination of disgust and despair at the idea of Ruiz with a bullet in his brain.

"I don't know the details, BeBe," Hugh had replied. "I only know we have to hold you here until we can extradite you to Florida after the hurricane."

She stared at the concrete floor now, then the concrete ceiling, then the concrete walls. She stared at the small window and the tall iron bars that went from top to bottom, as if this were a real cell, in a real jail, like she'd seen at the movies hundreds of times.

It is a real jail, you moron, she told herself.

What had been as bad as being hauled in for "questioning," was that Liz had stood by and watched it all happen, without ever coming to her sister's defense.

She'd tried to tell Hugh Talbot that they had to look for the Cubans—the people behind the boatloads of illegals that were Ruiz's "other" business, the black market big business that he'd disguised as a charity. She'd tried to tell Hugh, but Hugh didn't care. His job was simply to put her away for the duration.

She looked back to the iron bars on the window and wondered if the jail would be protected from the storm clearly brewing outside, or if anybody would care if BeBe Adams got washed away in a gale.

Ruiz might have cared back when she was his meal ticket.

But now even he was dead.

Closing her eyes, she knew she should cry for him, and yet she could not.

"Your sister is *where*?" Michael shouted as he stood in the living room of the house on the Vineyard, disheveled from the wind and rain. Liz had been neither disturbed nor elated when she'd seen Michael at the door not long after BeBe had been whisked off by Hugh. She'd been sitting in the living room, waiting for something, though she didn't know what, perhaps death.

Death had not come; instead, Michael had. He told Liz they had left Florida for New Jersey when he'd telephoned Hugh to see if there was news. Hugh's wife said he was out making ready for the storm, but that as far as she knew Danny had not surfaced. So Michael diverted the charter to Logan, then caught a Lear down to the island and prayed they could still land.

They could; they did; and his shadowing agents even managed to secure a vehicle, a canvas-topped Jeep.

"BeBe's been taken in for questioning in a murder," Liz repeated flatly. "The way she lives—the way she's always lived—sooner or later something like this was bound to happen." She listened to her words as if they were being spoken by someone else. She wondered why Michael was putting his arm around her, and then she remembered that he did not yet know about her and Josh.

"They have to know she has nothing to do with it," Michael was saying.

Liz shrugged. "Who knows."

Michael sighed. "Well, *I* know your sister better than

that. As soon as this storm is over I'll get Buzz Rangely on it."

Nodding mechanically, it took Liz a moment to remember that Buzz Rangely was a lawyer. *Oh, great,* she thought. Once the lawyers were involved, everything would be known. Every dirty little piece of their dirty little lives.

"Right now, the priority is to find Danny," Michael, in-charge Michael, continued. "Where is he, Liz? Why is he still gone?"

The flames in the fireplace licked one another as if trying to soothe each other's pain.

Before Liz could respond, footsteps sounded on the stairs. It was Evelyn and Roger. "If you've come to the Vineyard for a little sun, I'm afraid your timing is off," Liz said. She turned back to the fireplace and asked, "Where are Mags and Greg?" Please, God, she prayed, don't let them be here, too.

"We left them in Boston," Michael said. "They've gone to the house. I didn't think . . ."

"Thought I'd help board up the place," Roger said. "This could be a doozie. They almost wouldn't let us land."

A doozie. *Yes,* Liz thought, *Roger would call a hurricane a "doozie."* Perhaps he had inherited that word through DNA from Mother. Is that how DNA worked? Did Danny now say things that Josh always said? Did he react more like Josh than the rest of the family? Would he fit in better with Josh and his family? Would he want to be Jewish?

"Liz," Michael said after Roger and Evelyn left the room. "Where is Danny?" he repeated. "What happened?"

She studied the burning logs. "I want to go home," she said. "I want to go back to Boston."

Michael hugged her. "We can't go home, honey. We have to find Danny."

Tears drizzled down her cheeks. She wanted to break down into sobs, despite the fact that Michael would hold her and calm her and tell her everything would be all right when he didn't have a clue how wrong things were. She wanted to do it all, but suddenly she was so tired, so very, very tired.

"Hugh is combing the island for Danny," Michael said. "If he's still here, he'll find him." He nudged her. "Come on, honey, I'm going to take you into the bedroom. You're going to lie down and rest. I should give Roger a hand."

The thought of a presidential candidate nailing plywood across windows seemed somehow out of sync. She wondered if Josh was outside, boarding up his place, too. She wondered if . . . *Oh God,* Liz thought. Could Danny have gone to Josh's? Could he be there now? And if he was, what was he doing? The media was there. The media was everywhere.

She jumped up from the sofa. "I've got to go out."

"What?" Michael stood, steadying her with his arm.

"I've got to go out. Keith has the car keys . . ." She headed for the kitchen.

Michael grabbed her arm and stopped her. "Liz, what are you doing?"

"I think I know where Danny is." She wrenched her arm from his hand. "I've got to go." She marched into the kitchen, where Keith was on the phone, talking to God only knew who.

"Give me the car keys," she demanded. "Now."

Michael was right behind her. "It's okay, Liz. We rented a Jeep at the airport. I'll drive you."

She shook her head. "No. This is something I have to do alone."

• • •

Evelyn peered out the window as Liz backed down the driveway and wondered what the hell was going on. She hated not knowing things. She hated being shut out like she didn't matter, just because she wasn't an Adams by birth, just because she had ended up with Roger when she should have had Daniel. She hated being shut out because she'd not had any children, no heirs to the throne, unlike Liz.

She hated anyone knowing when she had made a mistake. Especially BeBe.

On the other hand, she thought with a small smile, sometimes things really did work out for the best.

She turned from the window and wondered what would happen when the media learned what was really going on behind the Barton/Adams closed doors.

Liz studied the trees that blew and bent before her, and the rain that pelted in the headlights. And then she saw it: the long, unmarked driveway where a signpost with an arrow reading "Miller" once stood, back before the name meant anything, back when it had been safe to have your name on a signpost because no one cared who you were.

She turned down the driveway and slowed the vehicle to traverse the ruts and the potholes and the other deterrents that provided a natural "No Trespassers" caution.

Liz had never seen the house from this side, only from the ocean side when she had walked along the beach so many times, spying, pretending to just happen to be strolling by, to just happen to be digging for clams right there in his front yard. As she rounded a final curve, the house stood before her, looked back at her, reflected in the headlights. It was big and gray and not unlike her family's house.

Only this house was all boarded up, without a sign of life.

Chapter 29

"Sit down, Michael," Liz said after she had returned to the house. It was after ten, and there had as yet been no word from Danny.

But on the ride back to the house, Liz had finally slipped back into her mind, into her body, and into what was left of her spirit. She had slipped back into herself because she had decided what must have happened to Danny, and she felt that at least he was safe.

Josh would take care of Danny. She felt as certain of that as she did that Danny had gone to Josh's house, that they had left the Vineyard together. She had not figured out what had happened to the van: that would come later, once the pieces had all been revealed.

And revealed, she knew they would be. Which was why she also knew that the time had finally come to make things right. Because despite everything else that she had done wrong, there was one thing that Liz could do right: she could tell Michael the truth before he learned it somewhere else, some other way, like on the evening news.

She'd brought him into their room—her room, actually, the room where she'd slept each summer, where she'd stared out at the stars and dreamed so many dreams, where she'd learned to go against her father's wishes by sneaking out to Josh. The room with the window where sand pebbles had grazed so many times, sands of time, grains of her heart.

Michael sat on the edge of the bed. It was a queen-size bed, with a headboard made of white birch logs, put there after they were married, replacing the twin wrought-iron bed that Liz had during her childhood. The rocking chair that had once been in there was also gone— the tiny space with the window dormer left no room for both the big bed and the chair, so Liz now was compelled to sit beside her husband, when she would rather have been further away. Los Angeles, perhaps. Or London.

She reached down to the chenille bedspread and pulled at the threads, the way she'd done when she was a kid, the way her kids had done. "I think I know where Danny is," she said, quietly, so no one but she and Michael and maybe God could hear.

"You came back alone from your secretive mission," Michael said with an edge to his voice that Liz did not recognize. "So he must not have been where you thought."

Liz sighed and closed her eyes. "It wasn't as much 'where' as 'with whom.' " She opened her eyes, looked at her husband, and spoke as clearly as possible. "I think I know who Danny is with."

Michael's eyebrows elevated as if to say, *So? Get on with it!* But he sat patiently beside her, in a politician's neutral pose, awaiting her next words.

"I think he's with Josh Miller," she said, more abruptly than she had planned.

His expression turned to a frown. "Miller? Why?"

Liz could not even force a half smile, not even for Michael, her husband, her mate—if not of soul, then at least her husband of years of loyalty, the builder of their family, with Liz so visibly by his side. Michael, her husband, the father of two of her three wonderful children. But she could not even force a half smile for him now, despite the fact that he was about to feel so much pain, pain that he did not deserve. She cleared her throat.

"Michael, remember when we were kids? That summer Daniel died?"

His frown deepened. "Of course I do." A hint of impatience crept into his voice. "What does that have to do with Danny?"

She took a deep breath, but part of it got caught somewhere in her throat. "I knew Josh Miller then," she said. "Did you know that?"

"He lived down the beach. Why wouldn't you?"

"Because Father wouldn't allow it. It was the one time in my life I disobeyed him."

She let her words have time to float in the air, then sink into Michael's mind.

"We were lovers, Michael." There, she had said it. The dreaded word that the media would use. The word that would destroy all that they'd worked for, all that they'd had, all that Will Adams had built.

Lovers.

Michael loosened the collar of his shirt. He took a small breath. She started to put her hand over his, but stopped. She did not deserve to comfort him when she was the one causing the pain.

He stood and went to the window, ducking so he would not bang his head on the dormer, staring mechanically at what was no longer the outside, but the back of a sheet of plywood, affixed over the glass to ward off the storm.

"Michael?" she asked.

He shook his head. "You were only . . . what? Seventeen when Daniel was killed?"

She closed her eyes, wondering why now, at forty-four, she was so ashamed of what they'd done as young lovers, before they'd hurt anyone, before they'd known that they would. "Sixteen," she said. "I was sixteen."

Michael laughed. "Jesus. I guess I'd just assumed you were a virgin when we married."

She nodded. "It's what I wanted you to assume. I didn't lie, but I didn't tell you the truth, either."

Her husband ran his hand through his light brown hair, lighter now by the strands of gray that the media predicted would be white by the time he was out of office, if, of course, he was elected.

Liz pushed her thoughts from the future and tried to focus on the past. "Josh and I . . . we were young."

"Who knows, Liz?" he interrupted in a whisper, then suddenly turned to look her in the eye. "Who knows about this?"

"BeBe knows. That's all. Only my sister." She did not tell him about Roger and Evelyn or about the night that they'd caught them. The fact that she and Josh had been seen having sex seemed so insignificant in light of the outcome.

Michael returned to the bed. "What about Miller? Is he going to use this against us?"

The "us" that Michael referred to, Liz knew, once again, was not him and her alone, but him and her and the entire political party. "I don't think so," Liz said. "Please, Michael, sit down."

He sat.

She took another breath.

"I loved him, Michael. It probably was puppy love, but I loved him, or thought I did. But he was off-limits. His father . . . my father . . . well, do you have any idea how that fuels the fires of teenagers?"

Michael did not answer. He simply looked at Liz, perhaps able to understand what she was saying, perhaps not. No matter what, she knew she must continue. For Michael's sake. For Danny's sake. Wherever he was.

"The summer Daniel was killed Josh ran away to Israel. That's when he joined the military."

Michael nodded. Of course he knew that. Those kinds of dates were embedded in the mind of the competition. Liz remembered that Roger had decided they should not play up the fact that Josh had fought for Israel, because Michael had not gone to Vietnam, because Michael had not fought for America, because, after Daniel's death, Will Adams made sure that Michael was sent a continent away from Vietnam to serve his country. So Michael had spent his time in Germany, far from the jungles and the heat and the post-traumatic stress that would haunt the other soldiers, the ones with no "connections." Roger had decided they should drop the whole issue of Josh fighting for the Jews because it could raise his sympathy vote and diminish Michael's.

Liz closed her eyes again. "When he returned, you and I were married."

Silence in the room was accompanied only by the concert of rain beating against the plywood on the window.

"You were in China that summer. At the young attorneys' conference."

Michael did not respond. It was as if somewhere deep inside him, he knew what was coming next, as if he were bracing himself for the inevitable. He did not respond, and he did not move. In fact, he barely breathed. Then, finally, he asked the most difficult question of all: "What does any of this have to do with Danny? And why do you think Danny is with Miller now?"

"God help me," Liz answered, closing her eyes, choking on the words, "but Danny is Josh's son, not yours."

.   .   .

Evelyn had not meant to gasp as loudly as she did. In fact, if she hadn't been so busy gasping she might have heard her husband come up behind her.

Roger grabbed Evelyn's arm. "What are you doing?"

She put her finger to her lips. "Be quiet," she warned. "They'll hear you."

Roger pulled her away from the door. "You're listening at their door. How dare you . . ."

She shook his hand free and walked down the hall, not quite believing what she'd just heard, not quite believing, yet believing very much. She, of all people, should know it could be true, that Danny was Josh Miller's son, not Michael's.

Roger followed Evelyn into their bedroom. He latched the door behind them.

"Okay, Evelyn," he said, "I want to know what you're up to."

Evelyn shook her head, her thoughts churning as they'd not done in years. If only this time she could turn this piece of knowledge to her advantage.

She sat on the deacon's bench that was nearly three hundred years old and thought of the past, and thought of the future. "Before the election," she said slowly to Roger, "I think you should ask Michael for the attorney general's slot."

Roger went to the window and stared outside. "It's premature, Evelyn. Whatever Michael does or does not decide to do with me, with us, after he's elected is his business. What's more important now is winning. We've got to find a way to increase our lead. . . ."

She stood up. "Aren't you listening to me? Don't you ever listen to me? Do you think I'm so stupid?"

Roger turned and stared at her blankly, the way he always stared when her mind was moving faster than his. "What are you talking about?"

She knew he would be angry that she'd heard what

she'd heard, that he wouldn't want to believe it, not of his sainted sister, Liz. She knew he'd be angry and yet some small part of her thought he deserved it. Deserved it for letting her marry him in the first place, deserved it for liking men better than her, deserved it for not being as good as Daniel had been, not ever, not even coming close. "Sit down," she said, crossing the room and making herself comfortable on the generations-old quilt that lay atop the maple hope chest.

Roger sat down.

"You accuse me of snooping, but there is a reason. I wasn't snooping, Roger, I was trying to protect us. To protect us and our future." She looked down at the red-white-and-blue squares that formed the quilt. "All these years, I kept the dirty little secret about Liz and Josh. I kept the secret because I didn't want anyone to be hurt. But something has happened now. Something that changes everything."

She tried to act as if she were somber. She tried not to reveal the building excitement she was feeling, as each moment told her this could finally make something work to her advantage.

And then she told Roger. She told him that the night they'd caught Liz and Josh making love had only been the beginning. She told him that they had resumed the affair even after Liz and Michael were married. She told him that Danny was Josh's son.

"So you see?" she finished, speaking to the now white-faced Roger who seemed to have aged at least twenty years right there in the bedroom in the last fifteen minutes. "Do you see why it is so important now to our future?"

He shook his head. "No, Evelyn. If what you're saying is true, I don't see that it has anything to do with us. It's between Liz and Michael."

Evelyn smiled. "And Danny and Josh Miller. Oh, yes,

and your sister, BeBe. Apparently she's known all along."
She held up her fingers and ticked off the names: "Liz.
Michael. Danny. Josh. BeBe . . . oh, yes, and the rest of
the world if the news gets out."

Roger scowled. "I'm sure Miller wouldn't want it to
leak any more than Michael."

"Only if he wants to show the world how unbalanced
the potential First Lady is. And who would want her husband in office if she went with the job?"

Roger paced the floor, the wide-boarded, uneven,
damn Yankee floor. "Well, I know Miller doesn't play
dirty. I doubt if he'd do anything so blatant to hurt
Danny. And if we're the only ones who know, it's not
going to leak." Then he was quiet and she was quiet and
slowly he raised his gaze to hers. "It's not going to leak,
Evelyn. Is it?"

A loud banging sounded on their door.

"Roger!" called Liz's frantic voice. "Hurry. Sheriff
Talbot is here. Oh, God, they've found the van."

"It's on Lobsterville Road. Across from Menemsha.
Looks like it's been there awhile."

Images raced through Liz's mind, as she tried to envi-
sion where Hugh Talbot meant, as she tried to figure out
why Danny and Josh had gone there, if Josh had gone at
all, if they had been together. They stood in a semicircle:
Liz and Michael and Roger and Evelyn and Clay and
Keith and Joe, curved around the front door where
Sheriff Hugh Talbot stood, rain dripping from his hat
down his shoulders, making his announcement.

"I don't understand, Hugh," Michael said, composed
as ever, as if he had not, just moments ago, learned that
his wife had been lovers with his opponent and that his
son was not his son after all. "If the van is there but
Danny isn't, where is he?"

Liz's stomach tumbled. She wanted to slide into Michael's arms, to feel him hold her upright, to lean on his strength, but felt it was no longer her right.

"We think the bike ferry is a clue," the sheriff continued. "It's on the other side."

"You think Danny took the bike ferry across the water to Menemsha?" Liz asked, then added, because she had to know, "Was he alone?"

"There's no evidence that anyone else was around."

Her heart sank.

The sheriff continued. "But the good news is, the van looks clean."

In other words, Liz wanted to blurt out, no one's bludgeoned him. No one's murdered my son the way BeBe supposedly had murdered Ruiz. The fact that her thoughts could be so dark sent shivers down her back.

"There's something else," the sheriff said. "Did Danny know the Watsons?"

"Watson?" Michael asked. He turned to Liz.

She shook her head. "Not that I know of." Once again she was embarrassed that she—that they—had been too busy to know something important in Danny's life— this time, the names of his friends. She searched her memory for someone named Watson . . . from college? From prep school? "No," she repeated. "No one named Watson."

Hugh Talbot scratched his day-old beard growth. "Too bad. I thought there might be some connection, because their catamaran is gone. We tried to figure if anyone saw them leave, but everyone's been so busy with the hurricane coming and all . . ."

Evelyn stepped forward, breaking the line of the semicircle. "Wait a minute," she said. "They're a couple of kids, aren't they? The Watsons? Don't they charter a boat?"

"Yeah," Hugh replied. "Well, they're not hardly kids anymore. A brother and sister. Reggie and LeeAnn. They charter the *Annabella*."

"I remember their father," Evelyn said, "from when we were kids."

"I've heard those names," Liz suddenly recalled.

"Me, too," Michael added. "They came to see Danny when he was in the hospital. I remember now. They came up from the Vineyard."

Liz turned back to Hugh. "So where is the boat?"

"We don't know where the boat is, Mrs. Barton. We've tried to raise it on the shortwave, but didn't get a response. We can't find the kids, either."

"Where's their father?"

"He's dead, ma'am. The kids own the boat now."

"Dead?"

"Yes. He was killed . . . well . . . he was lost at sea some years ago. In a bad storm."

"A hurricane?" Liz asked.

"Well," Hugh stuttered, "yes, ma'am. I believe that it was."

Danny huddled under the coarse Red Cross blanket that the Cuttyhunk Historical Society had on hand for emergencies like this. The smell of ham and baked beans wafted through the large room where it seemed that almost all the island's people—except those "too stupid or too stubborn," according to the harbormaster—had gathered to weather out the storm. Living here year-round apparently had its advantages: Cuttyhunk was self-sufficient and self-contained, with its own underground municipal power system, which meant folks here could wait out the hurricane in well-lit style, and look across the sound to the Vineyard, which could be in total darkness. On Cuttyhunk, the only thing they had to worry about was being washed or blown away. But even if that happened, the lights would still blaze.

LeeAnn walked toward Danny in the corner. She juggled two plates, and handed him one. He smiled at the beans and ham, the added coleslaw, carrots, and fresh-baked roll. "Nice place," he said. "Think I'll stick around."

She pulled up a metal folding chair and sat down beside him. "How are you doing, anyway, Danny?" she asked, digging a red plastic fork into her meal.

He shrugged. "Okay. I suppose I've had better lifetimes but I can't remember them."

"That's the beauty of past lives," LeeAnn said. "We don't know all the stuff we screwed up."

"Or all the stuff that we got right," Danny added, chewing on what had to be the best piece of ham he'd had in ages, certainly a far cry from the fodder of the campaign circuit. "Assuming, of course, that we got anything right."

LeeAnn laughed. Outside the wind seemed to pick up speed. Inside the harmony of neighbors' voices blended in sweet repose. All were music to Danny's ears—the kind of fairy-tale music that indicated all was well, and that all was happy, or, at least, happy enough.

"So when are you going to tell me the truth?" LeeAnn asked.

He wanted to pretend he didn't know what she meant. He wanted to pretend there was absolutely nothing wrong, that life was grand and he'd just happened to be in the neighborhood when he'd come to see them in Menemsha in the middle of a storm. He did not want to lie to LeeAnn, but he did not think he could tell her the truth. He was not yet ready to admit—maybe even to himself—what the facts he had learned really did mean, and what ramifications they would hold for the future, his and others; oh, yes, and the nation's, too.

He gulped another spoonful of beans and tried once again to assimilate the reality that his truth could affect an entire nation and become a chapter in the history books. He wanted to think these things through before he put them into words, if he decided to put them into words at all. But LeeAnn was sitting across from him, staring at him, waiting for an answer.

"Some stuff is wrong, yeah, you're right," he said. "But I don't think I can talk about it yet. Part of it, I know, has to do with me being trapped inside this lovely motorized chair. The rest of it . . ." He shrugged. "Too soon to tell. Too much heaviness."

"Is it about the election? God, Danny, I can't imagine being in the spotlight."

He eyed LeeAnn, in her T-shirt and her jeans, with her hair combed by the wind and her skin tinted by the sun. No, he was sure she couldn't imagine such a thing. *Freedom's just another word for nothing left to lose . . .* he remembered from an old Janis Joplin song. And LeeAnn, above all else, was free, would always be free.

He pushed his dinner around on the plate. "Sometimes I wonder what it would have been like to have been born to . . . nobody," he said. "Well, not nobody, of course, but to parents who had regular jobs, who took two weeks' vacation in the summer, who always knew where each other was at night because they were under the same roof."

"But I always thought your family was close," LeeAnn said.

"Close. Yeah. Close as long as we were where my grandfather expected. I wonder what's going to happen now that he's dead. You know, Lee, he was the axle that kept us all in motion. Without him here . . . poof. We may just scatter in a hundred million directions."

"One of those directions will probably be to Washington. Your father's ahead in the polls, isn't he?"

Danny hesitated, then nodded. And with his nod came the realization that if word about Danny did get out, it might clinch the election for Michael if everyone felt sorry for him. He hated to admit it, but for all the hiding he preferred to do, he really hoped his father . . . Michael . . . won. He deserved it, there was no doubt. As for Josh Miller . . . well, blood or not, Danny didn't even know him beyond what the media said, and beyond the few minutes they'd spent in congenial conversation out on the porch, before Danny had known he should have been doing other things, like looking for similarities in the color of their eyes, the shape of their skulls.

He had little to go on in regard to Josh Miller, except for the media and Uncle Roger, whose job it was to dissect the opponent and see where they could fill in the gaps, take up the slack, capitalize on the weak spots, and on and on and on around the ever-turning gears of the political machine. "Let's just say it's going to be an interesting election," he added. "In the meantime, I think we should stay here on Cuttyhunk. Far from civilization."

"I can't stay here," LeeAnn said. "I go back to teaching next week. A girl can hardly make a living as a sailor." She laughed, a light, carefree laugh, unencumbered by presidential elections and fathers who were not hers.

"Why didn't we stay together, Lee?" Danny asked. "We had fun once, didn't we?"

Her laughter stopped. "Sure we did, Danny. Some of the best days—and nights—of my life. But we're too different, you and me . . ."

"We're not so different," he said. "Oh, sure, our day-to-day lives were different. But we're just people, LeeAnn. Just two damn people who both probably get awful lonely sometimes."

She smiled. "Why, Mr. Barton, are you making a pass at me?"

Danny laughed. "The last pass I made was in football and you can see where that got me."

LeeAnn stood up and came to him. She set down her plate and put her arm around his neck. "I think where it got you is right here, right now, with me and with Reggie, wherever the hell he is, and with all these people who are strangers now but who I guarantee won't be strangers by the time the storm has passed. That's where I think it got you, Danny Barton. And I think it's one fine place to be."

Danny smiled. He straightened the blanket on his lap and wondered if, beneath it, the reflex muscle of his penis had kicked in. "Save the bullshit for someone it'll work with," he said. "Now, don't they have any dessert in this crappy place?"

Chapter 30

They were trapped inside the house by the wind and the rain and the fact that years ago Will Adams had set into motion a legacy from which there had been no escape. They were as trapped, Liz realized, as Danny was, bound not by a wheelchair, but by decades of one man's manipulation and misdirected expectation.

Liz had sequestered herself in the study, where she now sat on the leather swivel chair behind what would always, to her, be Will Adams's desk, despite the addition of Danny's computer. She wondered about the man who had controlled them all. Years ago she had asked why he wasn't the one who had vied for political office: he'd responded with a wink by saying that there are directors and there are actors, and that the most important thing you can do for yourself is to figure out which one you are.

"You're an actor, Lizzie," he had said, sitting right in this chair where she was sitting now. "You belong on the stage, not behind it. Your brother Roger is a director."

She had been about thirty, already the mother of three, and there was no question of the course of her life. "Daniel was an actor," she'd said to Father.

He'd looked off toward the bookcases that displayed, between books, photos of Daniel here on the Vineyard, photos of Daniel at the Beacon Hill house, photos of Daniel in parade at West Point. And Liz's favorite, the photo of Daniel twirling a skunk, the photo she'd taken the day he had left.

She remembered now that Father had not said whether he thought BeBe was a director or an actor. She remembered because it had bothered her, that he discounted her sister. Perhaps he'd thought BeBe was merely a member of the audience. A member who didn't count, who simply bought her ticket to watch others perform.

Passing her hand across the deep red leather desktop embedded into the centuries-old cherry, Liz realized that BeBe had not told Josh about Danny because she was vicious, but because she was angry at Josh, or angry at Liz, for what they had done. BeBe was angry because she did not understand what it was like to have lived a thousand years performing for Will Adams, never having the chance to have a mind or a life of one's own. She did not understand what it was like to never have had the courage to stand up to Father and say, "Father, I want to do this," or "Father, I do not want to do that," to never have the courage to tell him she no longer wanted to be one of the actors, or even a director, but that all she wanted was a little bit of peace to live her life, however faulty or flawed it might be.

She opened the center drawer of the desk and poked through the contents: a fountain pen that had long ago dried up, a packet of sticky-back notepads, three business cards—one from a carpenter here on the island, one from a dentist that Liz remembered Father had needed when his front crown broke on an ear of fresh corn on the cob, one from the boatyard that had bought the sailboat he'd decided to sell after Danny's injury. "I only bought the damn thing for your kids," Will had sputtered. It had been common knowledge among his own children that he did not like "the water," that he was neither a sailor nor a fisherman and did not even like lobster, a sacrilege for an old Yankee if ever there was one.

"If you're looking for Father, I doubt if he's in there." Roger said quietly from the doorway, resting his forehead against the woodwork.

Liz pulled the junk from the drawer and spread it on the desktop. "It's odd, isn't it, that a seventy-eight-year-old man's life can be reduced to this—to bits of paper and trinkets and leftover paper clips that may or may not have meant anything to him, but surely mean nothing to anyone else." She reached into the drawer again and fished out a small box that read "Ammunition—Colt .45." She remembered the gun that Evelyn had given to Daniel, but did not know if it had ever been used.

Digging a little deeper, she removed two keys: one brass, one silver, linked together on a plastic ring with a fluorescent red tag that read "Christopher's Wholesale Bait." She put them on the desktop. "Take these keys, for instance. What do they open? Were they Father's? And, if so, why are they on a key ring from a bait shop?"

Roger stepped into the room and closed the door behind him. "There are pieces of all of us that no one will ever know about, Lizzie," he said. "Even family."

Liz nodded slowly, knowing that she would never invade the private moments of Roger's unhappy life. She was oddly comforted, however, by the way he had begun calling her "Lizzie" again, as if she were a little girl again, as if she needed taking care of. Right now, that was not an unpleasant feeling.

"The Secret Service and the nurse are all out looking for Daniel," Roger said, then quickly corrected himself. "Danny," he said. "I mean, they're looking for Danny."

Liz half smiled. She had not caught the mistake. It was almost as if Daniel and Danny were sometimes one and the same anyway, one having arrived so soon after the other had departed. She wondered—not for the first time—what Daniel would have thought if he'd known that his namesake was Josh's, not Michael's.

She slid her palm across the cool leather again, then over the keyboard of Danny's computer, and asked, "Where's Michael?"

Roger moved closer to the desk. He picked up a paper-weight that sat on the top—a handblown glass "planet" crafted by an artist named Simpson, given to Father as a gift. Roger turned the planet over and over in his hands, gazing at the peaks and the valleys and the oceans and the land masses that emerged and then vanished. "Michael wanted to go with the others," he said. "He wanted to go, but the agents would not let him."

Liz nodded and tried to decide what it meant that Michael had not yet relinquished Danny as his own. Or maybe he was merely keeping up appearances, as would have been expected by Will Adams. She wondered why it was that sometimes Father seemed more like Michael's father than hers.

"I know this sounds crazy, coming from me," Roger continued, a small catch in his words, "but no matter what happens, I'm not going to abandon you, Lizzie." He had a crack in his voice she had never heard. "But I just wanted you to know that I believe they'll find Danny, and that everything will turn out okay."

Liz found herself fixating on the glass globe as well, wondering what was behind Roger's words.

"Danny's a bright boy," Roger said. "And he can be very independent. You know better than to let his wheel-chair fool you."

"But he's not the same, Roger. He's not like he once was."

"None of us is, Lizzie. Life changes us all."

The wind suddenly whipped a tree limb across the

window, startling them both. "Oh God, Roger. This is really the hurricane, isn't it?"

"Sheriff Talbot said the worst of it will hit land about two A.M."

"What time is it now?"

"Midnight. You should try and get some rest."

But Liz stayed in her father's worn chair, not yet ready to go to the room she shared with Michael, not yet ready to face him again. She studied the paper clips and the pen and the trinkets and the box of ammunition, and wondered if that was what Michael was feeling right now, that he had never really known the intimate parts of his own wife, any more than she had known all the pieces of Father.

Evelyn sat in the corner of the living room and typed *www.JoshMillerPresident.com* into Roger's laptop. The screen zigged and zagged and brought up a full color photo of the man who was her nephew's real father. There was a bit of a resemblance, although, lucky for Liz and the secret she'd had to maintain, Danny had taken more after the Adams branch of the family tree. But now that tree was about to be uprooted and tossed out to sea, hurricane or no hurricane, polls or no polls, because, unlike Roger, Evelyn was tired of being second best.

She wondered if she should send Josh an e-mail to let him know that soon all would be well, that she had a plan and that, this time, she was going to succeed.

It would, of course, be much easier to pull off if Danny returned. Because the plan might just be ruined if Danny turned up dead.

She clicked the mouse on an icon marked "We want to know what you think," and decided to let Josh know where Danny might be. And that she knew Danny was his son. The fact that she'd always paid attention to what was going on around her was about to pay off. And though Evelyn hadn't told anyone, she knew the Watsons the way she knew everyone and everyone's business, and she knew their catamaran, and she'd bet her sweet Yankee blue blood that she knew where they'd gone, and that Josh would be forever grateful to find out.

He was on his third beer, compliments of Reggie, who claimed to always have a healthy stash on board the *Annabella,* and who had ventured out in the storm to go back to the marina and load up the golf cart between wind gusts.

He was on his third beer and grateful that LeeAnn, too, was on hers, and that she sat close beside him, because he'd explained about how quickly his bag would fill up and how he wouldn't want to embarrass himself. Nor would he want to interrupt the others who were clustered in the room and were busy trading stories of hurricanes long past, seeming a bit pleased that they had someone new to listen, perhaps having told theirs and heard the others' too many times as it was.

"They don't have a clue who I am, do they?" he whispered to LeeAnn.

LeeAnn shrugged. "Who knows? But I'm sure it wouldn't matter."

He frowned and took another drink. "Why not?"

LeeAnn laughed. "What do you mean, 'why not?' What difference could it possibly make to them if you're the son of the next president or the king of Siam?"

Danny blew his laugh into the foam of his beer. He wiped his lip with the back of his hand. "The king of Siam? Jesus, LeeAnn, there is no 'Siam' anymore, is there?"

"How the hell do I know? I'm just a sailor."

"And a teacher."

"Right. Mathematics, not geography."

"And now if you'll be so kind as to wheel me to a corner, I will teach you something: the proper way to empty the catheter of a paraplegic."

She did not, however, wheel him into a corner. They went to the ladies' room, together, and no one in the room seemed to give it a second thought.

For the first time since his accident, Danny felt good. Danny felt whole.

When Liz finally emerged from Father's study, it seemed like the middle of the day, rather than the middle of the night, judging by the activity in the house.

Evelyn was playing with Roger's laptop. A fire was still going in the fireplace and Roger sat in front of it, reading one of Father's old *National Geographic*s. Michael was on the phone. It could have been a picture of any time over the last twenty-some years, except for the absence of one sister who was being held for questioning in a murder case and one son who was missing out in the hurricane.

Through the Norman Rockwell image of a family at rest, Liz was stung by a sharp flash of fear: what would become of her if Michael left her? They had been together so long they sometimes thought and talked and moved as one. What would become of her as half a person, an amputee of marriage as were so many of her friends? And what would become of the children? Would they stay with their father, would they abandon her? And what about Danny?

All those thoughts came and went in the split second it took for her to walk from the study, survey the room, and have Michael's eyes meet hers.

"Mom's right here," he said into the receiver while keeping those so blue, so familiar eyes on his wife. "I'll let you talk to her." He held the receiver out toward Liz, who did not have to ask; she knew it wasn't Danny, because Michael would have said.

"Mom?" came Mags's frantic voice. "Where's Danny? Will they find him soon? Oh, God, I can't believe we're stuck up here in Boston in this freaking hurricane and Danny is missing."

Liz blinked and looked at Michael. He had told Mags that Danny was gone. She wondered if he'd told her anything else. He turned away and walked toward the fire. "He'll be fine, honey," she said, her gaze following Michael. "He's probably taken shelter somewhere to get in out of the storm."

"Mom, it wasn't storming when he left, and he can't exactly duck into any doorway or hide under any rock. He's in a wheelchair, in case you forgot."

"No, honey, I didn't forget."

Through the wires, she could hear that Mags was crying.

"I'm sorry, Mom," her daughter said. "It's just that I feel so helpless . . ."

Liz knew that feeling. It was the same empty-shelled way she'd felt when Daniel had been killed and, again, after Danny's accident. "I know you do, honey," she said softly, "but we have to have faith that he'll be all right. Now put Greg on the line."

It was another minute before Mags would relinquish the phone to her younger brother, as if not wanting to let go of her mother's voice.

"If anyone calls the house," she cautioned Greg, "don't tell them that Danny is missing. There's no need to set off any alarms."

"I know, Mom," he said. "Dad already told me." Greg, the youngest, would take control, of that Liz could be certain, for Greg was quiet, intelligent—the most like Michael. She squeezed her eyes closed and reminded herself that of course he was more like Michael than Danny was. She opened her eyes and watched her husband stoke the fire, wondering how many times over the years such thoughts had crept into her mind, and how many times she'd denied them.

After she hung up the phone, she stood there a moment, not sure whether to speak with Evelyn in the corner, interrupt Roger, or go stand with Michael. She did not know where she fit anymore in this Rockwell tableau.

"You didn't tell them about BeBe," Liz said to Michael, feeling guilty that she too had forgotten for a moment about her sister.

"No," Michael replied. "Let's get Danny home first. Hugh has agreed to keep BeBe's predicament under wraps from the press. For now."

BeBe's predicament, Liz thought. So that's what the family was going to call it. She wondered if that was a spin Roger had devised, or if Michael had coined it all by himself.

The phone rang. Liz answered it, praying it would be Danny, or if not Danny, then BeBe to say that her nightmare was over. Liz knew she'd forgive her everything if only she would come home and be Liz's protective sister again.

"Liz?" asked a familiar voice on the other end of the line.

Her heart began to pound. It was not BeBe.

"I'm in New Haven and I just heard the news," the voice said. "Where is Danny? What's going on?"

Her eyes drifted back to Michael, then down to the floor. She dropped the receiver to her side and said, "Oh, God. It's on the news. It's on the news that Danny is gone."

Roger set down the magazine. Evelyn looked up from

the screen. Michael bolted toward Liz and grabbed the phone.

"Who is this?" he bellowed. "Leave us alone."

Liz shook her head and yanked back the receiver. "It's not a reporter, Michael," she said. "It's Josh. He just heard it on the news."

At that moment someone began banging insistently on the front door.

"Don't answer it." Michael slammed down the receiver. "Don't anyone answer the damn door. I am not going to have this family held under a microscope any more than it already has been." His eyes flickered toward Liz. She could not read the expression in them.

"Barton?" someone shouted from outside where the media surely lurked, where the microscope was waiting for some little germ, some circulation-boosting bacteria.

"Barton? It's Sheriff Talbot. Open the door."

Michael muttered "Shit," and went to the door.

He unlocked the bolt and opened the door. "Where is he? Have you found him?"

The sheriff stepped inside, water dripping off his worn yellow slicker. He shook his head. "It's not about Danny. It's about you. All of you. I have to ask you to evacuate. It looks as if the hurricane's going to hit us full force. You have to get to the Chilmark Community Center. Bring blankets if you can. And any bottled water or canned food you have on hand."

"I'm not going," Liz said quietly. "I need to be here if Danny comes home." Now that she knew Danny wasn't with Josh, she felt even more hollow, even more scared.

"Excuse me, ma'am," the sheriff said, "but Danny won't be going anywhere, let alone coming home in this storm. I can't force you to go, but anyone would be a damn fool not to, pardon my French."

Liz looked at Michael, not because she could not think for herself, but because it was second nature for her to make decisions together with him.

"We have to go," Michael said. "We're right on the water."

Liz paced to the window. "How can I?" she asked, as much to herself as to anyone. "What if he comes back and finds no one home? He's not like others . . ." She began to cry. She hated that she was breaking down here, in front of them all, but she could not stop.

Then the power blew.

They were left without lights, only the orange flames from the dim fireplace.

"Shit," Michael said again.

"You can't stay here," the sheriff said. "With no power you'll lose your water. And high tide is coming. There could be a surge . . ."

"Think about Mags," Roger said from across the dark room. "And Greg. Even if you want to talk to them, you won't be able to. You know the phones go as dead as the lights."

"Michael has his cell phone."

"Cell phones need to be recharged."

She knew they were right. She hated it that they were right. Slowly, she nodded. "Danny can't possibly come back until after the storm . . ."

Michael nodded, then turned back to the sheriff. "We'll be there, Hugh."

The sheriff nodded. "Great. Because this isn't a drill. Lives are going to be lost unless people use their heads."

After he left they began gathering what supplies they could. They extinguished the fire in the fireplace, then piled into the car. Sheriff Talbot's words about lives being lost rang in all their minds.

Chapter 31

Tuna was there. Liz watched him playing with kids she assumed must be his grand-children. She stood to one side of the big pine-paneled room that was the Chilmark Community Center, where so long ago at the celebrity auction she and Josh had their first date.

Tonight, there were even more people here than at the auction back then. There was an abundance of children—kids too young to be afraid. Instead, they seemed to find great excitement in this thing called Hurricane Carol that had brought them all together in this big, friendly hall.

She looked around the room, first toward the kitchen where tall aluminum urns perked strong-smelling coffee, then at the stage on the opposite side where the humble "Don't Tread on Me" flag of the Commonwealth of Massachusetts was raised next to the red, white, and blue of the U.S. of A. Between the kitchen and the flags a few hundred islanders and tourists sprawled in various states of dress and undress, chatter and quiet, laughter and tears, amid sleeping bags and cots and small mounds of pillows. The lights, however, burned brightly: the

Chilmark Community Center had a generator, a necessity on an island that, when it lost power, lost virtually all contact with the world beyond.

Not necessarily a bad thing, Liz thought, strolling toward the bulletin board, where full-sized colored sheets of paper were thumbtacked and taped.

Children's Story Time
Wednesdays and Fridays, 10 A.M.–Noon.

Flea Market, Saturdays, 8 A.M.,
Whalers' Lodge, Tisbury.

Teach Holistic Health.
Free the Spirit Within.

Liz did not read the rest, because she had no interest in freeing her spirit. She had always left that sort of thing to BeBe, who seemed to have been born to be free.

She turned back to the crowd and realized that for the first time in her life, she felt as if she did not belong. Families and neighbors gathered in groups, except, of course, her own. Michael was down by the stage, talking with voters, no doubt. Evelyn had volunteered in the kitchen: she was probably organizing them while gleaning the latest island gossip. Roger was off by himself: he had brought his computer and most likely was monitoring the polls. Keith and Joe and several more agents (who must have arrived with Michael, though Liz hadn't noticed) were commiserating, a chessboard between them. And Clay—a nurse without a patient—was there, napping or not napping (who could be sure?) to the beat from his headphones. Liz folded her arms, leaned against the bulletin board, and wondered what had happened to her wonderful family, and if it would—could—ever be whole again.

"Let's have a sing-along!" a young woman in gingham shouted from the stage.

Liz thought someone ought to tell the young woman it was almost two in the morning and that outside Mother Nature might right now be destroying their possessions, including their homes. As the first strains of "She'll Be Comin' Round the Mountain" began to fill the hall, Liz retreated to the ladies' room, wondering if BeBe was singing in a jail cell now, and if, somewhere, Danny was, too.

"This is against my constitutional rights," BeBe shouted at the bars that kept her inside the now darkened, eight-by eight-foot cell. "If you're going to hold me, you have to arrest me. And you have to turn on the goddamn lights."

A uniformed guard appeared at the door. "Look, lady, I don't like this any more than you do. But the power's out all over the island and there's not much I can do about it."

"You can get me out of here."

"Sorry. You're wanted for questioning in Florida. Murder is a capital offense. Until someone can get up here to get you, you have to stay put." He began to walk back through the doorway.

BeBe jumped up and grasped the bars. "Don't you know who my brother-in-law is? Don't you know I have a business worth sixty million dollars? This is illegal! You can't keep me in here!"

This time, the guard did not reappear.

"Power's out on the Vineyard," a salty young guy in a slicker announced, marching into the Cuttyhunk Historical Society and shaking rain from his hat.

Surprisingly, everyone cheered, as if they relished the

fact that they would always have lights when their larger, more popular sister did not. Perhaps it gave them some sense of power over the Vineyarders, Danny thought with a chuckle, then wondered if there wasn't a pun in there about power over power or not to be overpowered. Then he decided there was no pun there, that it was only the three beers doing his thinking.

The salty guy approached them, his wet hat now in his hand. "Looks like the *Annabella* has a problem, Reg," he said. Reggie was sitting on a blanket on the floor next to Danny, leaning against a book rack marked "Early Settlement."

"Shit," Reggie said. "What's wrong?"

"Well, if you asked the boat she might say she's having a hell of a good time. She broke free of the pier . . . or rather, the pier broke free of her, since it, too, is now out in the channel, dipping around like an apple in a bobbing tub on Halloween."

"Shit," Reggie said again and stood up, as if wanting to run out the door of the Cuttyhunk Historical Society, dash down the hill, and rescue the catamaran from her predictable fate.

Danny felt like the shit that Reggie kept referring to. He rubbed his hands on his head. "Oh, man, Reg," he said. "I'm sorry. This is my fault . . ."

LeeAnn leaned forward. "Oh, right, Danny. Like you brewed up this hurricane right there in your cellar."

"I talked you into taking me out . . . You didn't want to come . . ."

"Shit," Reggie said once more.

"The *Annabella*'s not the only one out there," the messenger continued. "Looks like there are at least a dozen boats trying to survive. But my guess is we've got gales over a hundred miles an hour."

Danny whistled. LeeAnn sighed. Reggie shook his head.

"It's worse than expected," Reggie said, and Danny took some solace from that.

"And now the Vineyard's in darkness," Danny said. He thought of his mother, stranded in the darkness. At least Aunt BeBe was there to keep her company, he thought. At least Moe and Curly were there. And Clay. Danny hoped they'd had the sense to board up the windows.

He wondered if his mother had run to Josh for protection.

Feeling suddenly queasy, he turned to LeeAnn. "Mind if we go outside?" he asked.

"Excuse me? I believe there's a hurricane ripping out there with hundred-mile-an-hour winds."

"Yeah, I know. But more than anything I could use some fresh air. And if I don't get some fast, I'll probably puke."

"Jesus," LeeAnn said lightly, "if it's not one end with you handicapped people, it's the other."

Danny did not take it personally.

"Feel better?" LeeAnn asked through the wind that whipped through the cracks between the boards covering porch screens.

Danny smiled. "Yeah. Actually, I've felt better since we boarded the *Annabella* than I've felt in four years. Maybe longer."

"You've only been in that chair three years, Danny."

"Guess I wasn't much happier before."

LeeAnn leaned against the windowsill and looked sincerely into his face. "You were going to be a doctor. That made you happy, didn't it?"

He studied his fingernails. "Yeah, well, things change."

The wind sang now, a low, ponderous hum. "But you

always said you were going to be an old-fashioned doctor who really cared about his patients. Someone as far from a politician as possible."

"Well, I'm still no politician. That hasn't changed. I guess the family torch will be passed off to Greg. He's a lot like . . ." he caught himself, for a second not knowing how to complete his sentence. He would have loved to share his news with LeeAnn, with someone, if only so he didn't have to feel its weight all alone. But it was news not to be shared. It was simply too ugly. To mask his discomfort, Danny laughed and said, "Greg's a lot like my father."

"Well, I think you'll make a better doctor, anyway. You're right about one thing. You're very different from your father."

Danny was struck by the thought that maybe LeeAnn already knew. She would have to know. How else could she be so certain he was different from him? She barely knew Michael; in fact, Danny couldn't remember if the two had ever met. Well, yes, he decided, there was that one time in the hospital. Had that been enough for her to make that judgment, or had she—had all the islanders—already known?

His stomach flipped again. His throat felt as if it were closing, his airway shrinking, as if a boa constrictor had wrapped itself around his neck and was squeezing tighter, tighter. He tried to force his thoughts from a visualization of his mother and Josh Miller, from a picture of them lying together—where? On the beach where Danny used to go clamming with Mags and Greg? Down by the cove? In the same bed where she slept with Michael?

An overwhelming pity for Michael—the man he knew as his father—rushed into Danny as strongly as the wind rushed outside. If Michael had known about Josh, he probably would have waited it out, waited for his mother to come to her senses, he loved her that much.

Maybe, Danny thought, he had waited too long. And

now the two men were fighting the biggest battle of all. Suddenly Danny wondered just how much of this election was about the White House, and how much was about Josh Miller's unresolved childhood jealousy—a conflict that Michael didn't deserve.

"Danny?" LeeAnn interrupted his thoughts. "I said you are different from your father. Does that upset you? I didn't mean to upset you . . ."

Danny blinked. "How do you know?" he blurted out.

"How do I know what?" she asked.

Pain crept around his eyes, around his throat, around his heart. "How do you know I'm different from my father?" Suddenly the image of Josh Miller repulsed him, and he did not wait for LeeAnn to reply. "If this storm is ever over, and we end up alive," he said, "I need to get back to the Vineyard. Then I need to get off-island and find my father. He needs me to help with the campaign."

The screen door slammed open. "LeeAnn?" barked a voice. "What the hell are you two doing out here?"

"Staying out of the rain, Jake," LeeAnn responded to the old man whom Danny had been told was the harbormaster, the keeper of the island or at least of all its comings and goings.

"Well, for chrissakes, you're not going to believe this, but your friend there has a phone call."

"Me?" Danny asked. He glanced back toward the Vineyard; the power was still out. He wondered if cell phones would work in the storm.

"Damnedest thing," Jake continued. "I didn't know we had a celebrity here, LeeAnn. Well," the old man said with a scratch of his beard, "you'd betta' take the call, young man. I think it's important."

Danny closed his eyes. "My mother?" he asked.

"Nope," the harbormaster replied. "Someone who says he's Josh Miller. And he sounds like he's pissed."

. . .

It was the middle of the night in the middle of a hurricane, and BeBe was stuck in the middle of a jail cell. The
guard had given her two chemical light sticks in case she
wanted to see: not that there was much to see except a
calendar with New England scenes taped to one wall and
a chrome sink and matching toilet in the corner. Still, one
might have thought a jailhouse would have an emergency
generator.

"We do," the guard had told her. "But it's on the fritz."

Fritz, BeBe thought now. What a stupid, stupid word.
Fritz, fritz. She ran the syllable over and around her
tongue just as the guard reappeared in the doorway.

"Someone to see you, Ms. Adams."

"A visitor? How nice. Just like a real prisoner."

"I'm not just a visitor." It was brother Roger's voice.
"I'm here to take you home."

"But I thought . . ." BeBe said, then quickly stood. "Is
it about Danny?"

Roger shook his head. "No word yet."

The guard glanced at Roger then back at BeBe. They
all looked ridiculously ghoulish in the glowing green
chemical light.

"I tried to tell your brother that we can hold you up to
twenty-four hours for questioning," the guard said, "but
he said in Florida, the law's only twelve hours, and that's
where you're wanted." Then he unlocked the old-
fashioned barred door. "You can't get off the island, anyway. And I want to get home and check up on my family.
This storm's a pisser." He pronounced *pisser* like *pissah*
in that exaggerated New England way that drove BeBe
crazy. But right now she didn't much care, because as the
guard said it, he swung the door open. She stood there
and stared at her brother.

"You came all the way to Edgartown just to get me? Are you an idiot? There's a hurricane outside."

"I'm not an idiot," he said, guiding BeBe from the cell, "but I have been. I decided to steal the Secret Service agents' car. I had to come get you, Beebs. I need your help. It's about Evelyn."

BeBe asked no more questions, but let him lead her down the corridor to the front door. She turned around to be sure the guard had not followed them. "They can only hold someone for questioning twelve hours in Florida?"

Roger shrugged. "I made that up. It's not as if he can check. The power's out, you know."

BeBe didn't know whether she should laugh or cry. Instead, she slapped her brother on the shoulder and said, "My big brother. At last you've located your balls."

Liz was washing out pots from the chowder she had helped make, wondering if this would be considered the upper-class rendition of a soup kitchen. It was almost six A.M.: the worst of the storm was, hopefully, over. Yet Liz couldn't sleep, she was far too restless between the sounds of the rain and the wind and the incessant back-and-forth guilt-chatter going on in her mind.

From the big room, melodic strains of semi-sleeping drifted on an occasional softened whisper of one person to another, all trying to be respectful of their neighbors who now lived on the next cot and not down the street. As Liz put away the last big pot, Hugh Talbot came into the kitchen.

"We're lucky the media left the island with Josh Miller and didn't know your husband was on the way," he said. "Imagine what fun they'd have with the next First Lady serving soup to the hurricane-homeless."

Liz did not bother to try to smile; she was too weary, she was too dead on the inside. She had avoided Michael all through the night; she had also avoided Roger, though, like Danny, he seemed to have disappeared. She had needed to keep busy. That was the real reason she had wanted to work in the kitchen: not for a photo op, but for an escape. She had even let Evelyn tell her what to do, how many potatoes to put in the pot, how much butter, how much milk.

"The press learned that Danny is missing," she said to Hugh. "I can't imagine how they found out." She did not want to accuse him, although aside from the family, he'd been the only one who had known. Still, she would not accuse him because she needed him on their side; she needed his help; she needed his cooperation.

Hugh shrugged. "I suppose the media has its own devious ways." He scratched his unshaven chin. "The storm's lessening a bit. I'm going to try and make it over to Menemsha to the Texaco station. They have a generator and a two-way. Maybe I can locate someone who saw the *Annabella*. Someone who maybe saw Danny."

She dropped the damp linen cloth. "I'm going with you."

He shook his head. "Sorry. Not allowed."

"I have to go, Sheriff. Danny is my son."

"I appreciate that, Liz." He spoke with the familiarity now of those who have been brought together by disaster.

"Danny . . . has special needs."

Hugh nodded. "Which is exactly why I'm going to the station. Maybe I can also rustle up someone on the mainland and see if they know how much longer before this storm is long gone to sea."

"Please let me come, Hugh. If I stay here one more

minute not knowing where Danny is, I'm going to lose my mind."

"I'll take full responsibility," Michael said from behind her. "In fact, I'll drive her myself."

Liz stiffened.

"We'll follow you down," Michael continued. "If a tree lands on the car, it won't be your fault."

Hugh hesitated.

"Please," Michael said as Liz gripped the edge of the sink, "please let us help find our son."

As Roger had said, he had stolen the car from the Secret Service agents. What he had not told BeBe was that Keith had caught him, and agreed to let him go to Edgartown only if he went along.

Which was why he sat in the backseat now, behind BeBe, and why she was stunned when Roger spoke up right there in front of him and said, "I know about Danny. And I know where he is." He drove with his face practically pressed to the windshield, trying to see through the rain that pounded the glass.

"What?" BeBe asked. "You know where he is?"

"I think he's on Cuttyhunk. I think he's with those kids—those friends of his. Reggie and LeeAnn. I didn't figure it out, though. Evelyn did." He wiped the fog that smoldered on the inside of the window, and then continued. "But that's not everything, Beebs. I know the rest, too. About Danny. About Josh Miller."

BeBe turned her head to look out the window. In the backseat, Keith said nothing, the silent Secret Service agent, privy to it all. "Fuck," she muttered. "How did you find out?"

"Evelyn. She overheard Liz tell Michael."

She raked her fingers through her tangled orange hair.

"Liz told Michael?" It wasn't difficult to picture Evelyn lurking in doorways, hearing it all. It was difficult, however, to imagine Liz telling Michael, to imagine her sister's guilt and her pain.

Roger nodded. "And I'm afraid, BeBe. That's why I had to come and get you."

BeBe wanted to ask what he was afraid of, but didn't want to in front of Keith.

As if reading her mind, the agent said, "I'm here to help you, BeBe. I care about your sister. I care about your family."

BeBe cast a sidelong glance at Roger.

"I had to tell him," Roger said. "Or he wouldn't let me come get you."

"But I already knew," Keith said.

Yes, BeBe thought, of course he knew. It was his job to know everything, to protect and defend. And to play chess and make it appear as if he wasn't paying attention. "Did my father tell you?" she asked.

"Yes. As soon as Miller made noises about entering the race, your father feared for what might be ahead. He knew he needed someone he could trust."

BeBe snickered. Father. Everywhere, always. "And do tell. What made you so special that Father could trust you?"

Keith paused, then said, "I was your brother Daniel's second lieutenant at Fort Dix. I was there when he was killed."

It was a moment before BeBe was able to digest the information: Keith had known Daniel. Keith was a friend. She swallowed with difficulty and asked, "So what about your sidekick? What's so trustworthy about Joe?"

"He doesn't know everything. But he is trustworthy. He is my son."

They drove another quarter mile before Keith spoke

again. "I've studied this from all angles, BeBe. And as I told Roger earlier, I had no doubt that Josh would not use this . . . *situation* . . . against Michael."

"Had?" BeBe asked. "Why did you say you *had* no doubt? Has that changed?"

It was Roger's turn to speak. "It has changed," he said. "Because of Evelyn. She's the one who figured out that Danny's on Cuttyhunk. Well, she did, but she didn't tell me. I brought the laptop to the shelter. I had an idea she'd been up to something—she'd spent a long time on the computer tonight. Anyway, thank God there is power at the center. I hooked up to the Internet and found an e-mail that she sent to Josh Miller. She told him where to find Danny. She's always been jealous of Liz. And of you. I'm afraid she sees this as a chance for some sort of childhood revenge." He paused, staring at the wipers, staring at the rain-drenched road.

"Did you tell Liz where Danny is?"

Roger shook his head. "I only told Keith. There is no way of knowing for certain where Danny is until this storm's over. We didn't want to get Liz's hopes up. . . ."

"And he wanted you there," Keith added. "For moral support."

A look of sadness passed over Roger's face. "I feel responsible for Evelyn," he said, "as if I should have sensed her, well, her craziness." He took a shallow breath. "The fact is, BeBe, she's completely out of control. We have no idea what she'll do next."

Chapter 32

She was not happy to be alone in the car with her husband, the man to whom she'd been wed for over twenty years. She was not happy and she had no intention of speaking; her shame had stripped her of words.

The windshield wipers slapped back and forth in front of their faces.

"No matter what you say," Michael said so quietly Liz could barely hear over the sound of the wind and rain, "I will always think of Danny as my son. I'm not without guilt here, Liz. When we were young, I was so eager to get my career started I didn't pay much attention to you. I know that."

She gave Michael credit for so many things: for being an outstanding politician who would, truly, make a great president; for being so smart that sometimes it made her head reel; for being so compassionate to his fellow man that it sometimes made her envious. She had given Michael credit for so many things, but never for realizing the things she'd always felt: that he had never given her enough time, that the goodness of their marriage could realistically only be measured in moments rather than months or years. She had not known her husband had been so aware.

From her own guilt, she found the need to defend his. "I know you did the best you could, Michael. I know Father had a lot to do with what we were—or were not— as a family. It still is no excuse for what I did."

He did not speak a moment, the politician's savvy to think first. To think, then respond, in kind.

"Did you love me when you married me?" he asked.

Liz was not startled by the question. She was too numb to feel anything so sharp. And she knew this was not the time to lie, that all that was left now was room for honesty, no matter how brutal, hurtful, or irreversible.

She studied the rain a moment, the slant, then the swirl, then the straight pounding drops splattering on the trees, the road, the hood of the car. The dark sky was now lightening a little—as if no one had told daybreak there was a hurricane going on. "I don't know if I loved you," Liz replied, aware that she felt surprisingly calm, surprisingly cleansed.

Beside her, Michael nodded, the slow, deliberate nod of someone who had already known the information he'd just received.

"I thought I was in love with Josh, Michael," she continued. "But you, well, you were my destiny. I think I'd know that since the first time we met at West Point. I think Father had already chosen you."

"It went back before that, Liz. My appointment to the academy came because of your father."

She rubbed her neck. That was something she'd never considered, never, not once.

"My family's position . . ." he continued, "the mills in Lowell . . . well, my family was in a terrific position to back your father's plan for Daniel, first on the state level. I think he wanted to use me, and my family, to help elevate Daniel straight to the top."

Liz stared straight ahead. "God," she said. "I never thought . . ."

"I know he was your father, Liz. And in many ways, he was like a father to me. But Will Adams the man was a master manipulator. Who knows what went on inside his head? But I do know that without him around, I'm beginning to realize that I'm not quite sure where the line is between your father's dreams and my own life. I'm not quite sure what's mine and what was his."

She sat there marveling at what she was hearing. She had never, ever dreamed that Michael could have critical thoughts about her father. She had never, ever dreamed that Michael did not receive from Father exactly what he wanted. "Yes, well," she said, "I guess I've been a little unsure, too. About where he stops and where I start."

They did not speak for a few moments, both of them steadily watching the taillights of Hugh's vehicle as it wound around fallen tree limbs and yellow and green wet leaves, torn from the branches too soon for autumn. Liz realized that she'd never considered the fact that Michael, too, had been affected by her father's death. Just because he'd been *her* father, not his, it didn't mean that his influence had been any less great for Michael. In many ways, she thought it had been even greater.

"Michael?" she asked quietly. "When we got married . . . did you love me?"

He was quiet, pensive. "I was in love with the future, Liz. You were part of that."

She put her head back on the headrest. "But you didn't love me," she said flatly, knowing the emotion could not come now, but would come later.

"I know this is going to sound, well, thin, Liz, but I have grown to love you. Very much. We have . . . we have a family. We have a life that I cherish. Beyond the political arena."

"Did you ever cheat on me?" she asked, unsure, for some odd reason, if she was prepared to handle the answer.

"No," Michael said. "Never."

She looked at him. "Never?"

He smiled. "Your father would have killed me."

A small piece of her heart smiled, too, and her tension eased. But her brief relaxation quickly dissipated as the Texaco station came into view.

Using their slickers as shields, Liz and Michael ran toward the shacklike building that hugged the Menemsha pier. Liz stepped over the swordfish weathervane that lay in a windblown, twisted heap of metal on the ground. As Michael opened the door, she grabbed hold of it to keep from being blown over, too.

Inside the cottage-sized, fishing-tackle-lined station, a tiny light glowed. Hugh had made it inside ahead of them; they followed the sound of his voice to a small room in the back.

"Cuttyhunk Harbormaster, this is Menemsha," Hugh repeated over and over, his voice straining to be heard over the wind that rocked the thin walls. "Cuttyhunk, come in, please."

The radio snapped, but there was no response. Hugh turned to look at Liz and Michael when they reached the doorway. "If Danny's on the *Annabella,* maybe someone on Cuttyhunk has seen them or heard their radio transmission. Cuttyhunk never loses power." His words sounded positive, but Liz did not miss the doubtful look in his eyes.

"Menemsha," came a sudden, crackly voice, "this is Cuttyhunk. Lost your lights, eh?" It was almost a chuckle on the other end, lost to the static over a short span of rough water.

Despite the sarcasm, Hugh smiled. "Glad to hear Cuttyhunk didn't go out with the tide."

Crackle. Crackle.

Liz held her breath, then gripped Michael's arm to restrain herself from jumping over the stacks of boxes of fishing tackle, grabbing the microphone, and shouting, "Where the hell is Danny? Have you seen my son?"

"At least if we went out with the tide, we'd be able to see where we were going." Laugh, laugh, crackle, crackle.

"Are you all okay?" Hugh asked.

"Safe and sound. Most everyone's here at the Hysterical Society. 'Cept of course the Howards."

Hugh laughed as if he knew the Howards and was not surprised that they were not at the "Hysterical Society," whatever that meant. Liz squeezed her husband's arm more tightly. Michael cleared his throat.

Hugh looked at him, then nodded. "I'm on a mission, Jake. We're looking for a few lost kids. From the *Annabella*. Do you know her?"

"The catamaran? Sure. Reggie and LeeAnn. We know them well."

"And?"

"And have we seen them?" Another chuckle, another crackle.

"Yeah, Jake. Have you seen them?"

"As a matter of fact, I'm looking at them right now. Sleeping on the floor of this shithole like a couple of babies."

Hugh flicked his gaze back to Michael. "Are they alone? Just the two of them?"

"Hell, no. Got themselves one passenger. He's asleep, too. A kid in a wheelchair."

Liz closed her eyes and felt Michael's arm slide itself protectively around her waist.

. . .

It would be at least a day, maybe two, they were told, before Danny and Reggie and LeeAnn could get a lift back to the Vineyard. A couple of days, depending on the weather, depending on the cleanup and how soon someone would venture across the sound, by air or by sea.

On the way back to the shelter, Liz let her tears fall. "Please, Michael," she said, "let's not talk about any more of this until he's back safely. Whatever you choose to do later, fine. But please, at least give me the luxury of enjoying Danny being safely home again."

"I've already made my choice," Michael said as they pulled into the parking lot of the community center. "I've decided to withdraw from the campaign."

Chapter 33

 He turned off the car, and they sat there silently, the rain splattering the windshield, forming a translucent screen separating them from the world.

"You can't do it, Michael. I won't let you."

"I can do whatever I want, Liz."

"No. Too many people are depending on you."

"Maybe that's part of the problem. Maybe I'm tired of having people depend on me."

"What about the party?" She'd heard that word so often, she, too, had sadly come to recognize it as the almighty. "And what about us?" she added. "What about your family?"

"The kids will be fine, Liz. Kids always are. No matter how hard we try and get them to do things our way."

"What about Greg? His political ambitions? If you quit now it could ruin his chances . . ."

"I'm not going to push him the way I . . . the way *we* were pushed. And this is a new century, Liz. A new millennium, remember? The party is not going to hold Greg responsible for the sins of the father." Neither of them mentioned the sins of the mother.

Their vision out the windows was blocked by the rain and by their tentative breaths that coated the glass.

"When did you make this decision?"

"During the night. Before we knew that Danny was okay."

Her body was weak and aching. She wondered if she— or any of them—would survive this hurricane, or this mess. "This is all BeBe's fault, you know. She told Josh and Danny must have overheard . . ."

"It's not BeBe's fault, Liz. It's not, and you know it."

Okay, so she knew it. The part of her that twisted inside her now, that made a big lumpy knot that sat inside her stomach, knew it was not BeBe's fault. "But she shouldn't have told Josh." Her voice was almost a whisper, almost a cry.

"It's doesn't matter, Liz. Maybe this should have come out years ago. But now we know the truth, and Josh knows the truth. I can't take the risk that he'll use it against us. I don't want to destroy the kids. Or you."

"I can't believe Josh would use this against you."

Silence a moment. A long, draining moment. "How well do you really know him, Liz?"

The truthful answer was one she cared not to admit. She had known him one summer, or part of one summer. She had known him one week, when Danny had been conceived. And she'd known him one day and one night, last night or the night before. Not how she knew Michael. Liz had known Josh far better in fantasy than she had in real life. She wiped a small corner of the window.

"Why?" she asked.

Michael did not answer right away. "You said Josh saw it on the news, about Danny being missing. Well, there's a good chance it was Josh who told them."

She shook her head and looked at her husband. "No. It couldn't have been him. Josh is the one who called me. He told me . . ."

Michael shook his head. "I'm sorry, Liz. But Roger checked with CNN. The story didn't break until half an hour *after* Josh called. He knew the story before it was aired."

She frowned. She tried to fit the pieces together. She could not. "But, Michael . . ."

"Please don't be naive, Liz. Politics is about getting ahead. With emotional costs never considered."

"But . . ."

He shook his head again. "I'm not going to wake up some morning and find that the media has revealed that Danny is not my son, that my wife had cheated on me with a member of the opposite party . . . excuse me, that would be *the* member of the opposite party. I'm not going to have the children held up to that kind of ridicule. I'm withdrawing as soon as Danny is back. And there is nothing you can say to change my mind."

"My guess is your sister-in-law is trying to switch sides," Keith said. They were still in the car, slowly picking their way across the island, as if they could outwit the storm.

No one seemed to care that they were with BeBe—an accused murderer. When BeBe had mentioned it, Roger had said, "You? Come on, BeBe. You didn't kill anyone." She'd taken comfort from that, thank God for Roger. She fidgeted with the seat belt now. "There's only one problem," she said. "Why would Evelyn switch sides?"

"Think about it. She's always been jealous of you and Liz. But she's played the martyr role, probably hoping to still cash in on some childhood dream. That would explain why she's stayed married to Roger even though, well, sorry, Roger . . ."

Roger nodded. "Evelyn has said many times she doesn't care if I have sex with a horse. I am her husband and she will not allow her birthright to be taken from her."

"Her birthright," BeBe muttered. "How asinine."

"Not to her," Keith retorted. "Anyway, now that this business about Liz and Josh and Danny is out, she's probably terrified the family will collapse and she'll go down with it. Unless she finds another route out."

"With Josh Miller?"

"Precisely. He's as close as she can still come to all those things she believes she deserves. If the information she's passed on to him can help him get elected, he may feel indebted to her."

"How?"

"Who knows? But don't forget, Evelyn comes from a grandfather whose life revolved around giving favors and cashing in on them."

"Favors," BeBe said. "I am sick to death of that word. Evelyn told me it had all been arranged for her to marry Daniel. One favor for another. Her grandfather to my father."

Roger scowled. "When did she tell you that?"

"The night I told her I knew all about Daniel. That I'd always known that Grandfather made sure Daniel's orders were for Vietnam." There. She had said it. She had told Roger the secret she'd held in for so long. "I'm sorry, bro. I seem to be saying a lot of things I shouldn't these days."

"It doesn't matter," Keith said from the backseat. "Because you're wrong."

BeBe turned. "No. I confronted Father. He did not deny it."

Keith shook his head. "It wasn't your father's idea," he said. "It was Daniel's. And it wasn't Evelyn's grandfather who pulled the strings. It was Evelyn."

He paused for a moment, as if to make sure he had BeBe's attention. He did. Then he continued.

"Evelyn's grandfather had had a stroke. He was fairly out of it. So she pretended to be him. She wrote letters on his letterhead. She made phone calls on his behalf, without telling anyone he had no idea what she was doing, or that he was nearly dead. It was Evelyn who made it all happen so Daniel would go."

BeBe interrupted. "But why? Why did he want to go to Vietnam so badly?"

"Because he wanted to be a war hero. He wanted to make your father happy. He thought that then he would feel as if he deserved to be president." The rain on the windshield did not drown out his words. "It was Daniel," he added. "Your father never even knew. Until it was too late."

The wipers squeaked. BeBe and Roger stared straight ahead.

Whispering now, BeBe asked, "How do you know?"

"Daniel told me," Keith replied. "The night he was killed. He explained that he'd needed Evelyn to get what he wanted. In return, I guess he really was planning to marry her."

BeBe closed her eyes. "I told her I knew," she said. "I told her I knew that Daniel wouldn't have been killed if it hadn't been for favor-swapping. I always thought it was Father . . . I hated him so much. And he hated me . . ."

Roger looked at her in surprise. "He didn't hate you, Beebs. If anything, he was afraid of you."

BeBe laughed. "For godsake, Roger, you know better than that."

"Think what you like, but Father was afraid of you. You reminded him of his sister, Ruth. She killed herself, you know."

BeBe snapped her head around. "She what?"

"She killed herself. Father caught her with a boy one night. She and Father had a fight. She went down to the dock and got into the boat and rowed out to the ocean and jumped. She couldn't swim. Her body washed up on the Cape."

BeBe could not say a word, for her mouth had dropped open and her brain had stopped working.

"He told me you look just like her," Roger continued. "He also said you acted like her. Stubborn. Independent."

"So he was afraid of me."

"He always felt guilty about his sister's death. That's why he never ran for president. He was afraid people would ask about her."

"I can't vouch for all that," Keith said, "But I know your father told Daniel you had accused him. Daniel intended to tell you the truth right after boot camp, before he shipped out. But then he was killed, and he never had the chance."

"Father could have told me."

Roger spoke up. "Would you have believed him?"

BeBe shook her head.

"By not telling you—by not telling any of us—Father kept Daniel's image intact."

"Untainted," BeBe added. "Perfect even in death." Both men were silent.

They were quiet for a long time, until they reached Tisbury. BeBe now wondered if the only secret left to tell was the one about the night before West Point graduation when Michael had been drunk and she had been, well, there. She decided that some things were best left alone, to keep in the scrapbook of the mind. With any luck.

"What do we do now?" BeBe asked as they at last pulled into the debris-strewn parking lot of the community center.

"Nothing," Keith said. "Leave everything to me." Then, as BeBe opened the car door, Keith stopped her. "Wait a minute," he said. "Did you say that Evelyn knew that you knew about Daniel?"

BeBe thought for a moment. "I used the term 'favor-swapping.' I don't know if I specifically told her I thought it was Father . . ."

"So she could have thought you knew she had done it. That she'd been the one to arrange Daniel's orders."

"Well, yes, I guess . . ."

"Great," Keith said, then added, "We won't be able to do anything about her until after the storm. So when you see her inside, keep your distance. Both of you. And tell Liz and Michael to do the same. Something tells me Evelyn is highly dangerous right now."

Evelyn tried to keep busy in the kitchen, pouring milk into pitchers, setting boxes of cereal on long tables set up in the back of the room, pretending that she was not looking out one small, unboarded window at Michael and Liz, that she was not aware they had been sitting in the car way too long and must be discussing something really important, like the fact that their son was not *theirs* and that their marriage was a ruse.

She smiled, smug in the knowledge that, indeed, there was a God after all, one who was throwing Evelyn a life preserver just as the Adams/Barton boat was about to sink: a life preserver named Josh Miller.

Josh, of course, now owed her big-time and she had every intention of cashing in her chips. Maybe an ambassadorship of her own—*hers,* not Roger's. *Hers,* well earned.

She had, of course, at one point, wanted Michael to win. At *every* point she'd wanted him to win, until that bitch BeBe had to interfere. Until Evelyn learned that BeBe had known all along.

"Isn't it a federal offense to impersonate a congressman?" Daniel had asked when he'd learned what Evelyn had done for him . . . for *them*.

Evelyn spilled a dab of milk, then wiped it with a sponge, thinking, knowing that it should have been BeBe who'd wound up dead. Dead and unable ever to reveal to the world the things she knew about Daniel's demise. But by the time Evelyn had a plan, BeBe had left Florida for the Vineyard. So she tracked down BeBe's boyfriend. It hadn't been difficult. In fact, it had been even easier when BeBe's assistant said, "I'm sorry, Mr. Arroyo no longer works for French Country."

Evelyn found him, driving the silver Mercedes. Then, with one of the guns from her grandfather's collection, she'd blown him away, tossed the gun into the Atlantic, and made one simple call to the police—all while Michael was making one of those god-awful speeches.

"I'm worried about my son," she'd told the desk sergeant, affecting a strong Cuban accent. She said that her son and his lover—a very rich woman—had a violent argument. The lover was outraged and spoke of revenge.

The rest, Evelyn thought now with another wry smile, was history. And the only back she'd had to scratch was her own. No favors required. Only her own common sense.

Liz sat in the car after Michael had gone back into the shelter. She needed to digest his words, their impact, and the effects it would have on her family. She no longer cared about the effects on the world.

Once, she had thought Josh would make a fine president. Once, when she'd thought she'd known him. But Michael was right. She'd not known him at all. Clearly Michael thought Josh had an inside connection to have learned of Danny's disappearance long before the media. An inside connection . . . a traitor on Michael's side? One of *theirs*?

Now, in addition to her shame over Danny's birth, in addition to her humiliation that the truth had come out,

Liz felt equally duped. She wondered just how much of Josh's appearance on the Vineyard was a coincidence, and how much had been planned. She also wondered if, when BeBe had blurted out to Josh that Danny was his son, maybe BeBe had been telling Josh something he already knew . . .

Which meant that Liz had some decisions to make. And she needed to start by repairing the damage between her and her sister. BeBe, who was . . .

Just as Liz began got out of the car, she noticed BeBe crossing the parking lot of the community center. Roger and Keith were at each of her arms—a trio of support against the still-blowing rain. *BeBe,* Liz thought, her sister, who should have been in jail.

"Not exactly Palm Beach, is it?" Liz asked BeBe, who shook the water from her yellow slicker and hung it on a rack with dozens of others.

BeBe turned to her sister. "Nope," she replied.

Liz put her hand on BeBe's shoulder. "We found him, Beebs. Danny's on Cuttyhunk. He's okay. He's with his friends."

They stood there, looking at one another, Liz hardly knowing her own thoughts, let alone BeBe's. She only knew that she wished they were children again, innocent children who stuck together, defending one another from enemies of their kingdom. Once, perhaps, they had thought those enemies were external—that they were people like Father. Perhaps they'd both learned that enemies can also come from within, those self-inflicted beasties brought on by ourselves.

"You didn't kill that man, did you?" Liz asked.

"No. But I would have if it could have brought Danny back, or if it could have changed what I did."

Liz held out her arms. They embraced, they cried.

"Oh, God, Lizzie, can you ever forgive me?"

"You? I'm the one who was such a fool, Beebs. I've been a fool and a liar and . . ."

"Stop," BeBe demanded, pulling away from Liz and wiping eyes—first her own, then her sister's. "We're not going to name-call and we're not going to point fingers. Deal?"

Liz laughed. "Deal. How's your jaw?"

"I'll survive."

"We're going to get the best lawyer for you, Beebs."

"Don't worry about me. Tell me about Danny. When's he coming home?"

A smile, a look of hope, a touch of anxiety all passed over Liz's face. "It'll be a day or so before the sea quiets down enough for the trip back."

"Why the hell did he go there? Christ. When I get my hands on him . . . "

"When you get your hands on him a lot is going to be different," Liz said. "Michael knows he's not Danny's real father. I told him. He has decided to drop out of the race."

BeBe stared at her and blinked. "He can't do that."

Liz shrugged. "I don't know what's right anymore, Beebs. It seems that since Father died . . ."

"Father was an ordinary human being," BeBe said, "just like the rest of us."

Liz took off her slicker and hung it on the coatrack beside BeBe's. The thought of anything about Father being ordinary seemed as unreal as these last hours had been.

BeBe took a deep breath. "All these years I thought it was Father's fault that Daniel was killed," BeBe said. "I was wrong. It was Evelyn's. And Daniel's. Evelyn did it, but Daniel let her. Together they arranged for his orders to Vietnam. Together they concocted the whole thing." She ran her finger along the windowsill.

"Daniel must have had a good reason," said Liz, the good sister, the trusting sister.

"He was trying to please Father. Which I guess for him was enough. But all these years, Lizzie, I blamed Father . . ." Her thoughts, her words trailed off into the air.

"Why didn't you tell me?" Liz asked.

BeBe shook her head. "I didn't want to upset you. What a moron I was."

Liz smiled. "Come on, moron. How about buying me a cup of coffee? And maybe, between us, we can figure out a way to get Michael to change his mind."

Chapter 34

Hurricane Carol finally blew out to sea. The Chilmark Community Center emptied by late morning—its inhabitants scattered to their respective homes to assess the damage and begin the cleanup of everything from broken tree limbs to swollen streams that flooded basements, from shattered windows to caved-in roofs. Most would, however, return to the community center by nightfall; it could be days before power would be restored and their homes would be inhabitable again.

At twilight, Liz, Michael, BeBe, Roger, Evelyn (who was kept at a precarious arm's length—orders from Keith, though Liz did not know why), and the Secret Service agents (one and all) came back to the center. Clay had insisted on staying behind at the house in case Danny made it back—so they left him with the Jeep and a warning to bring Danny immediately to the center if he, indeed, showed up.

Liz stood in the food line now and felt muscles ache from her shoulders to her ankles, but she was grateful. Although seven large trees had been uprooted on their property and one had landed on the back porch, severely damaging it, they had been lucky: a few fallen trees was no great tragedy compared with what might have happened to Danny, what might have happened to all of them. It amazed her how life—and the forces of nature—had a way of putting things in perspective.

Behind Liz in the food line stood BeBe; behind BeBe was Keith. In fact, he'd stayed noticeably close to BeBe most of the day.

BeBe leaned in to Liz. "After this mess is over, Keith wants to take me out for dinner. What do you think of that?"

Michael had overheard. "I think I'd like to know if his intentions are honorable," he said. "Because you deserve the best, BeBe. And don't ever forget that."

Liz smiled and took a cardboard cup of coffee. Then she reached for a bowl of chowder.

"Honey," Michael said, "I'll get that." He took one bowl for himself and one bowl for her, though Father was not in the room and no cameras were around.

Honey. It was only a word, yet with it came the reforming of a bond, the mending of a heart. They'd had no time to speak today, to hear one another over the symphony of chainsaws that worked at rebuilding their property. They had no time to talk, and yet, working side by side, they had spoken great volumes of what was important to each other, and what was not.

"I'm afraid our date will be on hold until the power's back," Keith said to BeBe. "Because only emergency flights are leaving today, and I intend to take you somewhere decent. Like London. Or Paris."

"Paris?" BeBe asked. "I could do some business while we're there. These people named Loudet are . . . well, were, interested in buying my business . . ."

"You're going to sell your business?" Keith asked. "Why?"

BeBe picked up a napkin. "Good question," she said. "Maybe I won't."

Just then the door banged open. The slam of wood reverberating against wood echoed through the hall. And then every motion, every sound, every breath among the crowd ceased as heads turned and eyes turned and the tableaux froze on Danny who sat there in his wheelchair.

"Danny!" Liz shrieked, dropping her cup on the table and starting toward him.

"Stop, Mom," he said, holding up his hand. "Where is Aunt Evelyn?"

Liz stopped. Danny looked tired. Danny looked angry.

"I'm right here," came Evelyn's voice. She came out from the kitchen, her straw tote bag over one arm. "Nice to see you, Danny. Glad you made it back."

"I'm sure you are," Danny said. "I would have thought you'd be working for Josh Miller by now."

Liz did not understand what Danny meant. She began to move toward him. "No, Mom," he said firmly. "Stay right where you are. Evelyn is going to tell us what she did. She'd going to tell us how she tried to sabotage the election by going to Josh Miller. She's going to tell us how she tried to frame Aunt BeBe over that man in Florida."

Silence deadened the community center.

Then Evelyn moved forward. "Now Danny, dear," she said, her voice not much more than a tiny tremble, "this is not the time or the place to air our family's dirty laundry. Besides, anything I've done has been for the good of all of us."

"Including murder?"

Liz heard the cry from BeBe's mouth, but, thankfully, her sister did not move.

Evelyn paled. Her eyes flicked around the silent, stone-still crowd. "Danny, you don't know what you're saying." She turned back to the crowd. "Poor boy, he doesn't know what he's saying. He must have been traumatized out there, lost at sea."

Liz held her breath. She noticed that Keith and Joe and Michael had jockeyed their positions without a word, without a sound. The three of them now flanked Evelyn, though she seemed not to notice. In the split second it took for Liz to wonder what would happen, Evelyn opened her tote bag and pulled out a gun.

A shiny, blue-silvery, hefty handgun.

Even after all these years, Liz recognized it immediately. It was the one Evelyn had given Daniel, the graduation gift that was now pointed at . . . Danny.

Liz screamed.

Danny ducked; Michael lunged forward and flung his body on top of the wheelchair, covering Danny. The trigger clicked. And the blast shook the timbers of the old community center. The gasps from the crowd were as loud and as the gunshot itself. And when Liz found the courage to pull her hand from her face, she turned just in time to see blood spurt from Evelyn's temple, to watch her sister-in-law crumple to the floor, the gun still in her hand, still pointed at her own head.

Chapter 35

Liz had insisted on a proper funeral, though, thankfully, Roger chose to have it on the Vineyard, not in Boston, not in the Second Congregational Church with the traditional "reception" at the Beacon Hill townhouse.

For Roger's sake—and only for Roger's sake—BeBe agreed to attend.

So two days after Hurricane Carol departed and twenty-eight years after Daniel was killed, the Adams/Barton family gathered on the back porch of the summer house in Chilmark and said good-bye to Evelyn Carter-Adams, or at least to her ashes. The service was brief: they could not mourn long, because Michael had decided to go on with the campaign—Danny had talked him into it. But the polls didn't lie: the gap was narrowing. Tomorrow they would be back on the road.

After the ceremony, BeBe said "No, thanks" to iced tea, and strolled across the lawn, down to the thicket where Daniel's skunks had once been. Stooping, she peeked into the brush: there were no skunks today; maybe they were gone, too, like so many people, so many years.

"Penny for your thoughts," said a voice behind her.

She stood up quickly, surprised to see Michael. "I was looking for Daniel's skunks," she said. "I guess they moved out."

"Or they moved on," Michael said with his presidential smile.

She grinned and wrapped her shawl around herself more closely, the early autumn chill creeping into the sunset. "I'm glad you're going to fight this, Michael," she said.

He shrugged. "They want me to," he answered. "My family." Last night Mags and Greg had arrived for Evelyn's funeral. Liz and Michael told them the truth about Danny's birth. There were no more secrets among those who mattered. Well, only one.

"For what it's worth," she said, "I'm your family, too."

He put his arm around her and stared off to the pink- and peach- and navy blue–colored sky. "Thank you, BeBe."

"Thank you? For what?"

"For never saying anything all these years. For having the class to never mention what happened that night before graduation."

She thought for a moment, then frowned. "What graduation?" she asked. "West Point?"

"Yes. Of course, West Point."

She followed his gaze out to the horizon. She thought about the years that had passed. The years and the life she'd had, which hadn't been so bad, not really. She thought about how unhappy she would have been tied to someone as stable as Michael, someone whose life was preplanned, ordained by children and commitment and responsibility, without deviation. She smiled, then shrugged. "I don't remember much about that night," she said. "I know there was a party. I know I had way too much to drink." They stood in silence, then she added, "I must have blacked out. Because I don't remember anything else."

Michael leaned down and kissed the top of her head, the pile of her still-orange hair. "Are you really going to Paris for dinner with Keith? Are you going to fall in love with a Secret Service agent?"

"Who knows? He's nice. He was a friend of Daniel's." As if to herself, BeBe nodded. "There are worse choices I could make. Hell, there are worse choices I *have* made."

"Well, he's trustworthy. We know that much."

"And he already has a kid, so I don't have to worry about him wanting to start a family."

Michael laughed, and rubbed her arm. "No matter what happens in the election, Beebs, I want you to know you are welcome to be as much of a part of our lives as you want. Always. Forever more. And there's another thing I have to tell you. It's about Father."

As much as she hated it, she felt herself stiffen.

"When all was said and done," Michael continued, "he didn't think you were so bad, either. In his will, he left Liz the Beacon Hill house and some cash; he left Roger his investment portfolio. And to you, my dear sister-in-law, he left about half a million."

"Dollars?" she asked.

"No. Clamshells. Of course, dollars. And something else, too."

"What?"

"He left you this house."

BeBe turned and looked back to the lawn, where her family was still gathered, where her family belonged. "He left me this house?"

"The one and only."

She unwrapped her shawl around her, then wrapped it again. "Well, I'll be damned," she said as tears came to her eyes.

. . .

It was after midnight before everyone had settled in for the night. Liz tried to sleep; she could not. Daniel was gone; Mother and Father were gone; Evelyn was gone. The summer house would be in BeBe's hands now; this would be the last night when Liz would feel free, free to roam, free to . . . be free.

She waited until she was sure Michael was asleep, then tiptoed past the room the agents were using, out onto the porch and down to the lawn. Then she walked, slowly. There was no moon out tonight, but that did not matter. Liz knew the way. She had never forgotten.

She went to the cove. She stumbled along the undergrowth; she pushed aside the cattails, the sassafras, the Queen Anne's lace. And then she was there.

Standing by the water, she listened to the night sounds: the high chirp of the peepers, the deep gulp of a bullfrog. She'd never heard a bullfrog there before; she took it as a sign that things had changed, that life continued.

Evelyn was dead. Shot by her own hand, shot because she'd been caught in her own trap of lies and deceptions.

But, thanks to her, Josh had tracked Danny down on Cuttyhunk. He had tracked Danny down to see if he was okay, then told him his Aunt Evelyn had leaked to him— and the media—the information that Danny was missing. Josh had warned him that Evelyn might be out to "cause trouble" and they all had better beware.

He'd also said that Evelyn had told him with a chuckle of sarcasm that Danny's "other aunt" was in jail in Edgartown, wanted for questioning in the death of Ruiz Arroyo. She'd admitted to Josh that she'd done that, too—"For the good of the family, not that they'd cared."

Josh was leaving it to Danny to contact the police: he said he felt it should be between them—without any public connection to Josh—without any proverbial Pandora's box to spring open.

Then Josh had told Danny that no matter what the outcome of the election, he would be there to talk to Danny whenever Danny wanted or needed; that he would not interfere in his life or with the lives of Liz and Michael, but that he would be there, and would consider it an honor to know him when, if, he ever wanted.

Then he added that he thought Danny was the most courageous man he'd ever known, to be willing to share with the nation—thanks to Michael's high profile—the pain and the honesty of being handicapped.

"Your visibility alone will help more people than you will ever know," Josh had told Danny. "I will keep our secret to protect both our families, but if you ever choose to speak out, I will say I am proud that you are of my blood. That you are my son."

Liz stood in the quiet, in the dark now. In the distance, the gentle surf touched the shore. In the distance, she knew, would be Josh . . . the faraway distance, not here. He would be in San Francisco tonight, maybe, or Seattle, or Salt Lake. He would be where his road was taking him, but he would not be here.

She looked up into the sky, at the stars that dotted the blackness. She thought about Anastasia, and youth, and love. She thought about how lucky she had been to have had it all.

And then Liz turned and left the cove, walking toward her life that maybe never would be perfect, but was rich and full and good.

Epilogue

 The room was a sea of red, white, and blue, alive with the cheers of a thundering crowd, charged with an energy that could be felt even as it was framed by the big-screen TV.

Liz sat in the living room of the hotel suite and watched the early returns, thinking how much Father had loved this—the action of the game—sometimes even more than the outcome.

She wondered what he would have thought of the game now, and of the price of it all: that the secrets of his children he'd tried so hard to protect had been too great to shield against the heartbreak of life.

Liz had seen Josh again, at the presidential debates, from a safe distance. She knew that time would find the right place in her heart to put his memory; she hoped it would work for him, too.

But, best of all, through Michael's forgiveness, through her children's patient attempts at understanding, Liz had been able, at last, to forgive herself.

Roger's and BeBe's support had helped, too.

After tonight, Roger would be leaving to build a new life. He'd been offered a coveted position at the

Smithsonian, where he would, Liz knew, be respected for his knowledge and his talents, where he would be able to find a place where he alone could shine, where he would emerge from the shadows of his brother and his brother-in-law before him, and from the stronghold of a marriage that was never meant to be. Liz hoped they would see him often, and that he would, in time, be able to forgive Evelyn, and come to peace with her agony, and with her death. She also hoped he would find someone—someone he could truly love, someone who would love him in return, the way she loved Michael, the way Michael loved her.

BeBe had cleaned out the house in Palm Beach and was in the process of moving her business to Boston. "I'm not going to sell out," she'd announced to Liz one day over the phone. "But I'm coming home. I've decided the winters in Boston are more agreeable than the summers in Florida. And besides," she added, "my family is there. Or, at least, closer."

She did not have to add that Boston was also closer to the Secret Service headquarters, closer to Keith.

BeBe had also decided what to do with her inheritance. "I'm blowing it on the kids," she said, then explained. For Mags, BeBe was starting a new division of French Country, a boutique line of French-inspired country apparel that she would train Mags to run after Mags was finished with college; for Greg, BeBe started a private fund, a savings account for his presidential campaign, which everyone figured would be around the year 2036.

BeBe also replaced Reggie and LeeAnn's catamaran with her cash and her thanks. Then she announced she was turning the house on the Vineyard over to Danny, as long as he promised to always leave room for the family.

So the summer house had been put into Danny's name, then closed for the season: next year, they'd return, as usual, as always.

Liz watched now as the TV screen cut to a picture of a map, enlarged with some states shaded in red, some in blue. Then the camera moved to a group of great-looking children—young adults, really, Liz realized—who sat at campaign headquarters, smiling and happy.

There was Greg, practicing a white-toothed politician's smile. Next to him was Mags, dressed like SoHo royalty, right down to the handmade silver hair clips BeBe had suggested that she wear. Then there was Danny, looking more handsome than ever, more like Will Adams than any of Will's children or grandchildren, yet with darker hair and a softer spirit—softer, more gentle, with the lines of despair now lifted from his brow, thanks, Liz knew, in part to the young woman, LeeAnn, whose hand he now held.

Maybe there would be a White House wedding.

"Come on, sister of mine," BeBe called as she entered the room carrying a red suit on a hanger. "Time to get dressed and go greet your public."

Liz smiled. "I can't believe this really is happening."

"Believe it," Michael said, emerging from the other bedroom—*their* bedroom, where they had made love last night for the first time since Father had died, for the first time since the nightmare had begun. "Believe it and hurry," he said, leaning down to kiss her cheek quickly. "We just got the word that Josh has conceded. We're headed for the White House, honey, ready or not."

On the other side of the camera, on the other side of the stage, Danny kissed the hand of the woman he loved. He had already promised her he'd go back to med school. He had already promised her he'd come back to the Vineyard and set up practice there, where he could keep an eye on his wife and the seven kids that they would—or maybe wouldn't—have.

The best part was, it no longer mattered, because just last night, LeeAnn had helped him beat the odds, and Danny Adams was able to love again and at last he felt complete, in his mind—the only place that it counted.

About the Author

Massachusetts native Jean Stone returns to Martha's Vineyard for *The Summer House*—her seventh novel from Bantam Books, and her third that employs the celebrated island as a backdrop for her characters. She is currently working on a sequel to *Places By The Sea*. A former advertising copywriter, she is a graduate of Skidmore College, Saratoga Springs, New York.

Jean Stone

First Loves

For every woman there is a first love, the love she never forgets. Now Meg, Zoe, and Alissa have given themselves six months to find the men who got away. But can they recover the magic they left behind?

_____56343-2 $5.99/$6.99

Places by the Sea

In the bestselling tradition of Barbara Delinsky, this is the enthralling, emotionally charged tale of a woman who thought she led a charmed life...until she discovered the real meaning of friendship, betrayal, forgiveness, and love.

_____57424-8 $5.99/$7.99

Birthday Girls

Abigail, Maddie, and Chris were childhood friends who celebrated birthdays together. Now, as they near the age of fifty, they must try to make each others' wishes come true.

_____57785-9 $5.99/$7.99

Tides of the Heart

In an attempt to make peace with her past, a woman goes to Martha's Vineyard to find the daughter she gave up for adoption thirty years ago.

_____57786-7 $5.99/$7.99

THE VERY BEST IN CONTEMPORARY
❦❦WOMEN'S FICTION

SANDRA BROWN

___28951-9 Texas! Lucky $6.99/$9.99 in Canada	___56768-3 Adam's Fall $6.99/$9.99
___28990-X Texas! Chase $6.99/$9.99	___56045-X Temperatures Rising $6.99/$9.99
___29500-4 Texas! Sage $6.99/$9.99	___56274-6 Fanta C $6.99/$9.99
___29085-1 22 Indigo Place $6.99/$9.99	___56278-9 Long Time Coming $6.99/$9.99
___29783-X A Whole New Light $6.99/$9.99	___57157-5 Heaven's Price $6.99/$9.99
___57158-3 Breakfast In Bed $6.99/$8 .99	___29751-1 Hawk O'Toole's Hostage $6.50/$8.99
___57600-3 Tidings of Great Joy $6.99/$9.99	___57601-1 Send No flowers $6.99/$9.99

TAMI HOAG

___29534-9 Lucky's Lady $6.99/$9.99	___29272-2 Still Waters $6.99/$9.99
___29053-3 Magic $6.99/$9.99	___56160-X Cry Wolf $7.50/$9.99
___56050-6 Sarah's Sin $6.99/$9.99	___56161-8 Dark Paradise $7.50/$9.99
___56451-x Night Sins $6.99/$9.99	___56452-8 Guilty As Sin $7.50/$9.99
___57188-5 A Thin Dark Line $6.99/$9.99	___10633-3 Ashes to Ashes $24.95/$35.95

NORA ROBERTS

___29078-9 Genuine Lies $7.50/$9.99	___27859-2 Sweet Revenge $7.50/$9.99
___28578-5 Public Secrets $7.50/$9.99	___27283-7 Brazen Virtue $7.50/$9.99
___26461-3 Hot Ice $7.50/$9.99	___29597-7 Carnal Innocence $7.50/$9.99
___26574-1 Sacred Sins $7.50/$9.99	___29490-3 Divine Evil $7.50/$9.99

- -

Ask for these books at your local bookstore or use this page to order.

Please send me the books I have checked above. I am enclosing $____(add $2.50 to cover postage and handling). Send check or money order, no cash or C.O.D.'s, please.

Name _____

Address _____

City/State/Zip _____

Send order to: Bantam Books, Dept. FN 24, 2451 S. Wolf Rd., Des Plaines, IL 60018
Allow four to six weeks for delivery.
Prices and availability subject to change without notice.   FN 24 4/00